The Orphans of New Lur
Book One of
The Anterra Collection

Upcoming works:

Catalyst
Coming 2020

The Tenebrous Miasma

Malatras

Newsletter and Website:
My website grows along with Anterra; blakevanier.com.
If you'd like the latest updates, please join my newsletter.
blakevanier.com/newsletter-signup/

The Orphans of New Lur

Book One of
The Anterra Collection

BLAKE VANIER

Cover Art: Daniel Kamarudin

Lettering: Hakim Yaacob

blakevanier.com

Dedication

This book is dedicated to my wife, Heather Passe. She has shown incredible patience working on this with me. She has read sections multiple times as I've ironed them out and is always there when I need feedback.

Table of Contents

1 Family   1

2 The Industrial District   8

3 Isis B.   24

4 A Second Chance   36

5 Flight from Home   49

6 On Their Heels   58

7 Ferin Forest   63

8 Blue Horin Bay   80

9 Captured   93

10 The Nero Assault   117

11 Kabel Reikyn   133

12 Gracie   148

13 Stone's Fortress   168

14 Kiats   188

15 Exploration   201

16 Taunting   216

17 A Stolen Dagger   226

18 A Disappointing Purchase   236

19 The Hunt   247

20 Lepisents   256

21 The Smoking Boy   273

22 Odoki   290

23 The Games   303

24 Recuperation for Body and Mind   323

25 The King   334

26 On the Other Side   353

27 A Cell of a Room   365

28 Practice Makes Perfect   384

29 The Moltrik Corusnigma   387

30 Now to Execute   418

31 Getting Out is the Hard Part   434

32 It Couldn't Be Worse   447

Epilogue   460

Thank You!   462

Acknowledgements   463

Glossary   464

About the Author   477

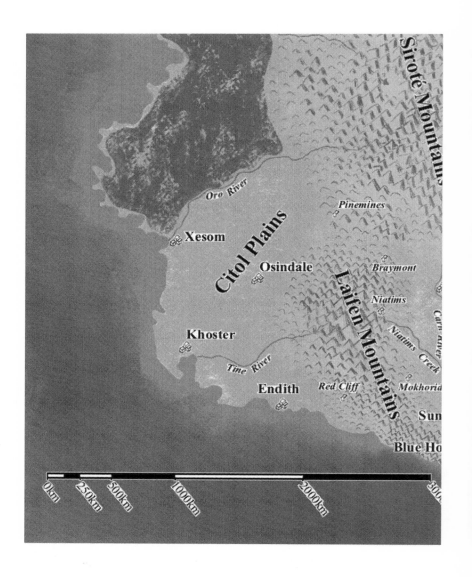

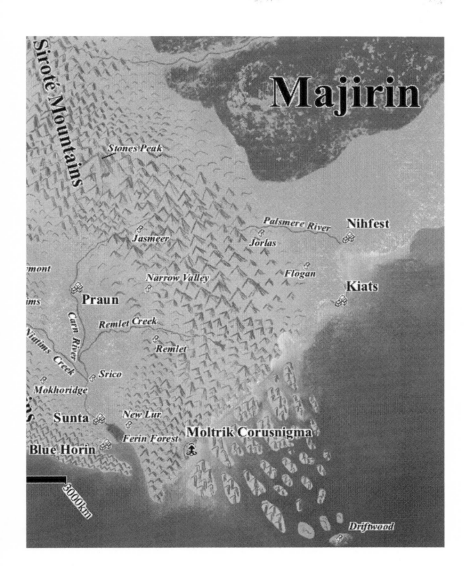

Majirin

Siroté Mountains

Stones Peak

Palsmere River

Nihfest

Jasmeer

Jorlas

Flogan

Kiats

Narrow Valley

mont

Praun

ims

Carn River

Remlet Creek

Niatims Creek

Remlet

Srico

Mokhoridge

New Lur

Sunta

Ferin Forest

Moltrik Corusnigma

Blue Horin

5000km

Driftwood

'I have lain with you for a thousand years and yet you still suffer. My first attempt to free you from your burden had been stifled. But now the gears of fate have once again brought to me an opportunity, to which my daughter is the key. She is once again among the living and my slumber is coming to a much-needed end. Though I have slept, I have grown strong. I will not fail you this time.'

1 Family

Fae

The relaxing buzz of the radio mixes with the sounds of clanging pans and running water. The smells of breakfast permeate Fae's cozy home. A sudden hiss from the radio slices through the beginning of a song. The kitchen noises abruptly stop, save for sputtering oil. A deep, energized voice emerges from the static.

"Hey, hey my fellow Humans it's Mr. X with a neeeews flash! If you've been holding your breath you can let it gooo. As long as Havityn Isidore doesn't throw any surprises at us, the smaller towns around Sunta should be safe from destruction and thank goodness for that! This is the sixth Havityn in as many months and what do our miniature overlords do about it? Nothing! So, if this makes you upset, tell a Mini about it… Just kidding folks, the Minis don't care. They hide behind their huge walls and watch as the Humans abandon their homes and flee for safety."

"But don't get down my friends. I've just heard first hand that the Minis are having serious trouble in Sunta. Who better to short the Minis' circuits than Catalyst? The resistance group has been throwing extra loads of gravel in the Minis' gears lately, and for the first time I can smell smoke coming from the higher-ups. Could this explain why more and more Humans are mysteriously disappearing? Are the Minis getting desperate? Regardless of the Minis' perverse motivation, you can bet this week's utility credits that Catalyst will rescue our taken brothers and sisters."

"Now bear with me for a second, because if you're anything like me, just hearing this name boils your blood, but I can't let his actions go unnoticed. You've all heard about the Human Mini sympathizer, Art Lively. Well, he just made some new agreement with them, pushing for peace. Let me tell you something, Mr. Live-little, if you're listening. We'll give them peace when they give us freedom!"

There is a short pause from the radio.

"Well, that's the latest from Mr. X, the only source of accurate, honest news. I'll be back tomorrow at the regular random time and remember—always keep a wary eye down."

With a crackling hiss, the unannounced broadcast ends and the same song snaps back into play. Rapid tossing of the sizzling vegetables brings the kitchen back to life.

Fae looks up from the frying pan to see a young boy walking down the steps alone, holding a bracelet and rubbing it with his fingers. Beads of sweat cause his light, wild hair to stick to his pale face.

"Sam, did you have another bad dream?" she asks. He does not respond. She sighs. "Nero, are you okay?"

The boy takes a deep breath, looking up. "What's for breakfast?"

"The usual scrambled breakfast. Would you like to help? You can whisk the eggs."

Nero flashes a smile at Fae, shoving the bracelet, far too big for his skinny wrist, into his pocket. Fae watches him fondly for a moment as he prepares the eggs with practiced skill. They move like dancers, perfectly in sync, quietly whittling away the tasks with smooth efficiency. The eggs, potatoes, sausage, onions, and peppers mingle together in a large steaming pan, carrying up and away a marriage of smells few could resist. Nero spreads shredded cheddar cheese over the top and Fae mixes it in with a large wooden spatula.

A girl yelps from the floor above. A patter of light footsteps follows. A muffled struggle ensues, accompanied by a large thud and flailing limbs banging against the floor. There is another patter of footsteps. A door slams. Nero quickly sits down at the kitchen table, just as two girls in worn pajamas scamper down the stairs, giggling to each other.

Fae looks up at them. "Victory, girls?"

A smile blossoms across Thea's face. Her eyebrows jump. "Korbin tried to put toothpaste on my face, but I woke up before he could!" Her short blond hair bobs around her head, while a dark, rectangular piece of metal hanging by a silver chain dances around her neck.

"Which was his first mistake." Iona yawns, affixing her long, dark hair into a ponytail. Her blue-gemmed pendant dangles low on a necklace.

Thea crinkles her nose, baring her teeth. "Me and Iona jumped on him," she says, imitating a pounce and hopping down a step. She wrestles with the air and pretends to dump something to the ground. "And took him down."

"Then I pinned him," Iona says.

"And I smeared toothpaste on his face!" Thea squeezes an imaginary tube of toothpaste. With a sour face, she pretends to smear it all over her victim.

Iona nods. "It was pretty good. He should know not to mess with us."

Fae shakes her head, smiling. "If only he would learn his lesson. Now come over here and help me set the table."

Nero jumps up to help set the plates and forks around the rectangular table. Before they finish, an older boy with dark shaggy hair jogs down the stairs. He lands on his toes at the bottom and stretches his arms out, yawning.

"So did you girls finally get Korbin?" Ryder asks.

"Oh yeah, we got him gooood!" The girls say in unison.

"Jinx!" Thea says, pointing at Iona.

Iona throws up her arms in protest, sealing her lips with a pout.

Fae brings over the frying pan to serve the steaming hot scrambled breakfast. The children settle about the table. Thea nudges Nero sneakily as she sits down. They eat without hesitation. Not long after, Korbin, who is slightly younger than Ryder, descends the stairs. His brown hair is short, and his face is slightly pink from a fresh cleaning. He sits down without comment and eats.

Midway through a mouthful of breakfast, with bits of potatoes in the corner of his mouth, Ryder turns toward Korbin. "So, I heard you got whooped this morning."

Korbin takes a sip of water. "Yeah they got me."

"That's it, no protests?" Fae raises a grey eyebrow.

"It was fair and square. What else can I say?" Korbin shrugs his shoulders and stabs through a piece of potato with cheese and egg stuck to it. Iona and Thea exchange confused looks.

Fae picks up her fork. "Well, good for you, Korbin. I think we're turning over a new leaf today."

Korbin looks at his food, shrugging once more before shoving it in his mouth.

"So, what are your plans for your day off from school?" Fae asks. "Are you going to play outside today?"

Ryder sits up straight, wiping the mess from his face. "Oh yeah, I just discovered some top-secret information this morning. I heard from my informant there'll be a Mini convoy delivering medical supplies to Sunta this afternoon."

Thea grabs the edge of the table, leaning forward. "Are we going to take them?"

Ryder gives her a small smile. "Of course, Thea, we wouldn't pass up an opportunity to get some medical supplies to Catalyst, especially when the Minis are traveling through our turf. It's our duty!"

Iona raises her hand, smiling politely at Ryder.

Ryder looks at her quizzically. "Why are you raising your hand, Iona?"

Thea lets out a disappointed moan.

"Ha!" Iona sticks her tongue out at Thea then turns back to Ryder. Her eyebrows are knit together, serious. "Is your information clean?" Iona asks sternly. "We've been hitting them regularly. They're bound to try something sneaky."

Ryder half smiles and nods. "Oh it's good, trust me."

The wrinkles disappear from her forehead and her shoulders relax. "What's the plan and what can we expect for their forces?"

Ryder pushes on one of his front teeth with his thumb. He takes a deep breath before looking up at everyone.

"Okay, so the convoy only has two-hundred—no make that four-hundred and fifty—armed soldiers, but don't be disappointed. The tricky part with this one is not the number of soldiers, but the timing." Ryder rearranges some of the food on his plate, making a little road through mounds of vegetables, potatoes, and sausage. He then forms small off-streets here and there. Finally, he positions a piece of egg covered in cheese at the entrance to the main road. "This is the convoy, which includes twenty-three vehicles." He starts the cheesy egg down the road. "The convoy's going to be moving fast, making it virtually impossible to intercept, except for here." The cheesy egg comes to a stop at a small bend in the road. There are mounds of breakfast all around it. "Here, they're going to have to slow down and clear out the blockade we'll build. Once they stop, we'll have a small window of time to hit them and hit them hard." He squashes the cheesy egg with his fork. He points to a mound of potatoes. "Iona, you'll be positioned in this building overlooking the ambush and redirecting our forces if needed. You'll also be watching for surprise attacks."

Iona nods. "Easy."

Ryder looks at Korbin. "I'll need you and your commandos to charge the front, making sure to hold them up and give us time."

Korbin smacks the table with his fist. "They won't know what hit them!"

"I'll take another group and hit the rear guard from the side. This should provide enough distraction and cover for Thea to slip in and secure the medical supply vehicle." Ryder looks at Thea. She nods back at him enthusiastically. He catches Fae's eye, then sees Nero playing with the remains of his food. "Nero, I have an important mission for you. Are you up to it?"

Nero looks up, shrugging. "If you think so. Korbin got mad at me last time you made me do something."

"Well he won't this time, 'cuz you won't mess up. Since Thea will be securing the supply vehicle, we'll need you to drive it."

Nero's jaw drops. "But I can't drive! I'm sure you'd do better."

Ryder shakes his head. "Sorry, I can't, man. We're all going to be tied up, so it has to be you. The driving is a minor detail. You'll pick it up quick… So, you in?" The color drains out of Nero's face while he stares right through Ryder. "Okay, excellent. As soon as we're done with breakfast, we'll head out." Everyone but Nero gives an excited whoop.

Fae holds up her wrinkled hands. The children fall quiet. "Just remember to be safe and to be home before dinner. Make sure to listen to Ryder and stay out of trouble." She sees the excitement wither from the children and pauses, lightening her tone. "Should I make you all some sandwiches for lunch?"

"Yes!" Korbin throws a hand into the air. "Could you pack some chips and snacks too?"

Fae lets out a short laugh. "Of course." The children quickly cram the last bits of food into their mouths and look hopefully at Fae, their cheeks bulging. "Well, I can see you are all quite anxious to get out of here. Go change. I'll clean today." Korbin, Iona, and Thea say quick thanks, bolting upstairs.

"Thanks Fae," Nero says as he slowly gets up, trudging upstairs after them. Ryder collects the dirty plates.

Fae puts a hand on his shoulder. "Thanks for including Nero. I'm sure he appreciates it."

Ryder sets the dishes into the sink. "Oh, sure. It's just tough sometimes since he doesn't really get as excited as the others. I'll make sure he has fun today."

"Good. I'm looking forward to hearing about it tonight. Please make sure to be home before Illi sets and be careful playing in the old industrial district, okay? Those buildings can be unstable."

"We'll be safe, especially if we have an awesome lunch to keep us busy."

"Oh yeah? Well then, I better get on that. I'll finish up here."

"You're the best Fae," Ryder says, heading upstairs.

Fae clears off a portion of the counter and slaps together a bundle of sandwiches. She fills up a little cooler with ice and drinks. On top of the ice, she sets the sandwiches, a bag of chips, and some fruit. She closes the lid, carrying the cooler to the front door. All the while, feet are slapping the floor above her. Just as she finishes cleaning her second frying pan, the children bound down the stairs, wearing an assortment of clothes and bags. Fae meets them at the door. They exchange quick goodbyes as they grab the cooler and scurry off. She peers through the window, watching her herd of misfits tear down the dilapidated street. They disappear behind a couple of dead bushes. She smiles to herself. As she turns back toward the mess of a kitchen, the smile fades. She rolls up her sleeves and attacks the remainder of the dishes.

2 The Industrial District

Nero

The children hurry up the street, energized by the scent of fresh air and the morning light streaming over the jagged mountains. Fae's well-kept blue home is an irregularity compared to the other neglected houses they pass. Their shoes crunch over the decrepit streets. The sound bounces off the houses on either side but is mostly lost in broken windows and crumbling walls. Rusted metal and debris litter the lawns of the inhabited houses, hiding the burnt brown grass and dried dirt within the Illi-bleached, peeling fences.

Iona and Thea proudly lead the way through the heart of the small town, where a few stores provide the essentials for life. A lone worker pauses from picking up trash for a moment to watch Ryder and Korbin wobble awkwardly by with the cooler swinging between them.

Just past the stores, the children scramble down to the bed of a creek. Its mellow flow of water weaves around rocks of various sizes and a smattering of rusting junk.

On the left side of the creek, a graveyard of abandoned homes overwhelms the horizon. On the right, machinery echoes from the inside of a few grey, water-stained factories of newer construction. A tall cement wall, starting many kilometers away, runs behind these factories. It turns sharply at the creek and continues for a long distance toward the mountains. A smaller, makeshift barrier of chain-link fence and roofing metal juts out from the wall, spans the creek, and continues through the rubble of homes to eventually encircle the town.

The children trek through the loose detritus and rocks of the creek. They stop to peel back an opening in the chain-link fence to squeeze through. Once on the other side, they come to a concrete storm drain that punctures the base of the cement wall.

Ryder steals a quick look toward the town and sets down the cooler. "The coast is clear, let's move quick." He drags a rusted metal grate away from the mouth of the storm drain.

Korbin uncovers a piece of plywood with a rope looped through holes in two of its corners and pulls out a flashlight from his backpack. He positions the rope around his waist and crawls into the drain.

Ryder heaves the cooler onto the sled and slaps the top of it. "You're good to go, Korb!" The wood scrapes against the dirt and concrete as the cooler slides into the darkness. "Alright, Iona, Thea, and Nero—go for it."

Nero watches as Iona vanishes. *Oh, I hate this part.* He closes his eyes and takes a deep breath. When he opens them, he sees the bottom of Thea's feet moving deeper into the drain. He quickly drops down and chases her silhouette made from the bouncing lights in front of her.

Ryder follows last and pulls the grate back over the drain from the inside. The dirt in the drain ends after a couple of meters, exposing cold concrete where gravel uncomfortably jabs the children's hands and knees as they crawl down the tight drain. The scraping of Korbin's sled muffles out the rest of the world.

A knot inside of Nero coils itself tightly around his lungs, making it hard for him to breathe. *What if this old pipe collapses?* Nero's head hits Thea's butt.

"Hey, Nero, slow down," she laughs.

Nero catches himself. *I've done this before. It'll be okay.*

They crawl for several long minutes when Nero bumps into Thea again. "Oops, sorry, Thea. Why'd you stop?" Nero asks, trying to peek around her.

Iona's hand drums the side of the cooler. "Move it, Korbin. You know I hate tight spaces." The drain swallows the sound and all that is left is their breathing. "Korbin?"

"What's Korbin doing?" Thea asks.

"I'm not sure; he just stopped."

"Is he alright?" Thea's voice begins to rise. "Did something happen to him?"

"I don't know, Thea. I can't see anything." Iona huffs and pushes against the cooler. "It won't move at all."

Nero struggles to look backward and sees the faint light of the day from the entrance. *Maybe we should turn around now, before we all get trapped.*

"Korbin!" Thea's sharp voice slices their eardrums. "Are you okay?"

There is a muffled cough from the other side of the cooler. "You must go back," Korbin whispers, "before it's too late…"

"What, Korbin? Speak up," Iona says.

"What's going on up there?" Ryder asks.

"Something happened to Korbin," Iona says. "I think he's hurt." She smacks the cooler again. "Korbin, what's going on?"

Silence. Thea squeezes her way beside Iona. "Korbin, are you okay?" Still, there is no response. "Korbin! Please talk to me."

"Bwah-hah-hah," Korbin breaks out laughing. "You guys are too easy!" His laugh continues to echo down the pipe and the cooler starts to move again.

The rest of the children fail to move for a long moment. "I'm going to kill him," Iona growls as she starts forward.

After crawling the rest of the way in silence, they arrive at a musty chamber crisscrossed with other drains. Light from a manhole entrance illuminates a corner, where Korbin is dancing and grinning from ear to ear. "Boo-ya. I got you guys so good!"

Iona punches his arm. "You're a jerk." She starts climbing up a metal ladder.

"Oh come on, that's what you get for double teaming me and putting tooth paste all over my face this morning," he says, rubbing his arm.

Thea walks up to him with her hands on her hips and shakes her head. "That was really mean. You scared me." She follows Iona up to the surface.

Korbin drops his shoulders. "Jee, so sensitive. I was just having a bit of fun."

The daylight is blinding. As their eyes adjust, the broken shells of old buildings take shape. Shattered windows and demolished walls provide glimpses of melted machinery. The chilling silence that permeates the surroundings is an eerie backdrop.

Ryder heaves the cooler from the access hole with a huff. "Let's drop the food off at our base before we start setting up for the attack," he says. "We'll take the long way to see if we can find anything cool."

The group navigates through the streets and over piles of rubble. Occasionally, one of the children scrambles over the debris and picks up a piece of wreckage, flipping it over in their hands and assessing its worthiness as an imaginary tool or weapon.

A faint scream cuts through the silence.

The children freeze. They strain their ears and hold their breath, waiting for something more. Pinpricks run all over Nero's body, along his back and under his scalp. His skin tenses, causing the hair on his arms to stand up. *Oh no, someone's just been eaten by a monster!*

"What was that?" Thea asks.

"Probably nothing," Nero says quickly. "We should head back home."

"Aw, spineless Sam," Korbin says. "Did you forget your blanky at home?"

"Quiet, Korb," Ryder says, surveying the empty husks of the buildings. He points down one of the streets. "I think it came from there."

"We should check it out. What if someone needs our help?" Thea starts to walk.

Ryder nods his head, putting the cooler down. "Everyone, follow me and stay close. Let's take a quick look."

Nero's eyes widen, and he waves his hands at Ryder. "Whoa whoa whoa. No, wait, what if it is some kind of monster or something?"

Korbin runs to the front with his chest out and his fists on his hips. "I'm not scared, let's go!"

"Korbin, be quiet!" Ryder hisses. "And chill out, Nero, there aren't monsters here." He steps out in front of Thea, walking carefully. He hugs the walls and stays in the shadows when he can.

Oh, this is so stupid. We're going to get eaten for sure. With a great effort, Nero wills his legs to follow the others, pulling up the rear.

Ryder sneaks around several buildings and sticks his head around a corner. "I don't see anything."

They look around the corner, bunched together. The street leads toward the cement wall surrounding the industrial district. One of the buildings to the right has collapsed onto the wall, turning the once impregnable barrier into a more manageable obstacle.

Nero steps back from the corner. "Well, I don't see anything either. Let's go back to base!"

Iona points. "Woo! I think I see something at the base of the wall where it's partially collapsed."

Ryder squints his eyes and nods. "Yeah okay, stay behind me. We'll just get a little closer to take a better look." He hunches over, ducking in and out of doorways and side streets at every chance. The other children follow him like a series of train cars, mimicking his every move. Ryder stops at a hiding spot where they see a small lumpy object lying among the rubble.

Nero's heart kicks against his ribs. With every pulse, it tries to escape from his chest, throbbing loudly in his ears. He holds his breath and looks around at the other children to see if they can hear the thunderous beats of his heart. They pay him no attention.

Korbin leans onto Ryder's shoulder. "What is it?"

Ryder shakes him off. "Geetooooff Korb. I don't know."

Iona moves her head forward. "It looks like a backpack."

A backpack with a monster in it! Nero squeezes Thea's arm. "What if there's a m—"

Ryder glances back at Nero with mild annoyance. "Shhhh, we're going in."

Ryder and the rest of the children jog over and crouch around the backpack. Nero hesitates but something draws him along, gently blowing his concerns away.

The backpack is bulging at the zipper, and several edges are outlined in its fabric. Ryder stands it upright and gently unzips the top, releasing a soft glow of white light that blossoms across his face. Gingerly, he slips his hand into the bag and pulls out a metal, cylindrical canister just bigger than a soda can. It has a matte black finish and brass colored trimming. There are two rectangular eyelets of silver glass along its length. A white shimmering light glows from within.

Korbin leans forward to get a better look. "What is it?"

Ryder turns it over in his hands and slides his finger over a series of engraved numbers and letters. He looks closely into one of the windows and then shakes it by his ear. "I haven't a clue, but it sounds empty. It's almost like it's just trapped light. Maybe it's from the Minis."

Korbin reaches for the bag. "Awesome. Let me get one too."

Ryder yanks it back. "Just hold on a sec! We don't even know what they are."

"I want one too," Thea says, squirming her way closer to the bag.

"I think we should just leave them," Iona says. "I don't like it."

The children continue to argue when Nero suddenly snaps back to reality. He pulls himself away from a strange, comforting warmth that is emanating from the canisters. He stands up. *Where did the bag come from? Who's the owner?* He looks up at the crumbling wall and notices a shoe hanging in a clump of rusty barbed wire. Stepping back from the circle, he looks around. In their excitement, none of them had done so earlier.

He sees a crumpled mass of a person lying in the middle of the street twenty meters farther down the wall. Without turning, he reaches for Thea and tugs on her shirtsleeve.

"Hey look, there's a body," he says, but she brushes his hand away, still arguing about the canisters with the others.

The body's arm jerks to life, and Nero jumps. It begins to rise, a puppet guided by a jerky master. Facing away from Nero, it moves its wobbly legs under its torso and begins to stand, its arms and head dangling lifelessly from its hunched back. It sways from side to side for a moment and then, as if it just remembered how to stand, it steadies and stretches. Suddenly, its head twitches to the side as though it has heard something. It turns.

The light plays over the outline of a man's face and shaggy blond hair, but as he continues to turn, the light is lost in a dark void of his left eye.

Nero jumps back and slams into Korbin.

Korbin spins around and pushes Nero away. "Dude, Nero, what the heck?"

"There's someone down there," Nero says as he turns back, thrusting his trembling finger toward an empty street.

Korbin jabs Nero hard in the ribs. "Imagining monsters again, Sammy?"

Nero scowls at Korbin. *JERK!*

"Stop being so mean, Korbin," Thea says. She shoves him lightly.

"Enough," Ryder says. He slides the canister back and zips up the bag. "We should get out of here. We can look at them back at base." Ryder turns to Iona. "Will you take the backpack with you, so Nero and I can go get the cooler? We'll meet you there."

Iona's jaw drops. "What? I told you I don't like those things. What if they're dangerous. What if Fae finds out?"

"I think we should definitely take them," Thea says.

Korbin reaches for the bag. "Here, I'll carry them."

"No!" Ryder pulls the bag away from Korbin. "Thea, you take the bag. Nero and I are going to be quick. Meet us at the base and don't mess with the backpack." He hands the bag to Thea. "Let's go, Nero." He gestures to Nero to follow.

Nero takes one last look down the empty street before jogging with Ryder back the way they came.

After the other children fall out of ear shot, Ryder speaks up. "Nero, you've got to stop pretending to see things."

"No, I really saw something this time!" Nero says. "I promise. It's the truth."

"So, what was it? Just some guy?"

"No… Well yeah but he had this one crazy eye that was all black. It looked like there was a hole in his head."

"Could you see what he was thinking?" Ryder chuckles.

"No, seriously, Ryder! He had this black eye and he just disappeared when I looked back! Do you think that was his bag?"

Ryder shrugs. "Who knows? If it was, then he probably shouldn't have run away." They jog in silence for a moment until Ryder starts to shake his head. "I really should have kept the bag with me. I just didn't want it to slow us down… Let's hurry". He quickens his jog.

In no time, they make it to the cooler and carry it together. They walk quickly and in silence. After navigating through the abandoned streets, they arrive at a large building that towers over the rest. An open doorway leads to a fire escape, where they begin to ascend many flights of stairs.

On the fifth floor, they hear a loud crash from above.

They run up the last two levels, leaving the cooler behind. Nero follows Ryder through a door that opens to a huge room. It is enveloped by dirty windows that look out over the industrial district and the surrounding grasslands. A gentle breeze circulates through the room dragging away the smell of old dust. There are chairs and upturned wooden crates placed around a large, rectangular table in the center of the room. Heaps of semi-organized junk litter the back wall and a few surviving shelves.

Korbin is there, standing over pieces of a broken wooden crate. He catches Ryder's eye and runs over to a heavy metal table off to the side.

"Hey Ryder, look what I can do!" Korbin grabs the bottom of the table and heaves it up on two legs. Junk slides off the top and clatters to the ground. With one more push, he pivots the table on its legs and it crashes down. The floor vibrates.

Ryder looks over the disaster. "What are you doing?"

Thea and Iona are both standing on crates by the large table in the center of the room, each holding a long piece of wood like a sword and wearing pieces of bent metal on their heads. Thea jumps down from a crate and runs over to Ryder. She grabs onto his arm and hides behind him. "He opened up one of the canisters and he's acting all crazy!"

Iona arrives next to them. "Korbin is picking stuff up and throwing it around like a thick-skulled ape!" Iona shouts, jabbing her wooden sword in Korbin's direction.

Ryder clenches his eyebrows together. "No, back up. Did you say he opened up a canister?"

"Yeah, I tried to stop him, but he took it from me!" Thea yells.

"Wait a second!" Korbin jumps in. "She was going to open it first!"

Ryder balls his fists. "I can't believe you did that, Korbin. You were supposed to wait! What if it's dangerous?"

Korbin shakes his head. "It's not dangerous, trust me. I had a good feeling. Plus, I feel great. Remember how hard it was to move that table in here?" He flexes both of his arms. "I bet I could take you easy. And now I'm probably even faster than Iona. Here, I'll open up another one to prove it's okay!" He runs over to the large center table where the bag is. The remaining five canisters are strewn about. He grabs one of them

"Wait, Korbin, just stop!" Ryder yells.

Korbin's eyes open wide in surprise. "Oh jeez, Ryder. It's not going to kill you."

Ryder hurries over. "Korbin, if you open that I'm going to tell Fae!"

With a mischievous smile, Korbin rotates the locking mechanism, opening the top of the cylinder. A thick grey mist vents out and collects in the air. It radiates white light, crackling with energy.

Korbin hesitantly takes a step back. "Just touch it, Ryder."

The anger disappears from Ryder's mesmerized eyes and he approaches the glowing mist, lifting his hand. The cloud dims and retracts from Ryder's outstretched fingers, but not quickly enough. As soon as Ryder touches the mist it disappears into his finger. There is a bright flash as the last bits of the cloud disappear. He jerks his arm away, stumbling backward. His face crinkles up and his legs turn to jelly. He falls.

Thea and Nero run over, but Iona keeps her distance. "Are you okay?" Nero asks.

Ryder gets up, holding his head. "I shouldn't have done that," he groans.

"Oh man, you should have seen your face! It was ridiculous," Korbin says, bursting into laughter. "How do you feel?"

"I feel strangely good... well, besides the headache and my tingling scalp. Is that what happened with you, Korb?" Ryder asks rubbing his temples slowly.

"Yep, same thing, except I didn't make that pansy face."

"Oh please, Korbin," Iona says. "You screamed like a baby."

"I did not! You're just jealous you didn't get one." Korbin walks over to the canisters. "I think there's one more!" He sifts through the three other canisters and grabs the only one that glows. "What should we do with the last one?"

Ryder sits down. "Leave it alone." He hangs his head while still rubbing his temples.

"Yeah okay." Korbin turns to the others. "Iona? Thea?"

"I don't want it!" Iona squeaks.

Nero takes a hesitant step forward.

Thea excitedly jumps before him. "Can I have it?"

Korbin shrugs. "Sure. It's the one you picked out first." Korbin grabs the canister in both hands and strains to open it. "Dang, it still won't budge."

"Let me have it," Thea says, wiggling in anticipation.

"If I can't get it, I doubt you can, but whatever." Korbin tosses it to her.

Thea fumbles with it for a moment until there is a click. A glowing mist hisses from the container. "Ha! Got it." She jumps. The mist forms another cloud. This one shifts about actively. With each new movement and shape change, there is a flash of light. Thea reaches out to touch it but the cloud jumps at her.

It disappears into her chest before she can even react. She yelps. Thea looks around at the others uncertainly and blinks repeatedly; a shiver runs through her body.

Ryder runs over and puts a hand on her back. "Are you okay? What happened?"

After a moment, Thea focuses on him. "I'm not sure, but I feel great..." She looks around the room for a moment, then snaps back to Ryder with a big grin. "Catch me if you can!"

Thea bolts off and Ryder and Korbin follow. The three children start playing a wrestling version of tag. Iona sits at one of the windows and Nero moves to the table, collecting Ryder and Thea's canisters on the way.

He looks at the white engravings on Thea's canister, which read 'SPEC UK741,' and then that of Ryder's, which reads 'EXP B113T6.' Nero grabs the only other open canister and it reads 'EXP R121T2.' He then picks up one of the canisters that Korbin discarded. 'EXP O-B302T9.' A sharp edge of shattered glass catches his finger. One of the glass eyelets is completely broken. *If there was a mist in this one… it probably got out when the glass broke.* He finally grabs the last one, which reads 'EXP X301T1' and inspects the glass eyelets for damage. His eye catches the slightest glint of light from within.

What? He puts the canister on the table and makes a dark seal with his hands to look in the eyelet. In the darkness, he can see a dim swirl of light. He jumps to his feet and twirls around holding the canister in the air. "This one isn't empty!" The others stop playing and jog over. *Oh no… I shouldn't have said anything.*

Korbin arrives first. "Give it to me! Let me see."

Ryder steps in front of Korbin's advance. "Lay off, Korb."

Korbin tries to shove past. "I just want to see it."

"Yeah. I believe that." Ryder pushes him back. "Leave Nero be."

"Really? I can have it?" Nero asks.

Ryder shrugs. "I'm not sure any of this is a good idea… I give up. Do what you want."

"But Ryder—" Korbin protests.

"Just leave it, Korbin. You already got one."

Thea jumps and claps. "Yay, Nero. Open it!"

Nero twists the locking mechanism and a very faint grey mist flows out. As it coheres, Nero's breath creates eddies in what looks like a distortion of the light; like ripples in water.

Nero reaches out and it makes only the slightest movement away. As soon as he touches the mist, his vision goes dark.

A lone floating orb, burning with soft white light hangs in front of him. As he reaches for it, he can feel something odd... something familiar... *What is that?* He resists the temptation of taking the awesome power that the orb promises. Its warmth brings with it a sense of completeness; filling a void Nero only now recognizes he has. Beyond this, he senses fear.

But why? This will help me fit in with the others. I need this! For the first time in his life, he realizes he is not afraid. *But if it isn't me... then... is it the mist? No way. That's crazy. Just take it!* He tries to shake his mind clear of the feeling but every time he reaches for the power he is frozen by an overwhelming fear, an all too familiar wall. *But why is it afraid? It's just a stupid cloud of mist... Am I about to kill it? Can it even be killed? Stop this, Nero! Just take it! You need it to fit in and be strong...* He makes one last push for the warmth but finally gives up and relaxes. *Is it worth it? I can't kill it...* Suddenly he is overwhelmed by a gut-wrenching flood of memories, good and bad from throughout his life. It is as if they are being ripped from him. His skin crawls as the darkness around him closes in, confining him into a smaller and smaller space. He tries to stop the memories, but they keep coming. Panic grips his chest and throat, making it hard to breathe. A hot lance of pain travels through his body and out his limbs. The burning orb brightens just before it disappears from his vision with a flash of violet. Suddenly, he feels like he is falling.

A faint voice echoes through Nero's semi-conscious mind. "Nero! Wake up!"

Nero opens his eyes to sees everyone huddled around him. The concern is apparent on their faces. The pain that had gripped him so entirely just a moment ago, fades.

Ryder sees Nero's eyes and lightly punches his arm. "That's for scaring us!"

Nero sits up, shoving Ryder away. "Don't hit me." A wave of hostility drives Nero to pounce on Ryder but Ryder's shocked face causes him to hesitate. *Why am I so upset?* He looks at the other children, who are equally surprised, and takes a breath. His blood cools. "I'm sorry, Ryder, I didn't mean it. What happened?"

"You touched it, just like everyone else," Korbin says, "but nothing happened for a second. Then you started to shake and passed out. It was weird. The mist kinda just disappeared, but you didn't absorb it. I guess you're just too weak," Korbin says.

Ryder helps Nero up. "Okay, everyone, give him a break and a little space to breathe."

"I knew this was a bad idea." Iona walks over to the window shaking her head. "Woo!" She points outside. "Uh, hey, there are a lot of trucks coming down the road," she says.

Thea presses her face to the dirty window to see a group of dark vehicles speeding toward town. "Are those Minis?"

"Yeah they definitely are. Probably military by their size," Iona says.

Korbin hurries to the window. "You think it has to do with the canisters?"

Ryder steps back from the glass. "We need to get out of here and get back to Fae. She'll know what to do."

The children grab their things and quickly follow Ryder down the stairs and outside. Ryder, Korbin, Thea, and Iona tear through the crumbling streets as fast as they can go. Nero struggles to keep up, but they slowly gain distance. His burning lungs and legs protest. He cannot even find the breath to yell for them to wait. By the time he makes it through the storm drain and back up the creek, the other children are far away.

Nero forces himself to continue. *Oh no, oh no, oh no. I'm going to get caught by the Minis! What am I going to do? What are they going to do to me?* He continually glances behind, spurred by a sinking feeling he is not alone. *It's just my imagination, calm down… There is no way they're already looking for me.*

When he finally makes it to town, there are no Humans in sight. Instead, Erohsian light infantry are everywhere. Their dark grey body suits are hashed with silver lines. Black visors come down from their grey helmets, only exposing the pale skin around their mouth. The Erohsians are moving around the town in groups of three, looking only slightly bigger than teenagers. One soldier in each group has a large metal backpack attached to a device they are carrying in hand.

Nero hides from view, his thoughts racing. *I just need to get home. It'll be safe there. If I can just make a run for it…* Desperation tramples caution and Nero jumps out of his hiding spot, turning toward home.

Just as he rounds the corner, he slams into an unusually tall Erohsian officer. He falls to the ground. The officer's light grey military uniform matches the hat sitting atop her hair. Once she regains her balance, her pale blue eyes take a moment to register Nero, and when they do, they turn ice cold. Nero scrambles to his feet but is roughly grabbed by one of the three soldiers with her. Nero barely takes notice of the pain shooting through his arm. His mind is ensnared by the glare of the officer.

The officer asks him what he's doing. *Oh no, does she know?* Nero barely squeezes out a response when she asks a second time. *Did I just say something about breakfast? Oh great, I'm doomed!* She talks with one of the soldiers. So many thoughts race through Nero's head, all he hears is gibberish. One of the soldiers with the large backpacks walks up to Nero and points a deadly weapon at him. Nero closes his eyes, shrinking away. The iron grip on his arm holds him in place. All the muscles in his body start to twitch and he holds his breath. *Oh please, no…*

Nero hears the button on the weapon click several times. He waits for pain that does not come. He opens his eyes, patting himself, frantically looking for wounds. *I'm not dead?*

The soldier with the device shakes his head. "No Aether, Ma'am. I'm not even getting a reading."

The officer looks down at Nero. Two evil eyes burn into him. "Alright Human, get out of my sight!"

To Nero's relief and amazement, the soldier tosses him in the most comfortable pile of rocky rubble he has ever fallen into. The Erohsians storm off without looking back.

3 Isis B.

Isis

A young Erohsian lieutenant in the standard light grey uniform stands stiffly in front of an officer's desk in an immaculately clean office. Light scintillates off small beads of sweat on his forehead. The only sound is the officer's fingers pitter-pattering over her glass keyboard. The lieutenant shifts awkwardly and looks out at the immensity of the capital. They are ninety floors up and in the center of the largest military complex in Sunta. In the distance, at the heart of the city, glass and cement skyscrapers of incredible height reach up toward the sky like slender stalks of prairie grass.

"Don't you have somewhere to be?" The ranking officer's voice stabs through the silence. Her eyes remain focused on her paper-thin computer screen.

The young man winces, but quickly regains a modicum of composure. "Yes ma'am!" He squawks with a shocking amount of vigor. His face reddens.

Isis finishes a thought, looking up at him with an unexpected fire in her pale blue eyes. "Then shouldn't you start, already?"

The man stares back at her, eyes wide, jaw slack, and knees on the verge of buckling. "Oh… yes, right away!"

Isis shakes her head, typing once more. *Pathetic. And command wonders why we have problems.*

The man looks over a holographic display emanating from the band on his wrist. "I have details from the latest report which you requested on the newborn ailment," he announces. Isis looks up at him with daggers shooting from her eyes, and the man hurriedly continues. She goes back to typing. "In the heart of Sunta, newborn numbers this month have reduced even further, which puts us down eight percent from the average five years ago. The ailment is now measurable in some of the smaller sections of Sunta as well."

Isis presses her fingers hard into her keyboard. Her fingertips turn white. "Lieutenant, do you happen to have any useful information? Even the Human cattle could have predicted that," she says without looking up.

"Yes ma'am, I was getting to the interesting part."

"Do you feel my time is unimportant?" She looks up at him. He shakes his head rapidly. "Well, then, maybe you should consider that the next time you speak. Stop wasting my time and leave me to decide what's important. Now please—what is this 'interesting' information?"

The man swallows quickly. "The Nesivians are showing the greatest reduction, followed by the Borukins in Kiats, with the Thumarians in Calahzan not far behind. The Humans, on the other hand, continue to show the most resistance. The ailment seems to be tightly connected with the population density and the natural Aether abilities of the race."

"And they're just figuring this out? Perhaps you have some ideas on what is causing it?"

The man averts his eyes. "No…"

Useless… "What else? Anything new on the Havityn?"

"The latest Havityn model confirms that Havityn Isidore won't hit the city and there's only a twenty percent chance of manifesting itself further. Currently it is at twelve percent localization. We are taking the proper precautions, just in case." Isis continues to type on her computer. The young man stands, silent and awkward.

Finally, Isis looks up. "Is that all?"

"Uh, no, sorry ma'am." The man looks at the holographic display and feathers several different views with a flick of his trembling fingers. "Oh, yes! The high royalty of the Borukins, King Ramas, has confirmed his visit in nine months!"

"That's good news." Isis pauses for a moment before she types a new note. "Okay, if that is all, I would like you to inform the office of the Secretary of Foreign Affairs that I need a copy of the preliminary itinerary for their visit for security review as soon as possible."

"Yes ma'am, right away," he says with a quick salute while he scurries out of her office.

Isis shakes her head and continues with her work. Before she can finish a sentence a small window on her monitor with red letters flashes.

INCOMING CALL: Lt. Co. Phillips

Isis taps the accept button on the screen and an Erohsian officer appears.

"Colonel, there is a situation that requires your attention. We got a hit on the DNA and retinal scanners two days ago in the outer districts of Sunta that match a class-two Human named Kabel Reikyn. He has known activity with the terrorist group Catalyst," Phillips says.

"Then standard triple S procedure applies, Lieutenant Colonel. Take two squads, scan, search, and secure the area. Why do you need me?" *Are you helpless as well?*

"Because, Ma'am, I don't have the authority to make sure we catch him."

"I'm not going to release more resources for a single class-two Human." Isis says. "If we arrest one, there'll be ten more in his place. As far as I know he's not a high priority."

"Normally, I'd fully agree, Ma'am. However, this Human has given us a significant amount of trouble. My squads tracked him to New Lur but lost him again this morning. In the process, they made several Aether scans that suggest he was in possession of multiple essences."

"Really? And out in the open like this?" Isis runs her thumb along the edge of her right ear, pensively. "Did they get a reading on their strength and cast?"

"There was an unusual amount of noise in the signal so there was no way to tell cast. Our extrapolation algorithm estimated the essences to be around a one on the Boltz scale. The stranger thing is, it was sporadically estimating values of four and higher..."

"Four! How did that slip by? Have the terrorists found a way to hide the signature?" Isis shakes her head. "Regardless, a class-four essence would cause a lot of trouble if one of the terrorist members absorbed it..."

"I agree, Ma'am. That's the last thing we need."

Were these the ones stolen from research? I don't remember any level-four entities being held there. Isis continues to play with her ear. "They must be transporting them. This may be our last chance to retrieve them before they're put to use. If we can locate him before night, we still may have a chance. Take four platoons of light infantry, fully geared. Split them into fire-teams of three. One Aether detector for each team. Search the area in and around New Lur. Have a levitraft ready with an equipped team of soldiers for me outside. I'll see you within the hour at New Lur."

"Yes, ma'am."

Isis salutes and ends the call. She finishes writing a couple of messages, then grabs a white ruler-shaped object resting in a charging slot. With a little pressure the object snaps around her wrist and a large holographic display pops up in front of her.

Good morning Colonel Belshiv.
Power Cell: 100% charged

Isis swipes the hologram away. She grabs her hat and coat, turning down the light grey hallway with an evenly illuminated ceiling. After a couple of elevators, she arrives at a large main floor lobby where a series of guards and scanners monitor a stream of people coming and going. She easily picks her way through the crowd, her eyes looking over the other Erohsians. A set of automatic doors opens at the exit.

Among the cars waiting for passengers, she is quick to spot the sleek lines of the levitraft supported by three landing feet. The dark, windowless vehicle shimmers in the light, showing off a surface that has a deceptive depth. Small, adjustable ducts for thrust and control line the bottom. Larger ducts are situated in the rear. An armed soldier stands on either side of the entry to the bright white interior.

Isis takes a slightly cramped seat next to the driver, nodding to him. The driver waits for his companions to sit down in the rear seats before sealing the hatch. The door closes like a set of jaws, accompanied by a whirring of gears.

The turbine engine ignites with a gentle, intensifying hum and virtual windows appear, revealing the surroundings. "Activating the Yerantol cage when you're ready, Ma'am," the driver says.

Isis closes her eyes and nods. The driver touches a button and Isis squeezes her armrests as she is thrust into a sudden gut-wrenching free-fall. The sensation lasts a few seconds before it subsides into uneasy weightlessness. The three landing feet retract, and the craft rises a meter off the ground. With a kick of the thrusters, they gracefully zip through the base.

On their way out, they pass rows of heavy infantry in their metal combat armor and an assortment of war vehicles. Off in the distance, a few light bipedal mech units are performing agility drills through a course of large cement obstacles.

Once outside the base, they follow a wide road lined with pristine, monotonous grey commercial buildings. The road eventually leads them to an imposing wall, one hundred meters tall, that forms the edge of the city. They go through the large gate and accelerate on the open road, passing a long line of traffic waiting to enter the city.

"Take us as high as you can without risking the Skimmers. I'd like to have a look around," Isis says.

The driver tips back the control stick and the levitraft shoots to the sky, revealing the landscape around for hundreds of kilometers. Off to the side, the Carn River runs from under the walls of Sunta and is swallowed by a thick forest. Glimpses of a silvery thread of the river shine through the forest as it extends all the way to the coast. A dark haze steams from the trees and blurs the blue of the ocean behind. A chill runs up Isis's spine as she recalls macabre reports of people lost to the forest. *If evil exists… It would be there.*

Halfway to their destination, they begin to glide down toward the ruined Human city of Lur. Eventually, they lose enough altitude to join the road once again. The road takes them through a ragged wall made of a patchwork of materials and ultimately to New Lur, a pathetic town that was reestablished to give the Humans some ownership. *To think we used to respect the Humans… now they're nothing but marginally useful cattle.*

The levitraft settles alongside several large transport trucks in the middle of town. Teams of light infantry are scattered about, banging hard on doors and interrogating the frightened Humans. The Erohsians have an air of supremacy despite their small size.

"Disengaging the Yerantol cage," the driver says.

Isis grabs her armrest as she suddenly feels like she is rocketing toward the sky. Her body clenches until she adjusts to normal gravity. Lieutenant Colonel Phillips approaches her as soon as she steps from the levitraft.

Phillips snaps her a crisp salute at the top of his helmet. "Ma'am, we have teams of three scanning and searching the town as requested. The other platoons are searching the surrounding fields and abandoned structures."

Isis taps her wrist computer, popping up a holographic screen. She pulls up a map of the area that shows soldiers as little red dots swarming around. "I can see that... Have you found anything yet?"

"No ma'am, just... cattle," he says with a bit of disgust. "And non-bonded, at that."

"Keep me informed and make sure that you do a thorough search of the old industrial buildings. If you haven't found him by dusk, triple the patrolling groups east of the town to catch him on the run to the mountains. He'll want to put as much distance as he can between himself and Sunta. He'll probably look for sanctuary among Borukin sympathizers. We can't let him get that far. Notify me immediately if anything comes up."

"Yes, ma'am." Phillips gives her another salute.

Isis gathers an additional team of three soldiers. She sets off on a direct path to the burning point of frustration in her mind, a well-kept blue house.

Once at the house, she pauses a moment to survey the blooming flowers filling the windows on either side of the main door. *How disgustingly domestic...*

Isis approaches the porch. Before she reaches the top step, the door opens. A strong, older woman steps into the doorframe lightly. She stands half a head taller than Isis, her expression guarded.

"What can I do for you, Isis?" the woman asks.

"We are going to search this dwelling, Nidella."

"You are welcome to come into my home. Your soldiers are not."

"I must insist," Isis says, face deadpan.

"Then I would like to talk to your father."

"This is outside of General Belshiv's jurisdiction. Step aside."

"I don't understand where you get all this anger."

"I'm doing my job. Apprehend her," Isis says to the soldiers with her.

The two closest soldiers respond instantly. Their combat suits give them an unnatural speed. Nidella reacts just as fast, evading their grasp. With an incredibly smooth motion, she grabs one of the soldiers, spins him around, and yanks his arm up behind his back.

In the middle of the action, Isis takes a stun baton from a soldier's belt and closes the distance. Before Nidella notices, Isis jabs the stun baton around the soldier and into her side. Nidella's body tenses. With a yelp, she releases the soldier, falling to one knee. Isis stuns her again and she collapses. The two soldiers quickly recover and grab Nidella's arms, hauling her upright.

Isis glares at the soldiers holding Nidella. "Send her to Capping and Extracting in Demeeurj and have Dr. Grantov run her through every scan his twisted mind can come up with. I want to know everything."

"Ma'am, we could cap her here and let you know immediately," the soldier that had his arm yanked behind him says.

Isis snaps her eyes to the soldier. "I know it's not fair, because you were probably born stupid and incapable, but I strongly suggest you stop thinking for yourself. If a cap would work on her, don't you think I would have asked for that?" The soldier looks at the ground. "Now, take her to Demeeurj tower."

The three-soldier team marches off with the stunned Nidella while Isis and the three soldiers from her levitraft enter the house.

Isis looks around the neat living area. A twinge of anger flares up with a thought of Nidella's comments. "Tear this place apart and bring me anything that looks suspicious. Scan everything."

The soldiers begin to sweep the house, scouring every corner. Isis walks to the kitchen, where she smells the lingering scent of breakfast. Her stomach turns over in hunger. A steaming kettle just on the verge of whistling catches her attention. *Why not?* She finds a silly looking mug and makes herself some tea. Isis pulls up information on her wrist computer while sipping her drink.

```
Name: Fae Underwood
Race: Erohsian
Dependents: Orphans 345567091,
    345567921, 345570159,
    345570159, and 345570160
Notes: Commonwealth volunteer.
```

Erohsian? That's a joke.

She sweeps away the holographic projection in frustration and paces about the house, stepping around the scattered contents of shelves and drawers. She eventually drifts up the stairs toward the echoes of the destructive search.

One of the soldiers meets her at the top step, something small and silver hanging from his hand. "Ma'am, I think I found something from one of the children's rooms."

Isis frowns as the soldier hands her a silver chained necklace. The pendant is a dark rectangular piece of flat metal. *Useless*—Her heart nearly jumps out of her chest when her eyes catch sight of a series of etched symbols on the necklace. She drops the mug she was carrying, snatching the necklace with her hand. "Ancient?" she asks, running her finger over the symbols.

The soldier relaxes a little and nods his head. "That's what I was thinking, Ma'am. I picked it up with the detector, so it may even be active."

A genuine smile forms on her lips. "Okay. We're done here."

*****

Isis's purposeful strides take her toward her levitraft. Just as she passes one of the uninhabited houses, a blur of something smashes into her. She jumps, tightening the grip on the necklace in her hand. The blur is a scrambling, young,

Human boy. Her anger flares immediately. One of her soldiers grabs him roughly as soon as he jumps up. She glares down at the skinny child and he shrinks away. *Pathetic Human...*

"What are you doing out here, boy?" Isis asks coldly.

"Umm... errrr, aaaaa." The boy looks around frantically for inspiration before his gaze finally rests at his feet.

"Hey!" Isis snaps. "What are you doing?"

The boy winces, looking up at her with his eyes, his head still downcast. "Breakfast?"

Isis shakes her head. *Unbelievable.* "Scan him just in case."

The soldier with the Aether detector approaches him and points his handheld device at the boy. The child clamps his eyes shut, visibly shaking. The soldier pushes a button on the top of the device where a red bar flashes and beeps. He tries it a few more time with the same results. The boy slowly opens one eye then the other, puzzled. He looks down at his body, tentatively patting himself in several areas.

The soldier shakes his head, frowning. "No Aether, Ma'am. I'm not even getting a reading."

Isis shakes her head in disgust. *Wow, a true gem among the cattle...* Isis returns her cold stare to the boy. "Alright Human, get out of my sight!" She jerks her head to the side and the soldier tosses the child into a pile of rubble.

*****

"It's ancient, alright," says the svelte Erohsian scientist. "And it's in amazing condition." He stands up from a lab bench, where the orphan's necklace is lying under a light on a flexible arm.

"Can you tell me anything about it, Alec?" Isis asks. They walk side by side through the lab.

"Come on, Isis, what do I look like, a miracle worker?" Alec asks.

"Well, I thought you were smart. And I don't say that often. Was I wrong?"

"Oh, please, you're just egging me on now."

"What? Are you not up for the challenge?"

"Trust me, Isis, I need no motivation to look into something like this," Alec says, rolling the piece of metal in his fingers. "You just need to understand that this is an incredibly rare piece. The majority of ancient technology I've seen has been inert, so it's going to take some time. But I can tell you this: compared to the other active pieces that have been discovered, this one is in superior condition. I have a feeling this piece is going to open up a new door for us."

"Is there anything you need that will speed up the process?"

"Besides the equipment I've been asking you for?" Alec thinks for a second. "Well, considering the condition of this piece, it must have been kept in a vault or a semi-sealed area, so naturally, you could expect there to be more treasures of the sort, which could increase funding and accelerate the deciphering process. Where did this come from?"

How could a bunch of orphans get their hands on this? "I need time to figure that out. For now, see what you can do. I'll be back later."

"Yes, Ma'am!" Alec mock salutes, his blue eyes glinting.

Isis shakes her head, smiling. She turns on her heel, quickly walking out.

After rising from the depths of the military headquarters, she arrives back in her office. The orange light of the sunset plays against her walls. She sinks into her seat and calls Lt. Co. Phillips. "Phillips, what's the status on the search around New Lur?"

"Colonel, we've been trying to reach you. We haven't found the suspect, but we picked up his trail leaving the old industrial district. I've sent a full platoon to follow. We also traced a faint essence signature through the old industrial district and found five empty canisters in what appears to be a hideout filled with junk. The canisters have no Erohsian markings. They look to be similar to what the terrorists have used. We compared several hair samples we found with our database and they belong to the orphans registered to Fae Underwood."

"Tell me you found those rats. Or at least that you set up surveillance on Underwood's house…"

Phillips pauses. "Sorry, Ma'am, as soon as my platoons finished searching the town and the industrial district, I set up patrols of the eastern area. As you requested."

Damnit! I shouldn't have been so careless… If they have absorbed those essences or have knowledge where they got the ancient technology… I need to find them. "Alright, Phillips, get soldiers back there immediately and monitor Underwood's house. Expand your patrol East of New Lur, toward the coast, and between New Lur and Sunta. There's no way to know where these orphans could have gone. I want your men to bring in everyone they find, and I don't care what rules they have to break… Do you understand, Phillips? I want those Humans!"

"Yes, ma'am!"

4 A Second Chance

Nero

Sunset is fast approaching when Nero finally makes it back to Fae's house, stumbling up to the door. He turns the knob and pushes, but the door is locked. He rattles the door.

Can't anything go right today? First, I mess it up with the mist, then I almost get vaporized by stupid Minis, and now I can't even get home! His head falls against the door with a thud as he fights back another round of tears. The door suddenly opens and Nero falls through.

"Nero!" Before he can catch his balance, he is caught in the surprisingly powerful arms of Thea. After a long moment, Thea lets go of him. "We were worried about you. What happened?"

Dried dirt outlines the tearstains below Nero's bloodshot eyes. He looks at everyone standing around the kitchen. A knot forms in his throat and a giant hole opens in his chest. The others are all home safely without him. His eyes dart desperately around the room for Fae, but she is nowhere to be seen.

"Where's Fae?" He slowly starts to take in his surroundings. Their nicely organized house looks as though it was hit by a Havityn. Cabinets are open, drawers are lying on the ground next to their contents, and virtually everything else in the house has been carelessly moved or broken. *What happened here?*

"We're not sure where she is. We just got back," Ryder says. "What happened to you?"

"You guys left me!" Nero exclaims. His voice settles, and he looks at the ground. "All by myself. And the Minis almost got me."

"I told you!" Korbin says, pointing a finger at Ryder.

"Korbin, stop. They don't use Human slaves," Ryder responds. "How do you know they even took Fae. What if she's just hiding?"

"Well, why'd they tear the place up then?" Iona asks.

Ryder turns to Iona. "They're Erohsians. That's what they do, ruin people's lives. I know running away seems like a good idea, but they've already searched here. Why would they come back? Fae will be back. They can't keep her for no reason." A silence falls over the group.

"You think the Erohsians took Fae?" Nero asks, his panic hitting a new level.

Thea lets out a sob.

"Take it easy, Nero. We're trying to figure that out. We don't know anything," Ryder says.

Iona drums her fingers on her thigh, thinking. "You have a good point Ryder. If you're playing hide and seek, the best place to hide is somewhere they've already searched. Besides, it would look a lot worse for us if they caught us wandering around in the middle of the night."

Ryder slaps his hands together. "Okay, so that's the plan. We just hang tight until Fae gets back. So, Nero, how'd you escape?"

It takes Nero a moment to let go of the thought of Fae and remember what he just went through. "I was trying to get home after you all disappeared when this horrible woman with a gang of soldiers grabbed me. The woman told one of the soldiers to shoot me just in case."

"Then what?" Thea asks, leaning forward.

"I'm not sure. The soldier pointed a gun at me, but I think it was out of juice, or whatever it uses, because he said 'there's no Aether.' Then they just tossed me in a pile of rocks."

"They were scanning you for Aether, not trying to kill you!" Iona blurts. "I think Aether is like a magical energy or something that lets you do special things. They must have been searching for something if they were scanning the whole town."

Thea suddenly jumps off the ground in a fit of excitement. "Is that what was in the canisters?"

Everyone looks at her with surprise. "What?"

Thea throws up her hands as if it were obvious. "The canisters we found today! Was that Aether inside of them?"

A large smile sprouts on Korbin's face. "I have magic?"

Ryder nods his head at Korbin. "That would explain a lot. Maybe someone from Catalyst stole the canisters and the Minis are searching for them."

Korbin throws out his arms. "No, seriously guys. I have magic? This could be the most awesome thing ever!"

"We don't know what you have, Korb, but I'm guessing it's brain damage," Iona says with a smirk. Korbin glares at her.

"But why'd they take Fae?" Nero asks.

"Oh no." Iona puts her hands to her cheeks. "What if they tracked us to Fae and think we're part of the resistance?"

Nero looks at the other children uneasily. "What does that mean?"

"If the Minis took Fae because they're looking for us," Ryder says, "then they could be back."

Wide-eyed, Iona looks at Ryder. "Unless they're already here…"

Thea jumps over to Ryder and latches herself to his arm. "What are we going to do? I don't want to be used as a lab rat." She finishes with a sob.

Ryder dismisses Iona in frustration. "Come on, Iona, that doesn't help." He looks back at Thea and tries to peel her away. "Look, if they were outside… we'd know." He steps back. "They probably won't be back until morning… So, let's be long gone by then." He looks around at everyone, his eyes calm. "We'll be alright. They can't get us if we run away."

"What about Fae?" Nero asks.

Thea nods. "Yeah, what about her?"

"We're just kids, what could we do to help if they took her?" Ryder asks. "We don't even know if she's still alive. Anyone caught with ties to the resistance can be punished by death or locked up for the rest of their lives. If we really want to help, we need to find someone to help and come back. It doesn't do her any good if we get caught too."

"You think they killed her?" Nero asks softly.

"I hope not… but they are Minis. What I do know is that if the Minis are looking for us, then we need to get as far away from here as we can."

"What if we're over reacting?" Iona asks.

"We'll call back in a few days," Ryder says. "Hopefully everything is fine, and we'll just come back… The alternative just isn't worth the risk."

Iona nods. "Okay, so run away—where?"

"We could go to the ocean. I bet we would be safe from the Minis there." Ryder looks around at the worried faces and catches Thea's eye. "Thea, you always wanted to go on a boat, right?"

Thea nods her head. "Oh, yes please."

Ryder smiles. "Well, then we'll go to the ocean and find a boat. We could travel the world until things cool down."

Now a smile spreads on Korbin's face. "That sounds good to me."

Ryder half-smiles. "Yeah. And when we've made some friends, we'll come back and take Fae with us."

The children nod while Nero's head hangs.

Ryder holds up his hands. "Okay, we first need to pack. Only bring what is absolutely necessary. A few clothes, something to sleep on, that kinda thing."

Korbin and Thea hurry up the stairs. Iona lags behind. "So what's the plan?" she asks.

"I figure we just need to get out of here as soon as possible. I'll grab our map and compass, and we can make a better plan at old Tom's house where the Minis won't expect us," Ryder says.

Iona looks at him. "That's not much of a plan."

Ryder puts a hand on her back. "We'll come up with something good, trust me. Okay?"

Iona nods hesitantly then heads upstairs.

Ryder pats Nero on the back. "Come on, man. Let's go pack."

Nero nods his head weakly, slipping off his chair. *I don't want to travel the world... and I don't want to go to old Tom's in the middle of night. I sure hope Fae's okay...*

He slowly follows Ryder upstairs, stopping at the top when he sees his favorite mug shattered on the floor. Nero sighs, dropping to his knees to collect the pieces. *It couldn't get any worse...*

When he finishes, Nero walks down the stairs, inspecting the broken fragments in his hands. Again, tears well up in the corners of his eyes. Just as he reaches the bottom step, a flash of light bounces off a window and refracts through his tears.

Minis? Nero ducks down from view, fear fiercely ripping away his despair. *They're here already?*

No.

What? Nero looks around but sees no one. He shakes off his confusion, his fears strangely drifting away.

He sees another glint of light, violet, coming from outside. *What's that?* He walks toward the back door, moving his head around to manage a better view. He peers through the window in the door, nothing to see. Helplessly curious, he slides the bolt and cracks the door open, carefully peeking out. Still nothing. He pokes his head out. A quick look around gives way to disappointment... *Wait, why am I disappointed?*

Just then, he notices a slight shimmer in the night air. If he squints and looks to the side, he can see a faint light. Before he realizes what he is doing, he steps out into the open, toward the light. His chest is tight. His palms are clammy. A couple of steps away, the shimmering air collects itself into a gaseous violet blob. Deep reds and yellows crackle with life from within.

Nero takes a sudden breath, pulling his arm back and covering his eyes with a hand. He squints through his fingers. *Another mist? Is this Aether?* The energetic, dancing light mesmerizes him. The different colors curl into one another, fading, then popping back to a strong violet. Suddenly, his heart jumps. *My second chance? I could be fast and strong like Ryder, and then they couldn't leave me...* With a newfound eagerness, he steps forward. *I'll get it this time!*

He pushes away the uncertainties that had stricken him in his first attempt and reaches for the mist. Just as he is about to touch it, the mist casually avoids his hand, moving just out of his reach. Nero takes another step forward. Again, the mist narrowly escapes his eager fingers.

What's going on? This didn't happen before. He takes another step forward, and then makes a quick reach for the mist. It reacts with an equal amount of speed.

His nose wrinkles in frustration. *What the heck?*

He readies himself on the balls of his feet and lunges for the mist. It evades him with ease. He regains his balance and runs after the elusive mist, reaching whenever he gets close. No matter how fast he runs, or how quick his hand moves, the mist is always just out of his reach. His breathing is short. A cramp in his side burrows into his organs with every ragged breath. Finally, he closes the distance and makes a desperate dive, hand outstretched.

The ground knocks the wind out of him. He lies there on his stomach for a moment without moving. *Maybe Korbin is right. I am too weak to absorb one.* He lets out a pent-up breath from his nose and dust gets into his eyes. He rolls over, rubbing them. *Why does this always happen to me? It's the stupid mist's fault, making fun of me like everyone else!*

Nero opens his eyes. Finding a small rock, he jumps to his feet. "Just leave me alone!" He winds up and throws the rock toward the glowing mist. The mist bursts, showering the ground and fading as it falls. Darkness overtakes the night, leaving Nero alone once more. He pats some of the dirt from his clothes and heads back inside.

By the time Nero makes it back to the stairs, his triumph has evaporated and his stomach feels like a large stone. *Maybe I should just stay back by myself. I can't do anything. If I go with them, I'm just going to slow them down and be a pain...* Thea's scream cuts through his gloom, sending a jolt down his spine. Ryder and Korbin rush to the girls' room in a stampede of feet.

Thea is on the ground, tearing through the piles of items the Erohsians had scattered. "My necklace is gone!"

"What?" Ryder asks.

Thea looks up at Ryder, eyes brimming. "They took it! The Minis stole it!"

Ryder's jaw drops. "Wh—why weren't you wearing it?"

Thea throws what she had in her hands to the ground. "Because I'm afraid of losing it... It's the only thing I have left."

Ryder glances at Iona. She is touching the blue gemmed necklace around her neck. He walks over to Thea, sitting down beside her, his hand on her back. "Look, Thea, we'll get you a new one, a better one."

Thea turns sharply to Ryder. "I don't want a new one! I want mine!"

Ryder flinches. "Okay, sorry. Well, then, I guess we'll just have to get it back."

Her eyebrows lift. "Really?"

Ryder puts his hand on her back again. "Oh, yeah. We're going to be the greatest treasure hunters on the entire planet. Your necklace will be at the top of our list."

Thea wipes a tear from her eye. "But how are we going to get it from the Minis?"

"It's going to be hard, and it may take a while, but as long as we don't give up, one day it'll be back around your neck. Will you promise me you won't give up?"

Thea puts her hand to her bare neck, nodding. "Okay, I won't give up."

Nero straightens himself up. *Maybe if I go, I'll get another chance to absorb a mist. I can't give up, either!*

Ryder helps Thea up. "So, Iona, you know you have nothing to hide, since you didn't touch a mist. If you don't want, you probably don't have to come."

Iona turns back to Ryder. "Who else is going to run the boat and find the treasures?"

Ryder smiles. "Aren't you afraid of the monsters we might find?"

"Come on." A small smile creeps up one side of her mouth. "Haven't you known me my entire life? I'll probably have to protect *you* from the monsters."

Ryder's lips come together with a playful glare.

Korbin jumps in to the middle of the room. "I can't wait to fight the monsters! I want to be just like Captain Konquer." Korbin suddenly freezes. "I'm going to go pack." He disappears.

The pit in Nero's stomach opens again. He tries to swallow, his throat dry. *I can't do monsters. I can't even get a stupid mist. I'd probably just get eaten. If the Minis don't want me, maybe it is safer to just stay behind.*

"Okie-dokie. Well I should go check on Korbin. That last look concerns me. We'll see you downstairs soon." Ryder thumps Nero on the back. "Come on, Nero."

Ryder and Nero enter their room to see Korbin collecting a pile of action figures on his bed.

Ryder eyes the pile. "Yo, Korb, what're you packing?"

Korbin glances up at Ryder, his face innocent. "My Combatmen 3977 collection with all-terrain vehicle and field med station along with their arch nemesis The Spider Murderess!"

Ryder picks up a muscular soldier: green short sleeves ready to burst, metal spiked shoulder plates, two clenched fists, and a snarling face with bulging veins to match. "Your Combatmen, Korbin? Can you wear Captain Konquer?" Ryder says, waving the soldier around.

"No."

"Can you eat the good Captain?"

"Um, no, he's made of plastic. That'd be stupid."

"Well, then, you must be able to sleep on him."

"No way, Ryder! He's my favorite, plus his spiky shoulders would probably hurt—if not—pierce a hole through all your organs!"

Ryder hands back the figurine. "Yeah, that's kinda my point. I know you look to Captain Konquer for inspiration, but we can't use him where we're going."

Korbin's shoulders drop. "So, don't bring him?"

Ryder nods. He adopts an adult-like tone. "Now, Korbin, just because your bed is something you can sleep on doesn't mean it'll fit in your bag, so don't try."

Korbin punches Ryder in the arm. "I'm not stupid! Jeez…"

Ryder hops away, smiling. He winks at Nero then gestures with his head to their beds. "Come on, Nero, let's try to pack our desks since those will be useful…"

Korbin glares at Ryder.

Nero smiles, walking over to his bed. *I have to go with them, they're all I have; my only family.*

It takes twenty minutes before everyone is downstairs with their backpacks. Ryder and Iona cover the counter with food.

"Alright, this is all the food we can find that won't go bad," Ryder says. "Everyone bring as much as you can."

Korbin shakes his head. "Can't, don't have any room."

Ryder's shoulders drop. "Come on, Korb, seriously? Captain Konquer?"

Ryder and Korbin lock eyes for a moment before Korbin lets out a grunt. He dumps several action figures from his bag onto the kitchen table. He walks back to Ryder, glaring. "Alright, gimme the food. I just hope if Fae comes back, she'll look after them for me."

Nero's resolve melts away. *Fae...*

Ryder hands Korbin cans of food. "Of course she'll watch our stuff. I bet the first thing she'll do when she gets back is put them in your room."

And wonder where we are...

"And with all of us out, she'll have this place cleaned in no time," Ryder says.

Will she be sad? Lonely? Nero looks around the kitchen, recalling fond memories of cooking.

Thea pauses from filling her bag. "Do you think she'll be okay?"

Ryder nods. "Of course she will. She's super strong and, besides, we'll be back as soon as we can to make sure everything is good."

"Do you think she'll be mad at us?" Iona asks.

Ryder shakes his head. "She'll understand that we had to go because of the Minis."

But I don't have to...

Ryder grabs several items and thrusts them at Nero. "Here, pack up."

Nero looks at the food in Ryder's hands for a long moment. "I don't think I'm going..."

"What?" Thea gasps.

Nero looks down at the floor. "I'm going to stay, just in case Fae comes back. I already got scanned. The Minis won't really care about me."

Korbin zips up his bag and sets it down on the counter. "You're just scared!"

Nero's head slumps. He uses the long sleeve of his shirt to wipe at tears rolling down his cheeks.

Ryder punches Korbin in the arm. "Shut up, Korbin." Ryder walks around the counter, putting a hand on Nero's shoulder. "It's okay, Nero. Fae will be happy that you decided to stay back. Though, I can't say I'd want to be you when she makes you help clean this mess." He squeezes Nero's shoulder. "You're probably the brave one to stay behind." Ryder pats him on the back one last time and looks to the others. "Okay, everyone, let's get going."

The children finish stuffing their bags and make their way to the door. Thea gives Nero a hug and the rest say their goodbyes.

"Tell Fae we're sorry for taking all the money and food," Ryder says. "We'll be back, so keep out of trouble."

Nero waves them off as they disappear in the night. *It's not because I'm scared. This is just where I belong…*

He walks over to the couch by the window, sitting down with his head in his hands. A memory of another time overtakes him.

Fae walks over to Nero. He watches the children run off on their first adventure on their own.

"Come with me, Nero. I want to show you something."

She leads Nero up the stairs to her room. A sliver of light from a crack in the curtains shines on an old four poster bed. Nero follows, and Fae pulls back the curtains, letting the light flood in. She guides Nero to the wall opposite the foot of her bed.

A large painting hangs from the wall. A group of people stands in the foreground to the right and a single woman stands to the left. They all watch a lone man ride away with two swords crossed on his back. Two similar wooden swords of different lengths are crossed underneath the actual painting. The swords are carved from a dark wood, light grain running their length. Their edges are scorched.

"Nero, do you know what this is?" Fae asks. Nero shakes his head. "This is something that has been in my family for a very long time. It is similar to the story of Nero, who you took your name from, but it is much older. The story is about a young man named Vadik. He was humble, not especially brave, not especially talented, but he had a very good heart. One day, his village was overrun by a terrible enemy. The strong and powerful people in the village, the ones that you would expect to save the day, left the villagers to their doom. Vadik realized that something must be done, and even though he was scared, he rallied the villagers and fought back. The villagers from that day forward looked at him with new respect. He knew that more fighting was to come, so he made two very special swords. He continued to fight for months and he did so wonderfully with his powerful Aether Blades—as they were called in legend. One day, he was summoned by people from a distant land who were also fighting the same horrible enemy. They said that they found a way to stop the enemy, if only they had more people to fight. Vadik offered his help, but wouldn't let any of the other villagers come, because he knew many wouldn't return. This picture is of the day when he left the village."

"What happened to him?"

"No one knows." She smiles, scratching his back.

Nero returns from his memory. Fresh tears soak his hands. *Am I just making excuses because I'm scared? Do I really belong with them?* Nero shakes his head. *What am I supposed to do?*
Go!

5 Flight from Home

Iona

Low on the horizon, the golden moon Aurysy, bathes the lifeless remains of the crumbling homes in a yellow light. Higher up, the outline of Stybris is barely visible. Bright yellow meteor impacts and other scars on its surface give away the otherwise dark moon. Around the two moons, a countless number of stars poke holes through the night's sky. Hidden in the deep shadows cast by the forlorn structures, the children look back on their town.

"Think Nero will be okay?" Thea asks.

"Don't worry. He'll be fine," Ryder says. "If they let him go once already, then there's no reason they'd take him now. I'm sure him and Fae are going to have a blast together."

"Yeah I bet," Thea says. Her voice carrying a hint of a smile.

Ryder slinks out of the shadows. He runs along the makeshift barrier to where it meets another structure.

Iona hesitates as Ryder dips into an old building. *Stupid Nero. Why can't he just be like the rest of us? He's always making things difficult.* With one last look toward the town, she follows the others.

At the back of the building, Ryder moves over a few rocks. He peels back a thin piece of metal covering a hole in the wall, allowing the children to crawl through. On the other side, they scuffle along a crumbling road. Dark trees loom overhead, like menacing figures, rustling in the light breeze. The road leads them up a small hill where the outline of a huge mansion cuts into the horizon.

Iona's mouth is suddenly very dry, and she looks around, half expecting to see Nero.

Korbin stops. "Are you sure Old Tom isn't here?"

Ryder faces Korbin. "Yes, Korb, I just made that story up for fun."

"Jeez, Korbin," Iona says, storming forward. "Are you going to take Nero's spot now?"

Korbin jumps. "What? No way. I'm just joking," he says with a hint of timidity.

Ryder hurries around Iona. He leads the way through a broken gate and up to the front of the large house with a pair of dark doors. The hinges scream in protest and the bottom of the door scrapes as Ryder pushes into the house. Once everyone is through, he seals them inside. Dirty windows light their path as they step around the old furniture. A set of stairs with a broken railing plunges into the utter darkness of the basement.

Korbin stops at the top of the stairs. "Can I turn my flashlight on now?"

Ryder walks down the stairs, rummaging through his bag. "Just wait until we're down and out of sight. We don't need to risk anyone seeing the light."

The stairs groan with each step as the children descend into the basement. Ryder's flashlight beams across the dark room, revealing old dusty shelves and a table pushed against one of the back walls. The air is warm, old, and touched by the stink of mildew. More flashlights blink on behind him and dance about the basement from one dark corner to the next. Ryder pulls out a map from his bag. He lays it out across the table, smoothing it flat with his hands and placing a couple of cans of food on the corners to hold it down.

Iona is first to join Ryder. "So, what are you thinking?" she asks after they both look over the map for a moment.

Ryder takes a deep breath. "Well we only have three opt—"

The screech from the hinges on the front door sends a thrill through Iona's body.

Korbin flashes his light at the stairs. "Tom!?"

Thea grips Ryder. "Minis?"

Iona squeezes her flashlight. *How'd they get here already?*

Ryder clicks off his flashlight and sets it down on the table. "Shhh, quiet. Turn your flashlights off and stay here. I'll be right back."

Iona, Thea, and Korbin huddle together in the dark; a few slivers of moonlight pierce the darkness through large gaps in the floor. They hear Ryder's light steps leaving them and then the groan of the old stairs.

Iona holds her breath. *You're alright, it's just some stupid animal or something. The Erohsians would make a lot more noise if they were chasing us.* She starts to breathe again. *Unless they sent special units—stop it!* She shakes her head.

There is a loud thump of bodies thrashing against the floor. She instinctively ducks down with the others, looking toward the ceiling at the far end of the basement. The sound stops after no more than a moment. *Oh, please be all right, Ryder.* The floor creaks and footsteps move toward the basement door. She tenses when the staircase begins to groan. Multiple sets of feet clap down the stairs. A flashlight appears, floating in midair, slowly scanning the area.

"It's okay, everyone," Ryder says. "It's Nero!"

Iona exhales her pent-up breath and clicks on her flashlight with the others. *At least it's not the Erohsians...*

Thea jumps up. "Nero! What are you doing here? I thought you were staying at Fae's."

"Well..." Nero's flashlight moves around the ground. "I was, but then I saw that you guys left the matches and some food, so I figured I'd bring them to you before you traveled too far. I ran like crazy to get here. I'm glad I caught you."

Ryder holds out his hand. "Well, thanks, Nero. I'll take them from you."

Nero looks down at Ryder's hand, grabbing the shoulder straps on his backpack. He adjusts the weight of the pack and looks back up to Ryder. "I was thinking—um—Well, if it's okay, and since I'm already out here... could I just come along?"

Thea runs up to Nero and gives him a hug. She steps back, smiling. "Of course, Nero!"

Iona turns and walks over to the map. *Great... He's just going to slow us down.*

Ryder thumps Nero on the back. "Welcome aboard! But seriously, enough wasting time, we really need to figure out our plan."

Nero points his flashlight at Ryder. "Wait. You don't have a plan yet?"

Ryder glances at him. "We were about to work on it. Then you came and scared us." Ryder walks over to the map. Iona and the rest of the children gather around. Ryder places his finger on the foothills in the southern part of a mountainous area. "We're here." The mountains run north to south and end abruptly at the ocean on either end of the continent. A river drains from the mountains to the west and then hooks south through a city to the ocean. Ryder points his finger at the city. "This is Sunta, and we definitely want to stay away from here." He puts his finger next to a bay, where there is another city on the opposite side of the river from where they are. A thick forest runs along the river with small skull and crossbones printed along its perimeter. "This is Blue Horin, the closest place other than Sunta. I say this is where we go and look for a boat or something to get us away."

"No, that won't work." All the children look at Nero. He pushes forward, pointing to the forest. "You forgot this forest. We can't go through this."

"Why not? It's the quickest route," Ryder says. "It's either that, north along the foothills around Sunta which puts us in the open, or through the mountains to the Borukins. That's just too far for us to travel on our own. We need to get to the city and find some help."

Iona's tongue is dry and sticks to the top of her mouth; a problem she usually has when Nero is around.

"Are you sure?" Nero bends down to look closely at the map. He starts to tap it frantically. "It's called Ferin Forest. FEAR-IN-FOREST! Other than that, and the cute little Human *skulls,* I don't see any reason not to…"

Korbin smacks Nero on the back. "That's the spirit, let's get some monsters!"

"Weren't you just scared of the dark?" Iona asks.

Korbin glares. "I was only scared for you and Thea."

"Pff, yeah…" Iona looks away.

"This is our first time ever leaving New Lur!" Nero says. "Did you ever think the monsters might be bigger than you? Why would they put skulls all over the place? Can't we go another way?"

Korbin lets out an exasperated sigh. "If you're so scared, then go back to Fae, Sam."

Nero looks at Korbin, eyes glistening.

"Easy, guys," Ryder says. "The Erohsians probably just put them on the map to scare people. Or maybe it's just really old. If there are animals still there, they will probably be just as scared of us as we are of them."

Nero looks down and rubs his eyes. "Yeah, all of the animals except the ones that want to eat you…"

Ryder puts his hand on Nero's shoulder. "Come on, Nero, it'll be okay. The worst thing is the Erohsians. The forest will give us a nice place to hide. And if it's dangerous, they'll never think we'd go through it." He pauses. "Any choice we make is a risk, and I think this will be the best. Besides, we're stronger and faster now. I think we'll be okay."

Iona drums her fingers on the table. "Yeah, that sounds good. Plus, it should only take a couple of days to get to Blue Horin, which is about all the food we have." *I don't like the skulls, though…* "We just need to be really careful in the forest."

Ryder claps his hands together. "Okay, that's the plan! I say we walk as long as we can through the night and tomorrow on short rests. Then once we get to the cover of the forest we can sleep for a while. Grab anything here that might be useful, and let's get moving!"

*****

A gentle summer breeze carries a crisp scent of freshness through the abandoned buildings. It does little to enliven the children, who have succumbed to a zombie state of motion, late in the night. With dragging feet and an all-too-often stumbling gait, they follow Ryder. Their slog is occasionally interrupted when Ryder squints at a compass for bearing.

After Nero falls for the third time, Ryder stops next to a tree growing from the middle of a broken structure. "Alright, let's rest here for a bit. It won't do us any good to hurt ourselves now," he says. He throws his own pack to the ground and lays down.

The rest of the children try to find a comfortable spot among the rocks and dirt. They quickly fall asleep.

Illi's light is just spilling over the horizon when Ryder wakes them. Too tired to protest, the children eat a quick snack and continue.

Squirrels dash between the increasingly sparse ruins of old buildings. They scurry up trees that are growing in size and number with every passing minute. The children duck under cover whenever they see an Erohsian craft zipping through the air, but nothing ever comes close enough to give them a true fright. It does, however, provide enough motivation to keep them going, even on their tired and sore legs. Eventually they encounter the creek from town. They take a quick break to splash the cool water on their faces, rinsing away some of their fatigue. As the day wears on, a haze begins to settle in the trees. With the thick forest canopy and cloud cover, the light from Illi is largely filtered out.

Ryder tromps through the first set of ruins they had seen in the last hour, throwing his backpack down. "Holy cow, I'm ready for a break." He kicks off his shoes and gingerly starts for the creek. "I think we're deep enough into the forest that we can rest and start to take our time. I don't know about you all, but I'm going to soak my feet in the water."

After splashing in the creek and soothing their swollen feet, Ryder leads them to battle—against their dinner. The simple process of opening a can of beans proves to be a significant challenge without a can opener.

With mangled cans strewn about and relatively full bellies, the children set out the little sleeping gear they have in the corner of the ruins. When they finally get situated, they are snuggled close together.

Iona's palms begin to sweat as she pulls a cover over herself. She rubs them on her shirt. *I hate when they do that.*

"Are you sure we'll be safe?" Nero asks, curled between the wall and Thea.

"Aw, Nero, are you afraid of a monster coming to snack on you?" Korbin mocks.

"Shut up, Korbin," Thea says. "It's spooky here."

"I'm not scared at all," Korbin says.

"Ha, Korb. Is that why you're wedged in the middle?" Ryder asks. "Hey, everyone. If Korbin was an animal, he'd be a big ugly cockroach."

"A cockroach? Oh, come on, Ryder, don't do it," Korbin says, his voice laced with dread.

There is a pause and then Iona starts. "Is it because they run away from anything bigger than them?"

Ryder shakes his head.

"How about because they are scary-looking?" Nero asks.

"Nope."

"Because they have a crusty shell?" Thea asks.

"What does that even mean, Thea?" Korbin asks.

"You know, because you have a hard head?"

Ryder shakes his head again. "That's not it either, guess again."

"Oooh! Because they're always in the dark?" Iona asks.

Ryder lets out a snort. "Ha, no but good one! Nero was closest."

"Uh," Nero holds his finger to his chin. "Because they are scary looking but gooey on the inside?"

"Yeah! Nice, Nero."

Thea ruffles his hair.

"That's such crap," Korbin says. "I'm not gooey on the inside."

"You totally are a scaredy-cat," Thea says.

Korbin sits up. "Yeah? Well if Ryder was an animal, he'd be a pretty little lady bug," he says, holding up jazz hands.

"Oh, because he is friendly and pleasant to be around?" Iona asks.

"Psh, no."

"Because you can tell their age by looking at their back?" Thea asks.

"What?" Everyone asks simultaneously.

Thea looks about. "Well because his back is getting more muscular, right?"

"Gak." Korbin puts his finger in his mouth.

"That's actually a myth about the lady bug spots," Nero says. "How about because they are extremely effective hunters?"

Korbin looks at Nero sidelong. "Are you serious?"

Nero nods. "Yeah, Fae loves them for her flowers. You should see them go after aphids. It's actually kinda scary."

Korbin waves his hand. "Well, that's not it, either. It's because he's girly and stuff."

"Oh yeah!" Thea says. She sits up and gives Korbin a high five. "Girls are awesome. Nice one."

"No, that's not what I meant."

Thea frowns. Her face becomes very serious. "Then what?"

Korbin flushes. "Uh, never mind. Girls rock. It's Nero who's the scaredy-cat."

Thea waves her hand at him and turns to the others. "Oh, I've got one," she says with some attitude. "If Korbin was an animal, he'd be a goose."

Korbin throws up his hands. "Come on, not again."

The children laugh for some time before they all drift off to sleep.

6 On Their Heels

Isis

"Ma'am, you shouldn't be here."

Isis throws an empty can of beans to the ground. "None of us should. You should have found them before it got to this."

Phillips kicks the ground with his light infantry boot. He nods. "If they can confound our tracking so effectively, perhaps we are underestimating them. Regardless, I take full responsibility. I should lead this group after them."

"If we are going to violate protocol and enter the forest, then I can't risk you screwing up any further. There still might be a chance if we can catch them before they go in too deep."

"Yes, Ma'am."

"Alright, everyone," she says into her helmet com. "Pair up. The distortions may be severe. If I tell you to hold your position, do so."

The visor on her helmet blinks with ten green affirmation dots from the soldiers in her group.

"Com, is your equipment ready?"

"Yes Ma'am. I'm boosting our communication signal, and I have my Aether sensors activated."

"What's the background level?"

"Four-hundred milliSorvin."

"Let's move, then. Wedge formation. I'm on point. Phillips, I want you staking every fifty meters to start. Shrock, you're scouting the trail."

"Samós," Shrock says, moving forward.

Isis throws a bundle of rope over her head and hefts her Aether rifle. She starts into the forest.

*****

Phillips hammers a stake between moss-covered roots. From the other end, he pulls out a collapsible shaft with a little flag.

Isis looks back to see a trail of the flags weaving through the dense forest. The colors of the forest have been muted. "Com, what's the background?"

"Nine-hundred milliSorvin and still rising. Moltrik, Pahzan, and Icor Aether detected. We are experiencing initial Moltrik Aether shifts."

"Any reaction to our presence?"

"Not that I can tell, Ma'am. According to the map, we are still outside of the restricted boundary."

"Shrock, how's the trail?"

"Easy, Ma'am," he says from ten meters ahead. "Unless they're playing with us, they don't appear to be covering their tracks."

"Let's hurry."

*****

"Com, background?" Isis breathes in the sauna-like air, sweat dripping down the bridge of her nose.

"Eighteen-hundred milliSorvin. Holding constant, Ma'am. We're currently in a significant Pahzan shift."

Obviously. "Are we still being followed?"

"I believe so. I'm picking up lifeforms all around us."

"They're cressen. I know it," one of her soldiers says.

"Quiet. It could be anything." Isis looks back to the last flag marker. It appears thirty meters in the wrong direction. *I could have sworn it wasn't that way...*

Suddenly the air is frigid.

"My helmet!" One of her soldiers yells. "It's melting." He frantically fights with the straps to remove his helmet.

"Don't take off that helmet," Isis says.

Before she can close the distance, his helmet comes off. His pupils instantly dilate. He looks around, horrified. "They're all around us!"

The soldier turns and runs.

"Grab him," Isis says, pointing.

Everyone moves in different directions. One of her soldiers manages to tackle the stray.

"Hold your positions," Isis says. Her soldiers are spread out, confused. "We are experiencing visual aberrations. The forest is trying to spread us out. Com, can you sort this out?"

There is an explosion of light, appearing to come from several different locations. Like a kaleidoscope, the visuals are fragmented.

Com lands on his butt, the Aether equipment smoking in his hands. "Damn. How is that possible? It's Aether-hardened."

"Forget it, Com, we'll have to do this the old fashion way," Isis says. The soldier that lost his helmet continues to yell. "Get him sedated or put his damn helmet back on."

There is a scream. Isis turns to see a soldier fall on his face and get pulled into a bush. He scratches at the ground to slow himself, grabbing a root. The other soldiers move to help, but they only get spread out further.

"No one move!" Isis closes her eyes. She tracks her movements and that of her squad through the past until she is back in formation with her soldiers. She visualizes their positions, picking out the soldier being attacked.

Isis moves. Eyes still shut. The man's screams are muffled at first, then suddenly clear.

She opens her eyes and sees more than half of the soldier in the brush, sliding once again. Isis dives for his hand. He grabs her, desperate. She plants her free hand, swings her feet underneath herself, and leans back. His slide stops. She raises the Aether rifle from its sling on her suit, aiming into the bush. The weapon kicks back as bolts of Aether burn through the bushes. Isis falls back as the tension in their grip vanishes. The soldier scrambles free of the bush, his lower leg bleeding, his suit below the knee shredded.

His grip on her wrist tightens. "Cressen. The eyes. I saw them. We've got to get out of here."

She punches him in the chest, startling him. "Pull it together, soldier."

He nods, still shaken. "Yes, Ma'am."

She lifts him up, once again following her memory to return the way she came.

Phillips grabs the injured man. "What's the plan, Ma'am?"

"We need to gather the others and pull out. Cover me." Isis takes the rope from over her shoulder, tying a rock on one end. She consults her memory and throws.

"Shrock. Grab the rock, I'll pull you back." She feels a tug on the line and reels it in.

His image bounces as if he were in a mirrored room. Eventually, the images consolidate. Shrock looks around. "Holy crap, that's... something."

Isis throws the rock again.

An Aether rifle barks multiple times. Isis ducks, feeling the heat on her cheek.

"Hold your fire until we regroup!" Soldiers curse in the distance.

Isis repeats throwing the rock until she pulls everyone in.

One soldier's arm is bleeding. Claw marks run from the top of his shoulder to his wrist.

"I want five looking out. I want you firing every ten seconds, or if you see something. Anything. We need to dissuade the cressen before they group."

Aether rifles sound continuously. Shrock and two other soldiers run out ahead with rope, searching for their next stake. With each find, the group moves forward. The visual distortions lessen quickly. Their pace picks up. The soldier who lost his helmet calms down. When they finally reach Phillips's first stake, Isis calls a rest.

Phillips steps next to Isis. "I'm glad you were there, Ma'am."

"So you wouldn't have to tell me you couldn't get into the forest?"

"No, because you got us out. I didn't react quick enough."

How am I going to explain this mess to the general?

"What are we going to do now?" Phillips asks.

"You're going to follow our other lead, east into the mountains of Boruk."

"What about the kids?"

If I couldn't get through… "The forest has them now."

7 Ferin Forest
Iona

A house burns, the dancing flames are so large they seem to lick the night sky. The heat forces her to turn away, and she sees Nero staring into the flames. His horror takes her breath away. She tries to call out to him, but her mouth is too dry to form the words.

The dream slips away as quickly as it came.

What's that sound? Iona is immersed in blackness; muffled groans barely register in her mind. *Is someone crying?* The fog slowly begins to lift, clearing her mind with it. A host of aches and pains from the long day before wake with her. Her mouth is parched. She imagines drinking a glass of water the size of her head. *But why is someone crying?* Suddenly, she remembers where she is and opens her eyes.

Rays of light spill through gaps in the forest canopy. They streak through the haze in the air and illuminate the ground. She lifts herself on her elbow and notices the other children are stirring as well. Nero's body twitches. He lets out weak whimpers and moans, face glistening with sweat.

Thea rolls over. "Nero, wake up!" She uses both hands to shake him.

Nero's eyes snap open. He looks around. "What's going on?"

Thea sits on her feet. "You were having a bad dream. Are you alright?"

Nero throws his blanket off, standing up. "What? No I wasn't." He turns his back to the group and walks away from their little camp.

Thea looks quizzically at the others.

Korbin props himself up on one arm. "That's the way it always is, Ryder and I have just learned to ignore his little night terrors."

"I had a dream last night, too. And I never dream," Thea says. "Maybe it's just because we're away from home."

Korbin shakes his head. "No, he has them most nights. For as long as I can remember. But don't worry, you'll get used to sleeping right through them."

Iona rubs her eyes and lies back down. *Jeez, Nero's a mess.*

*****

As the creek leads the children deeper into the forest, the pine needle carpet gives way to large roots weaving snakelike through the thick plant growth. Colorful birds sing to each other in the treetops and dart from one branch to the next, hunting for insects. As Iona looks, she stumbles over something and looks down at it.

"Woo!" She jumps back as the grey rock sprouts legs and a head. It scurries off into some bushes. "Neat," she says to herself.

Korbin reaches deep into a tangle of vines and pulls free a large stick. He thrusts it into the air. "Ah ha!" He lowers it and points it at Ryder. "Ryder! I challenge you to a duel!"

Ryder continues to walk. "We should save our energy, Korb."

Korbin glares at Ryder then snaps the stick at Thea. "Thea! I challenge you to a duel!"

A smile spreads across her face but disappears just as fast. She frantically looks for another stick. She finds one and tugs it free. "Very well. As a prize, I'll give you a quick death!"

Thea lunges at Korbin. The two begin to spar and chase each other through the moss-covered trees.

*****

An hour later, the haze and the cloud cover have grown thicker. The children's energy is sapped from them just as the colors of the forest have been drained away. In some places, Iona feels a stifling heat and just as suddenly she is cold. She notices a slow drip of water from a tree. Sometimes, a drop disappears midair.

"What the heck?" She looks closer. Every time a drop disappears, another drop falls from out of nowhere a little way to the side. "That's strange…" A bird flies overhead, the same type she noticed earlier. Instead of being orange and green, its feathers are different shades of grey. Iona frowns and looks up at the sky through the holes in the canopy. "Hopefully, the weather doesn't get too bad. It seems like everything is gloomy."

Strangely, a part of her feels light and free. She rubs her fingers on her palms, expecting them to be sweaty. They are not. She moves her tongue around next, expecting it to stick to her mouth. Her mouth feels normal. *Weird.*

Ryder shakes his head. "Yeah, it is. At least we're semi-covered if it starts to rain."

"I like it here. It's really cool!" Nero says. He walks with pep to his step. "I've never seen anything like this before."

Iona shakes her head. *I guess it goes with his depressing personality.*

"Like that!" Nero points to a tight group of semitransparent butterflies. Their glowing wings seem to be moving with the exact same wing beat. The butterflies flutter in and out of existence.

"Oh, weird." Thea runs up to them, hands out. She tries to catch one, but they all pass through her hands as if she does not exist. "What the heck is going on?"

Nero runs up to the butterflies and cups his hands about them. As his hands close, the butterflies fold in on themselves until they all disappear. He opens his hands slowly and a single, solid butterfly is perched on his palm, fanning its glowing wings slowly.

"Isn't it awesome?" Nero asks. "I call it a butterfire!"

Thea looks at it closely. "Yeah. How did you catch it? Was it just one the whole time?"

"Uh yeah… What do you mean? I just grabbed it. It wasn't hard at all." Nero moves it to his finger, smiling, and skips off. With a jump, and a thrust of his arm, the butterfire flies away. Immediately, the butterfire unfolds and multiplies once more.

For hours, they follow the widening creek until a thick wall of bushes and foliage bars their path. They move down to the bank of the creek and hop over rocks to proceed. Past the bushes, the creek spills into a large river that is spanned by a massive cement bridge.

"Oooie! That's a big river," Korbin says. "It's a lot bigger than it looks like on the map."

"Seriously." Ryder squints at the bridge several hundred meters farther up the river. "Let's see if we can use the bridge to cross."

The children slide down the steep banks and skip across the rocks at the edge of the river.

"Holy cow, this is huge!" Thea says. "Who made it?"

Ryder shrugs. "I don't know. Maybe this is why the Minis don't want people in here—because they're trying to hide this."

Iona nods. "Fae always said that the Erohsians took all this land from Humans. I wonder if Humans made it."

Korbin puffs up his chest. "Of course they did. It's huge! I can totally see Humans making something this awesome."

He takes off running along the bank and the others hurry to follow.

Dark scars and pockmarks cover the bridge. Massive chunks of the four-lane road are completely missing. It is as though a giant had tried to use the bridge but had punched holes through with her feet.

Korbin kicks the detritus, throwing up his arms. "Trashed! Just like everything else…" He picks up a large rock and heaves it into the water.

Iona scrambles about the chunks of cement on the bank, climbing to the main level. Large legs of a statue, broken at the waste, stand to one side. "I think there's enough left we can use it to cross," she yells down to the others. "We just need to be careful."

Ryder joins Iona, tracing the expected path with his eyes. "Let's get this over with."

The children zigzag between large gaps where chunks of cement hang from reinforcing rebar. Through the gaps, Iona can see dark shadows the size of Ryder moving about the murky water. *Those are big fish…* She squeezes a bit closer to the wall as she shuffles through a narrow section of solid ground.

At the far side, the bridge has collapsed into the banks of the river. The children climb and hop over the pieces of cement until they reach bushes and trees. The growth consumes the old road almost entirely.

Ryder tries to peer through. "Oh gosh, this should be fun." He looks up and down the bank, noticing the same barrier. He walks around the bushes, first on his toes, then crouching to get a better view. "I think we can make it through here if we crawl." He points to a small gap running along the base of the copse.

Korbin sighs. "This stinks."

Iona plops down on her hands and knees. "Suck it up, Korb."

She plunges into the bushes. Grunts and yelps follow her as the plants and twigs prick the others. Tangles of vines and branches catch her shoulders and arms, but she squirms and tears through. Eventually, she pops out the other side.

She stands up, shaking loose bits of plant matter from her hair and body. The bustling sounds of the forest hit her from every direction; singing birds, stridulating bugs, and squawking animals. *I've never been anywhere with so much life.* She turns her attention to the other children emerging from the bushes covered in a collection of leaves and twigs. Again, an incredible feeling of lightness overwhelms her, and she sees Nero crawl out with a smile on his face. "Are you enjoying this, Nero?" Iona asks.

Nero nods. "Yeah, I like it here. It's beautiful."

Korbin struggles through the last bush, jumping to his feet. He shivers and shakes his body. "Oh gosh, that was horrible. Do I have bugs all over me?" He spins around, trying to see his back.

Iona lets out a sigh. "Come on, Korbin, there aren't any—" She bites her breath as she catches a glimpse of a sizable, black mantis hanging on his pack. "Wait, Korb. Stop. You have a big bug on your backpack."

"What?!" Korbin flails his arms and jumps like he is on fire. The bug flies through the air, landing on its back.

Nero hurries over and squats next to the bug. He picks up a stick to flip it over just as a rock smashes it. The rock bounces away, leaving a crumbled mass of twitching limbs behind. Nero spins to Korbin, who is standing victoriously wiping his hands.

Iona's vision suddenly takes on a tint of red just as Nero shoves Korbin in the chest. "What the heck, Korbin! Why'd you do that?"

"Whoa, Nero, what's your problem?" Korbin takes a step back, his hands up. "It's just a bug."

"So? You didn't have to kill it!"

"It was totally going to attack when it flipped itself over. Why do you think it was on my back?"

"Yeah, it looked real dangerous crawling about minding its business, you jerk." Nero holds Korbin's gaze fiercely.

Iona sees the anger and frustration boiling off Nero. *What's going on with Nero? I've never seen him make a stand like this.*

Korbin shrugs. "Whatever, Nero. Stop being so sensitive."

Thea points at the bug. "Hey look!" It has just stopped twitching. A marble-size bright spot of light rises from the bug. A faint mist follows next and swirls about, obscuring the orb. "Ooooh, what's that?"

Korbin reaches down to touch it before Ryder can stop him. The mist is drawn into him. He springs up straight, looking at the others with dazed eyes.

"Dang it, Korbin, why do you always have to do stuff without thinking?" Ryder asks. Korbin does not respond. "You alright?"

Korbin blinks a couple of times until his eyes clear. "Yeah, I'm good. It felt like the stuff at our hideout, but now I have this strange desire to crawl through the forest and hunt for green bugs."

"Does every living thing have mist in it?" Thea asks.

Korbin shakes his head. "I've killed lots of bugs and this is the only time I've ever seen that."

Thea looks at Iona. "Do you think it's Aether?"

Iona shrugs. "I don't know. Why would this bug have Aether?"

There is a long pause. Ryder begins to tramp off. "Alright, team, let's keep moving. We can ask someone later."

The group gathers themselves to follow Ryder through the persistent haze of dull colors. The huffing and puffing of the children create a strange uneasiness in Iona's stomach. She tries to put her finger on it but cannot. *You're just being silly.* Her palms begin to sweat. She wipes them on her pants.

There's nothing bad in the forest, remember all the birds and...

"Hey, something doesn't feel right," Nero says.

Korbin stops. "Aw, Nero, are you still crying 'cuz I killed the bug?"

Nero glares at Korbin. "No, seriously, something's changed. What happened to all the animals?"

Korbin raises his eyebrows. "What are you talking about? We haven't seen any animals besides some birds and bugs."

"No, he's right, listen." Iona holds up her hands, looking around. A faint breeze stirs the tops of the trees. "No birds, no bugs, nothing running around. There are no sounds at all."

Korbin looks at Iona. "What does that mean?"

"I haven't got a clue. But something's going on."

"Maybe it's just different on this side of the forest, or it's just that time of the day." Ryder looks up into the trees then along the ground. "I think the best thing we can do is keep moving forward. I'm sure it's not a big deal." Ryder flips out his compass and frowns. He shakes it briefly then stuffs it back in his pocket. "Oh, and just in case... keep your eyes open, but like I said—I'm sure it's nothing."

They proceed to meander through plants and over roots and logs until they reach a small clearing with a soft mossy ground cover. The children instantly collapse, releasing sighs of relief as their feet rejoice.

Korbin rubs his hands over his scratched forearms. "Hey, Ryder, this was a wonderful idea man. Next time we should cross the Blishin Desert, and just for fun, we won't bring any water. That would almost be as awesome as this."

Ryder rolls his eyes. "Stop whining. It's not that bad."

Iona hops up, looking around the clearing. "I think something lives here." She walks away and jumps. "Woo. There's a huge animal over here."

The children scramble over, where there is a large four-legged animal lying on its side. It looks like a giant wolf. It is easily bigger than any Human adult and its fur is a mottled, streaked grey. The animal does not move. The children surround it.

Nero's mouth drops. "Oh wow, that's cool! I wish I were that color."

"What is it? Is it dead?" Thea asks.

Korbin picks up a long stick. "Let's find out."

"Maybe you should leave it be," Iona says.

"It'll be alright. I'm just going to poke it a little." He walks as close as he dares, poking the animal in the ribs. Korbin springs back and waits for a reaction that does not come. He creeps back to the creature, jabbing it with more force. The creature's eyes just barely open. It takes a large breath. "Hey, look, it's alive! It must be on its deathbed. Maybe I can get it to move." Korbin readies another jab.

Nero wrestles his way past Korbin, standing in front of him. "Come on, Korbin, just let it be."

Korbin stops, looking at Nero. "What's your deal, Sam? You're being really annoying. Look, it's barely alive, and I want to see if I can get it to move a bit. Just get out of my way."

"No, Korbin, leave it alone," Nero says.

Wow, really, what's happened to Nero?

Korbin pokes Nero with the stick. "Come on, stop being such a baby. What if it has more of that mist stuff in it?"

Nero looks at Korbin with shock. "You want to kill it?"

Korbin shrugs. "Why not? It looks like it's going to die soon anyways. We would be doing it a favor."

"It'd be a waste if it died for nothing," Thea says. "We could put the Aether to good use."

Nero looks at Thea, his mouth open. She looks away. "You're going to just let him kill it?" Nero asks.

"Thanks, Thea," Korbin says. He pokes Nero again. "Is the little baby going to try to stop me?"

"Come on, Korbin," Iona says. "Just let it be. It's not worth it."

Korbin spins on Iona. "Look, if we're going to fight the Erohsians, we're going to need all the Aether we can get. So, no, I will not let it be." He turns back to Nero, shoving him to the side.

Nero lands next to the animal with a grunt. Suddenly, the animal's black eyes snap open. It jumps to its feet, towering over the children, hackles raised.

Before the children can react, it destroys Korbin's stick with one chomp and roars, exposing its long, sharp teeth. They stumble backward, tripping. A stench of rot jolts their senses and steals their breath. They are up and running immediately. The creature lets out another deafening roar, leaping after the children.

Panic squeezes Iona's body, and no matter how fast she runs, it does not seem fast enough. The clear image of the razor-sharp teeth runs through her mind. The burning in her legs finally becomes unbearable, and she ducks behind a tree. The other children huddle beside her and they wait, gasping for breath. The monster is nowhere to be seen.

"Oh my lord, Korbin, you jerk!" Iona punches Korbin in his arm. "You should've just let it be."

Korbin rubs his arm and looks fiercely at Iona. "Jeez, we're all in one piece, aren't we? No harm done."

Iona throws her arms in the air. "Yeah but gosh, that thing could have eaten us all."

Ryder nods his head. "Did you see how big the teeth were compared to Nero's little head?"

Korbin holds his hand up showing the size with his fingers. "They were huge! Would have chomped right through him if it wanted."

Thea seizes Ryder's arm roughly. "Wait!" She looks around. "Where's Nero?"

The memory of Nero, his pleading eyes rolling back in his head as he crumples to the ground runs through Iona's mind. *Oh no.* "He's with the monster." The words slip from her mouth.

Ryder grabs Iona by both shoulders, looking into her eyes. "Did you see what happened?" Ryder waits a moment and shakes her. "Iona, come on, this is important. There still might be a chance. Did you see the monster get him?"

Iona looks down at her feet then at Ryder. "No, but he was right there next to it. I think he passed out. I guess, I just figured. I mean, why else do you think we got away?"

"Typical Nero, too scared to save himself." Korbin kicks a large root. "I guess there's nothing we can do about it now."

Tears flow from Thea's eyes. "We can't just leave him!"

Korbin plucks a slender stick from the ground. "What do you expect us to do?" He swings it so hard, it whistles through the air. "Fight the monster with sticks?" He looks at Thea and snaps it in half. "You heard Iona, the monster got him. There's nothing we can do. He would probably want us to save ourselves."

Iona looks down at the ground, shaking her head. *Dang it, Nero! Why couldn't you have just run?*

Ryder pulls up a much larger stick from a clutch of vines. "We might not be able to do anything about it, but I don't like the thought of leaving without knowing for sure. He would do the same for any one of us."

Korbin looks at him in shock. "What, are you kidding me? He would totally leave us. He's the biggest wuss I've ever met."

"We only have each other and I don't think he'd leave any of us." Ryder looks at the rest of the children. "We'll keep our eyes open and be very careful. First sign of the monster and we'll head out. Okay?"

Thea wipes the tears from her eyes. "Okay."

Iona lifts her head, nodding. "Yeah, that sounds good."

Korbin looks at them and chucks the broken stick into the forest. "This is ridiculous! Now we're all going to get eaten!"

"Korbin, this is your fault!" Ryder says with a poke of his finger causing Korbin to jump. "Either come with us," Ryder gestures off to the forest, "or go on without us. But stop complaining."

Korbin looks into the forest and sighs. "I'll come. Who else is going to protect you wimps?" He kicks about the plants, pulling out two fist-sized rocks. "Lead the way."

Ryder hits his palm with the thick stick. "Okay, then, let's go." He moves out from behind the tree, walking toward the monster's clearing. "Keep your eyes open."

Iona winces with every step. *How are we going to sneak up on the monster when we're making so much noise? It's going to jump out of a bush and get us before we even know it's there.* Iona turns toward the bushes. *You're just seeing things, calm down.* Iona's heart is thumping painfully against her chest. Her breathing is fast and shallow.

"Ah, right there!" Korbin jumps back, throwing a rock at some bushes. "Holy cow, I just saw something."

Ryder peers in the direction of Korbin's throw. "What? Where?"

Korbin pokes the air with his finger. "Right there, in those bushes. It was like a glint of light or something. I just saw a flash of it."

"Come on Korbin, you're being dramatic. We need to stay quiet," Iona says.

Ryder nods. "Yeah, man. I bet it was something that just caught Illi's light at an odd angle."

"What light, Ryder?" Korbin throws up his hands. "Everything is dark here. There's hardly any light to shine off anything!"

"I don't know, Korbin, maybe there was a quick break in the clouds or something. We're all scared but we need to keep going. The faster we go, the faster we get this over with. Now be quiet."

Ryder moves along without waiting for a response. The rest jump in line to follow. Other than the sounds they are making; the forest is completely silent. Iona glances at the bushes but sees nothing. She takes a couple slow, deep breaths, forcing herself to stop looking. *It's probably just a squirrel or something, no big deal.*

"Look there!" Korbin yells, throwing his other rock into the forest.

Iona nearly jumps out of her skin.

Ryder again looks in the direction of Korbin's throw. "Where, Korb? I don't see anything."

"Over there, by the big tree with the moss and the broken branch." Korbin moves his head around, looking at different angles.

Ryder shakes his head. "It must've been another glint or something."

Korbin looks at Ryder with wide eyes, face pale. "No, man, I saw two eyes! They were glowing gold and they disappeared when I looked at them."

Ryder walks up to Korbin, putting his hand on his back. "It's probably just some little critter that's interested in us."

Korbin shrugs Ryder's hand off. "Interested in a snack."

Ryder sighs. "Come on, Korb."

Thea jumps with one hand on her chest, the other pointing into the forest. "Eyes!"

They all look at her shaking finger, following it to the forest. Nothing is there.

Korbin spins to Ryder. "See? I'm not making it up! We need to get out of here!"

"Dang it, Korbin, you're freaking everyone out. Just chill," Ryder says.

Iona throws up her arms. "Seriously, Korbin, I thought you wanted to fight some monsters? This is ridiculous. There's nothing out there."

Ryder begins to walk. "Alright, we need to g—Oooh I just saw something."

Okay, everyone's lost their minds. Iona looks quickly in the trees. *There's nothing there; everyone's just panicking.*

Thea jumps again, pointing. "There. I saw eyes and they were looking right at me."

Iona looks at the others. "Come on, what's going on here? We all just need to take a couple deep breaths." A clicking sound that quickly accelerates rings through the forest. The children freeze. "What was that?"

Korbin puts his hands on his head. "I think we should head back. Nero's gone." He glances at the others. "I mean, come on, how would he survive something like that? It's Nero. He couldn't survive his room in the dark if there wasn't a night light."

Ryder pushes forward. "It's going to be okay. We just need to keep moving."

Thea runs to Ryder, grabbing his arm. "I'm really scared, please make it go away."

Another set of clicks comes from the forest. The children spin around, trying to see the source. Suddenly, Iona sees a set of golden eyes blink in and out of existence, taking her breath away with them. *Eyes!*

"Come on, let's move." Ryder trudges through the forest at a brisk pace, pulling Thea along by her hand. The clicking rings throughout the forest and multiple sets of glowing eyes are visible at any one time.

Pressure begins to build in Iona's body. *We need to go! They're all around us. Just run!* She can barely keep herself from surrendering to the fear.

Thea starts to pull ahead of Ryder, dragging him along. "Come on! We need to go faster. They're coming!" She tugs on Ryder's arm. "Come on!"

Ryder stumbles along. "Stay calm, Thea!" He says in a high-pitched voice.

"No! We need to run. Can't you see? They're coming for us!" She rips her hand free and runs.

Iona can hear rustling in the forest all around her. "Run!"

The children sprint as fast as they can through the thick forest. The clicking is now short and is coming from every direction. Iona glances back. Eyes appear and disappear from every angle. Her legs start to burn again, her breathing becomes frantic, but she urges herself on.

"Hey, wait up!" She hears from behind her.

Iona looks back and to her surprise there are no golden eyes. Instead... *Nero?* She looks back again. He is running desperately, waving his hands. *But how?* "Hurry, Nero," she says, pausing to let him catch up.

He is running with two dull pieces of fruit in each hand. "What—are—we—running from?"

As soon as he is within reach, she grabs his wrist, pulling him on. "We need to keep going!"

Nero stumbles while Iona drags. They finally come upon the other children, bent over and sucking air.

"Iona!" Ryder says, looking at Nero. "Where'd you find him?"

Nero instantly collapses.

Iona shakes her head and shrugs, unable to speak.

"Why are we running so much!" Korbin says in between breaths as he kicks some vines.

Ryder turns his attention back to the forest, which is now quiet. He wipes his forehead clean of sweat. "I think we're safe."

Thea pulls Nero halfway up, locking him in a tight embrace. "We thought you got eaten by the monster." She lets go and looks at him. "How'd you escape?"

"What?" Nero picks himself up.

"What do you mean 'what'?" Ryder asks. "There was a huge monster that was about to eat you. How'd you get away?"

"Um... well, actually, I, ah... just kinda woke up and it—I mean, this tree was there. With this fruit!" He holds up the fruit like a prize.

"That's it? You just woke up? What happened to the monster?" Korbin asks.

"The monster?" Nero looks at his feet. "It... wasn't there. It must have wandered off or something."

"But why didn't it eat you?" Korbin asks.

Nero shrugs. "Maybe it didn't want to. I don't know." Nero looks at the others for a moment then fidgets with the fruit. "This fruit is really good. Do you want to split it with me?" He struggles to peel back a hard rind, exposing a grey, juicy pulp. He holds it up to Iona's nose.

The fruit smells harsh with an acidic edged. It burns Iona's nose, forcing her to pull back her head. "Oh, that's disgusting. I can't believe you're eating that."

"Really? I like it! It tingles in your mouth like that fizzing candy. Anyone else?" They shake their heads. Nero shrugs, eating. "So, why were you running?"

"We were coming back to look for you when these things with golden eyes and no bodies started hunting us," Thea says, her eyebrows raised. "They were all around us, making this clicking sound like they were talking about how tasty we all would be."

Nero smiles. "You were coming after me?"

Thea relaxes, smiling. "Of course."

Suddenly he takes a breath, looking around. "But what happened to the eyes. Are they still around?"

Thea's eyes widen. She looks at Ryder.

Ryder shrugs. "I don't know. I guess we got away from them. I don't see or hear them anymore."

Nero lets out his breath. "Thank goodness. Well, shouldn't we get moving?"

Iona studies Nero, a tinge of guilt poking her chest. *He must have thought we'd just leave him...*

Ryder smacks Nero on the back and pulls out his compass. He visibly relaxes when he opens it. "Yeah, that's a good idea. I'm really glad we're all back together."

As they walk, life slowly returns to the forest. The birds are sparse at first, but soon they are back in the same numbers as earlier. The clouds start to break up and Illi's light pours through, washing away the dull haze and cleansing the children of their fears. Soon, they are joking with each other.

After several hours of walking, the thickness of the forest abates, allowing them to move with ease. A peachy glow from Illi as it sets, alights the few clouds remaining in the sky.

Ryder finally stops at a nice flat section with soft ground cover. "I think we can safely say we are out of that mess. Let's call it a day and try to get a jump start tomorrow morning so that we can reach Blue Horin by midday."

They unpack their sleeping gear, scrounge together some food, and fall victim to their extreme exhaustion.

8 Blue Horin Bay
Iona

A figure shrouded in shadows holds his arms out, gently calling to her, like a father would call his child. She desperately wants to go to him, but she is unable to close the distance no matter how hard she tries. The figure slowly fades away.

Iona blinks the grogginess from her eyes. She sees treetops swaying gently with a light blue sky behind them. She hears a rustle and sits up. A well-rested Nero is bending over the backpacks, collecting food.

Ryder pushes himself up, rubbing his head. "Hey, Nero, what'cha doin?"

Nero pauses to look at Ryder. "Just looking to see what's for breakfast."

Ryder yawns. "Jeez, you're up and moving quick this morning." His face is dirty and his hair is a mess.

Nero looks at Ryder seriously. "Wish I could say the same about you all."

Ryder smiles. "I like it, Nero, let's get these lazy bums moving. Barrel Roll!" He whips the blankets off and rolls back and forth over the other children, occasionally stopping to tickle and terrorize.

"Alright, we're up," Thea says. "What's for breakfast then?"

They put together a sorry-looking breakfast, which they eat in no time. On sore feet and tired legs, they continue their journey. Nero leads the way, tossing and catching the piece of fruit he found from the forest.

Iona marvels at the strange lightness in her chest. She tries to shake the feeling with little success. *I need to be on my guard. There could still be danger.*

Ryder snaps his compass shut, looking at Nero. "So, why are you in such a good mood?"

Nero shrugs. "I don't know. I just like it here. It's peaceful."

Ryder raises one eyebrow. "Yeah? I guess so, if you don't include all the monsters trying to eat us. What really happened with the thing back there?"

"Nothing exciting... It's not a big deal. You wouldn't believe me anyway."

Ryder gives Nero a playful shove. "Oh, whatever, just tell us."

Nero takes a deep breath. "Okay. So, after Korbin shoved me and the animal roared... I just kinda blacked out, I think."

Korbin hurries alongside them. "Ha! I can believe that."

"Come on, Korb, let him finish," Ryder says.

Nero hesitates for a moment. "So, I woke up under the tree—like I said—and the yellow and red striped animal was lying near me—"

"What?" Korbin looks at Nero. "What yellow and red striped animal?"

"The big animal that roared," Nero says. "The one you were poking with the stick."

"It didn't have red and yellow stripes." Korbin turns to Ryder and shakes his head. "Can you believe this? He's already making stuff up." He turns back to Nero, contemptuous. "I bet next you're going to tell us you fought it with your bare hands and scared it away."

"What?" Nero says. "No! I'm not making this up. It's the truth."

"Oh right, I believe you. I bet the real reason it didn't eat you is because it was afraid you'd upset its stomach."

"You're such a butt!" Nero runs ahead, hanging his head.

"That was super mean, Korb," Thea says. "You don't always have to be a jerk."

"Yeah, but you heard him. The creature wasn't yellow and red. It was grey."

Thea shakes her head and jogs up to Nero, who is pulling his rusty-brown colored bracelet from his pocket with his free hand.

"Korb, you've got to be more gentle," Ryder says. "Maybe he was just really scared. Sometimes your memory gets a bit twisted when you're scared. I bet it was a horrible experience for him."

"It's just so annoying when he's so scared of everything and *now* he's making stuff up!"

"Cut him some slack, Korb. You were being just as big of a wuss, so you have no right to be so hard on him."

"Woo!" Iona smacks Ryder in the chest, pointing with her other hand. "Look!"

Someone covered in rags and filth is walking toward Thea and Nero, who have frozen in their tracks. Suddenly, the figure launches at Nero, grabbing his wrist and yanking his arm into the air. Thea jumps on its arm but the figure shrugs her off with little effort. Iona, Ryder, and Korbin run to help, but are tossed away.

The figure wrenches the fruit out of Nero's hand. "Where did you get this?" From the depths of the rags, a woman's voice crackles as if it had not been used for months.

Nero reaches up with his hand and tries to pry his wrist free from the iron grip; tears are streaming down his face. "Let me go!"

The woman shakes his arm, scowling. "Do you have mo—" Her eyes fall on his bracelet and she freezes. The wildness she possessed just a moment ago vanishes and she slowly looks at the other children who are circling her for another attack. "Where are your parents?"

"We don't have parents," Korbin blurts out.

Iona glares at Korbin fiercely. "Shhhh!"

"Orphans?" She says quietly to herself. She looks once more at the bracelet in his hand and her scowl vaporizes, leaving behind sudden shock and horror. She pulls her hand away from Nero's wrist as if it had burnt her. The fruit falls from her hand and she stumbles back in a complete daze, tripping over her feet and landing on her butt. She stays there, her pale, blank face frozen.

The children hesitate for just a moment before they run. This time Ryder stays with Nero. They run as far and as long as they can, before Nero can go no further. Nero falls over and lies on his back, gasping for air. The others stand in a circle, doubled over, taking deep breaths.

Finally, Iona stands up straight. "What the heck was that?"

Ryder shakes his head. "No idea."

"I'm so tired of running!" Korbin starts to kick the dirt and leaves gathered about the ground. "The whole world is crazy!"

Thea nods her head. "Yeah, that was really weird. As soon as Korbin said we didn't have parents she changed…"

"Maybe she's an orphan too?" Iona says. "And couldn't bring herself to steal from us when she found out."

"I guess that would make sense." Ryder shrugs. "Maybe she's just wacko. The important thing is, we all got away this time."

Iona turns to Korbin. "But seriously, Korb, don't go telling everyone we don't have parents."

Korbin looks at Iona, holding a stick that he was about to break over his knee. "What do you mean? I just saved us," he says.

"We got lucky, for all we know it could have just as easily gone the other way. What if she decided to kidnap us because we weren't with anyone?"

"Fine. Whatever. Just don't make me run."

Nero is just starting to catch his breath.

Ryder pulls him up. "Alright, let's keep going."

*****

The children reach a gentle slope before the trees start to thin rapidly. Off in the distance, they can see the crest of a hill. There are several tall watch towers spread out along the top.

Thea jumps up and down. "Civilization!"

Ryder smiles, looking at Iona. "What do you think we should do? I'm guessing those are guard towers. Think they'll have a problem with us passing?"

Iona clenches her teeth. "I don't think we have a choice." She points up the hill. Two small four-wheelers are racing toward them.

Several tense breaths later, two Human soldiers dressed in Erohsian military uniforms come skidding to a halt, spraying up dirt and plants. The two soldiers jump off the four-wheelers. The shorter of the two swings his gun around from his back.

"Come on, Walter, they're just kids," the taller soldier says.

"Yeah?" Walter's steel gaze is heavy on the children. "What are you kids doing out here?" The children cannot take their eyes from the weapon. "Speak up!" he says, jerking the gun.

The taller soldier steps forward, pushing the barrel of Walter's gun away. "Hey, dip stick! What's wrong with you? They're just kids, you dim witted entity."

Walter's face turns red and Korbin muffles a laugh with his hands. Walter shoots him a deathly glare that shuts him up.

The taller soldier steps in front of Walter. "There's no reason to be scared of us. We might be dressed in Erohsian uniforms but it's only because they supply the equipment to guard the city." He smiles at the children. "So, what are you kids doing out here so early and all by yourselves?"

"Oh, we aren't alone!" Iona says. "Well, actually, I mean our parents live in Blue Horin."

The tall soldier raises his eyebrow. "Well, what are you doing in the Forest? You know it's very dangerous, right? You shouldn't be out here by yourselves. What are your parents thinking?"

"Uh, well we really weren't, except for this last part. We're coming from visiting our aunt." Iona looks at the soldier, then at the ground. "She's a hobo in the forest and our parents wanted us to try to convince her to come home."

"You mean that creepy old goat that wanders the area? She's your aunt? Well she's as sweet as a mouth full of dirt. I'm guessing it didn't go well?" Iona shakes her head. "Well, I'm sorry to hear that. She doesn't deserve kids as nice as you, but excuse me, it's none of my business. So how are you kids getting back to the city?"

"Just walking," Iona says.

"Walking? That'll take hours. There's no one to come get you?" Pete looks at the dirty, disheveled children and his face relaxes. "Oh. Well, if you were looking for something to do, I'd recommend the open market around piers fifteen through twenty. The people are friendly. They're more likely to be looking for help if you were interested in working. I also heard there's some decent cheap lodging in the area. Anyway, my name's Pete and the cranky one's Walter." He signals at Walter with his thumb. "We can carry a few of you to the hill, at least, if you'd like a ride?"

"I ain't dealing with this crap." Walter turns and storms off to his four-wheeler. He rips on the throttle and sprays up more dirt and plants, accelerating up the hill.

Pete shakes his head. "He's always like that, if you were gonna ask. Luckily, his shift is almost over, and I can get away from his constant complaining about money. So, care for a ride? I think two of you could fit on the back."

Ryder steps forward. "No, sir. Thanks for the offer. We'll walk up together."

Thea jumps forward. "But—"

Ryder throws her a stern look. She closes her mouth and wilts down.

Pete nods his head, smiling. "I understand. Well, you all have a good day. I'll try to keep Walter busy until you all pass, so he doesn't get a chance to harass you. Good luck. I'm sorry I can't help more." He jumps on his four-wheeler and drives up the hill.

"I think he realized we were on our own," Iona says.

"Yeah..." Ryder nods. "It's probably pretty obvious."

*****

As they crest the hill between two of many watchtowers, a dark blue ocean spreads out along the horizon spotted with ships of all sizes. The ocean swells toward the coast where it had taken a bite out of the land, creating a large bay. The city wraps around its edges with many piers poking out from the coast. The city itself has clusters of skyscrapers close to the water and fans out toward a ring of agricultural areas.

Thea throws her hand over her mouth. "Holy cow!"

Korbin lets out a deep breath and relaxes. "Finally, something that isn't a heap of junk!"

"Wow, we do have a ways to go," Ryder says. He starts down the hill with long strides, head first into a gentle breeze tinged with sea salt. "All I can think about is some real food... so let's hurry."

Most of the day passes while the children slog toward the city. They catch a fortunate break in the form of a public transportation bus. It takes them all the way down to the water and drops them off at Pier Eighteen, just outside the open trade market.

They are inundated by an incredible variety of smells, noises, and people of all shapes, sizes, and looks. The crowd flows in currents and electrifies the air as people barter through rows of vendor stands that fill the center of a square.

Shops form the perimeter of the market with the ocean on the far side.

There is a dark skinned, longhaired race that pokes out from the crowd, several heads taller than the Humans. They make the Erohsians look like children by comparison. Their deep voices are easy to pluck from the hustle and bustle of the market. They wear sleeveless shirts, and some have ivory tattoos on their arms.

A waft of fried seafood and baked goods from Pier Eighteen pulls the children forward. Before they reach the pier, they are distracted by a burst of flame, erupting from the center of a gathered crowd. Gasps of awe dispel their concern and they squeeze their way to the front where they find a woman in a tight grey outfit addressing the crowd. Behind her is a raised platform with a grated metal floor and poles sticking up from the corners. A series of large gas burners are set up below.

She turns to the crowd, holding up her hands. "And for my final act—since I can't seem to keep a man around to dance with—I will dance with fire."

"I'd dance with you!" a man from the crowd yells.

The performer looks in the direction of the voice, squinting. "Oh, it's not that I can't get a man. It's just that they always seem to burst into flames." She holds out her hand. "Are you still interested?" The man is silent. After a moment, she shrugs. "And that's why I'm single." The crowd laughs.

The performer turns on the gas to each of the burners under the grating then pushes play on her portable stereo. She jumps on the grating, places her hands on her hips, and taps her foot impatiently. After a long moment, fire spreads from the grating like a fountain of surging water, forming the shape of a man. She stops tapping her foot, looking at him with a cocked head. The man of fire puts his arms out, shrugging. She waves her hand at him and turns to the crowd. "It looks like men of fire are no better than men of flesh. Always late." The crowd lets out a muffled chuckle.

The performer turns back to the man of fire and reaches out her hand; he takes it just as the brass instruments and drums from the stereo kick in. They dance around the grate and each other, spinning and twisting about their locked arms in a series of seamless moves synchronized with the music. As the instruments hit their climax, the performer jumps into the air and the man of fire twists, catching her hip with one arm over his head so she is parallel with the ground. He holds her above his head, rotating her so the crowd can see her straight on. After a slight pause, the man of fire lowers her to the ground. His form collapses in a reversal to how he was formed. The performer takes a bow and the crowd cheers.

She hops off the grating, grabs a bucket, and places it at the front of the crowd. "If you liked my show and you want to show your appreciation, then I'd be happy to take your money. If you didn't like my show, I'd still be happy to take your money." She takes one final bow. "I'll be here again tomorrow. Tell your friends!"

After the children break free of the disintegrating crowd, Thea turns to the others. "That was sooo cool! How did she do that? Do you think the fire guy was real?"

"It didn't seem real," Nero says. "What if it was just magic?"

"Oh, shut up, Nero, it was totally real," Korbin says. "How else would he catch her?"

Ryder puts his hand on Nero's back, walking toward the pier. "At the rate we're going, we'll have a million questions by the time we find someone to ask. Let's at least get some food so we can think on full stomachs."

They make it to the pier, which is nothing more than a platform for more vendor stands and stores running along the sides. The booths down the center have fresh fish displayed in packed ice. Tanks of water are filled with crabs and lobsters crawling along the bottoms. Large stoves are covered with food. Some stands have delicious-smelling fried food on sticks. Others have creatures that look neither edible nor enjoyable to eat. Ryder leads them to a stand that has the simplest selection and orders sandwiches. They leave the pier and hurry to a calm section of the market along the ocean where there is an empty picnic table.

Korbin eyes the bag on the table. "What'd you get us, Ryder?"

Ryder reaches into the bag and pulls out small packages wrapped in white paper. "Not sure. I asked for something not too expensive and good. So, hopefully it's good." He hands out the packages to the others.

Iona tears open the paper, eagerly chomping into the large fish sandwich. Her stomach hurts from the shock of warm food. For the next five minutes the children scarf down their meal while Illi falls into the horizon.

"I'm stuffed," Iona says as she leans back, surrendering to the remaining bit of her sandwich. *I needed that.* "So, what's the plan?"

Ryder swallows and clears his mouth. "Umm…" He looks up at the quickly darkening sky. "I guess we need to figure out where to sleep for the night. Tomorrow we can start to look for a boat we can jump on or something."

"I hope we don't have to sleep on the streets," Nero says. "I bet that's where all the bad people come out."

"Can we rent a room at an inn or something?" Iona asks.

"Yeah, maybe. I just don't want to spend too much of our money," Ryder says.

A small dark boy, with matted hair and a dirty old button up shirt that has the sleeves rolled up, slides next to Thea. "Hey!" Thea squeaks, moving as far over as she can. "I couldn't help but hear you're looking for a place to stay."

Ryder glares at the boy. "Did anyone ever teach you to mind your own business?"

The boy's mouth opens in mock shock. "Excuse me. I only thought you could use my help. Seeing that I know the area, I know of a few safe spots to spend the night." He stands up. "But I guess I was wrong," and starts to walk off.

Ryder jumps up from his seat. "Wait! Maybe we can use your help."

The boy sits back down. "See? I can always recognize fellow orphans, though it seems you all are still fresh." He looks at the others. When nobody says anything, he smiles. "My name is Totos, and for a small but reasonable price I can show you a safe place to turn in. Off the streets. For free." He grabs the remaining bit of Iona's sandwich and casually starts to eat. She glares at him, wiping her suddenly sweaty palms off on her pants.

"What's the small price?" Ryder asks.

Totos swallows the remains of the sandwich and licks his fingers. "Ten Anterren."

"I'll give you five now and five later."

"Deal!" Totos holds out his hand and Ryder gives him a paper bill. "Okay, follow me."

They leave the comfortable market behind, to be replaced by commercial buildings and warehouses. The ships along the piers are huge, made for business, not comfort. In the fresh moonlight, the details of the ships are hidden, but they look like a combination of freight and old battleships. Totos begins to sing, swaying side to side.

"Have you heard of an isle, where the beaches are gold?

The water is warm, the wind never cold.

The treasures are endless, greatest of lore.

With all the food you can eat and all the drink you can pour.

Have you heard of an isle, where no boat can go?

Many have searched but no one may know.

Blood for your boat, every action worthwhile.

Is the price you must pay to reach Cainin's Isle."

Iona cringes. *This is torture. If the singing doesn't kill me, it'll probably get us caught for trespassing.*

Totos leads them to a door on the side of a warehouse. He fiddles for a moment then opens the door on smooth hinges.

Totos turns to the others. "Please, after you."

Ryder looks at Totos then into the dark doorway. "Are you sure? This place doesn't look abandoned."

"Well, it's not, so you'll have to make sure you're out by morning."

Ryder hesitates. "I don't know. We really don't need any more trouble."

Totos shakes his head. "No, no, no. No trouble at all. Trust me. Here, I'll even give you this, so you can get in tomorrow." He hands them the tool he used to open the warehouse door. "The doors only lock from the outside, so getting out is easy." He hands Ryder a fancy-looking lock picker. Ryder still hesitates. "Either this or one hundred Anterren for a room at an inn... or sleeping on the streets, where you're just begging for trouble."

"Errrr. Fine." Ryder moves through the door. Korbin, Thea, and Iona follow.

The door closes behind them, plunging the area into total darkness. The children pop on their flashlights, revealing crates all around, stacked almost to the ceiling.

Totos takes them to a large metal crate in the back of the warehouse, pulling up the locking mechanism to the double doors. One door after another swings open. There are blankets and pillows strewn across the inside.

Iona looks at the castors the large crate sits on. *Wheels?* Iona shines her light on Totos's face. "This seems really nice. Where are you going to sleep?"

Totos covers his eyes. "This is my favorite spot and I've been collecting for a while. This isn't my only place, so you all can have it for a couple weeks if you need."

Iona lowers her light. "What's the catch?"

"No catch, just the ten Anterren... Unless you wish to pay me more?"

Ryder pulls another few bills from his pocket, handing it to Totos. "No, ten is just fine."

"I call this pillow!" Thea says as she jumps into the crate onto a red, body-sized pillow. Korbin follows and they start to wrestle.

"Come on, wait just a second." Iona tries to grab one of them without going into the crate. "Get back here!"

Korbin looks at Iona then jumps at her. He grabs her wrist, pulling her onto the blankets. "Whatcha going to do now?"

Thea jumps on Korbin's back while Iona struggles to free herself. "Korbin, hold on!" Iona gasps.

Ryder shakes his head, turning back to Totos. "Thanks for your help."

Totos smirks. "No, thank you. You've done more for me than you can imagine." Totos signals with his head for Ryder to go into the crate. "Here, let me help you with the door before I leave."

"Thanks." Ryder steps into the crate and turns to watch the wrestling match between the others.

One of the double doors closes with a thud. Iona pushes Korbin off but his tight grip on her arm prevents her from standing. "No, stop!" she yells.

The other door closes and the locking mechanism screeches shut. Everyone turns to the door. Iona pushes Korbin away, her heart beating uncomfortably.

Ryder shoves the doors, but they are firmly shut. "Let us out!" He bangs on the metal with both fists. The rest of the children join in.

Suddenly the crate starts to move, throwing the children off balance. The vibrations of the wheels on the hard cement floor resonate through the metal walls.

"Where are they taking us? What's going on?" Thea asks.

Iona slides down the wall in one of the corners. She hugs her knees and shakes her head. *We're trapped...*

9 Captured
Nero

Nero looks out at the piers and the dark boats floating on the water. *I wonder where those ships have been... or who could be watching us.* He hurries to catch up with the singing Totos, who is leading Ryder and the others.

There's something about him I don't like... I guess there isn't much I can do, unless I say something. He plunges his hand into his pocket, grabbing his bracelet. *But then they'll just make fun of me for being scared.*

He glances at the ships then into the shadows of the buildings, feeling like he is being watched. Totos turns the corner of a warehouse, disappearing into its shadow.

Hey!

Nero whips his head around to look behind him, then around the docks. He puts his hand on his chest, where his heart is thumping against his ribs. *I'm definitely losing it.* Suddenly, he catches a glimpse of a faint violet light to the side of the building up ahead. *What's that?* Nero hurries over to the building, staying in the shadows as much as possible.

He carefully pokes his head around the corner, seeing the light further away, off behind another building.

"Errrr." Nero runs after it.

He turns the corner and again, the light is further away. "What the heck!" The run turns into a sprint. He continues to chase the light, but every time he turns a corner, it is farther away. He speeds around another bend. This time, the light is gone. He searches the lane, but there is no sign of it.

"Dang it!" The darkness of the quiet alley creeps in on him. He turns around. *Where am I?*

He sprints back the way he came, hesitating at each turn, struggling to remember where to go. *Dang it, dang it, dang it!* All the warehouses and alleys look the same. *What if I can't find them? Where will I sleep? What if I can't find them tomorrow?* He sprints down another alley. *Why do I always get separated!* "I'm so stupid!"

Finally, Nero pops around the corner of a warehouse back by the piers. He slows down, trying to recover his breath. *Okay, this looks familiar. I just need to remember exactly where I left them. Maybe I can yell to get their attention.*

He walks up to the warehouse where he last saw Totos. Muffled voices are coming from inside. Nero jumps behind a pile of old wooden pallets stacked to the side. The large garage door in the front of the warehouse rolls up with a clanking of metal. It jerks to a stop. Suddenly, the night seems quiet.

A man in black steps out from the opening. "Alright, hurry it along. Get the cargo back to the ship before the Cap'n gets upset."

Two other men and a small boy tug on a rope attached to a giant crate with wheels.

Totos! What's he doing?

The first man leads the group down the road to the water line. Muffled banging and voices echo from the crate.

Who's in the crate? Nero gulps. *No no no. What's going on?*

As the crate moves along the edge of the bay, Nero scuttles through the shadows of the buildings in a frantic haze of thought. He follows as the man in black leads the crate to a pier below the silhouette of a large warship. From a distance, Nero watches the crate stop. A ramp extends from the boat and other workers pull the crate aboard. The ramp retracts, and the people disappear.

This can't be happening! Nero jumps out of his hiding spot, running back to the warehouse. He searches for his friends, yelling out to them and hoping his suspicion is wrong. After several hours, exhaustion and reality settle heavily upon him. He wanders back to the picnic table where they had all eaten dinner and falls into a fitful sleep.

A roaring fire consumes everything, and a person screams.

Nero wakes up in a cold sweat, his heart racing. *Stupid dream.* He blinks his eyes a couple of times, rubbing them with shaking hands. The morning light is still dim, and the ocean breeze carries a bite. He crosses his arms for warmth. *Where am I?* The memories of the night before stab him like a searing hot poker. He curls up into a ball and forces his eyes shut. *This has to be another bad dream.*

Nero opens his eyes again; this time the memories of last night are there to greet him immediately. He rolls onto his back, covering his face with his hands. *What am I going to do?* When he removes his hands, he notices a pair of covered legs sitting at the bench. Nero freezes. *Maybe they haven't noticed me...*

"I thought you were going to sleep all day," a woman's voice says from above. He looks around carefully, expecting to see someone walking up to the table.

"You, under the table. Get up here."

One of the feet starts to tap. Nero builds up the courage to scoot himself out from under the table, peeking his head over the top.

The woman is sitting at the table with both hands palm down. There are two white boxes between them. She is wearing a bland combination of typical working clothes. Her short brown hair just barely makes a ponytail. She gives him a thin smile. "Sit. I'm not going to bite."

Nero cautiously sits, keeping a constant eye on her.

"Are you hungry?" She opens one of the boxes, sliding it over to him. Inside are baked fish over eggs and seasoned potatoes.

Nero ignores the food. *She looks familiar.* "Have I met you—" He jumps out of his seat and spins to run away. Just as his body starts to move forward, his arm stops, and she yanks him back to his seat.

"Hey. I said I wasn't going to bite," the woman says with a snarl, squeezing his wrist. Nero looks at her in utter terror and the woman drops the curl to her lip. She lets go of his wrist, releasing a rush of blood that tingles his arm like an army of ants. "Look, I'm sorry. I'm having a rough go of things at the moment. Will you hear me out for just a moment?" she asks. "Please?" She says the word as if it is as foreign to her as breathing water.

Nero gives her a curt nod and the woman smiles. She reaches into her pocket and pulls out the fruit she took from Nero in the forest. It is dark green with red speckles all over it. "I just wanted to apologize for taking this. It was wrong of me." She puts the fruit in front of Nero. He stays stationary. They look at each other for a moment. "So, why were you sleeping under the table? And where are your friends?"

Nero rubs his wrist, glaring at her. "Why should I tell you?"

The woman's face remains unchanged. "You're right. It's none of my business, but you're better off on your own if they abandoned you."

"They didn't abandon me!"

"Easy now. Friends will only get in the way. They did you a favor."

"I told you. They didn't ditch me. They were taken by—" Nero bites his tongue.

The woman raises an eyebrow. "Taken? What happened? Were they taken by the police?" Nero shakes his head. "Alright then. Who?"

Nero looks down. "I don't know... I think they were taken to some huge boat in a crate."

"That's bad. I hope they weren't particularly important to you."

Nero looks at her sharply. "Yeah, they are important to me! They're the only family I have."

She opens her mouth to say something, but then closes it. Her callousness falls away. "Look, if I had to guess, they were taken by traffickers. They'll probably be sold as slaves on another continent."

"What? Slaves are illegal. I've got to go to the police or tell someone!"

The woman grabs his hand. "Hold up, kid. If there's money in something, then it'll always exist. Slavery can be quite the lucrative business, especially when you're selling a bunch of kids that no one cares about." Nero's mouth drops, and she rolls her eyes. "Don't take it personally. It's just reality. Do you know anyone in Blue Horin?" Nero shakes his head. "And I'm guessing you're running away?"

"Kinda."

"Well then, there's no one here to miss you if you get taken. Unfortunately for you, most of the city officials will turn a blind eye. These ruffians provide certain legal 'services' at a reasonable price, and they do it by not-so-legal methods. As long as the city isn't endangered, the officials would rather not know how they do business."

"What am I going to do?" Nero bites his lip but cannot prevent tears from gushing out.

"Okay, cut it out, tears never solve any problems. You're so damn pitiful it makes me want to drown myself..." She says, disgusted. She grimaces. "Sorry, maybe that was inappropriate. Can you show me where the boat is? Maybe we can figure out something that might help your friends."

"What?"

"Don't tell me you're deaf."

"No. But you're going to help?" Nero looks at her, his eyes bloodshot.

"That's what I said."

"Why?"

Her face turns hard. "Maybe I feel bad for how pathetic you are. Does it matter?" Nero shakes his head. "That's what I thought. Now collect the breakfast and show me which boat."

*****

Nero and the woman duck behind a building, peeking out from the corner at the huge battleship. It has several large turrets on its top and a green alligator creature painted on its hull. The creature's legs are just visible at the water line. At the prow, the creature is snarling, its white teeth ready to chomp.

The woman pats Nero on the back. "Yep, just what I thought. If your friends are on that boat, they're screwed."

Nero looks at her in shock. "What?"

"Definitely taken as slaves. We need to collect some info if we want to even consider doing something about it. For all we know, the boat could leave within the hour."

"Couldn't we just ask someone on board?"

"That's a battleship, if you didn't notice. It doesn't shoot hugs and kisses. They'd kill you and not think twice of it. If you threatened one of them, they'd cut off their own leg before they gave us any info. Trust me, it's not something you're going to be up for. We need a different angle."

They watch for a while. The crew bustles on the main deck. A lone man dressed in casual clothes walks along the path from the market area.

Nero points. "Hey, that's one of the soldiers we ran into just outside the city. I think his name's Walter."

The woman scowls. "That scumbag. I've run into him a few times. He's a total prick; what I wouldn't give to see him strung up. I bet he's the one who tipped off the traffickers about you."

"Why would he do that?"

"I told you. Money. People will do anything for money these days, and, if you're willing to make some moral sacrifices, it's especially easy to come by. It wouldn't take a genius to figure out a handful of children coming from the forest aren't from the city."

They watch as a guard escorts Walter into the ship. Fifteen minutes later he is shoved down the ramp. He walks hastily away.

The woman taps Nero's shoulder. "Alright, kid, meet me back at the table where I found you. Eat some breakfast."

"What are you going to do?"

"I'm going to extract some information," she says with a curt smile. "What's your name?"

"Nero."

"Nero? That's not your real name, is it?"

Nero looks down. "No, I gave it to myself. I like the story of Nero the hero."

"Well, you have a lot to live up to with a name like that. I'll see you at the table. Don't go wandering off. I had enough trouble tracking you down the first time."

"What's your name?" Nero asks, hesitant.

The woman stares at him without blinking. "I committed autonomicide. I am no one." She strides down the path after Walter.

What the heck does that mean? Nero waits several minutes before he leaves his spot and walks back to the table. He picks through his breakfast, glancing up at anyone walking near his table. *Maybe she won't come back.*

When he finishes eating, he worries about his friends for a long time until he catches a glimpse of her. He sighs with relief but feels the stress of her presence weigh down on him instantly.

The Woman reaches the table, a smug smile on her face. "I didn't think I could find so much pleasure in helping someone else," she says, almost to herself.

"Did he tell you anything?"

"Everything. As though his life depended on it." She sits down and pulls one of the breakfast boxes to her. "It turns out he IS the coprophagist who got your friends in trouble." She takes a couple bites of her breakfast. "How did they fall for that rat trap anyway? What did they do, just walk into a crate? At least you had brains enough to avoid it."

Nero fiddles with the lid of his box. "Actually… I got distracted. By the time I found my way back, they were in the crate."

She shakes her head. "Your friends deserve what they got. If it were up to me, we'd leave them. It's survival of the fittest in this world. The weak don't deserve to make it."

Nero's mouth drops open. "But…"

She puts her hand in front of his face. "Don't even start. I'll still help. I'm just saying, if they're stupid enough to get caught in a crate, then being a slave is about the best they can do." Nero's mouth continues to hang open. She ignores him. "Walter told me they're planning to leave the bay tomorrow morning. He even felt so bad for what he did, he gave me all his money." She smiles at Nero, but he remains catatonic. "So, being as we have some cash and time, I think this is about the best scenario for rescuing your friends we could ask for. What's your plan?"

"What?"

She raises an eyebrow. "I just have to say one of my pet peeves is when people complain about something and then don't do anything about it. And here you are, complaining about your friends while you don't even have a plan to rescue them." Nero's mouth opens and closes like a fish out of water. "I guess I was hoping for too much, seeing as your name is Nero. I'll try not to dwell on it." She crushes a potato under her fork. "You must have some sort of skill if you and your friends managed to pass through the forest. Can you fight?"

Nero shakes his head. "The others did most of the wrestling, I usually just watched."

"Wrestling! Did you have any sort of training, or have you just wasted your life so far?"

"I'm just a kid," Nero says, eyes swelling with tears.

The Woman closes her mouth, taking a deep breath. "Okay, that's alright. We can still manage. Sorry, I don't have a good sense of what a normal childhood would be like." She squashes another potato with her fork and licks it off. "You're a bit scrawny, anyway, so fighting doesn't seem like it'd be your strong suit. How about Aether? Have you taken an entity or an essence?"

"A what?"

"An essence…" Her eyes scan the area. She takes another bite of food. "Essence is the stuff that connects our world with Aether and it's what makes using Aether possible. Humans can absorb them, which lets them use Aether. Do you have any idea what I'm talking about? It's like a floating blob of mist." Nero's eyes light up and the woman smiles, but just as quickly, Nero's shoulders drop, his excitement fading away. "Marks's blade, you're dramatic. What's wrong?"

"Well, me and my friends found some canisters with stuff in them in the old industrial district of New Lur. My friends absorbed them. I tried, but it didn't work…"

"How so?"

"I touched it and wanted to absorb it, but it kinda just faded away or something. I don't remember. I passed out. I keep seeing more of those things and I try to get them, but I can't."

"More essence? Was there a dead person nearby?"

Nero shakes his head. "No, but Korbin absorbed something from a dead bug in the forest. The ones I see are just by themselves."

"Where do you see them?"

"That's actually the reason I got separated from my friends when they got captured. I thought I saw one."

"Here? Are you kidding? There's no way you'd see an essence just floating around a city. It must have been some reflected light, but I doubt you saw an essence. You said you found the others in canisters?"

Nero continues to play with the food container. "Yeah, we think a Catalyst member stole them from the Erohsians. That's why they're chasing us..." Nero trails off and looks at the Woman, uneasy.

"The Erohsians are after you?" She smiles, slapping the table. "So, I should give you kids more credit. That's something to be proud of, as long as they don't catch you." She pauses a moment. "So, you and your friends dimwittedly decided to escape through the forest? Whose idea was that?"

"Ryder's. He thought the Erohsians were just making the danger up."

"Well, they're not. You all may be the first to pass through the forest and survive in fifty years. And you're probably the first kids to try. How did you find the fruit? Was that with the canisters?"

Should I mention the big creature, or is she going to think I'm lying like Korbin? Nero looks at his hands, playing with a fork. "I found a few next to a big tree."

"A few? What happened to the others?"

Nero hesitates. "I ate one when I found them and another a little later. But I don't see what the big deal is. I think they taste really good." He pulls out the last fruit and starts to pull away the tough peel. "Have you tried it before? My friends all think it's disgusting." Nero hands the Woman half. "Here, try it." He starts on his. The Woman watches Nero but does not eat hers. Nero finishes his half, looking at her. A tingling sensation spreads outward from his stomach. "You don't like it, either?" The Woman looks at Nero, eyes squinted, leaning forward. *Did I do something wrong?* "What's the matter?"

The Woman shrugs "Apparently, nothing. I was just waiting to see if you were going to die," she says casually.

"What!?"

"The fruit you just ate is from a Katashne'n Tree. It's a very expensive delicacy."

"Is it poisonous? Why didn't you stop me?"

"I didn't stop you because you said you already ate one. Naturally, I didn't believe you, so if you died, it'd be suitable punishment for lying." She smiles. "But you didn't, so good job being honest."

Nero looks at her in horror. "How do you know I'm not going to die!"

"Because if you were, you'd already be dead. Or screaming. The Katashne'n trees have a lot of Aether in them, and they're only found in areas with high background levels of Aether, such as the Ferin Forest. If you couldn't have handled it, the Aether released from eating the fruit would have burnt a hole right through you. Which—as you can imagine—would be quite painful. Does your stomach hurt?"

Nero puts a hand on his stomach, looking at her, worried. "Well, now that you mention it."

She waves her hand at him. "Oh, shut up, you're fine."

"If it is so dangerous, why's it considered a delicacy?"

"Because finding a tree is almost impossible, which makes it rare, expensive, and if the sudden jolt of Aether doesn't kill you, it can make even the oldest person feel like they're young again. Occasionally, someone is lucky and stumbles upon a tree. For whatever reason, though, it's near impossible to find it a second time. It's like it can only be found if it wants to. You probably could have paid for all the food you have eaten in your entire life, with what you ate just now."

The color drains from Nero's face. "Could we have used it to trade for my friends?"

"Probably not. The traffickers wouldn't expect anyone to mess with them, but they aren't stupid enough to deal illegally in the city. Especially if it could be a set up by another group.

No, they'll just deny it the entire time then try to steal it from you when you're not looking."

"So, why didn't I die, then?"

"That's a good question. I've never heard of someone who can eat a Katashne'n fruit like you. You must have an impressive Aethersotto."

"What's that?"

"Aethersotto is a measure of how well you interact with Aether. It also affects how you perceive the world. Hmm. Maybe you're a Natural."

"What's a Natural?"

"A Natural is a rare Human born with Aether. They can't absorb essence. I didn't think they had such a high Aethersotto, but I've never met one, so who am I to say? Their true potential doesn't show until they come of age, though you should still have enough ability to do what needs to be done to save your friends. Have you ever used Aether?"

Nero shakes his head. "I don't think so, but I can always tell when my friends are doing something they shouldn't."

"You're referring to being scared, which you'll have to get over if we're going to work together." She takes the remaining half of fruit and squeezes one drop of juice onto a piece of fish from her breakfast. A shiver runs through her body when she eats it. "I don't know how you do it," she says as she hands him the fruit. "If you enjoyed it, you might as well finish the rest before we start the tests. The fruit is going to go bad soon anyway."

"Tests?"

"Well, we have to see if you're worth a damn and figure out what you can do. So, eat up." Nero does as he is told. "Aether allows for the manipulation of energy. It acts like an extension of your body and requires an input, just like anything else. Nothing is free in this world, and it sure isn't easy. Get that straight in your head right now." The Woman picks up a piece of the fruit's rind. "Are you ready to try? How do you feel?"

Nero nods, swallowing the last bit. A strong tingling sensation runs up his spine and over his scalp, energizing his muscles. The euphoric sensation is followed immediately by a wave of hostility. He clenches his fists and curls his lip. *What's going on?* He lets himself breathe for a moment, relaxing.

"This is a few steps above where I'd start if I had the choice, but I don't have the time or the tools to hold your hand, so we're going to start here. I want you to try to knock the peel off my hand."

Nero reaches over, poking it off.

"No! Not like that." She grabs the peel from the table. "What does that prove?"

"I'm just doing what you say!" he shoots back. "You don't need to yell at me." Nero notices his fists are clenched. *Whoa...* He takes a breath, relaxing his hands.

The Woman looks at him curiously for a moment then takes a breath as well. "Yes, you're right. You accomplished what I asked quickly, so I shouldn't complain." She holds her hand up to Nero. "I want you to use Aether this time."

Nero focuses on the peel and tries to knock it off with his ferocious glare. *Come on, move!* Nothing happens. His frustration grows. "How exactly am I supposed to do that?"

The Woman lets her hand fall to the table. "All objects—living or inert, rocks, water, people—are made of energy, and by sensing this connection between energy and matter, we can manipulate the object. In order for you to interact with the peel, you need to impose your essence on the world."

"My essence?"

"Yes, your essence," the Woman says. "Assuming you can use Aether, your essence is what does it. Can you feel it?"

Nero thinks about the tightness to his full stomach and the hardness of his seat. "I don't know. What's it supposed to feel like?"

"It's like a sixth sense. I'm not sure how to describe it; it's just there. Like, how would you explain smell?" She thinks for a moment. "Probably like eating with your nose, but through air. Hmmm. In that case... you could describe it like another body you probe the world with using Aether. Like little feelers. Does that make sense?"

"No."

"It's like another part of your body. It's throughout your body, but it's different. When you get the hang of it, you can move it just as easily as moving your arm. You must've felt something like it."

"I haven't. Are you sure you know what you're talking about? Maybe I can't use Aether."

"That's not an option. You'll be next to worthless to me if you can't. So, figure it out! You need to feel it. I can't do everything for you."

He snaps. "Yeah, but you can at least help. Figure out a better way to explain it and maybe I will!" Again, he forces himself to take a breath. *Where'd that come from?*

"Wow. You have some fight in you after all. I like it, but if you use that tone with me again, I'm going to cut out your tongue and feed it to the fish. Understand?"

Is she serious? Nero uses his fear to beat down the hostility raging within him until it is a gentle simmer in the back of his mind. He nods.

She smiles, an evil glint to her eye. "Good. Now give me your hands. I have an idea."

"What are you going to do?" he asks.

"I'm going to use Aether on you and see if I can tickle your essence a bit."

"Are you sure it's safe?"

The Woman reaches out both hands. "Almost entirely."

Nero reluctantly takes her hands. He feels a tingling in her skin and looks up.

"Can you feel that?" The Woman asks.

"I can feel it tingling in my hands."

The Woman's gaze intensifies and the tingling crawls up his arms into his body. A sudden chill begins to grip him, numbing his fingertips. There are goose bumps all over his arms. He looks up at the Woman in alarm and she lets go. The tingling withdraws immediately, dragging through his body from his core to his hands. Just as it disappears, something rebounds inside of him and oscillates for just a moment before fading away, something with substance but not of his body. He pokes at it with his thoughts and he feels something respond.

"I think I can feel it!" Nero says.

"That's more like it," she says with a hint of a smile.

"What did you do? It was freezing."

"I can use Aether that controls the flow of energy, so I was pulling heat from you, though it wasn't nearly as easy as I expected. You definitely have a high Aethersotto, which should make you interesting to work with," she says. "Now, let's get this job started. You felt your essence, that's the first step. Now we need to get you to exercise it. In order to move something, you need to probe the world with your essence and build a mental picture of the object you're interested in. This helps solidify a connection. When you feel like you have a firm grasp on an object, you can exert your essence on it through Aether and move it. Just keep in mind, your ability to move something is only limited by how well you focus your essence. Aether is unhindered by distance and has many more freedoms than our normal experience of the world." She picks up the peel, rolling it over in her hand. "Now, typically when you want to interact with something, it has little to no Aether in it, but because Aether will react better with Aether, interacting with something like this peel will be easier. Especially because the Katashne'n tree reacts well with all types of Aether. Does that make sense?"

Nero looks at her blankly. "Umm…"

"Okay, moving forward." She hands him the peel. "Tell me what you feel from the peel."

"Strange. Like I just licked a battery. Same as when you used Aether on me."

"Yes, good. The peel poorly contains Aether now that it's been opened, so you're feeling the Aether spilling off. Now try to use your essence and feel for the presence of the peel."

Nero closes his eyes and pushes on his essence. It responds in his leg. *No, not there.* He pushes it again. This time he feels it in his other leg.

"Sometimes it helps to focus if you slow your breathing and let everything else go. Try to relax with each breath."

Nero collects himself and takes a few breaths, again pushing the strange hostility inside of him to the back of his mind. He notices an odd tension about this newfound essence of his. *What's this about?* It is a tension that runs through his whole body, a tension resisting something, some external pull. He examines the tension then with a breath, lets it go.

A whole new world of light explodes in his mind's eye. The table, the path, the buildings off in the distance, and most of the people in the area are etched with a white light. The Woman in front of him is a bright mass of swirling red light. Her features are all but impossible to determine. *Wow.* He looks down at the white table and then at his hand, which looks exactly how he would see it if his eyes were open. The peel on his hand emits a gentle pulsing violet light.

Nero twitches. He suddenly notices his body being stretched in every direction. His hand begins to dissolve. The light from the world starts to collapse in on him. It turns into an avalanche. His body continues to fly apart. He instinctively clenches his body and resists the pull, creating the same tension he felt earlier. The cascade of the world stops, the light retreating. His mind is once again void of light.

"What are you doing?" The Woman asks.

Nero opens his eyes. To his relief, everything is normal. He is on his back and the Woman is standing over him.

"Will you stop messing around?" she asks. She pulls him up, sitting him back at the table. "What happened?"

"I don't know. I was relaxing and then suddenly I saw all this light. It started crashing in on me."

"Hmmm, maybe you should try to breathe a little more. You were probably just holding your breath."

I don't think I was... What happened?

"Now try again, while breathing. We don't have all day." She puts the peel back on his hand.

I don't want to do that again. He closes his eyes once more, but this time he lets himself maintain the tension in his body. He pushes with his essence and feels it respond in his hand, bumping against the peel. *Cool.* He probes the peel, building a mental picture as if he were feeling the shape of a rock in the dark with his fingers. In his mind, the peel begins to feel tangible. He pushes directly against it, causing it to jump off his hand.

The Woman is smiling at him when he opens his eyes. "Good job. I wasn't expecting you to make it jump." She sets the peel at the end of the table. "Okay, now knock it off the table."

Nero closes his eyes and pushes out with his essence, extending it to his surroundings. His essence crawls over the table, feeling the cracks along its length, but as it reaches out further it becomes harder for him to control and maintain. His essence snags on the peel. He struggles to home in on it. It is easy to separate from the table, but it takes him some time before he can fully grasp it and when he does, he forces it away. The peel jumps off the table.

"Excellent," the Woman says. "You're catching on quick." She holds the peel on her hand. "Now, knock it off my hand."

Nero pushes out his essence, struggling to distinguish the Aether from the Woman and the Aether from the peel. He probes the peel from every direction and worms his way between it and the Woman's hand, which he then probes in detail as well. Slowly he is able to discern the difference.

When he does, the separation of the two is quick, and he is able to knock the peel out of her hand.

"And I was really dreading this whole thing, but now that you seem semi-capable you might just have a chance of not getting taken as a slave with the rest," she says with a smile. "Just remember, forces balance, so anything you push or pull on with your essence will affect your body, just as if you were pushing or pulling with your arms. If you practice, you could hold yourself up with your essence." The Woman collects all of their trash. "Follow me."

Nero hops up. "What are we doing now?"

"I'm going to teach you something else. Pay attention. What do you think is more powerful than any amount of Aether in the world?"

"Umm… Havityns—"

"No, the brain! Do you have a good brain?"

Nero shrugs. "It seems to work. I think."

"Confidence helps too… Anyway, what I'm trying to say is if you use your brain, you don't have to work so hard. Being lazy can be incredibly powerful."

She leads Nero down a side alley and jiggles the locked handle of an old, metal door. "If we wanted to get into this door, how do you think we would do that?"

"Use a key?"

"Well, yes, Master of the Obvious. But, if we didn't have a key, we would either have to bust the door down or pick the lock. Busting the door down takes a lot of work, so let's avoid that for now. If we wanted to use Aether to pick the lock, we would have to manipulate the tumblers in the lock just like someone with a pick set, which takes a good amount of skill. But what do we know about a door?" She pauses for a fraction of a second. "When we turn the handle, it retracts a latch that lets the door open. When we close the door, the latch gets pushed in. Do you get what I'm trying to say?"

"To open the door, all we need to do is push the latch in?"

"Yes! And since we can do that easily with Aether, it's possible to open the door without a great effort. Unfortunately, most people know about this trick, so it isn't terribly useful. Nonetheless, a good example of how to use your brain. Let's give it a try." She focuses on the door and after a moment turns the handle, swinging it open. "I had to pick this lock, since it specifically locks the latch in place, but we can still practice execution even if it's unlocked."

"How do you know all of this? About Aether and stuff. I thought you were just a hobo," Nero says.

The Woman's eyebrows rise as she looks at Nero. "I had another life at one point. I'm not going to share it with you, but what I will say is it required a large array of unconventional skills."

"If you know so much, then why can't you just teach me to pick the lock?"

"The fine skill to manipulate several different objects simultaneously is a bit out of our time budget." She reaches over to the latch on the door and pushes it in. "Now that the door is unlocked, the latch moves. I want you to try to push the latch in using Aether. We'll keep the door open to see how you're doing. Close your eyes if it helps"

Nero looks around. "Are we going to get in trouble?"

She glares at him.

He closes his eyes and pushes his essence into the world, feeling the edge of the door. The latch is apparent, though not nearly as substantial as the Aether in the peel. No matter how hard he tries to form a connection with it, the latch remains unmoved. After a long while, he looks at the woman. "I can't do it. It's not the same as the peel."

"You can't?" she asks venomously. "You give up after only a few tries because it's hard? You poor thing, you must have had such an easy life growing up. Well, wake up!" She pokes him in the chest. "LIFE IS HARD, Nero, and the only way you'll get anything out of it is if you take it. Your friends' freedom depends on you and you alone. I'd rather throw myself off a cliff than play mommy with you, so if you want to save them, figure it out. But let me warn you now, if I ever hear you say, 'I can't' again, you'll regret it." She looks down at Nero. His eyes are brimming with tears. "Do you want to save your friends?"

Yes. He nods.

"Good. Now remember, it's all the same. It's all energy. It's just a little different. Figure it out."

Nero wipes the tears from his eyes, setting his jaw. A fury swirls inside of him. *Stupid woman. I'll show her. I CAN save my friends.* He jabs aggressively at the latch with his essence. No success.

"Stop and breathe. Don't let your anger control you. Collect your emotions, accept them, and then let them go, or you'll never save your friends."

My friends. Nero breathes and lets his anger go. He struggles to bring his thoughts back to the task. He pushes out his essence once again, feeling the latch. It is still insubstantial. *It sure doesn't feel the same... but if it's different...* He pushes against it gently and with constant pressure. A hint of a different substance shimmers at his touch. He bears down on this new feeling and it grows more solid. *It is just different!* He grasps the latch and pushes it in.

"Good!" The Woman's voice startles Nero. "You keep pulling through! Now again."

She has him push the latch in several more times until she closes the door. "Now let's see if you can push the latch in while it's closed. It's the same thing, you'll just have to sort through more material. Remember, the only resistance your essence feels is the resistance you make. If you ignore the door frame, it's no different than what you were just doing."

Again, Nero struggles for a long time to reach the latch. Every time he tries to ignore the frame, the latch disappears as well. When he focuses on the latch, the frame becomes distracting. Frustration builds with the sweat on his forehead.

I will not give up! Finally, he separates the frame and the latch enough that he pushes the latch in.

Nero throws his arms in the air. "I did it!"

The Woman looks at him then at the door. "Did what?"

"I pushed the latch in… I think."

"Did you now? But what was our intended goal?"

Nero looks at the door. "To open it?"

"Hmmmm."

"Okay." Nero puts his hand on the doorknob, trying to push the latch in once more. It turns out to be exceedingly difficult to keep his concentration on the latch while pulling the door open. After he manages to open the door without turning the doorknob, the Woman has him do it again and again while she tries to distract him.

On his tenth attempt, the Woman tickles his ear using a stick but he still succeeds. Nero's stomach growls.

The Woman looks at him, surprised. "Wow. Didn't we just eat a couple of hours ago?"

Nero fiddles with his feet. "I'm sorry, we can keep practicing."

"No, you've done well," she says, patting him awkwardly on the back. "You've earned something to eat. It'll be a good time to go over our plan."

*****

Nero and the Woman sit at the edge of a walkway, their feet hanging over the water, eating banana bread.

Nero kicks his legs. His strength and the comforting tingle that ran over his scalp earlier are gone. So is the uncomfortable hostility he could barely control. *Was that always in me?* He looks out at the water. *I wish Thea were here.* He looks up at the Woman. "Shouldn't we hurry up and try to rescue my friends?"

"No. We'll wait. This is their last night in port, so the crew will try to get out and have some fun while they have the chance. They should be a touch more relaxed."

"Okay. How are we going to do this?"

"I'm going to sell you as a slave."

Nero chokes on some bread. "What? I thought you were going to help!" *She's going to sell me like the others!*

"Stop fussing. Do you have a better plan for getting inside?"

"Uh…"

"Precisely. Someone needs to free your friends from the inside and this seems like the easiest way. They'll probably be locked up tight. If we convince your captors you're sick and need to be quarantined, then you may have a little more room to escape."

Nero feels his pulse rise. "Couldn't we just sneak in together?"

"Uh, no. You wouldn't be able to keep up with me. And who would create the diversion for the escape? Certainly not you by yourself." She pauses. "We're only doing this because you want to. So, let me know if it's too much."

Nero looks down at the water, pushing away the panic. "Okay, so you sell me as a slave. Then what?"

"Well, you'll have to escape and free your friends," she says calmly.

Nero's starts to panic. "How am I supposed to do that?"

She sighs. "That's why I've been trying to teach you to use your brain. You'll have to figure it out on the fly. I'll make you a little poisonous blow dart so you can kill anyone that gets in your way."

"Kill!?"

"You're a piece of work, aren't you?" The Woman throws her hands in the air. "Fine, we can make it a non-lethal dart if it'll make you feel better, but that'll take longer to kick in. They're your friends, so if you're willing to take the risk…"

Nero smiles, nodding. "I'd like that better."

She shrugs. "Whatever suits you. So, once you have your friends, stay put until you get my signal. I'll give you an hour from when we separate." She pulls a small digital watch out of her pocket. "Put this on. The sailors shouldn't care about it when they take you."

"What's the signal?"

"Not sure yet... think on the fly, right? I'll be sure to make it so clear, even you wouldn't miss it. Once you hear the signal, get to the main deck of the ship and head to the side opposite the pier. There'll be a rope ladder with a small boat at the bottom. If they pursue you, they're going to be pretty upset. So, don't get caught. Get to shore as fast as you can and run like crazy to the Market. There should be enough people there that they'll give up. If not, I hope at least someone will intervene. We'll set up a hotel room you all can use after."

"This seems like a crazy plan."

She smiles. "Exciting, right?" She hops up. "Once you're free, you're on your own; I'm not playing babysitter." She pulls him up by the arm with little effort. "Alright, let's make you a tranquilizer dart."

She leads him through the Market, collecting things as she goes: a souvenir blowgun as long as Nero's forearm that is dyed black with carved notches, some paper, a few pieces of leather, strips of cloth, apples, and finally, after many stops, ingredients for the knock-out potion. Once the Woman is satisfied, she rents a room in a hotel.

Nero watches as she fashions several darts out of a porous woody plant and carves a groove along their sides to help collect the sleeping potion. She makes Nero a small leather strap for his wrist to hold the darts. He examines it while she mixes up the potion.

She puts two apples on the table and grabs the dart gun. "I'm going to take care of a few things. It will be a while, so in the meantime, practice with this." She puts a dart in the blowgun, firing at the apple. It sinks deep into the center. "Real easy." She tosses the blowgun to him, walking out.

As soon as the door closes, he loads the blowgun and fires. The dart ricochets off a lamp and sticks into the wall. He lets out a deep breath. *Maybe she won't come back and I won't have to go through with this crazy plan...*

10 The Nero Assault

Nero

The light flowing through the curtains is just starting to dim, while a pit of despair grows unabated in Nero. He lies on his back, staring at the ceiling. Finally, the door opens and the Woman walks through. She is carrying two small bags and some sticks. Nero does a double take when he sees she is wearing a pretty, light yellow summer dress, hair loose.

She glares at him. "I don't even want to hear it. I'll do whatever it takes to get a job done. That includes wearing dresses." She tosses him one of the bags. "There are some pieces of candy left, if you want them."

"Thanks." Nero opens the bag and swallows a few chocolate-covered raisins. "So what's going on?"

"Everything's in order and the time is approaching." She sets the rest down, then notices the apples on the table. Darts litter the area, but the apples are relatively unharmed. "Did you manage to hit one?"

Nero puts down the raisin he was about to eat. "A few times."

"Well, I hope you get it right when you need to." She grabs the blowgun and starts to shave off the dark stain with a knife, making it look like a stick. She takes the leather pouch she made for the darts, filling it with a thick paste. "Once you're free and get a chance, all you need to do is put the darts in here. They'll be covered with the sleeping potion so you can use them when you need them. Just remember, the potion will work faster closer to the head or the heart, especially close to large arteries. Now, take off one of your shoes and loosen the laces."

The Woman grabs the sticks, the blowgun, a long piece of cloth, the darts, and the holder. She takes the leather dart holder and ties it to his ankle, then stacks several darts into the blowgun, sealing them in with wads of cloth on both ends. Using the sticks and the blowgun, she makes an ankle brace with a wrapping of cloth, then roughly pulls his untied shoe back on and over the brace. Nero winces, but keeps his mouth shut.

She steps back to look at it. "Perfect, now you just need to act pathetic, and we should have an excellent little disguise."

Shouldn't be a problem. Nero's nerves make it hard to breathe.

"Remember to watch the time. Should be about nine-ish when I create the distraction."

Nero looks at the little numbers on his watch. "Okay."

"You're going to need your energy, so I got you some fish and chips for dinner. You can eat it before we leave." She walks over to the bag on the table, pulling out a white box.

Nero looks inside, without a hint of an appetite. *I couldn't eat anything if my life depended on it.* He looks back at her with a lack of enthusiasm.

"I don't care if you're not hungry, you're going to eat the food with or without my help," she says coolly.

Under the constant stone-cold glare of the Woman, Nero manages to finish the entire meal.

"Good work." The Woman stands up, heading for the door. "I need to get something from the front desk. We'll leave when I get back."

As Nero waits, a sharp pain grows in his stomach. His vision starts to blur. By the time the Woman gets back, he is nauseous and he can hardly focus on anything. "I'm—not feeling so—good."

The Woman smiles. "Excellent." She rolls a wheel chair next to him. "Hop on."

Nero struggles to move; everything hurts. His dinner is threatening to come back up. *What's wrong with me? I don't think I can do this.*

The Woman pulls him onto the chair, tying his hands and feet together.

She's really going to sell me as a slave! The whole room sways back and forth; cold sweat breaks out on his face.

A blanket falls over Nero, covering his tied hands and feet. The next thing he knows, he is outside. She pushes him down the walkway that runs along the edge of the water.

I need to escape... Nero pushes with his feet, but his strength is gone. They reach the pier and approach the same ship that swallowed his friends.

He tries to lift himself one last time, but a firm hand from the Woman dashes his hopes. They reach the ramp to the boat, where she talks with a few men. The conversation nears an argument, but no matter how hard he tries, he cannot make sense of any of it. Finally, one of the men throws Nero over his shoulder. The sudden pressure on Nero's stomach makes him feel like he is going to pop. He tries to focus on the man's feet, but they move in a blur. The cool breeze, which was the only thing comforting him, disappears. The air grows thick and warm.

They travel down stairs and through endless corridors before the man opens a large metal door. Suddenly, Nero is thrown into a cage. He hears a click, then silence, though he has a feeling he is not alone. Lying on his back, Nero fights the nausea. The musty animal stink seeps through his nostrils, making it all the harder.

The aching abruptly begins to fade. The nausea vanishes shortly after. *Was this part of her plan?* Nero pushes himself upright. For the first time, he looks around his prison. He is in a small, metal barred cell in a room full of cages. Most of them are empty, except for a few strange animals. One cage has a

Nero-sized orange cat with long white barbs lying against its back. Another cage has two huge, light-blue birds with short powerful beaks and four-centimeter-long black talons. The last cage has a grey crocodile-like creature that is several times the size of Nero. All of the animals stare at him.

Nero shifts uneasily, checking his watch. It is ten minutes after eight. *Oh man, I really need to get out of here.* He looks at the door to his cage and his eyes fall on a small lock securing the latch. His hopes plummet. *Oh No! How am I going to do this? She didn't teach me how to pick locks! I knew this was a bad idea...*

You're whining.

"No I'm not!"

The cat growls at him.

"Yeah, yeah..." *Great, I'm losing it and I'm trapped in here with myself.* Nero looks around the room with its grey metal walls. *What would the crazy woman do if she were here? She would pick the lock, of course...*

A board by the door catches his attention. There are locks hanging from hooks, and each one has a number above it. All but four of the hooks have locks. The empty hooks have keys. Nero scrambles to the door of his cage and looks at the lock. It has '22' written on it.

Yes! Now, I just need to get the key... A tingling sensation runs over his scalp and through his entire body. The hostility he felt working with the Woman returns. *I will not be trapped in this cage!* He grabs the bars and strains to pull them apart.

Stop and breathe. Don't let your anger control you. Collect your emotions, accept them, and then let them go, or you'll never save your friends.

Nero stops. The bars have not moved. *My friends. I need to think.* He breathes out, struggling to silence the hostility. With more effort than before, he manages it. *Alright, the key.*

He closes his eyes and reaches out to the room, pushing his essence toward the board. By the time he reaches something solid, any contact is fleeting. His ability to maintain focus at this distance is excruciatingly difficult. Frustration begins to consume him, but he forces himself to exhale. His mind clears, slightly. *How am I supposed to grab the keys if I can't even feel them?* He looks at the board, easily spotting the key on the hook with the label, 22. He turns around and slides down the bars. *I don't have much time... I need to figure this out.* He thinks back to his first attempt to use his essence when the world of light appeared to him. *Was that something I can use? Was that Aether?* He grabs the bars of his cage. *There's only one way to find out.*

Nero closes his eyes, searching for the tension pulling on his essence. Once he can feel it, he lets some of the tension go. Faint white lights appear out of the darkness, taking shape as the bars of his cage. He relaxes further. The details of his surroundings creep outward like growing crystals. Suddenly, the pull on his essence increases. The world starts to collapse. He grits his teeth, resisting the pull. With a considerable effort, the collapse slows. The world returns to a semblance of normality. The pull on his essence continues, but after a while, he finds that his subconscious begins to do the work. He relaxes, inspecting the world.

His surroundings are defined in white—the cat and the crocodile-like creatures included—but the two birds have a swirling green light that obscures their features. He picks himself up, looking at the glowing white board with the keys. *Okay... Here we go.* He reaches for his essence, pushing it forward. A thick white tentacle that looks like it had been caught in a garbage disposal sprouts from his chest.

"Ah!" He jumps, losing his concentration. The tentacle retreats. *That is so creepy. Is that my essence?* He pushes again, and the tentacle reaches out. A chill runs through his body. *Definitely creepy.* He moves the tentacle up and down, feeling it respond when it touches the bars of his cage. As he pushes it out further, it becomes more ragged. He focuses on his essence, clearing his mind with deep breaths. The tentacle thins and becomes more solid. *Okay, this is good... I think.* He pushes his essence forward again, and it maintains its shape until it reaches the board. Almost as if he were touching it with his hand, he finds the key, wraps around it, and tugs. The key comes off the pin with a surprising amount of effort. It clatters to the ground. *This is really good!* The two birds flap their wings. Nero drags the key across the floor to the edge of his cell.

He fights against the pull on his essence, forcing it to where it was before. His perspective shifts back to the normal version of the world. The key with a 22 written on it is within reach. *I can do this!* A wave of triumph rushes over him. At the same moment, the buzz over his scalp disappears, taking the hostility swimming in the back of his mind with it. *What's going on with me?* He shakes his head. *Friends first.*

Nero pulls apart his ankle brace, extracting the blowgun equipment from the tangle of cloth. He ties the leather strap onto his wrist and inserts the darts. Moments later, he is fumbling with the lock and is free.

The birds squawk, looking back and forth from him to the other animals.

I don't know how to help and I need to find my friends. Nero turns his back to the birds, walking toward the door.

Another squawk pierces his eardrums, causing him to duck. The birds flap their wings and bob their heads.

"Shhhh!" He checks his watch, twenty minutes until nine. *This is stupid...* "Alright, hang on." He goes to the board, grabbing the three single keys. *Okay, important point number one is that I don't want to get eaten.* He looks around the room for ideas. *Maybe if the door is open they'll ignore me.*

He slowly opens the heavy metal door to the ship, peeking out. No one is around. *I like cats. Let's start with him... or her?* The cat jumps up, arching its back. The barbs stick straight up, a low growl coming from its throat.

"Easy there, kitty." Nero holds his hands out.

Another squawk rings through the room. The cat turns to the birds, more relaxed. Sensing his opportunity, Nero slips the key into the lock and takes one slow deep breath. In a jerky fit of motions, he turns the key, removes the lock, throws the latch, and dives into the nearest cage. All the while, the cat watches with its head cocked at an angle.

Nero pulls the cage door shut, spinning around. *That was close!* The cat has not moved. "Arrgg. Come on, get gone!"

The cat looks at Nero one last time before it canters off. Once Nero is satisfied the cat is a long way off, he moves to the grey crocodile. It tries to snap at Nero.

Jeez. "You're welcome!" He says as it waddles away.

He reaches the birds. They fly out with friendly squawks.

Nero smiles. *That could be a good distraction. Using my brain!* As he walks toward the door, it hits him he has no idea what to do. *How am I going to—*

Suddenly, a young girl's face pokes around the door. She is about Nero's age, her face is smudged with dirt and stricken with fear. "All of them! Do you know how they escaped? Somebody is going to be in big trouble! The Captain is going to peel their skin off with a butter knife!" she yells.

Nero's mouth opens, but nothing comes out. Panic boils in his stomach.

Anger flashes across the girl's face. "Don't just stand there! We need to get them back, or he's going to take it out on all of us!" The girl runs into the room, grabbing two sturdy poles with wire loops at the end. She gives one to Nero and runs out. "Come on!"

Nero takes a couple sluggish steps after her, then stops. *She must think I'm part of the boat. Can I use that to my advantage? I bet if I just panic like the girl... Yeah, that works with my strengths!*

Nero starts to run down the halls of the ship aimlessly until he crashes into a man dressed in a dark uniform.

The man holds up his hands to stop Nero. "Hey, hold on a second. What are you doing?"

"Animals escaped!"

The man's jaw drops. "The big grey one too?"

Nero slowly nods. "I need to check on the jail. Where is it?"

The man shakes his head. "I don't think so. You're going to help me bring the animals in."

"I can't." Nero tries to move by, but the man bars his path. *What am I going to do? I can't waste time!* Nero panics. He pulls out a dart, kicks the man in the shin, then sticks the dart into his arm.

"Ow! What the heck?" The man pulls the dart out of his arm and grabs a handful of Nero's clothes. "You wanted to check on the jail? Well, I'm going to give you a firsthand tour of the inside, you brat!"

The man drags Nero down through the narrow bulkheads. The crew is running and yelling. They hardly glance at the two.

At last, the man stumbles through a door. The room has six prison cells, one of which has Nero's friends. They scramble to the bars when they see him.

A small guard stands up and greets the man dragging Nero. "Please, tell me you've come to relieve me of this job."

The man holding Nero shakes his head. He moves his mouth. Nothing comes out.

The guard puts his hand on the man's shoulder. "Hey! You alright?"

Nero feels the man's grip go slack. A moment later, he crumples to the ground.

The small guard tries to catch the man, but instead falls with him. "What's wrong with him?"

Nero shrugs. As soon as the guard turns his back, Nero sticks him with a dart.

"Hey!" The guard jerks up, pulling the dart out of his neck. "That hurt." He grabs Nero's arm. "What do you think you're doing?"

Nero's whole world is buzzing with adrenaline. He can hardly put two thoughts together. "Sorry?"

"Sorry isn't going—to—cut it…" The guard puts his hand on his head. "Whoa. All of the sudden, I'm feeling pretty funny." He collapses to the ground.

Oh, thank goodness that worked! Nero fumbles with the keys on the guard's belt and approaches the cell door. His friends are hanging onto the bars, watching with mouths open.

"Holy crap, Nero. What are you doing?" Ryder asks.

"Uh, rescue mission." Nero fumbles with the keys.

"Don't ask stupid questions, Ryder." Iona pushes open the door. "Thanks, Nero. I didn't think you had it in you." She walks over to the two collapsed men.

"I'm shocked, too," Korbin says walking through the door. "Umm, thanks."

"Seriously, Nero, this is amazing." Ryder pats him on the back.

Thea runs out of the cell to hug Nero. "Thanks, Nero. I knew you'd come for us!"

"These guys are knocked out cold, Nero. What'd you do?" Iona asks.

"That crazy woman made sleeping darts for me to use." Nero shows them the blowgun. "Though I can't hit anything with it."

"What crazy woman?" Iona asks.

Ryder steps between them. "He can fill us in later once we're out of this mess. First, we need to get out of here."

"Hold on a second," Nero says. "Actually, we need to wait here."

"What?" Korbin says. "That's stupid. We just got out!"

"Yeah, but—" Nero can feel all eyes on him. "I'm waiting for a signal."

"What kind of signal?" Iona asks.

"Umm. I'm not totally sure. I'll know it when it happens."

"Alright, Nero, you got this far. But we'll take it from here." Korbin walks toward the door.

Ryder puts a hand up to Korbin. "Hold on, Korb. You're right. Nero got this far, so if he says we wait, we'll wait."

Korbin's mouth drops open.

Ryder picks up one of the men's wrists. "Help me pull these guys in the cell, just in case they wake up."

Nero can't help but let a smile slip. *I'm doing well!*

Ryder and Korbin pull the two men into a cell, locking it.

Korbin dusts off his hands. "So, how much longer do we need to wait around, Nero?"

Please, hurry up. "Not much longer. I hope." Nero glances at his watch. It is four minutes past nine. *Should we just go now? What if the signal doesn't come, and we're trapped? What if I already missed it? More guards could come at any moment!* Nero forces himself to wait. "The woman said I would know the signal…" *If she follows through.*

Each time they hear footsteps running down the hall, they hold their breath.

Korbin jumps up and fidgets with his hands. "I've had enough. We should really go," He swings his arm through the air, pointing at the door. "If we stay any longer, we're just going—"

KABOOM!

The explosion sends a shiver through the ship, jarring the children to the bone. They almost fall over. The lights dim. Red warning lights and alarms go off. Everyone turns to Nero, open-mouthed.

Good Lord! Nero forces a half smile. "I think that was it."

"Uh, you think?" Iona says. "Who is this woman?"

"I don't know, but she's crazy," Nero says with extra emphasis.

"She's certainly not messing around," Ryder says. He steps forward. "So, I guess up and out?"

Nero nods.

"I'll lead, then." He cracks the bulkhead open and peers through, waving everyone forward. "Okay, stay close, and follow me."

Ryder leads the children through the maze of the ship's innards, losing their way several times. Fortunately, they easily blend in with the other children and the crew pays them no mind. The warning siren hits a new note when they reach the exit. Red flashing lights illuminate the dark night. Cool fresh air fills Nero's lungs. He runs to the edge and looks down the railing in both directions. He spots something hanging over the edge. The rest of the children follow as he runs toward it.

Nero sees a small boat at the bottom of the ladder. "Here's our exit."

Ryder glances over. "Good. Alright, one at a time. The rest of us will hide. Thea, you're first."

Thea descends the ladder while the others wait in the shadows. A few sailors run within meters of their hiding spot, but none notice. After Iona climbs down the ladder, Nero, Korbin, and Ryder make the trip. The little boat rocks dangerously back and forth as the children settle. Ryder unlatches the ladder and rows toward shore.

Korbin thumps Nero on the back. "That was great, Nero. I would've never guessed you'd rescue us."

Thea pushes Korbin. "Whatever, Korb." She looks at Nero, beaming with excitement. "I knew you'd come get us."

Ryder pulls back on the paddles. "I'm seriously impressed. I'm not sure any one of us could have done better."

Korbin's smile fades. "Speak for yourself. If Nero did it, I could do it."

Nero feels a strange glow from the pit of his stomach. A grin spreads across his face.

"How the heck did you do it?" Iona asks. "The ladder alone must have weighed a ton."

"The Woman from the forest helped me," Nero replies.

Iona raises an eyebrow. "Huh? You mean the one that attacked you?"

"Well, yeah, but she actually turned out to be... helpful. She taught me how to use Aether!"

Korbin chokes. "The crazy hobo woman taught you to use Aether? Did little magical fairies and an army of goblins help you, too? Why would she help anyways?"

"I don't know." Nero looks at the bottom of the boat. "Maybe she felt bad that you all were going to be sold as slaves."

Suddenly the sirens fall silent. The warning lights turn off. Voices from the crew are now audible over the short distance. A sailor stops at the railing, peering over the edge. He yells something to the upper decks of the ship. A spotlight zooms over the water, tracing back and forth. Korbin jumps next to Ryder, grabbing a paddle. They both row frantically, zigzagging the boat across the water.

Several more spotlights burn holes through the darkness. One passes within a meter of the boat.

Nero clenches his seat. "Hurry up. We can't get caught!"

Ryder pulls back hard on the row. "No duh." Sweat glistens on his forehead.

Nero watches as a spotlight sweeps around, heading straight for them. He puts his head down, closing his eyes.

"Dang it!" Ryder yells. "Faster, Korb, we need to get to shore."

Nero opens his eyes. The boat is flooded with light, the spotlight pointing directly on them. The voices from the ship zip over the water like an angry mob.

They hit the edge of the walkway, unloading as fast as the boat will let them in the glow of the giant spotlight. Nero looks back at the pier, using his hand to block the light. Men are yelling and getting closer.

Ryder grabs his arm. "Come on!"

"The Market!" Nero yells. They all start to run.

The children sprint down the walkway. Ryder is pulling Nero as fast as he can go. They make it to the outer edge of the Market area, passing a restaurant with an outdoor patio. People at the tables are staring toward the waterfront.

Ryder glances back and speeds up. "Run, Nero. Faster! They're not stopping!"

The Market is surprisingly empty; everyone is standing at the edge of the bay, chatting amongst themselves. Suddenly, Nero's collar tightens around his neck. He is yanked backward, out of Ryder's grasp. Ryder looks back in shock. He is quickly taken by another sailor. Large hands cover their mouths. The sailors drag them back the way they came as they struggle uselessly. Three other men spread themselves out to shield the two children from curious onlookers.

The sailor holding Nero leans close, whispering into his ear. "Your friends might've got away, but that just means there's only two of you to take the punishment. And the Cap'n won't stop until he's satisfied." Nero can hear the smile in the man's chuckle. "The boys and I start a little bet in these situations. I'll put my money on you not surviving half an hour."

A deep grizzled voice sounds from behind the guards, freezing them in place. "Excuse me, gentlemen."

The sailors holding Nero and Ryder spin around. A huge figure, easily a half-meter taller than the thugs, looms in the darkness. The lights from the surrounding buildings shine off his dark skin. He has long braided hair and scars lining the side of his expressionless face. A toothpick hangs from the corner of his mouth.

The sailor holding Nero steps forward. "Who you calling gentle?"

"Forgive me." The man dips his head. "I'm going to have to ask you toilet scum to leave the children alone," he says with an air of indifference.

The sailor growls. "Mind your own business, or we'll smash your face in."

The stranger opens his hands to the children. "Unfortunately, this *is* now my business, so—" He pulls out his toothpick and rolls it in his fingers, then shrugs. "I guess I could use a makeover."

"You're going to regret this." The sailor signals and the other men charge.

The stranger flicks his toothpick in the face of the nearest sailor and plants his foot in the middle of the man's chest, propelling him backward. He dodges as the heavy fist of a second sailor whistles toward him. He pulls the arm past him, driving a knee into the thug's gut. With catlike celerity, the stranger spins to strike the third in the side of the face with his foot.

Landing nimbly on the balls of his feet, he casually regards the scene; two standing sailors still gripping the children's arms, and three men on the ground. He touches his face and speaks without a hint of exertion. "Not much of an improvement. I would give your friends a hand if I were you. They don't look so good."

The two sailors let go of Ryder and Nero. Then, with an encouraging nod from the stranger, they help the other three up and shuffle them back toward the ship.

Ryder steps toward the huge man. "Thank you, Sir. That was amazing!"

The stranger looks down at Ryder. "Beating up someone weaker than you is not something to be proud of. Why were they chasing you?"

"We just escaped from their boat," Ryder says.

"Did they kidnap you?"

Ryder nods. "Yeah, yesterday."

"Where are your parents?" He asks.

"Uh, they're at home," Ryder says.

Iona, Thea, and Korbin appear next to Ryder and Nero, breathless.

The large man looks at the children then back to Ryder. "I don't believe that. Do you have a place to go?"

"Yeah," Nero says.

The man turns on Nero. "And you have a plan for tomorrow? What if they search for you?"

"We'll manage," Ryder says.

"Oh, yeah? It looks like you had everything under control just a moment ago. I'm sorry I interfered. Goodnight."

The man starts to walk off, but Thea runs up to him, hugging his massive leg. "Thanks for saving them, Mister."

The man stops and looks down at Thea, still holding his leg. He pushes her away. After a moment, he turns to face the children, looking at Nero intensely. "Where are you staying tonight?"

Nero takes a step backward.

"I know you aren't from Blue Horin," the stranger says. "Just tell me what your plan is, and I may be able to help."

"At a hotel," Nero says.

The man shakes his head. "That won't work. If you had something to do with the explosion tonight, the Traffickers will hunt you down. They have a reputation to uphold, and they'll intimidate anyone that has information on you. That includes the employees at the hotel. Is there anyone you can trust?"

Nero hesitates, then shakes his head. "I don't think so."

The stranger's gaze falls on Ryder. "This is how you plan to *manage*?" He pulls a small metal cylinder out of his pocket, twirling it about his fingers several times until he catches it in his fist. He closes his eyes. A low grumble rumbles from his throat. "Alright, I can provide you with a safe place to stay tonight."

"What?" Ryder asks.

"It's the best option."

"How can we trust you? How do we know you're not just going to lock us away somewhere else?" Ryder asks.

The man twists the metal cylinder apart, pulling out a toothpick. "You have no reason to trust me, but I promise I won't do anything to harm you or your friends. As a Borukin vow, that should be worth something. Let us at least talk about this in some privacy," he says, nodding his head toward a few people watching them. Ryder glances around, then looks back at the stranger. After a moment the stranger pulls out a set of keys from his pocket. "Here," he says, holding them out to Ryder. "These are my keys to everything I own. A gesture of good faith. I'm leaving now, with or without you. You better make up your mind."

Ryder hesitates but then steps forward and takes them. "Okay, lead the way."

The large man gracefully moves through the side streets. After ten minutes, he stops at a back door in a dark alley. "This is the back of my shop. Please, open the door for me."

The stranger helps Ryder select the key and the door opens to a soft glow. "My name is Sosimo," he says. "I guarantee you'll be safe here, but do as you will. If you decide to go, please leave my keys." He dips his head and disappears inside the doorway, ducking under the frame.

Ryder turns to the others. "So, what do you think?"

"He doesn't seem too bad, just sad or something," Thea says. "He did save you guys, so that's something."

"Yeah, but Totos didn't seem too bad either. And look where that got us," Korbin says, throwing up his arms.

"That's a good point," Ryder says. "But, what else can we do?"

Nero steps forward. "There's the hotel room, but it's back the direction we came."

Ryder pushes on his front teeth with his thumb. "That's risky. We could bump into men from the ship. Besides, there might not be someone to help us. And like the guy said, anyone could tip them off if we're seen."

Iona nods. "We're going to have to take a leap here. He hasn't done anything that makes me nervous yet. Plus, he just gave us all his keys. That's a pretty big risk on his part. I say we go in and feel it out. We can always sneak out later if something doesn't feel right."

"I agree," Ryder says, nodding. "Well, let's hope for the best." He leads the way inside.

11 Kabel Reikyn

Isis

Isis's head falls to her chest again. She jerks. The morning light is just spilling over the horizon. It illuminates the city of Sunta and the walls of her office. She sets her jacket—which had been lying on her legs—to the side as she stands up from her desk chair. She stretches; a yawn grips her and a shiver runs through her body.

Isis grabs one of the canisters found at the children's hideout and walks to the window. *How could they have been so stupid to go into the forest... If I can't find them, then I need to find Reikyn.* She moves back to her desk, uses her screen as a mirror to fix her hair, then calls Lieutenant Colonel Phillips.

Phillips pops up on her screen, wearing light infantry gear and a clear visor. "Ma'am. I was just about to contact you."

"Tell me you found Reikyn."

"I'm sorry, Ma'am, we haven't yet."

"Are you telling me you can't find one person with two companies? Are you telling me you're incapable of performing your duty? Are you telling me that I need to find someone else for your position? Because that's what I'm hearing, Phillips, and I'm in no mood for this type of news. You've had more than enough resources to find this man. What's your excuse?"

"I understand, Ma'am, and under normal circumstances I would agree with you. But the intel on our target hasn't been accurate up to this point. It's moving at a much greater speed than a class two Human on foot should, and it took out one of my squads."

"*It,* Phillips?" Isis asks.

"We're tracking something hostile, that's for sure, but some of the samples we took from the contact point with squadron three don't agree with anything we've seen before."

"Elaborate, Phillips. I don't have all day. How could one low class Human do this?"

"I'm sorry, Ma'am. I think this is something you need to see for yourself. This situation needs to be reassessed."

"Damnit, Phillips, this is hardly something I have time for."

"I know, Ma'am. I wouldn't request your presence unless it was serious."

Isis taps a button that says 'location' below Phillips' name. The screen toggles to a map of the mountains many kilometers from the foothills. She selects, 'Travel to,' 'From Current Location', 'Immediately', and 'by Levitraft'. Her computer outputs total distance and estimated time considering travel and vehicle availability. She flips back to the visual of the Captain. "I'll be there in a little over an hour. I hope—for your sake—this is worth my time."

"It is, Ma'am."

Isis reaches toward the 'end call' button. "Did you find anything on the runaway orphans?"

"No, Ma'am. I have people watching the forest to see if they were flushed out... but considering the trouble we had, I don't think we'll find them."

Isis nods, ending the call. A countdown of the estimated arrival of her levitraft shows on the screen. She watches the numbers tick down as frustration smothers her mind. Her whole body yearns to lash out. *Alright, enough. This isn't solving anything.* With difficulty, she imagines herself in a scene where she is commanding a group of generals looking to her with the utmost respect. *In time. Solve these problems, and you'll be one step closer.*

When she opens her eyes again, several minutes have elapsed on her levitraft countdown. She swipes it away, pulling up a map of Sunta, New Lur, Ferin Forest, and the mountains. *If they went into the forest, where were they going?* She pans the map over, so Blue Horin Bay comes into view on the opposite side of the river. *It does look to be the shortest route from New Lur to any other location. Is there any chance they could have made it through?* She runs her thumb over the edge of her ear. *If they have information on more ancient technology, then I have to assume they made it… It would be careless otherwise.*

She switches her screen back to the home menu and calls her assistant.

A video feed appears. "What can I do for you, Ma'am?" He asks.

"I'll be leaving momentarily. Make a flier from one of the pictures of the children and put Fae's name on the front, urging them to come home. Send it to me when you're done. Gather all the info on the children you can. Where they came from, medical records, history. Also, send me any information on the terrorist member we're tracking. I would like to review all of this on my flight."

"Yes, Ma'am. I'll have that ready as soon as possible."

"Good." Isis ends the call and starts another to Dr. Grantov. The call is unanswered. She calls back—three more times—until someone picks up.

A meticulously groomed old man in a lab coat appears on her screen. "Do you bedevil everyone like a spoiled child to get what you want?"

"When I call, Doctor, I expect you to answer."

"Science is the only thing I must answer to. What do you want?"

"What's the status on Fae?"

"Who?"

"Fae Underwood. An old, non-Erohsian woman?"

"The subject expired last night," Dr. Grantov says casually.

"What? Were you planning on informing me?"

"Would you like me to inform you when I go to the bathroom, too? My science cannot wait for such trivialities."

"Did you at least discover anything before you killed her?"

"Killed her? I barely got through the first layer of her consciousness before she died. It was hardly my doing. There needs to be a certain amount of will to live in order to survive the scans you ordered. It helps when a patient resists; it makes following the memory threads easier and calibrates the intensity of the sweep. Without resistance, the Aether used in the sweep was amplified greatly and it burned through her like a dry field of wheat. It was a noteworthy demonstration of mind control—but overall a disappointing subject. If she was hiding something, she took it with her."

"How could you just burn her up like that? I thought you were the best in the field."

"If it was so important, you should have told me she wasn't Human. Variables can make all the difference in an experiment. I'll tell you what, if you find me someone younger, I'll unravel the details of their mind so thoroughly you'll be able to see the reactions in their brain when they first started to comprehend language. They might not survive the process, but I'll have their mapped consciousness stored for your viewing pleasure."

"Hold up. What do you mean, not Human?"

"Her Aether profile didn't match a Human."

"And so what did the DNA results say?"

The Doctor shrugs. "Not my purview. Look, I must get back to my current experiment. We're just passing the delicate transition to the fourth layer of a subject's consciousness with a new technology. It's a very exciting time. Good day." He ends the call.

Isis closes her eyes. *Damn him. She wasn't supposed to die…*

She taps several commands into her wrist computer.

DNA request denied. Fae Underwood has been cremated.

What? How is that possible? She types in several more commands.

Request for cremation expediated. Unknown otherization.

Why? Is this General Belshiv cleaning up his mess once and for all?

*****

Shortly into the trip, while the levitraft gains elevation, the computer on Isis's wrist beeps with a message. The holographic screen shows the message has several attachments. She reviews the flier, then makes a call.

An image of an Erohsian Colonel sitting at his desk pops up. "What can I do for you, Isis?"

"Hello, Colin," she says with an air of fondness. "I'm sure you've heard that I'm pursuing some Human children?"

"I did. It seems a little below you."

Isis smiles. "I'll take that as a compliment. Would you keep that opinion if I found active ancient technology in their possession?"

"Assuming I believe you… But then, I'd wonder how you lost them in the first place."

"We never had them in our possession to begin with. They're proving to be more difficult than I expected."

"What do you need with me, then?"

"You're still in charge of the Blue Horin region, correct?" Isis asks.

The man nods.

"There is a chance the children are heading in your direction. Would you be able to commit some forces and do a search?"

"Under whose authority?"

"Look, I'm not asking you to cause any trouble. Just a simple search. Our General would hardly be upset with you if you found them. And with the discovery of a trove of ancient tech, it would surely lead to a promotion. Plus, I'd owe you one."

"A trove?" Colin's left eyebrow rises.

"It's likely, considering the condition of the first piece we found. We need to learn where it came from."

"Just a sweep, then?" Colin asks.

"Yes, and I have a flier to post around the city for them."

"It's interesting timing for your request. There was an explosion on one of the Trafficker boats last night. We got reports that a jagupine and adolescent toroc escaped."

"The jagupine shouldn't cause too much trouble, other than eating small pets… or children, if they're alone. They like to pounce from the trees and are quite stealthy. You could get some goats and put a class three tranquilizer mixed with oil around their necks then release them into the wooded areas of Blue Horin. Monitor their vitals. If one goes down, your jagupine should be close. The toroc is going to be a big problem if you can't catch it quickly. It could grow to thirty meters. If the local sea life doesn't keep it fed, then the next best thing will be the populace of Blue Horin Bay. They like to bathe in Illi's light after meals. They're creatures of habit, but they're smart. Make sure you catch it the first go-around."

"Thank you for that encyclopedic recital. I'm sure I can handle a couple of zoo animals."

"I'm sure you can… Do you know what caused the explosion?"

"They're saying a gas leak. I'm confident that's a lie. We're still investigating. There are rumors that sailors were brawling shortly after the explosion in the Market."

Is this all a coincidence? A flush of excitement runs through Isis. *Could they have made it through the forest?* "Do you think you could manage a quick search of the traffickers' boat? Maybe the children were involved."

"You can't expect me to search a trafficker's boat. That'd be a bigger nightmare than I'm willing to deal with. But, since we'll be patrolling the city today, anyway, I'll have my soldiers post the flier and keep a look out. I'll inform you if we find anything."

"Anything you can do is much appreciated, Colin. Just be aware: if you find them in Blue Horin, they passed through the forest. Their Aether levels could be formidable, so caution should be exercised."

The man shakes his head. "I see how you wait till I agree to help before you give me all the details. Coming from you, though, I'm not surprised. If that's the case, maybe they were involved with the traffickers last night... I'll inform my men. I'm not going to have a battle erupt in the middle of Blue Horin so I'll order them to keep their distance if they find anything."

"That's understandable, Colin. Thank you. And also, be wary of any large Aether signals if you're scanning. They were somehow interfering with our scans when we were tracking them before."

"It doesn't sound like you were tracking them, then. Don't worry I can handle these children," Colin says. He ends the call.

Isis smiles. *Excellent. Just a touch of luck, and everything could end up working out.*

She opens the next attachment from the message, which is a report on the terrorist member Kabel Reikyn. It has race as Human, his birthdate, and a few citations and comments from the past. *Useless.* Finally, she opens the last attachment, which is information on the children.

```
Orphan 345 567 091:
```

Name: Unregistered
Acquired: (22-10-2705) Found
    in the streets of Sunta
    alone.
DNA Results: (24-10-2705) Male
    Human
Birth Date: (??) Appears to be
    two years old.
Transferred to: (04-11-2705)
    Fae Underwood

Orphan 345 567 921:
Name: Korbin Keramar
Acquired: (12-07-2708) Parents
    killed in a vehicle
    accident. No other surviving
    family.
DNA Results: (13-07-2708) Male
    Human
Birth Date: (21-01-2704)
Transferred to: (17-07-2708)
    Fae Underwood

Orphan 345 570 158:
Name: Unregistered
Acquired: (04-08-2709) Dropped
    off by a group of spirit
    hunters passing through
    Sunta.
DNA Results: (09-08-2709) Male
    Human
Birth Date: (??) Appears to be
    three years old.
Transferred to: (14-08-2709)
    Fae Underwood

Notes: Dropped off with two
 other orphans, relation is
 doubtful.

Orphan 345 570 159:
Name: Unregistered
Acquired: (04-08-2709) Dropped
 off by a group of spirit
 hunters passing through
 Sunta.
DNA Results: (09-08-2709)
 Female Human
Birth Date: (??) Appears to be
 four years old.
Transferred to: (14-08-2709)
 Fae Underwood
Notes: Dropped off with two
 other orphans, relation is
 doubtful. Blood sample is
 contaminated. Recommend a
 retake.

Orphan 345 570 160:
Name: Unregistered
Acquired: (04-8-2709) Dropped
 off by a group of spirit
 hunters passing through
 Sunta.
DNA Results: (09-08-2709)
 Corrupted
Birth Date: (??) Appears to be
 three years old.
Transferred to: (14-08-2709)
 Fae Underwood
Notes: Dropped off with two
 other orphans, relation is

```
doubtful. Blood sample is
corrupted. Necessary retake
as soon as possible.
```

She looks for the retake of the blood samples, finding nothing. She shakes her head. *Worthless Humans. They truly are cattle.* She closes the holographic display on her wrist computer and turns to the displays. The shear mountains are quickly approaching while the small shadow of the levitraft moves rapidly over the ground hundreds of meters below. Her mind continually rolls over all the items on her task list.

They enter a canyon carved by the river below. The levitraft threads its way through the natural curves until the driver turns it above a rising off-shoot. They gradually meet up with the road, which takes them to a grouping of large Erohsian military vehicles. Pairs of Erohsian light infantry are patrolling the heavily wooded area with their weapons drawn.

Pine needles crunch under her foot as Isis exits the vehicle. The light infantry from her levitraft take up positions around her. *Patrolling pairs is standard procedure—in military hot zones. What's going on?*

Lieutenant Colonel Phillips approaches her, tips up his visor, and salutes. "Ma'am. Thanks for coming."

"You better get to the point quick, Phillips. Why does this look like a combat zone?"

"I'm sorry, Ma'am, but I'm still trying to process the situation. Let me take you to the contact point with squadron three and I can go over the details."

"Fine, then get on with it already," Isis says.

Phillips nods and starts through the forest in silence. After several minutes, they reach a gully cutting between large grey boulders. The boulders and the trees are covered in Aether burns. Soldiers monitor equipment scanning the surroundings.

"As I said earlier, we're not sure what we're dealing with," Phillips says. "You can see from the random markings of weapons fire that whatever they engaged was either numerous or fast."

"And your guess?"

"Fast, Ma'am. The engagement reconstruction was able to link only one set of tracks."

"What did the survivors have to say?" Isis asks.

"We believe two soldiers were taken as hostages. We're unable to question the other survivors due to medical issues, so—unfortunately—nothing. I've had the area almost fully scanned. I believe we have an accurate rendering of the conflict. May I go over the results?"

"Yes, and be specific," Isis says. "I want to know everything."

"We were having a hard time tracking our target on foot due to its speed, so I took a guess on its path and sent squads ahead hoping to cut it off. The first member of squadron three was poisoned with something organically-based. It has reduced him to a catatonic state. The next soldier was killed over there." Phillips points to a group of Erohsians huddled around a body fifty meters away.

"How was he killed?"

"All that is left is his suit, bones, and ash. It's as if he was consumed by fire, but there's no sign of flame, just one scorched hand print on the sleeve of the suit."

"There's a lot of energy stored in the chemical bonds in a body. If there wasn't a fire, where did the energy go?"

"We're doing the best we can, Ma'am, but we currently don't have an answer. We are confident that this is a new weapon."

"Weapon? The scorched hand print would indicate to me that this was done by hand."

Phillips nods. "Yes, but there's no Aether ability capable of doing this to a person. It's got to be something else. I'm thinking the Humans have created an abomination."

"Don't be dramatic, Phillips. We can handle anything the Humans throw at us. They're just cattle, after all. What happened next?"

"The team regrouped and began to fire. Two more soldiers were poisoned. They're both in a deep coma. The next two soldiers were killed with blunt trauma from blows that left nothing of their helmets intact. The seventh soldier was burnt the same as the other. The last two soldiers were incapacitated briefly then forced to follow as our target left the area."

"Do you have people tracking the enemy?"

"Yes, Ma'am, but I ordered them not to engage."

"Good. Keep me posted if anything comes up. Otherwise, be prepared for a new set of orders, and send me all the data you've gathered."

"Yes, Ma'am."

Isis walks off from the surveying soldiers, pulling up the holographic screen on her wrist computer. She selects her commanding officer, General Lark, and calls. The General appears on her screen.

"Sir, we have a situation."

"Go on."

She takes a breath. "The terrorist Kabel Reikyn is a larger threat than we had originally anticipated. He has incapacitated a squadron of light infantry and has taken two hostages."

"One class two Human did this?"

"It's possible Reikyn isn't actually a Human. Two of the soldiers that were killed were reduced to ash."

"Pahzan Aether?"

Isis shakes her head. "There was no fire." *Fire is the release of energy… but if there was no fire what happened to the energy?*

"How could he be burnt to ash without a fire?"

"Not burnt. Consumed," Isis says slowly, letting the word roll off her tongue as its significance finds roots.

"What?"

"If I had to guess, instead of a fire releasing the energy in the chemical bonds, the chemical bonds were broken down and the energy was harvested or consumed. We've never seen anything like it before."

"This sounds like something right up your alley. I want you to handle this personally."

"Yes, sir. I'll coordinate the soldiers appropriately. I'll need permission to deploy mid-infantry though, and a couple jumpers wouldn't hurt."

"Yes, of course. And you can have two fully-loaded vultures, as well as the appropriate ground support. Take your whole damn battalion if you need it. Just handle the situation, and do it discretely. Play it off as a training exercise."

"A good idea, sir. I'll arrange that."

"No, Isis, you're not getting it. I want you there. I want you using that big brain of yours in the thick of it—not second hand where there's less flexibility. We cannot afford to have this leaked, especially when we're so close to finalizing an agreement with the Borukins."

"How would this affect our fledgling alliance?"

"They already think we're weak enough. We don't need to give them more of a reason to lean toward the Humans."

"How much of a threat do you perceive the Humans to be?" *They're nothing. The Borukins are fools to respect them.*

"You've only ever known them as a crushed and hopeless race. We oppressed them for a reason: they're a threat if we don't take them seriously. The Borukins remember the Humans as they were, not how they are. We need to prove to them we're useful allies. We can't let them think the Humans still have strength, no matter how little. With Catalyst growing, it's becoming more difficult. The terrorists are gaining momentum, and the Borukin King could be instrumental in crushing them and keeping them down. So much so, that for the Axiom of Delue, I'm going to be forced to as act as a diplomat in Kiats during their games."

"And what will going to the Games accomplish?"

"It's the political dance, Isis. We need to soften the King up to an idea of an alliance with us. That involves pretending to be entertained by their crude demonstrations of Aether. The last thing I want to worry about right now is an unknown weapon on the loose, threatening our control. I need you on this, Isis. Entirely."

"Sir, I can't be tied to this area. I'm currently tracking the Human orphans and I'm close. I can feel it."

"So, what progress have you made?"

"I have a hunch they're making their way to Blue Horin. Colonel Colin is going to keep his eyes open and post a flier I've made to trick the children to returning home—if we don't catch them first."

"That's it? A hunch? Let me see this flier."

"Just a moment, sir." She pulls up the file, sending it to him.

General Lark's eyes walk over the screen as he studies the flier. "Isis, you don't have a choice in this matter. I'm not asking you. I'm removing you from the tracking of the children. Send the artifact to the research and development section in the Demeeurj Tower immediately."

"Sir, I assure you. I can do both."

"Being your father's daughter only buys you so much leeway, and you're burning through it quickly. Handle the threat. Fast. I want this terrorist hunted down. I want to know everything about this new weapon. I want you to do it with a low profile. Do you understand, Isis?"

Isis hesitates for a moment. "I do, sir." *This is absurd.*

"Good. I want an update at 18:00, and three times a day following."

"Yes, sir." *I have better things to do!*

"Good hunting, Isis, and don't worry about the orphans. I'll set up patrols over the entire country in case they make a run for it. They won't escape."

"Thank you, Sir."

The General ends the call.

And another step back. Damnit!

12 Gracie

Iona

The rumbling of wheels continues to slow.

"Are they coming again?" Nero whispers. He is packed in tight next to the other children, surrounded in darkness.

"Shhh." Iona closes her eyes. *We'll be alright...*

The rumbling finally stops with one last jerk. The heavy breathing of the children turns the air of the container thick. Heavy footsteps vibrate through the floor, slowly coming closer. When the footsteps stop just outside the container, so does the children's breathing.

There is a muffled knock on the top of the container from outside. "It's safe." The lid of the container cracks open. A blinding light floods in from behind Sosimo, who is wearing a beige long-sleeved shirt and pants. "Sorry if I scared you," he says with little emotion. The scars on his face stretch oddly as he moves the toothpick about his mouth.

Korbin jumps out first. "Heck no!"

The rest of the children clamber from the container, scrambling out the back of the large trailer to Illi's glorious light and fresh air.

"Was there any trouble?" Ryder asks.

"The container I hid you in shields Aether, so the Erohsians didn't detect anything suspicious," Sosimo says. "It should be safe to ride upfront in Gracie now. So, stretch your legs a bit and get in. I'd like to put as much distance on these wheels as we can before night." He closes the trailer, walking toward the front of his faded green, well-worn truck.

"Hey, Mr. Sosimo?" Thea says, stepping forward.

Sosimo turns. "Yes?"

"I was just thinking." She looks to the ground for a moment, then at him. "You wouldn't look so scary if you smiled sometimes."

"Is that so?"

"It is. I've never met anyone so sad as you... Well, Nero can be pretty sad sometimes, and he's scared a lot, and Korbin was pretty sad when we made him leave his toys, and this one time our pet mouse named Mousy died and we were all really sad, and even when I lost my necklace I was really *really* sad... but I've never seen anyone as sad as you. You're so sad it makes me want to hug you, but you're so big it's kinda hard." Thea walks up to him, hugging his leg. "I can barely get my hands around your leg and all, but I'll still try because maybe you'll cheer up." Thea looks at him. "Why are you so sad? Did you lose a pet or something?" Sosimo purses his lips. "Is it because you're so tall, and you always have to bend over to go inside, and maybe your back hurts? Or maybe because your truck is so old. You could always buy a new one. Or at least paint it. It looks like pea soup, and I hate pea soup." She scrunches her face, sticking her tongue out.

Sosimo pats her on the head. "You're so full of life, little one. I hope it rubs off." He turns away, pulling himself into the front of his truck.

Ryder walks up to Thea. "Jeez, Thea. You shouldn't talk to people you just met like that. It's rude."

"Yeah but he's so sad," Thea says with her hands out, leaning forward. "I just couldn't stand it anymore."

Ryder nods. "Yeah, he is." He looks at the grassy, flat landscape, pointing. "I'll race you to the bush!" Ryder takes off and the rest of the children run after him. When they finish running, they pile into the truck. Ryder and Iona sit up front with Sosimo. The others scramble into the back.

After forty-five minutes of driving in awkward silence, Iona finally breaks it. "So, you said earlier that we're going to Kiats?"

"That's correct," Sosimo says.

"Tell us about it," Iona says after a moment.

Sosimo moves the toothpick to his front teeth and chews it for a moment. "Kiats is the Borukin capital, on the other side of the Siroté Mountains. It's a beautiful city."

Iona waits for more, but Sosimo stays quiet. "Umm, it sounds nice," Iona says. "Why are you helping us again?"

"Because you need it."

"That's it?"

"Yes. I couldn't turn my back once I saw the size of the mess you're in. I'll help you until we figure out what's going on with your guardian, Fae."

"Do you think you'll be able to contact her?" Nero asks.

"There's no way to say, but I know some people. We'll try. You all made a tough decision leaving her. Considering how intently the Erohsians are looking for you, it was the best decision. You would have been in their hands by now if you had stayed," Sosimo says. "Now I want to know how you ended up in this situation." No one says anything. "Come on, speak up. I should know, since I'm in the middle of it now."

Another moment of hesitation passes until Thea jumps into their story at a dizzying pace. All the while, Sosimo listens without saying a word. She flies through the story of the canisters, the Erohsian patrols, and their trek through the forest.

Sosimo holds up his hand. Thea stops. "Holy Stone, girl, we're going to be driving for a couple days. There's no rush."

"I'm sorry," Thea says.

"Don't be sorry, just let me think for a moment," he says. "It would seem the Erohsians are after you because of the essence you absorbed from those canisters."

"What's an essence?" Thea asks.

The coldness in his face diffuses ever so slightly. "Essence is what gives people the ability to use Aether. In order to become stronger with Aether, people need to practice and exercise their essence. Humans, on the other hand, have the ability to absorb essence, which increases their Aether abilities proportionally to the strength of the essence. The problem with this is, the essence is imprinted with the owner's personality, so it's not just Aether abilities you're getting. Many Humans have lost their minds in their quest for power by absorbing too strong of an essence, or too many. It's something you should take very seriously." Sosimo looks at all the children. "Have any of you noticed strange or different behavior among you all?"

Iona looks back at the others as they look around, shaking their heads. She catches Nero's eye but he pulls it away quickly. *He's acting different...*

"Well, at least there's nothing majorly different," Sosimo says. "What you did was outrageously stupid."

Ryder looks back at Korbin, glaring.

"It was horribly risky, and you were lucky to come away from it sane. Ideally, for your first essence, you'd absorb an entity."

"What's an entity?" Thea asks.

"It's the most basic form of essence. They're naturally forming and have very little imprint. They're unlikely to make a large impact on the person that absorbs them."

"Are you sure we're all okay?" Nero asks.

Sosimo shakes his head. "I didn't know you before, so I can't say."

"Would you, like, hear voices or something?" Nero asks. "If it was a bad one?"

"No, it's more of a fundamental change. The person affected wouldn't really know," Sosimo glances back to Nero. "Why? Are you hearing voices?"

Nero shakes his head. "No... I'm just wondering."

"Good. Now, it seems since the Erohsians are after you, the only responsible thing is for me to train you to use Aether when we get to Kiats."

Korbin bounces in his seat. "Sweet! Can you use Aether? I really want to do something awesome!"

"Settle down, Korbin. You children are giving me a headache," Sosimo says, putting his hand on his head. "Ask me again tomorrow. We need to finish your story. Going through the forest... That was a brave decision and it was probably the only reason you slipped by. Not many people dare to venture into Ferin Forest."

"Why's that?" Iona asks.

Sosimo lets out a sigh. "About a hundred years ago, when the Erohsians first started to develop weapons of Aether, they were at war with the Humans. The Erohsians hoped to dominate the Humans before the Humans could build up momentum, so they pushed a large-scale attack up the Carn River toward Bahsil, a city now buried under Sunta. The battle was horrific. Both sides pushed all of their resources to stop the other. In the end, though, the Humans weren't prepared for the technology of the Erohsians. They were overwhelmed, but it nearly cost the Erohsians their entire army." Sosimo shakes his head. "There was so much death in the week-long battle that the essence couldn't dissipate fast enough. It soaked into the land, creating a spatsentzin."

"What's a spatsentzin?" Iona asks, spitting the word out.

"It's a land that has a large amount of essence trapped in its surroundings. It drastically increases the amount of background Aether, making the physics quite interesting. Unfortunately, the essences trapped in these areas are usually from large battles, so the land is tainted with an ugliness that can make them extremely dangerous." Sosimo moves the toothpick around his mouth. "Hmm. Since you're young, you're still mostly pure, and your desire for power is minimal. The forest might not have recognized you as a threat, which would explain why you made it out with little trouble."

"Little trouble?" Korbin slaps the seat in front of him. "We were chased by monsters!"

Sosimo glances at Korbin. "Why are you slapping Gracie?"

"What?" Korbin asks.

"I said, why are you hitting my car?"

Korbin pats the seat. "I didn't hit it very hard," Korbin says. Sosimo remains silent. "I'm sorry, I won't do it again."

"And, don't be so quick to label a creature a monster. Many are just misunderstood, and no more dangerous than you or I. Understand?"

"Yes, but—" Korbin is silenced by Sosimo's raised hand.

"Many great warriors have been lost to Ferin Forest. If it wants you, it gets you and there's not a thing you can do about it. Especially if you're a bunch of children. You're lucky to have slipped under its nose. Now, as for those creatures you encountered—" Sosimo says, eying Korbin. "The big one, I'm not sure about. There are many odd creatures that live in the forest, so it's hard to say. I do know who owns the golden eyes. They're called cressen, or golden-eyed demons. They are creatures of Aether. They only show their eyes when they are stalking, or preparing to attack. They're guided by an anterraktor, which is an extremely powerful creature. In stories of old, they were said to be the planet's guardians. I have a theory that the anterraktor in the Ferin Forest is a Creature of Aza."

"That name sounds familiar. What are those?" Iona asks.

"Creatures of Aza are truly evil," Sosimo says, the corner of his mouth turning down. "It's any animal that has its essence tainted in such a way they gain an unquenchable thirst for killing. Something changes within them, and they no longer just hunt for food. They're also very capable with Aether, which catches many off-guard." He shakes his head. "Nasty stuff. Anyway—if I had to guess—the cressen were herding you and preparing to attack. I don't know why, but they let you go."

Thea takes advantage of the pause and continues her story, finishing with their capture. She nudges Nero in the ribs, and he hesitantly takes over, telling how the woman from the forest found him.

"And she said she committed autonomicide?" Sosimo asks.

"Yeah, what does that mean?"

"It's a Borukin tradition when someone wants a fresh start. They give up their name and everything attached to it in the hope of finding a new self. It's odd that this Human would practice this. Anyway, continue with your story."

"She then spent the whole day teaching me to use Aether and coming up with a rescue plan."

"Come on, Nero, you can't use Aether!" Korbin says.

"I can, too!" Nero picks out a small wrapper from his pocket. "I'll show you! Hold this on your hand." He hands the wrapper to Korbin.

Korbin puts the wrapper on his palm, holding it up. "Good, cuzz I gotta see this! Whatcha going to do?"

Iona turns in her seat to see Nero and Korbin. *Woo, he's serious about this. Maybe he's telling the truth.*

"Watch!" Nero glares at the wrapper with squinted eyes. A few tense seconds slip by. Nero shifts in his seat.

Korbin's arm begins to droop. "Gee, you're making my arm tired from holding this up. Awesome."

Iona looks out the window to the rocky cliffs surrounding them. *Too bad...*

"I did it before. I swear!" Nero says while his shoulders drop.

"I bet you did." Korbin crunches the wrapper in his hand.

Iona's vision turns a tint of red. She turns back to watch.

Nero's face begins to boil. "Shut up, Korbin!"

"Enough," Sosimo says, an edge in his voice. "I will not have fighting while I drive." Several minutes of silence follow. "What happened after Nero freed you all?" The calm back in his voice.

Thea starts without hesitation. "After we escaped the boat, you came in and rescued us!"

"Yeah, that was awesome!" Korbin says. "If Sosimo were an animal, he'd be a giant gorilla!"

"What, Korbin?" Sosimo asks. "Did you just call me a gorilla?"

"Is it because they're big and strong?" Iona asks.

Korbin throws up his hand for a five. "Nice job, first try."

"Thanks." Iona returns the five with a lack of enthusiasm. "Your insightfulness knows no bounds."

"I got one," Thea says. "If Mr. Sosimo were an animal, he'd be a mountain that almost touched the sky."

Ryder lets out a sigh.

The corners of Sosimo's mouth turns down. "An animal mountain? What's going on?"

"Sh." Thea puts a finger to her lips. "It's a game we play."

"And Thea doesn't always follow the rules," Ryder says. "Is it because mountains are big?"

"Nope!"

"Is it because they're scary?" Nero asks.

"No again!"

"Is it because they are rock hard?" Korbin says, flexing his arms and waggling his eyebrows.

"Please, Korb," Thea says, squeezing his arm. "Those are jelly, and you're not even close."

"Does anyone care to fill me in on this game?" Sosimo asks.

"We're trying to guess why Thea chose to compare you to a mountain," Ryder says. "We usually don't get it. She can be a bit special."

"Thanks, Ryder, I am! Any last guesses?" Thea asks.

"No," Iona says. *This should be good.*

Thea sits up straight. "Okay, so Mr. Sosimo is a mountain because, to someone that doesn't know them, mountains are dangerous and intimidating. They'll probably end up dying by falling off a cliff or starving. But, someone who knows the mountain can live there peacefully. They can find water and food. Maybe they even know where some gold is or something. And they also know where all the secret paths are, so if someone else tries to get them, they're safe."

There is a moment of silence before Ryder speaks. "Who wants to break that one down?"

"Is it because you think he can give us shelter and take care of us but also teach us things at the same time?" Nero asks.

"Exactly!" Thea says then gives Nero a quick hug.

The corners of Sosimo's mouth quiver with the hint of a smile. "That is quite the game."

"So, speaking of gold, can you teach us to fight like you did?" Korbin asks.

Sosimo shrugs. "If you're willing to have the discipline, I'll teach you what I can."

Korbin pumps both of his fists. "Awesome."

"How was it you were conveniently there to save us when no one else was around?" Ryder asks.

Sosimo raises an eyebrow. "You're still suspicious?"

Ryder shrugs. "It's just a question that's been bothering me."

"It was luck, if anything. I'm usually only in Blue Horin briefly to tend to one of my stores there. It just so happened a woman roped me into having dinner with her."

"Ooh, were you on a date?" Thea asks.

"Is that why you were dressed up?" Iona asks.

Sosimo nods. "If that's what you want to call it… she ended up not showing, but while I was waiting outside the restaurant, I heard the explosion. Nero," Sosimo pauses for a moment. "What did the woman who helped you look like?"

"Like she was going to hurt someone. Mean, and mostly scary. Kinda like she hated everyone."

"But what color hair did she have?"

"Oh. I think brown."

"Was it short and did she wear a yellow dress?" Sosimo asks.

"Just for a little. How did you know?"

Sosimo looks down the road for a long moment. "I think the woman set me up. Clever."

"Ooh, you have a crush on her!" Thea says. "Was she pretty?"

Iona snorts.

"Do you want to marry her?" Thea asks, squirming about her seat.

Sosimo shakes his head. "If I knew how much trouble you'd be and how many questions you'd ask, I would have thought twice about helping you at all."

"We're not asking that many questions," Korbin says.

"What kind of store do you have?" Iona asks.

"Ooh, do you sell awesome weapons?" Korbin asks.

Sosimo takes his eyes off the road for a moment to look at Korbin. "I have a few candy stores spread out in Blue Horin, Sunta, and Kiats."

"Candy?" Korbin asks with shock.

Thea bounces on her seat. "Candy! I love candy. Do you have any now? I like the gooey worms that make your face go—" She squints her eyes and pinches her face together.

"I do, but nothing sour. You can have some later tonight. It's the best chocolate you'll ever find."

Thea closes her eyes, dancing her feet around. "Mmm, chocolate. That's good, too!"

"If you have so many candy stores, then why don't you buy a new truck?" Iona asks.

Sosimo lets out a huff. He pats the steering wheel. "I couldn't replace Gracie so easily."

*****

Sosimo leans over the yellowed map covering Gracie's hood. He taps northeast of Blue Horin and Sunta on the opposite side of a mountain range. "Here we are, just outside the town of Red Cliff, about one-thousand kilometers from Blue Horin."

The children lean in, slurping from bowls and standing on Gracie's bumper.

"Why's it called Red Cliff?" Thea asks.

"Because the cliffs are red," Sosimo says. "There is a large castle-like mansion built into the cliffs which brings in some tourists."

Iona squints against Illi as it rises. "I thought we were over here." She points to the larger mountain range east of Sunta. The smaller mountain range, containing the town of Red Cliff, meets up with the Siroté mountains in the shape of a lambda, with Sunta and Blue Horin nestled between the two. "I thought we are going to Kiats."

"We're going to skirt Erohsia by staying on the far side of the Laifen Mountain range. This is our best bet to avoid any more Erohsian patrols." Sosimo traces an arc that passes along the north west edge of the mountains. "This is a big day. I hope to cover about fifteen-hundred kilometers and camp somewhere in the north end of the Laifen Mountains. From there, we'll have an easy drive to Jasmeer, a Borukin mountain town, where we can try to stay in real beds with some old friends." He traces his finger over a path that cuts through the Siroté Mountains. "This mountain road is eight hundred kilometers long, and slow in spots." Finally, he taps on a star labeled Kiats by the South-East coast. "From there, we'll have another thousand or so kilometers to the capital of Boruk. If all goes well, we should be at my shop in Kiats in three to four more days."

"What do you mean, if all goes well?" Iona asks.

"Well, there are two main concerns. The first is this ol' girl." He pats the hood of his truck. "Hopefully she'll pull through for us. Gracie's dependable, but occasionally throws a little temper tantrum."

Korbin leans forward. "And the other?"

Sosimo looks at the children. "Today, we're going to make a run along the Citol Plains."

"What's wrong with that?" Iona asks?

"Well the only reason we'll be safe from the Erohsian patrols is because this is right at the edge of Drebin Territory."

"Who are the Drebin?" Thea asks tentatively.

Sosimo frowns and inhales. "The Drebin—as they call themselves—are a group of fanatical religious followers made up of any race they can convert. It's actually ironic—they're the only instance of all the races of the world working together. They believe in a savior that will come back and cleanse the world of all suffering and unify the races."

"What's wrong with that?" Thea asks. "It sounds like something I'd want."

"The idea's nice. Their means, on the other hand—can be quite horrible for someone in their way."

"Can't people stand up to them?" Korbin asks.

"The Drebin are not afraid of death. They believe they'll be reunited with their savior when they die. It's not a virtue you want in an enemy. To make it worse, each traveling group of Drebin is led by a seeker who is said to be the real-world projection of their savior. Their Aether abilities are formidable—to say the least—and they absorb the essence of anyone that falls in battle. They only grow stronger and more difficult to defeat the longer the fight goes on. If a seeker is killed by chance, then another Drebin will absorb their essence and become the new seeker. It's a tough situation and they'll fight to the very last one."

Iona drums her fingers on her leg. "Couldn't a Human absorb the essence of the Drebin or whoever falls in battle so the seeker can't?"

"Drebin essence is very potent. Humans who attempt this usually lose their minds. They'll either become a Drebin or a seeker—unintentionally. There have been attempts to capture the seeker, but the Drebin are extremely fanatical, so they'll do pretty much anything to free them. It usually causes more problems."

"So, what if they catch us?" Nero asks.

"We're going to do everything we can to avoid that scenario."

"I kinda want to meet them," Thea says.

Sosimo raises an eyebrow and looks at her. "You'd regret it as soon as you did."

Iona looks carefully at the map. "So, it seems like the best plan for us is to just shoot through this section as fast as possible."

"That's what I hope to do," Sosimo says. "We'll be at a higher risk for about eight-hundred kilometers after we pass north of the Tine river with no safe towns in between. Fortunately, only the Erohsians are looking for us so I think we'll do this with little trouble."

"How far can your truck go without filling up?" Iona asks.

"With my trailer, Gracie can haul us four hundred and fifty kilometers, so—"

"But you said it's eight-hundred kilometers without fuel!" Nero blurts out.

"No, I said we'll be at higher risk for eight-hundred kilometers. It's actually closer to a thousand kilometers where there won't be a safe fill up station."

Nero's mouth falls open.

"I'm not finished." Sosimo looks at Nero until Nero closes his mouth. "With a full tank of fuel, we'll only be able to go about four hundred and fifty kilometers. This can be easily remedied by bringing extra fuel with us," he says, eying Nero. "The real danger comes in needing to stop and fill up. As long as we're not being chased, we should do just fine." Sosimo reaches for the edges of the map and folds it up. "I'll give you all specific tasks to help speed up the process."

"Is it always this dangerous when you head home?" Ryder asks.

Sosimo shakes his head. "Not at all. Usually I make the trip right from Sunta, and spend the night at a small town called Praun before I make it to the Boruk pass."

"Why Praun?" Thea asks.

Sosimo shrugs. "It's on the way, it's a nice big city, and has a beatiful fountain which reminds me of Kiats. I stay there when I'm coming and going from Boruk… I guess just old habits."

Iona holds up her finger. "So, let me get this straight. You're only risking your neck to help us? Why? I still don't understand."

"You're the first people who might be able to help me. Something my friends tried to do, but…" Sosimo's eyes drift off toward the horizon.

"What do you mean?" Iona's heartbeat slows.

"It's time to go, Iona. Everyone, get your stuff together."

*****

Sosimo stares off into the distance while they drive over a small hill leading away from the Tine River, his posture erect, his hands tight on the wheel. "This is it. In eight hours, we should be through the worst of it, and hopefully in no more than twelve, we'll be done driving for the day."

A tense quiet falls over the passengers as Gracie rumbles over the rough road.

"So you're going to train us to use Aether?" Korbin asks eagerly.

"I'll try."

Thea wiggles in her seat. "Can you use Aether?"

"Can I use Aether?" Sosimo rolls the toothpick in his mouth. "It's not quite that simple. Do you even know what you're asking? Do you know what Aether is?"

There is a long silence until Iona finally speaks up. "Magic?"

"Hmm." Sosimo chews on his toothpick. "Just as much as a card trick is magic to someone that doesn't know how it's done."

There is another silence. "Well, then, what is it?" Thea asks.

"Doesn't Aether allow people to manipulate the energy of their surroundings?" Nero asks under his breath.

Sosimo glances back. "Yes, that's correct. Do you know what Aetheratin or Aethersotto are?"

"Um… the Woman said Aethersotto is kinda like how well you interact with Aether?"

Sosimo nods. "That is an indirect result of Aethersotto. In basic principle, it comes down to energy and power." Sosimo's posture relaxes and the edge to his voice softens. "Imagine you had a jug of water. Aetheratin would be how much water you could hold in the jug and Aethersotto would be how quickly you can empty the jug. Now imagine Aether instead of water and your essence instead of the jug. The ratio of these two values determines how someone would use Aether. Let's take Borukins for example. We have very little Aetheratin but very high Aethersotto, which makes our bodies practically a straight conduit for Aether. We have barely enough Aether to lift up a large rock, but if we use Aether from another source, we can do some incredible things with our Borukin skills. Our culture is entwined with our talents, which are demonstrated during the Borukin Games."

"What are the games?" Korbin asks.

"The Games were started by our great King Stone, who led us to freedom from the Creators. When the battle was over, he wanted us to continue to hone our skills without war, so he created the Games. They happen every time the planet Delue is in Axiom and last for four weeks."

"What does in Axiom mean?" Iona asks.

"It has to do with the Aether tides. Delue is the one planet in the solar system with the greatest effect on Anterra's Aether. About every three years, this year being one, when

Delue is in alignment with Illi and Anterra, we call that in Axiom. The Games display every aspect of our abilities with Aether. The earlier competitions are focused on the finer skills of Aether, such as Aether-weaving. It's a beautiful art that requires a tremendous amount of talent. When the Aether tides are high, manipulating Aether is easier, which allows us to push the limit on what is possible."

"Is there ever fighting?" Korbin asks.

"There are competitions of combat, but fighting isn't everything, Korbin. These games are more than just proving might. They are also a means to bring pride to our race through tradition and a common cause. For example, one of the most anticipated games is Capture the Orb, which is an Aether game for children."

"What do the winners get?"

"There is no medal, but it is a great honor. If a child does well, they may be invited to go to the last day of the Games, where Stone's Trials are concluded. A unique aspect about this game is any race can enter."

"Wait, so Humans can enter?" Korbin asks.

"There's only an age limit. Generally, race diversity is encouraged. I don't think a Human has ever brought the orb to the other side, though.

Korbin bounces in his seat. "Awesome. Can we do it? I want to be the first Human to capture the orb!"

"If you're still in Kiats next summer, and I'm satisfied with the progress you've made with training, I'll see what I can do. Unfortunately, the Games have become more aggressive and violent. Capture the Orb is no exception, and I'd be worried one of you would get injured. Even back when I was younger, there were hints at this change, but there was still honor. My brother," Sosimo says, as though the word is thick and hard to flick off his tongue, "was a great competitor for a while." He is solemn, and silence falls over the vehicle.

"What happened to your brother?" Thea asks.

"He lost touch with what was important and we lost everything." Sosimo stares down the long road, touching the side of his scarred face. "I'd rather not talk about it."

*****

Nero looks back.

Iona shakes her head. *Alright, chill, Nero, there's no one there.*

They begin to climb up another moderately large hill.

"This is it. When we get to the top, we're going to fill up Gracie. Everyone remember what to do?" Sosimo looks at each of them.

Nero frowns at the bare crest of the hill. The yellow and green grass of the rolling plains stretches out in every direction from the edge of the foothills. "Shouldn't we stop where there's a place to hide?"

"If there are places for us to hide, there are also places for the Drebin to hide. Up here, at least, we won't have any surprises."

At the top of the hill, Sosimo pulls Gracie to the side of the road. The children scramble out before the truck is turned off. Iona climbs to the top of the trailer and scans the horizon. Sosimo hurries to the back of the trailer and opens the ramp while Thea unlocks the gas cap for the truck. Nero grabs the large crank-operated pump, Ryder and Korbin lift one large drum of gas, and Sosimo hauls another. They insert the pump into the open drum and start to fill the truck by spinning the pump crank as fast as they can. Ryder and Korbin alternate cranking, each breathing heavily by the time their turn is over. Nero and Thea scramble to the top with Iona.

Kobin finishes his turn and throws his hands over his head, taking in deep breaths. "How's it looking up there?"

Iona looks over the side. "So far, so good. Could you all go any slower, though?"

"You want to come down and help?" Korbin asks with his arms out in challenge.

Nero walks over to Iona. He taps her shoulder. Suddenly, her palms are sweaty.

"Hey, I have a weird feeling. Do you see anything over there?" He points down the hill way off in the distance, from the direction they came.

Iona squints, shielding her eyes with a hand. "You always have that feeling, Nero. I don't see anything."

Several minutes later, the first drum is emptied. Sosimo starts on the second. He spins the crank faster than Korbin and Ryder without resting. They look at him in awe.

"Seriously, Iona, are you sure you don't see anything?" Nero asks.

Ugh! She shakes her head. "There's nothing there Nero, stop stressing out."

After another few minutes, Sosimo empties his drum. They begin to pack up, and he calls the children down from the top of the truck. "Not bad, everyone." He catches Nero looking off in the distance. "See something, Nero?"

Nero points. "I'm not sure, do you? Way, way off in the distance."

Sosimo covers his eyes from Illi, shaking his head. "I don't see anything. Regardless, I'd feel them if they were dangerously close. I think we're clear. I'm glad you're being especially vigilant, though."

Iona hops in the truck. *Especially stupid. How can he be scared now, but not in the forest?*

Moments later, they are back on the road and moving down the other side of the hill, safely on their way. Many more kilometers pass while Illi sets to the west. Eventually, they hit an intersection and turn right, back into the Laifen Mountains. The road is considerably smoother, allowing a strange quiet to fall over the truck.

"Oh, yay. That's much better. Those bumps were rattling my brain loose," Thea says. "How much longer?"

"We'll drive a few more hours before we start looking for a camp site." Gracie begins to groan as the road gets gradually steeper. "Come on, girl, we're almost done." Sosimo pats the wheel affectionately.

The failing light illuminates a much smaller set of grass covered mountains. The road ahead disappears as it weaves between them.

After a few more hours' drive, Sosimo pulls off the road, out of sight and into a small meadow next to a river. He cooks a simple meal in the back of his trailer before the tired gang lay down for the night.

*****

"This should be the last of the dangers for this trip," Sosimo says as they coast down the road from the Laifen Moutains to more grasslands. "Just this last bit through Erohsia and then we'll be at the Borukin Gate. The edge of Boruk."

There is a large river in front of them with a long, dark body of mountains beyond that. They have sharp peaks scratching the sky that make the Laifen Mountains truely look like hills.

After another hour and a half, they join up with a road alongside the river. The river follows the mountains for a little before taking a turn right for their heart.

"What river is this?" Thea asks.

"It's the Carn," Sosimo says. "The one that passes through Sunta. You crossed it in Ferin forest."

"Wow, it's so much smaller here."

"It covers a lot of distance to get to Blue Horin and there are a lot of mountains to feed it."

The mountains continue to grow. They shoot straight up from the hills, towering a thousand meters above the road. They are covered in a blanket of pine trees with large rocks and cliffs in between. The only break in the mountains is the gash carved into them by the Carn. Two large cement turrets, with impressive cannons poking out, stand in front of the canyon mouth. A thick wall runs over the river and spans the entire opening. Gracie stops at a large, grey metal gate and a Borukin guard steps out of the wall from a small door. She is the same size as Sosimo, wearing forest green long sleeves and a helmet. None of her hair is visible. After reviewing Sosimo's papers and eying the children for a long while, the guard signals for the gate to open, letting them pass. Sosimo loosens his grip on the steering wheel and they continue on the gently winding route through the mountains.

13 Stone's Fortress
Iona

After several hours of driving along the winding canyon road, where the faces of tall cliffs block almost all the light, the canyon opens. A large town spreads across the valley, homes sprinkling the sloped sides of the mountains.

Thea plasters her face to the window. "Wow, I can't believe there are so many people up here."

"Why not?" Sosimo asks, not taking his eyes from the road.

She pulls her gaze off the town and blinks for a moment before shrugging. "I don't know. With all the steep mountains and stuff, I didn't think people would live up here."

"You'd be surprised where you can find people. Nowadays, Jasmeer is a little worse for wear, but ten years ago, it was bustling."

They drive through the center of town, where Gracie blends in perfectly with the other rugged vehicles. The buildings and the longhaired Borukins walking the streets all share the same appearance: well-worn.

"Why is everything so much nicer than where we're from?" Korbin asks.

"The Erohsians have all but enslaved the Humans over the last hundred years," Sosimo says. "Lur used to be a thriving city before the Erohsians scattered and repressed the survivors. They haven't left the Humans much to work with."

Iona glances about the buildings. "These buildings seem weird, but I can't figure out why."

Sosimo's shoulders lift ever so slightly. He looks at her. "What's one of the most obvious differences between Humans and Borukins?"

"They're dark-colored," Thea says.

"Humans can have dark skin too Thea."

"Yeah but you *all* are dark colored."

"That's just skin color. It provides a bit more UV protection but it's not applicable to this conversation," Sosimo says. "What else?"

Size... Iona drums her fingers on her thigh. "Woo! That's it. It's all a little bigger."

"That's correct. Everything's about twenty-five percent bigger, to accommodate our larger size."

Sosimo pulls Gracie off the main road, working his way through the streets toward the edge of town. They snake up the side of a mountain and pull into the driveway of a large, two-story house.

Sosimo turns in his seat to face the children. "Just wait here a second. I'm going to see if anyone's home."

Iona ducks her head to see the full house through the window. "Who's house—"

The door slams shut. Sosimo walks around the back of the truck. He opens the rear hatch, pulls out a package, then walks toward the house, patting down his clothes with his free arm.

Ryder shrugs. "I guess we'll just have to wait. So, what do you all think of him? He seems pretty cool, just a little quiet."

Korbin nods his head. "Oh yeah, super cool. Can you believe how big and strong he is?"

"I think he's warming up a bit," Thea says. "We almost got him to smile once."

"Yeah, we did," Iona says, smiling. She turns to Ryder. "I think we can trust him."

Just then, the children see the door open in front of Sosimo. A well-dressed Borukin with rolled up sleeves and long hair appears. He is half a head shorter than Sosimo and he has white markings on his forearms.

They embrace. Sosimo hands the other man a package. After a few moments of talk, Sosimo signals over his shoulder to Gracie. The man's eyes widen in disbelief. He glances to the truck, then to Sosimo. Sosimo nods several times as they continue to talk. Finally, a smile appears on the other man's face and he smacks Sosimo on the shoulder. He says one more thing, then turns to go back inside. Sosimo looks at the ground as he walks to the truck, distracted.

"What's going on?" Thea asks when Sosimo opens the door.

"What?" Sosimo shakes his head. "Oh, sorry, I was just trying to remember if nakok were good pets."

Thea's eyebrows jump up. "What are nakok?"

"A nakok is a mining animal with incredibly sharp claws. I can't imagine why anyone would have them inside a house." Sosimo grabs the keys from the dash. "My friend Gorton seems to have a few as pets, so we'll find out soon enough. He's invited us over for dinner, and to spend the night. I just hope nakok don't eat Human children," he says with a serious look. The children's faces freeze in a mixture of curiosity and horror. "We can only hope for the best. Let's get our bags and go eat." Sosimo closes the door.

"Is he joking?" Nero asks while looking at the others.

"Yeah, definitely," Korbin says with a nervous laugh. "Right?"

The others nod with varying degrees of enthusiasm.

Ryder claps his hands. "Alright, last one inside is nakok dinner!"

The children frantically struggle to sort out their bags, yelping and grunting as they poke each other. One by one, they sprint off and trample through the front door of the house.

Korbin spins around. "Who was last?"

Iona looks back. *Probably Nero.*

Sosimo follows them in while shaking his head. He places his shoes off to the side. "Shoes off."

The children kick off their shoes so they land in a mess on top of Sosimo's. They set their bags next to the stairs. In their thick, loosely-fitting socks, they follow Sosimo toward the smell of heavily-spiced cooking. Sosimo suddenly freezes and bends his knees. A patter of clawed feet echoes through the house. Several brown creatures swarm around his legs. The creatures slip and slide on feet covered by boots that individually wrap each toe. Their black beady eyes lock onto the children and they barrel forward on long front legs. Their rough, scaled skin scratches Iona's arm as they plunge into the midst of the children, forcing them to jump out of the way.

"No, please stop!" Nero yells out from under the three licking nakok. "Ew, stop! Not in my mouth!" Nero's legs thrash under their hairless bodies.

"Hey!" Gorton's voice booms.

The nakok pull their tongues back, turning to Gorton. He is holding a shiny piece of metal. They sit back on their haunches and reach up for it. Their dexterous paws flex with excitement. Gorton walks over to the front door, waving the metal in the air. The nakok follow each motion with their whiskered snouts, mesmerized. He opens the door, tossing the metal outside. The nakok begin another round of sliding as they run outside.

"Yeesh, they can be a handful," Gorton says, wiping his hands on a red cooking apron that says 'King of the Kitchen.' White tattoos of interwoven patterns run up his arms. "Sorry about that. They've never tackled anyone before." He pulls Nero up by one arm, half a meter off the ground before setting him on his feet. "Holy smokes, are you filled with air?" He turns to Sosimo. "Looks like these young ones are going to need a bit of work, especially after that impressive demonstration of bravery."

Sosimo smacks Gorton in the stomach with the back of his hand. "Cut them a little slack, they're only Human."

Gorton flinches, but a smile creeps across his face. He grabs Sosimo's shoulder. "You look good, my friend."

"Oh, get off it," Sosimo says, pushing his arm away.

Gorton kneels down next to the children. "Looks like you children are tougher than you look if you cracked Sosimo's stubborn shell. He's been utterly intolerable for too long," Gorton says in a low voice. "I'm grateful for it, and it's a pleasure to have you as company. My name is Gorton. And yours?" He shakes each of the children's hands as they introduce themselves. He stands and turns to Sosimo once more. "Are they with that Catalyst group you're working with?"

Sosimo flashes him a look. "No. We just happened to bump into each other in Blue Horin."

"All the better," Gorton says. "Now, let's get ready to eat!" Gorton swings an arm around Sosimo's neck, pulling him into the kitchen. The children follow.

In the large kitchen, a Borukin woman the same size as Gorton and two Borukin teenagers are preparing food on stone countertops. They all have long, dark braided hair.

"Hey hun," Gorton says with his arm still around Sosimo's neck. "It looks like Sosimo's finally out of his funk!"

The woman sets a wooden spoon to the side of a pot on the stove and turns to face the newcomers. She is wearing a blue apron that reads "Queen of Everything."

The woman smiles affectionately, embracing Sosimo once Gorton frees him. "It's about time, Sosimo."

"I know. I'm sorry," Sosimo says.

"And thanks for the chocolate. You're making my day in more ways than one." She looks down to the children. "Who are these little ones?"

Gorton introduces the children. "This is my wife, Kas," Gorton says. The two Borukin teenagers, who are both easily a head taller than Ryder, walk over. Gorton grabs them around the shoulders with a grin. "These are our kids, Taris and

Centara." Taris, the girl, wears a "Grill Master" apron. She is taller than her brother, who wears a "Duke of Dicing" apron.

After quick exchanges and last-minute preparations, the Borukins set the large table with bowls of steaming rice mixed with spices, vegetables, and beef. Thea unabashedly stands on her seat to reach the food in the middle of the tall table.

"So, why do the nakok wear cute little boots?" Thea asks between bites of salad.

"The boots are to cover their exceptionally sharp claws, so they don't shred the place to ribbons," Gorton says.

"Though they cause plenty of other trouble anyway," Kas says.

"Hey, they're great pets."

"Did you ever find your watch?" Kas asks.

"Not yet, but I have a good idea where it might be," Gorton says.

"How about that necklace you like?"

"I'm sure the necklace and the watch are perfectly safe."

"Buried in the backyard somewhere?"

"Yes, perfectly safe in the backyard somewhere." Gorton lets out a sigh and turns to the children. "Nakok like to hoard precious metals, so—unfortunately—jewelry tends to go missing."

"It was Kas's idea to bring them to Jasmeer to help with mining," Sosimo says.

"Aren't Borukins a little big for mining?" Iona asks.

"That we are," Kas says. "Borukins love to work in the earth, especially quarrying stone. It was only after we developed the proper tools and skills that we started mining. This makes nakok all the more valuable to us. They have an incredible sense of the ground, if tunnels are safe, and where to look for shiny stuff. They can also tear through the ground as easy as sand using a little bit of Aether."

"They can use Aether?" Iona asks.

"Not like a person, but Aether none the less," Kas says. "Their abilities are limited to a few tasks that relate to digging or searching for precious material."

"Jasmeer exploded when Kas brought them here," Gorton says. "The people made her the mayor because she brought in so much work and figured out how to use them effectively."

Kas sighs. "Yeah, but that was a while ago. Unfortunately, the Creature of Aza really screwed everything up."

Gorton shakes his head. "It shouldn't have. Borukins should have bounced back better than this."

"It seems like all of Boruk is losing its way these days," Sosimo says.

"Hey now, Gorton," Kas says. "It might be slow, but people are starting to move. Tell Sosimo about your plans for the mining camp in Stone's valley."

Gorton smiles at Sosimo. "After ten years, I've finally convinced enough Borukins to head up and work on the old mining camp to actually make some progress. Kas is even allocating a generous fund for the effort. I'm hoping it'll encourage some new developments down the road. We're meeting the workers up there tomorrow... You should come." He nods and smiles. "Yeah, I like that. Come up, it'll be fun."

Sosimo shakes his head. "No. It'd be best if we get back to Kiats."

Gorton turns to the Humans. "Did you know Stone's peak is one of the largest mountains on Anterra? It would take you years of training and weeks of hiking and climbing to get to the top." The children shake their heads. "In the valley, there's a place called Serenity Falls with natural water slides and water falls you could play in. Doesn't that sound fun?"

"I've never been on a water slide before!" Thea says. "Can we, Mr. Sosimo? Please?"

"She has never been on a waterslide before... that is just heart breaking." Gorton cracks a small smile, looking at Sosimo. "It would be cruel not to take them. Why are you in such a rush to get back anyway? Come on, I know you. A little vacation won't kill you."

"Is the detector array still functioning up there?"

Gorton looks at him suspiciously. "Probably—what are you thinking?"

"I'm not going to get a better opportunity to find an entity than using the detector array. The children have absorbed an essence, except for Iona and Nero, and I'd like them all Aether-capable."

"Saraf would kill you if he found out you gave them an essence. Wait—does this mean you're coming?"

Sosimo looks at the children. "What do you think? Feel like camping for a couple more days?"

"Yeah!"

"Great," Gorton slaps the table. "If you're coming up, you can absorb every essence you find and I won't tell Saraf a damn thing!"

"Gorton!" Kas snaps.

Gorton throws a hand over his mouth, glancing at his children. "Sorry, hun, I'm just excited. Sosimo's coming camping!" Gorton hops up from the table and rubs the top of Sosimo's head playfully. "I'm going to find you all some gear."

Kas watches him leave the dining room. "Sometimes I wonder how he survived the military, even with your help."

"He has good energy," Sosimo says, "and he knows how to use it when it counts."

*****

Hours before Illi rises, Gracie works her way up a canyon road that follows a tributary of the Carn River. By mid-morning they reach an enormous valley surrounded by steep, impenetrable mountains. Light green grass and wildflowers of purple, red, orange, and yellow cover the valley floor. There is a lake at the opposite side of the canyon entrance. It rests below a summit that sits higher than the rest, lost among the clouds. On either side of the huge mountain, waterfalls pour into the lake.

Neat.

In the center of the valley is a cluster of dilapidated stone buildings. Many Borukin vehicles are spread out around the perimeter, tents and supplies filling the spaces. They find their own spot for Gracie, unpack some stuff, and have a quick snack before Gorton moves off to rally the Borukins for work. The workers begin on the large dining hall at the center of the camp, then move on to the smaller cabins on the outskirts. They patch the roofs and walls first, followed by work on windows and other repairs to hold back the weather. The swarm of tireless Borukins and the children strive to bring life back to the camp as the day passes by. The trio of nakok run around, tripping the workers and stealing their shiny tools, always bringing them to Nero as a prize.

Iona watches as Nero receives the latest tool. He plays with the nakok until he convinces them to run off somewhere else. *Why do they like him so much?* Nero looks at the new tool and marches off in search of its owner.

When Illi starts to fall, a giant bonfire is lit just to the side of the river. The Borukins sit about the fire, eating, laughing, chatting, and telling stories with a buzz of energy that invigorates the children. It is late into the night when they finally crawl into their tents, exhausted.

*****

Wisps of a dream slowly release her and the image of the shadow-shrouded man beckoning fades to nothing. Breakfast aromas eventually drag her into consciousness. Iona pulls her warm sleeping bag over her shoulders and tucks her cold nose inside of it. *What did that man want?* Details of her dream quickly dissolve, even as she fights to remember. Eventually, her bladder reminds her once more that she needs to get up. She reluctantly slips out of her sleeping bag and throws on a jacket. She crawls over the fitfully snoozing Thea and into the morning light.

Nero is nibbling on his breakfast at a collapsible table. His hair is messy and his skin is pale. He moves sluggishly, as though he hardly slept.

Sosimo immediately serves Iona a plate of food from a small portable grill he is using. She sits opposite Nero. At the other end of the table, the Borukin children are fiddling with a strange box. Wires poke out of the top.

A few moments later, Gorton appears. He walks over to Sosimo. "I can serve myself Sosimo."

Sosimo fills a plate with food. "If you served yourself, there wouldn't be enough left for the others."

"Are you calling me fat?"

Sosimo raises an eyebrow and hands Gorton his plate.

"Let me just see that spatula for a second."

"No."

"I worked hard yesterday. I think I earned it."

"I'm very proud of you," Sosimo says dryly.

"Gimme the spatula." He reaches around Sosimo but Sosimo blocks him with his back. "You really don't want to mess with me, Sosimo."

Sosimo spins around, throwing Gorton off balance, snatching the plate from his hand and standing back. "Or you could not eat." Sosimo says, holding the spatula and the plate of food to either side.

"You are still miserable."

Sosimo smells the food. "I doubt your stomach will agree."

Gorton grabs the plate. "We'll see about that." He turns around with a smile on his face, finding a seat.

Kas is out next and is met with a plate of food, equally as fast. She smells it. "Smells as good as I remember."

The rest of the children eventually stumble out of their tents. Sosimo is the last to sit with his own food.

"So, are you heading up to the array today?" Gorton asks.

"Yes. As soon as we get that Aether detector working." Sosimo signals with his head to the box the Borukin children are working on. "After we're done, I was hoping to take the children up to the falls. Are you interested in joining?"

"That'd be fun. You all want to do that later, after work?" He asks. Centara and Taris nod their heads. "Alright, as soon as you're done messing around, we'll meet you at the falls."

"Perfect."

Iona's palms suddenly become sweaty. She wipes them on her pants, irritated.

"Wasn't there a Creature of Aza in the area?" Nero asks.

"That was ten years ago," Gorton says. "We hunted it down with nearly a hundred Borukins and dispatched it, following the necessary protocol."

"Protocol?"

"Killing a Creature of Aza is very difficult, so there are some protocols to ensure success," Sosimo says. "The first step is to break its vessel and expose its essence. Then, you have to keep the vessel from forming a new shell. Without a shell, the essence will slowly burn away, until the World Essence can claim it once more. It took three weeks before this one was finally pulled back."

"No need to fear, little one," Gorton says to Nero.

"Umm. I'm not." Nero looks down.

Iona rolls her eyes. *Yeah...*

*****

Forty-five minutes from camp, on an old mining access road, the children stumble out of Gracie to gather around Sosimo.

"This is an Aether detector." Sosimo pulls out the textbook-sized device the Borukin children had fixed. "It can measure Aetheratin, Aethersotto, and even the locations of energy signals. It's one of the more useful things the good-for-nothing Erohsians made," he says with distaste. He kneels on the ground, so the children can see, and flips up a black screen. The screen becomes white when he turns it on.

"Before we start our search, I'm going to measure your Aether abilities." He removes a little handheld scanner from the device. The children eye the scanner with suspicion. "It doesn't hurt. Trust me." He points it at himself, pulling the trigger. A green light from the handheld device glows, and after a moment it beeps. "Look." He points to the display. "This is my Aetheratin... four hundred joules. A joule is a measurement of energy. Not very good, but on the higher end for a Borukin. And here," he points to another number, "my Aethersotto is seven hundred and eighty kilowatts, or seven hundred and eighty thousand watts, where a watt is a measurement of power, which is a joule per second. Very high by Human standards." He turns the scanner to the kids. "Who's first?"

Korbin jumps to the front. "I'll go!" The scanner beeps, and a shiver runs through his body. "Jeez, that felt cold."

"In order to test your Aethersotto, the scanner draws a little energy from you." Sosimo looks at the display. "Good! Your Aetheratin is sixteen kilojoules, and your Aethersotto is one hundred and ten watts."

"That's it?" Korbin's shoulders drop.

"That's not bad, especially for a Human your age. It also means you probably absorbed an essence of a safe size, which is good." Sosimo points the scanner at Ryder. "Alright, you're up. Good Aetheratin! Eighteen kilojoules, and your Aethersotto is ninety watts. Interesting combination. Your ratio of Aetheratin to Aethersotto is quite a bit higher than typical."

"What does that mean?" Ryder asks.

"It means you'll be better at sustaining Aether for a long time at a modest intensity." Sosimo then moves to Thea. "Here it goes Thea... Whoa."

"What? Am I okay?" Thea tries to look at the display.

"You're okay, Aetheratin and Aethersotto ratio is really well balanced…"

"That's good then, right?"

"Yeah, it's just not common among wild entities or races, so you rarely see Humans with a ratio like this. The Drebin seekers are one group that has a ratio in this ball park. It's part of what makes them so effective in combat."

"So, what are my values then?" Thea asks.

"Twenty kilojoules for Aetheratin and two hundred and thirty watts for Aethersotto. It is a bit high, but not too concerning for your first essence."

Thea beams.

"That doesn't make any sense!" Korbin says. "When me and Ryder absorbed our entities, there was a big explosion, but nothing happened for Thea!"

Sosimo shrugs. "Each Human reacts differently, so that isn't always a clear indication of an essence's potential. The next time you two absorb an essence, it'll probably be pretty tame. Something else to remember is that your Riner Ratio, which is a ratio defined by your Aetheratin and Aethersotto, is now set for life. As your skills develop, your Aetheratin and Aethersotto will increase proportionally to your individual Riner Ratio. So, Ryder, for example, you'll always have a much higher relative Aetheratin than Aethersotto, no matter what essence you may absorb in the future."

"You should measure Nero since he claims to be able to use Aether," Korbin says.

"Is that alright, Nero?" Sosimo asks. Nero nods and Sosimo points the scanner at him. The scanner beeps with a red light on top. Nothing happens. Sosimo frowns trying again, but still, the scanner beeps with the red light.

Korbin tries to peek at the detector in Sosimo's hand. "So, is his Aether zero?"

"Easy, Korbin." Sosimo puts the scanner back into the detector. "Well, we weren't expecting anything, since he apparently didn't absorb an essence."

"What was it, then?" Korbin looks at Nero with a sneer. "Lower than zero?"

Sosimo turns to Korbin sharply. "Korbin, enough." He shies away. "I've noticed you can be a real jerk sometimes. It's tiresome." He takes a deep breath and pushes a few buttons on the detector. "Okay. Let's get on with what we came here to do."

Iona looks at Sosimo carefully. *Is it zero? What isn't he saying?*

Sosimo lowers the detector so the children can see. The screen has black, evenly-spaced circles radiating from the center. They all have numbers on them. "These circles represent distance, so we know how far away a signal is. We change the numbers so we either get a larger or smaller view of the area." He points to a pole sticking out of the ground. Metal arms sprouting from it give it the appearance of a cactus. "That's one of the detectors in the array. It was used to hunt the Creature of Aza. They magnify the signal we're trying to measure, which increases our search area to hundreds of meters." He hits a button, and the whole screen turns green.

"That doesn't look very helpful," Ryder says.

"Hold on a second." Sosimo frowns at the detector. He fiddles with a few buttons until the screen returns to normal, leaving a clump of green blobs at the center of the rings. "Okay, that's better. The green signals at the center represent us. If we touch them, the scanner will estimate the Aether statistics of each one. It's not as accurate as the scan we just did, but it can be useful when you can't get close. We don't want to track ourselves, so let's get rid of those." He touches a few buttons and clears the screen of the green signals at the center.

"I just told the detector to ignore any Aether signatures within ten meters of us. This works because we each have a unique energy signature."

Sosimo pushes a button on the detector, and the distance indicators constrict. New circles with higher numbers appear from the edges. Just past the two-hundred-meter circle, there is a faint green dot. "We may be in luck. Let's go get it." Sosimo begins to hike up the side of the mountain through the loose, rocky terrain.

The children struggle to keep up with his long powerful strides. He relentlessly leads them higher. Finally, Sosimo stops, and the children, huffing and puffing, clamber up next to him. Nero takes a few more minutes to catch up.

"Alright, I think we're close enough to track it directly," Sosimo says without a hint of exertion. "I only want Iona and Nero to come with me."

I don't want one! Iona's nerves cinch tight about her stomach. The same uneasy feeling she had back at their hideout with the canisters comes back.

Korbin and Thea protest in unison.

Sosimo holds up his hand. "Wild entities can be skittish; they can pick up thoughts and desires of other creatures. If we all go up there and we aren't mindful of our thoughts, it may spook."

"But I thought entities were just misty things," Thea says.

"They still react to their surroundings. If there's a threat, they'll try to move away, some faster than others. Some will even dissipate into the environment, only to take shape again several days later. It's for the best if we do this alone. We'll be quick." Sosimo looks back at the detector.

"Come on," Ryder says, signaling with his arm. "Let's find a place to rest." He walks off in the opposite direction, reluctantly followed by Thea and Korbin.

Iona and Nero gather around Sosimo. He shows them the screen. There is one faint green dot at the outer edge. "This dot is the gal we're looking for. Move slowly and try not to get too excited." Sosimo leads them toward the glowing dot.

Iona swallows. *I really don't want one.*

After a short hike, Nero taps Sosimo on the shoulder and points. "Is that it?"

Sosimo looks up, squinting. "Wow, good eyes," he says after a moment

Iona follows Nero's arm. *Where? I'm usually the one to see stuff first.*

Sosimo pulls the two children behind a tree. "Okay, so who wants it?"

Iona shakes her head. "I don't want it."

"Okay, next one is yours." He turns to Nero. "That means you're up. Move slowly. Try to stay calm. Breathe deeply. We'll follow you a short while longer, but then you're on your own."

Nero leads the way, moving quietly, as if the entity can hear him. Just when Iona sees a strange shimmer in the air, floating aimlessly, Sosimo pulls her to the side. They watch Nero approach the entity, reaching for it.

Suddenly, there is a flare of light from the center of the shimmer. The entity takes a more substantial appearance. It dives at Nero and he yelps, falling and covering his head with his arms.

"Woo," Iona gasps, grabbing Sosimo's arm.

The entity spirals about Nero's body, looping around his torso and between his arms in a chaotic blur. Nero slowly opens his eyes and jumps to his feet. He dances around in circles, shaking his arms and trying to brush the entity away. His hands pass right through the blur as it continues to coil about his body. Finally, the entity detaches itself from Nero and hovers above his head in a morphing blob of mist and light before it zooms off into the distance. Nero turns to Sosimo, his face white as chalk. He does not move.

Sosimo runs up to Nero in a few quick bounds, leaving Iona behind. He grabs Nero's shoulder. "Are you okay?"

"I think so. What happened?"

Sosimo lets out a breath. "I've never seen anything like that before. Entities will move away a bit if someone tries to touch them. If they get really scared, they'll disappear. Either way, they're slow. But that one…" Sosimo shakes his head. "I don't know what happened."

Nero looks up at Sosimo with a long face. "Is there something wrong with me? Is that why I can't absorb entities?"

Sosimo shrugs. "You look fine to me. Maybe your body is different, and you can't absorb Aether. That would explain why the detector couldn't get a reading on you… Or maybe you aren't Human."

Not Human? Iona's chest begins to tighten.

"What does that mean?" Nero says with a sense of horror.

"It's not the end of the world. You are who you are. That's what matters. Your actions in life define you, not your label."

"Well maybe I'm a natural," Nero says. He wipes his nose. "How about that?"

"What's a natural?" Iona asks.

Sosimo moves his jaw forward, making the toothpick in his mouth stick straight up. He stares at Nero for a moment, then turns to Iona. "A natural is a Human born with Aether. They are incredibly rare, so it's unlikely. And besides, you should've still responded to the Aether detector." Sosimo pats Nero on the back. "I'm sorry I don't have the answers for you, but hopefully we'll figure something out in Kiats. Let's meet up with the others. We'll see if we can find another entity and let Iona try."

When Sosimo, Iona, and Nero reach the others, Korbin jumps up quickly, rushing over. "So, what happened? Did Iona get an entity?"

Iona opens her mouth but Sosimo speaks first. "Unfortunately, no. It eluded us before we were able to get close. We'll have to keep looking."

Korbin looks at Nero's hanging head. "I bet Nero scared it away."

Sosimo's eyes fall hard on Korbin. "Korbin, you are trying my patience." Korbin shrinks away as Sosimo looks at him for a long moment. Sosimo finally flips up the screen on the detector and begins scanning for another entity.

They search the mountain for several more hours and to Iona's relief, they are unsuccessful. Eventually, Sosimo calls it a day and drives them back to the valley, where they pass through the camp. They take an old dirt road leading to the large mountain and lake. To the children's delight, the mountainside is perforated with a number of natural waterslides and waterfalls. They all feed into the cool, crystal clear lake. The laughter of the children is so full, even Nero's poor mood evaporates and he joins in on the fun.

After a few rides down the water slides, Iona wanders over to Sosimo. He is sitting on a large boulder, looking at the Aether detector. A long-sleeved shirt still covers his arms.

"Hey, can I ask you a question?" she asks.

Sosimo looks up from the detector. "Sure."

"What happened when you scanned Nero? There's something you weren't telling us."

"You don't let anything slip by," Sosimo says. "Sit down. I'll try to explain." Iona scrambles up the warm rock next to Sosimo. "If I were to scan any living thing on this planet, I would get a reading. It might be zero, but nonetheless, I would get a reading."

"So, what did the scan say?"

"That's the weird thing. I couldn't scan him at all. It's like he wasn't even there."

"What does that mean? Could he really not be Human?"

Sosimo pushes a few more buttons on the detector. He shakes his head and sighs. "I can't say. This detector could be broken."

"What were you trying to do?"

"Do you remember when I was first showing you the detector and the screen turned completely green?"

"Yeah, was that normal?"

"Well, a little bit of weak background noise is expected. Aether can come from any number of places, but this was very energetic—a four on the Boltz scale. Do you know what the Boltz scale is?"

Iona shakes her head.

"It's used to quantify Aether. It combines someone's Aetheratin and Aethersotto into a single value that can be used to effectively compare Aether abilities, regardless of Riner Ratio. It is also logarithmically based, which means a two on the Boltz scale is ten times higher than a one, and a three is ten times higher than a two. A small difference in the Boltz value can be pretty significant. I'm a 3.3 on the Boltz scale, and the other children are less than a one. A four as a background value is very odd. I was hoping that it would show up again, but I'm not having any luck. I'll get a spike occasionally, but that's it. It's probably just a weird glitch." Sosimo moves the detector to the side and sighs. "This has been a strange day."

A car coming down the dirt road catches their attention. It parks next to Gracie and Gorton, Kas, and their children hop out. Taris and Centara head directly for the lake while their parents walk toward Sosimo and Iona. More cars begin to trickle down the road to the lake as well.

"It looks like there was a bit of an incident with the Drebin," Kas says. "I need to head back soon to play Mayor."

"Was there an attack?" Sosimo asks.

"There was," Gorton says. "They attacked the Gate and completely destroyed it. They went right through town and turned up the road toward Stone's Peak before our army could intercept."

"How did we stop them?"

"Our air support was able to slow them down enough that our army caught up with them. There wasn't much else to do at that point but fight. From what we heard, it wasn't pretty; eight Borukins were killed. There were two Seekers in the group. Unfortunately, before the army could finish them off, they both escaped into the mountains with some survivors, heading for the border. The army set off after them, but the

Drebin were too quick in the poor terrain. The military is now ensuring that they don't double back."

"Two seekers," Sosimo says. "I think we're lucky we only lost eight. But the Drebin must have known they didn't have a chance. What would motivate them to push so deep into our mountains?"

"They're still assessing, but maybe there's something up here," Gorton says. "Which means King Ramas is going to want the mountains searched thoroughly, and the people in charge will most likely be staying in Kas's town, and in these cabins. We should prepare to receive them."

"Looks like you have a lot of work to do." Sosimo looks out at the children playing in the water, then at Iona. "I bet it'd be best to stay here for a couple of days to let things settle. The road to Kiats is going to be crowded."

Gorton slaps Sosimo on the back. "That's good, because I could use more help."

14 Kiats

Iona

Gracie completes a gentle right turn and the canyon disappears. An expanse of green, sprawling farmland unfurls before them. The road bobs along the large rolling hills covered in crops at different stages of growth. Every fifty kilometers or so, towns interrupt the fields.

Several hours pass by and the rolling hills settle into a gentle slope running all the way to a deep blue ocean. Lines of white capped waves stretch across the horizon and roll into the shore.

A dense blanket of leafy trees abruptly overruns the farmland, where the afternoon light ignites red stone buildings poking through the canopy. The city dips down and back up with the beaches and cliffs of the varying coastline. Only at the heart of the city do the stone buildings become the distinguishing feature.

Thea throws her hand over her mouth. "Oh, wow."

"Neat," Iona says.

"My Kiats," Sosimo says. "It's hard to be gone for so long. I'll take the long way to show you the best of it."

Once Gracie pierces the thick layer of trees, the number of buildings and homes surprise the children. The Borukins they see walking about are dressed slightly more formally than those in Jasmeer. Almost all of them have long black hair and ivory tattoos. As they approach the coast, the buildings increase in size, and the stonework becomes more elaborate. The stone structures push the trees back, and the sky opens.

"Oooo, can we swim in that?" Thea asks, pointing to a large stone fountain with water spraying from the top and to the sides.

"That's not for swimming. It was a donation to the city of Kiats from one of the greatest stoneworkers of all times, Tyra Wintello. It's hundreds of years old. This is the fountain that is replicated in the Human city Praun, which I mentioned before." Sosimo points to the other side of the road where the building facades are made of intricately carved stone and red granite pillars support the roof. "If you look carefully, you'll be able to see Stone's Coliseum, where the Games are held."

The buildings part and a portion of Stone's Coliseum peeks through. It sits like a gargantuan stone bowl on a flat table. Enormous granite pillars, as tall as some of the surrounding buildings, support the edges.

"Woo. Where'd they get all that stone?" Iona asks.

"Anterra is bigger than you can imagine. It's just a matter of finding and digging it up. The Coliseum is actually three separate stadiums that have different arrangements for the events. Its size is quite daunting, even for someone who was raised here. Now look, here." He points to the other side where there is a long field of grass; individual statues stand around the perimeter. "That's the Lawn of Royals. It has a statue of every Queen or King of Boruk since our emancipation from the Creators."

Sosimo turns Gracie along the cliff-line that drops off to the ocean in levels like steps made for a giant of unimaginable size. Rectangular pools of turquoise water are framed in stone and spill through falls to pools below. Walkways and benches line the edges of the cliffs at each level, and small bridges span channels of gently flowing water. Between the pools, large flat areas of stone are filled with Borukins in lines. They all follow the motions of a master. Back on the main level, monuments and museums meld perfectly with the landscape as countless Borukins stroll the paths between.

"Can we swim in those?" Thea asks.

"People are only allowed to swim in the lower area, by the ocean."

"Aw, that totally stinks. Those look fun."

After driving along the coast for a few minutes, Sosimo turns Gracie away and weaves through the streets before parking in an alley.

"This is my store, and where I live. I'll show you around, and then we can come back for our gear," Sosimo says.

From the truck, he leads them from the back door of his store through aisles of storage. Longhaired Borukins in starched, beige uniforms move through the aisles with purpose. They all glance at the children and move past Sosimo without raising their heads. Iona smells the sweet candy, but finds her mouth is dry.

"I'll show you where we make the chocolate and other candy first," Sosimo says. He opens a door, leading them downstairs toward the sounds of machinery.

Rows of different machines split the room into sections. Borukins dressed in white move around from one task to the next.

"Neat. Why so many machines?" Iona asks.

"Making candy is no simple business, especially if you want to do it right. All of these machines serve a purpose and to really do it right, we have to keep the basement closed to control the humidity," Sosimo says. "Many of these machines are older than myself. It was a challenge finding them, but I tell you, it was worth it. The chocolate they make is unrivaled."

He walks them through the aisles and—again—the employees stay clear of his path. "That one, there," he says, pointing to a giant machine with a belt drive running a stone grinder, "is over a hundred years old." He reaches the end of an aisle and inspects one of the grinders, running his finger over spilled sugar. He signals to the closest worker. "You. Come here."

The worker jumps and approaches Sosimo. "Yes, Mr. Mantle?"

Sosimo points to the sugar on his finger. "What is this? Are we running a wood shop, or a candy store?"

"A candy store, sir."

"That's what I thought. Clean this up and check the rest of the machines. This kind of mess is unacceptable. You know better."

The worker nods his head, which is beaded with sweat. "I'll do it right away, sir," he says, walking swiftly away.

Sosimo shakes his head, letting out a frustrated breath. "I don't ask for too much, do I?"

"Why is everyone scared of you, Mr. Sosimo?" Thea asks.

Sosimo stares down on her. "What?"

"I was just asking why everyone around you sweats like they're about to take a spelling test that their life depends on."

"They're just focused on their work, Thea. I like to keep the store running smoothly."

Thea shakes her head. "They're definitely scared of you. Maybe you're too harsh. Fae always tells Korbin the only thing that should be harsh is sandpaper, not people. But he doesn't listen."

"I do, too!" Korbin says.

"Yeah, well then how many times has she said that?" Thea asks. "Just last week when Nero—"

"All right, children. Enough," Sosimo says. "Let's go see the storefront."

Sosimo leads them back to the storage area. They walk through a door that spits them out behind the sales counter, opening to a large candy store. The space is split into sections for each different type of candy. Borukin customers mill around quietly. Repurposed candy machines line the sides, filled with pieces of wrapped sweets.

"Candy!" Thea says, running out from behind the counter and down the aisles. She stops at the different bins, bouncing for a moment then running off to the next display.

"Sorry, Sosimo," Ryder says. "She's a spaz."

"It's okay," Sosimo says softly, not turning to look at Ryder.

The Borukins in the store all watch Thea run until one of the employees grabs her by the wrist.

"This is not a playground, child," the employee says, biting. She starts to walk her toward the door. "Run around somewhere else."

"Hold up, Tierney," Sosimo says, walking toward her.

Tierney looks up with surprise. "Mr. Mantle! I'm so sorry. I didn't know you were here. I don't know who this child belongs to, but I'll remove her immediately and you'll never see her again."

Thea's panicked face turns to sheer horror. Tears begin to build up in her eyes.

Sosimo looks from Thea to Tierney, who is equally horrified. There is a flash of realization before his rigid posture gives way and his face is ridden with sorrow.

Thea begins to cry.

"Please don't fire me, Mr. Mantle," Tierney says. "I know children aren't allowed unattended. I'll watch more carefully. It won't happen again." She turns around, yanking Thea with her.

"Stop," Sosimo says with difficulty.

Tierney turns around and Thea weakly tries to unclench the woman's hand from her own.

"Please," Thea says between sobs. "I didn't know. I don't want to go."

Sosimo drops down to one knee. "Come here, Thea. It's okay."

Tierney looks at them in surprise before she lets Thea go. Thea runs to Sosimo for a hug. He pats her back until her crying subsides.

"Oh, may Stone help me. I'm sorry, Mr. Mantle," Tierney says. "I didn't know they were with you. I thought you wanted nothing to do with children."

"I know, and I haven't had the right attitude. I'm sorry if I've been too hard on you. I've turned into a tyrant because I was too afraid of losing this store as well."

"You're a great boss. Your candy stores are the best—"

"Don't. There's nothing more to be said. I'll do better." Sosimo stands up, brushing the knees of his pants. He takes a long breath. "Could you prepare the list of ingredients we need for the store? I'd like to restock over the next few days."

Tierney nods. "Yes, sir. Right away." She turns away.

"Tierney," Sosimo says sternly.

Tierney spins back around. "Yes, sir?"

Sosimo's face softens. "Thank you."

A look of confusion flits across Tierney's face. Then, a small smile creeps into her expression. She turns purposefully away.

"Mr. Sosimo, sir," Thea says, tugging on his pants. She is still recovering from crying.

"You don't have to call me sir, Thea."

"I'm sorry I got in trouble."

Sosimo ruffles her hair. "You did nothing wrong." Sosimo looks over the Borukin customers watching the scene. He turns back to the children. "Let's collect our belongings, and I'll show you where we'll be staying."

Sosimo leads them out the back of the store to collect their belongings from Gracie. He takes them up a stairway in the alley to the second floor.

Sosimo slides the key into the door. "This is where I live." The back door opens to the side of a wide-open kitchen that flows into the dining room. "We'll be doing most of the cooking ourselves, so you'll get very comfortable in here."

Sosimo takes them through the living room, where double sliding doors expose a stone training room with spongy grey floors. "This is where I'll be training you to use Aether," Sosimo says.

The children fan out. Korbin runs to a rack of wooden staffs and swords. "Are these your weapons?" Korbin asks. "Where are your real swords and stuff?"

"Those are Borukin styks. They're made of special wood," Sosimo says. "In the hands of a Borukin, they're just as effective as any metal weapon."

"How is that possible?" Iona asks.

"With Aether and skill. Unfortunately, they won't be any use to you all, since Humans don't have a high enough Aethersotto to use them effectively."

"What are these?" Nero points to a rack with an assortment of patterned crystal rods, gloves with gems, and pendants. "They're amazing."

Iona looks at the rack. *They're not that amazing...*

"Those are Artifacts. They're infused with Aether. They will be the tools I'll use to teach you all."

"Oh, sweet," Korbin says. "Can we shoot fireballs and blow things up like Captain Konquer?"

"Who's Captain Konquer?" Sosimo asks.

"A silly action figure Korbin is obsessed with," Ryder says.

"Only because he's the most awesome fighting machine ever!" Korbin says, kicking against the air.

Sosimo frowns. "These are serious tools, Korbin. I expect you to treat them as such, and I expect you to act like an adult in the training room. Understand?"

Korbin drops his arms to his sides and nods.

"Good." Sosimo's face lightens and he looks over the children. "Now, over the course of our training, I'll go into detail about the different types of Artifacts and how they can be used, but it'll be some time before you'll be ready for them. You must master the basics, or further down the road these tools will only cripple you," Sosimo says, looking at the children. "We'll also be doing Roroonki here, which are the traditional Borukin morning exercises. They are a combination of calisthenics and meditation. They will help to build strength and to focus your young minds for the day." Sosimo shuffles the children out of the room, taking them up to the next floor, where there are several bedrooms and bathrooms. They are quick to split up and claim their beds.

As Sosimo is taking the children back downstairs, Korbin stops, looking up another stairway. "What's up there?"

"I keep a private work shop and some storage up there. It's locked, so don't bother exploring," Sosimo says.

"Are you going to show us that later?" Iona asks.

"Perhaps. We'll have to see. For now, why don't you make yourselves comfortable and settle in? Don't fool around in the training room, or I won't train you. It is a place to be serious. Right now, I need to talk with Tierney about the supplies the shop needs and run a few errands."

"Why don't you have someone else pick up the supplies if you own the shop?" Ryder asks. "It seems like that'd be a boring job."

"It is what you make it, Ryder. I like to hand-pick the ingredients myself a few times a year, to ensure quality and consistency. I'll be back in a little bit with some food, and then we can start on dinner."

"Remember to be nice!" Thea says as he turns away.

Sosimo nods. "Yes, Ma'am."

He leaves the children to themselves. As soon as the door shuts, Thea runs and jumps on one of the couches in the living room. "This place is almost as nice as Fae's. This couch is bigger than my bed!"

Ryder sits next to her. "Everything is big here, and Kiats is way nicer than New Lur and even Blue Horin."

"Yeah, I hope we get to swim in the ocean and play in those ponds," Thea says. "But I kinda miss home. I feel like it's been forever since we've been there."

"At least we're far away from the Erohsians and the Drebin," Iona says. "I feel safe here. The Borukins seem like nice people."

"Yeah, I just hope Sosimo cheers up more," Thea says. "Like Gorton. He was fun."

"And Kas, I liked her," Iona says.

"But Taris and Centara were total wusses," Korbin says. "I could totally take them."

"Pff, they were twice the size of you, Korb," Ryder says. "And you probably just have a crush on Taris."

"Whatever, that wouldn't stop Captain Konquer."

Ryder shakes his head. "They seemed cool enough, though. I can't believe they fixed that detector."

Korbin shrugs. "I could probably do that."

"I hope we get to play in those waterfalls by that camp again," Thea says. "That was the most fun I've had in my entire life!"

"Do you think Fae's okay?" Nero asks.

The energy from the other children washes away.

"I hope so," Ryder says. "We'll have to ask Sosimo about it later."

$$*****$$

"I appreciate all the work you did with me over the last few days," Sosimo says. "Now that all of the pressing jobs for the store are done and we've enrolled you in school, we can start to train with Aether."

"Do we really have to go to school?" Korbin asks.

"Borukins believe in practical experience. I told them you'll be apprenticing at my candy store, so you only have three days of school a week. You'll manage if you want to train with me."

Korbin dips his head. "Yes, sir."

"Now, on to Aether. There are many levels of complexity when it comes to using Aether. Many of these will take you your entire life to master. To start, we'll simply work on getting your Aether flowing. In a few weeks, we'll move on to Fundamental Aether."

"What's that?" Ryder and Korbin ask at the same time.

"Jinx!" Korbin says.

Ryder glares at Korbin before quickly turning his attention back to Sosimo.

"You got jinxed," Thea says, dancing in a circle.

Sosimo looks between the children. "What just happened?"

"Korbin just jinxed," Thea says, pointing to Ryder with big gestures. "Now," she points to Ryder again, "can't talk. It's very serious."

"You really can't talk, Ryder?"

Ryder smiles at Korbin then Thea. "Can now."

"You totally ruined it, Mr. Sosimo," Thea throws her hands up and slumps over.

Sosimo moves the toothpick in his mouth. "You children are a different species. I don't understand half of what goes on in those little heads of yours. Your attention span must be measured in breaths. Now, we focus."

Thea stands up straight, giving Sosimo her complete attention.

"Good. Back to the question that was asked before that little incident. Fundamental Aether is everything you can do with Aether that is not cast specific. There are passive abilities, like an increase in strength, speed, and endurance. There's also how you may perceive Aether. Then there are active abilities. Those are focused on using your essence to affect the world."

"So, like moving stuff without touching it?" Ryder asks.

"Yes, exactly," Sosimo says. "But as I said before we'll start with working on controlling the flow of your Aether." Sosimo walks over to the racks of Artifacts and grabs a glove made of golden chain. Red stones are set into each of the fingertips while pieces of polished wood decorate the rest.

"This is a Pahzan lepisent. It converts Aether into heat. I'm going to have you use this to melt ice cubes."

"What good is that?" Korbin asks.

"This is just the start, Korbin. When you're better trained, you can use a lepisent like this to release a stream of hot Aether."

"Awesome! When do we do that?"

Sosimo shakes his head. "When you master the basics." He brings a pitcher of ice to the children. "Now watch."

Sosimo puts on the perfectly fitting glove and holds an ice cube in his fingers. The ice slowly melts, water trickling down his fingers to the floor. "As easy as that. Now, Ryder, you're up first."

Ryder slips on the large glove and holds up a piece of ice. "Okay, what do I do?"

"The glove will do all the work. All you have to do is let the energy flow. Just relax and think about melting the ice. Once you get it, the next challenge will be controlling the flow."

Ryder closes his eyes, breathing slowly. After a few moments, a few drops of water fall.

"That's it. Keep it coming," Sosimo says. The ice quickly melts. "How'd that feel?"

Ryder removes the glove. "Weird. Like I was losing something. At first I didn't want to let go. Once I relaxed, it felt better."

"It'll only get easier from now on." Sosimo holds the glove out to Thea. "You're up, Thea."

Thea puts on the glove, and Sosimo places a piece of ice on her hand. In a moment, the ice cube is nothing more than steaming water on her hand.

"Wow, Thea, not bad."

Thea's grin covers her entire face. She hugs Sosimo's waist. "Thanks, Mr. Sosimo."

"Okay, Thea, let me have the lepisent so Korbin can go. Typically, we don't hug in the training room."

"That's a silly rule," Thea says. She hands Korbin the glove.

Sosimo puts an ice cube on Korbin's fingertips. "Okay, Korbin, just relax and let it flow."

Korbin looks at the ice cube. Nothing happens. He shuffles his feet, glaring at it. His head starts to tremble. A red glow fills his face, and a vein on his forehead bulges.

Sosimo holds up his hand. "Whoa, Korbin, hold up. You're going to pop something if you push any harder."

All the children burst into laughter.

Korbin's face stays red. He spins on the other children, throwing the ice cube at Nero's chest. "Is that funny, Nero? If it's so easy, why don't you do it? Oh wait, I forgot. You can't!"

Sosimo whacks Korbin's arm with the back of his hand. "That's enough." His voice booms. The color drains from Korbin's face and he shrinks down. "Go to your room. I will not tolerate this in the training room or anywhere else."

Korbin stands straight. His face curls in anger. "You can't tell me what to do."

"You're in my house and you're under my training. You'll do as I say or leave." Sosimo says, but Korbin hesitates. "Now!" Korbin jumps, scurrying off to his room.

Sosimo walks over to Nero, who is hanging his head. Sosimo awkwardly pats him on the head.

"I could do it. I swear," Nero whispers.

"Be strong, Nero." Sosimo kneels down. "If you and Iona would like to explore the city tomorrow while we practice, you can. It might be more interesting than just watching us train. Borukins respect Humans, so you shouldn't have any trouble with the people. There's even a park close by you can explore."

Nero looks up at him. "All by ourselves?"

Iona slumps. *I don't want to get stuck with Nero.* "Yeah, do you really think that's such a good idea?"

Sosimo nods. "I think it'll be good for both of you. At least try it tomorrow."

"Okay, fine," Iona says. "Just tomorrow."

15 Exploration
Iona

The Borukins smile at Iona as she walks down the busy streets, Nero in tow. Iona rubs her fingers on her palms, noticing they are sweaty.

Nero slows down. "Do you think we should be going this far?"

I knew he would be a downer. "Come on, just a little bit farther. Look, the park should be just down there."

Iona leaves Nero by himself as she walks down the road. By the time he catches up, the buildings have come to an end and a giant park is revealed.

Dirt paths separate thick, tall trees and foliage from open areas of green grass. Borukins lounge on picnic blankets while others disappear down paths that cut into the thicket. Little stalls are set up around the edge of the park, selling a huge variety of things. Iona and Nero stop at a booth with giant red, purple, and orange flowers.

"Woo, neat," Iona says. The flowers move with her hand as she waves it back and forth.

Another vendor has colorful figurines of blown glass and souvenirs of Borukin royalty.

Iona suddenly feels a surge of energy, right when Nero grabs her arm.

Iona spins around. "What is it?"

"Did you hear that?"

"I hear a lot. There's a lot to hear." *Does he want to go back again?*

Nero shakes his head. "Nevermind." He looks off toward the park. "I'm going to check something out."

What? Is he losing his mind? It takes her a moment to realize he is already walking through the crowd.

Nero ducks into one of the naturally wooded areas. Near the other side, he hides behind a tree, looking out. Iona crouches down beside him. A Borukin woman is arguing with a male vendor of another race, who is smaller and lighter of skin. He has a portable vendor display that looks as though he could carry everything on his back.

The Borukin throws up her hands, accentuating the definition in her strong arms. "That's a ridiculous price."

"Not if others will pay it," the smaller man says, his face cold.

"It's an intelligent and noble creature. They're rare enough, yet you'll sell it to someone that'll eat it as a delicacy."

"Some think they're evil," the man says. "I've heard the stories where they kill entire families. Maybe the world is better off without them."

"They're misunderstood. They've suffered a near extinction because of it."

"Lady, in the end, I'm a businessman. I can hardly concern myself with such trivial matters. This is the price, no matter what you plan to do with it."

"I could just report you," the woman says.

"You could," the man says calmly. "But you have no proof, and they can't search my stuff without it." The man puts his foot on a light-colored wood box. "Even with proof, I would disappear before the police arrive. Your only options are to pay the money or leave."

"Or I could just take it," she says, voice low.

"You could try but I'm prepared to deal with thieves with or without the law."

Nero clenches the side of the tree. "I'm going to save it," he says in a whisper, not facing her.

"Save what?" Iona asks.

"The creature in the box." Nero turns to her. "You going to help?"

"The guy said that it's evil."

"It's not."

"How do you know?"

"Just cause."

"You can't," Iona says.

Nero flinches. "What?"

"You can't just take it."

"I can't?" His face hardens and a strange fire glows in his eyes. "I can and I will. It's the right thing to do. If you're too scared, then leave." Nero starts to sneak around behind the vendor's stand.

What has gotten into him? It takes her a moment to regain her composure. *I guess I should try to create a distraction.* Iona walks toward the vendor and the woman, who are still arguing.

Iona grabs a small, blue sphere with a swirling green light from the vendor's collection. "Ooh, this is pretty. I'm going to go show my friend. I'll be right back." She walks off.

The vendor removes his foot from the crate, grabbing her by the shoulder. "Hey there. Not so fast."

Iona slumps her shoulders. "Oh, come on. I'll bring it right back. I won't be gone long. Just a second."

"Are you out of your mind?" the vendor asks. "No way, little girl. Give it back and get out of here. You've had your chance to look."

Iona holds it out of his reach. "Please, mister!"

"No." He snatches it away.

Iona stamps her foot, frowning. "You're mean."

"Both of you are out of your minds." He looks at the Borukin and Iona. "I'm running a business, not a charity."

"Well, then, how much do you want for it?" Iona asks reaching into her pocket and holding out some money. "I've got ten Anterren, but I'll only give you five."

"It's worth two hundred."

"For a little light!? What a ripoff," Iona says. She cocks hear head to the side. "Is that all it is?"

The vendor puts the sphere back. "It's an Ethnohap gem that I acquired from the Aquarians, across the Sirean Sea. They are very rare."

"Where's that?" Iona asks.

"Bah." The vendor waves his hand at her. "I told you to get out of here. I'm not about to give world lessons to an untraveled youth as yourself." The vendor spins Iona around, pushing her away. "Now go away."

Iona slowly walks away and glances back. Nero is nowhere to be seen. The small box has not moved. *What am I going to do? Was that long enough?* She catches a glimpse of something off in the trees moving away. *Nero?*

Iona hurries, following Nero to a clump of large bushes. A small, black furry creature is clinging to him with dark, stick like arms no thicker than her pinky finger. He removes a beige hood from its head, revealing a beak-like mouth and large blue eyes.

Iona's chest is incredibly light. She smiles at the creature. "She's cute. Or is it a he? How did you release it so quickly?" Iona tentatively reaches out, scratching its head. To her surprise it has four arms and stick-like legs as well.

Nero strokes the creature's head. "It wasn't too hard. There was a little latch on the box, so I just snuck around and popped it while you were talking to the guy."

Suddenly a shadow blocks out Illi. Iona and Nero spin around.

"That was an impressive little move you two just pulled. I couldn't believe my eyes when I saw what you were doing." The Borukin woman says with a smile. "Now what do you plan to do with your prize, young man?"

"It's not my prize," Nero says quickly.

"Then it seems we're on the same page. I would be very happy to see the zarta back in the wild where he belongs," the woman says.

"But we can't just let him go here. He'll be captured again," Iona says.

"Here, he would. But I can take him away. I'm from an old mining town named Jasmeer. There are plenty of secluded areas where he can live in peace."

"Did you know the Drebin were just near there?" Nero asks.

The woman nods. "That's actually why I'm in the city. I heard things have settled down, so I can head back immediately."

"How can we trust you?" Iona asks.

"Well, we could let the zarta decide," the woman says. "Have you named him?"

"It's a boy?" Nero asks.

"I believe so. Girls are typically lighter in color."

"Okay, then let's name him Jacob," Nero says.

Iona frowns. "That's no fun."

"Jacob's a fine name." The woman scratches the top of Jacob's head.

"So, how do we let him decide?" Nero asks.

"Zarta's are very smart and good at reading people's intentions. That's why he was hooded." She points to the hood on the ground. "If he's willing to come to me, then that should be sufficient proof."

"What will you do with him?" Nero asks.

"I'll take him back home and tend to him until he's ready to be released to the wild," the woman says.

"You swear on your life?" Iona asks.

"I promise on my life and on the lives of everyone I love that I'll do what's best for Jacob and help him back to the wild," she says.

Nero wiggles Jacob loose and holds him out to the woman. She slides her fingers into Jacob's hands. After a moment, he releases Nero's arms and clings onto her.

The woman smiles, petting his head. "He's in good hands."

"Why did the guy back there say they're evil creatures?" Nero asks.

"Well, this little guy is going to grow much bigger than me, and he'll be very good with Aether. He'll start to project more robust arms as pure Aether, which will make him pretty intimidating. As long as people don't threaten him, he'll be quite peaceful. But if he's pushed, he'll push back. Hard. That gives them a bad rep. Kinda like a bee or a wasp." The woman glances back in the direction of the vendor. "I've got to hurry before any trouble turns up. My name is Herith. Yours are?"

Iona and Nero introduce themselves.

"If you're ever in the area, you're welcome at my house. You've earned my respect, and I'll never forget that. I hope to see you two again someday." Herith moves away.

Iona turns to Nero. "I can't believe you rescued that creature. No offense, but I thought you were scared of everything."

"His name's Jacob."

"I know. I'm just surprised. That was really nice."

"Yeah, well. It was the right thing to do."

"How did you know it was there?"

Nero hesitates for a moment. "Uh. I don't know. I just had a feeling. Thanks for your help. You did really well…"

"That was exciting. Do you think Jacob will be okay?"

Nero nods. "Yes. Herith seemed nice enough."

"Yeah she did. Well, we should head back soon; Sosimo's training is probably almost over." Iona smiles at him. "You know; you're not so boring after all."

A small smile spreads on Nero's face. He blushes as he looks away.

*****

"So, what do you want to do today?" Iona asks.

"Should we explore the cliffs?"

"Nah, we did that yesterday. Let's go to the west side."

Nero shakes his head. "No way."

"Aw, are you chicken?" Iona asks. "It's been weeks since we've been over there."

"Hey. Last time we went there, you got us sooo lost, I had to hold your hand because *you* were scared."

Iona blushes. "It wasn't that bad."

"Yeah, it was. I had nightmares about it for a week."

"About being lost?"

"No, about holding hands."

Iona punches him in the arm. "You jerk." She turns away from him, smiling to herself. *I'll have to make up for getting lost.* She waves her hand over her head. "Come on. I won't get us lost this time."

Nero sighs. "Fine, but I'm not holding your hand."

Iona marches forward, pretending not to have heard.

After a few minutes of walking in silence, Nero suddenly grabs her arm, pulling her to the side. He squats down and peers into a cluster of bushes at the base of a rough stone building.

"What is it?" Iona asks.

"I hear something." He moves around for a better position. "Look there, at the bottom." He points into the bush.

Iona follows his finger with her eyes and just at the bottom of the bush is a chirping baby bird. She looks up and sees a nest a few stories high in a nook by a window. "The poor thing must have fallen out of its nest. Do you think it's okay?"

"The bushes probably broke its fall, but I don't think it'll survive down here."

"That's so sad. I wish there was something we could do."

Nero eyes the building and its rough stone face. "We could put it back."

"Are you crazy? How do you suppose we do that?"

"Well, look." He grabs a stone emerging from the building. "The stones have enough grip. We could climb up there, then work our way along that edge where there's a little more lip, which will take us to the window."

"But it's so high, what if you fall?"

Nero raises his eyebrows. "So I'm getting voted to go?"

"I'm not doing it. That's just stupid."

"Aren't you always giving me a hard time for being scared?"

"Yeah, but that's because you're scared of little things, like the dark and exploring and strange sounds. Where do you get the nerve to climb to your certain death?"

"Jeez. Thanks for being optimistic. If we don't help it, then it's dead. At least help me pick it up."

Iona grabs his arm before he reaches into the bush. "Wait. You're going to need both hands when you climb. Give me a second." She empties her satchel and puts the baby bird inside, wrapped in cloth. "Here, just be careful." She feels a surge of energy and sees his eyes are clear and focused.

"Sure, no sweat." He tenderly puts the satchel on and climbs. When he is a story up, his foot slips. His hands stay firm.

Iona gasps. "Nero! Are you sure this is a good idea? I certainly don't!"

Nero looks down at her. His face is red and glistening with sweat. "I'm already halfway up. Would you stop your nagging and help me?" He climbs a little higher.

Me, nagging? "You're lucky I care at all!"

Nero turns back down again. "What did you say?"

"I said… just don't fall."

Nero shakes his head, continuing to climb. "Very helpful," he mutters to himself.

"Hey! I heard that!" *What did he say?*

Nero makes it to a ledge. Hugging the wall, he shimmies across, two stories high. At the window, he pulls the satchel around. There is hardly enough room to balance. Iona holds her breath, clenching her fists. Using only one hand, he slowly reaches into the satchel and removes the baby bird, placing it back in the nest among two other babies.

Nero looks down at Iona. "Alright, it's back. I'm heading down."

"Be careful!"

Nero works his way back across the ledge with little effort and starts his way down, which proves to be much more difficult than going up. He struggles to see good places to put his feet and hands, and it takes him several minutes to lower himself half way. Suddenly his right hand slips and he swings around like a barn door, barely gripping on with his left. Just as his left foot slips off the wall, he turns and jumps, landing hard at the edge of the bushes and the stone path.

He rolls onto his back and curls his knees to his chest, with his eyes tightly shut. "Ooh, that hurts."

Iona runs over. "That's your own fault! I told you not to fall."

"It was a controlled descent."

"Oh, is that what that's called?"

"Yeah, it is. Maybe if you would've been a little more helpful I wouldn't have had to."

"I told you this was a stupid idea. Are you okay?"

Nero moves his ankle weakly. "I think so. I rolled it a bit when I came down. At least the baby bird's back in its nest."

Iona smiles. "Yeah, I'm glad you rescued the poor thing."

*****

"Are you two love birds going off by yourselves again?" Korbin asks Iona and Nero. The children are at the breakfast table.

"Shut up, Korbin," Iona says.

"Iona and Nero sitting in a tree," Korbin sings. "K-I-S-S-I-N-G. First comes love, then comes marriage, then comes a baby in the baby carriage."

Iona punches him in the arm. "That's not funny."

"Yeah, Korb, cut it out," Ryder says. "They're just hanging out together."

Korbin glares at Ryder. "Whatever, Ryder, you're the one that always complains about Iona not being around."

Suddenly, Iona is overcome by an extreme heaviness in her chest.

"Settle down, children," Sosimo says in a whisper. He joins them at the table. "Can we please eat peacefully this morning?"

The children turn their attention to breakfast and are soon scrounging for the last bit of crumbs on their plate.

"Why are you sad, Mr. Sosimo?" Thea asks.

"I have some bad news." All the children turn to him. "I had someone poke around back where you're from, and they discovered Fae's death certificate in the Erohsian public records. It said she died of natural causes." Sosimo looks at them with sad eyes, waiting for a response.

"That's a mistake." Tears well up in Thea's eyes. "You must have found a different Fae."

"I'm sorry Thea, but it is no mistake," Sosimo says. "I double checked everything."

"This is crap!" Korbin hits the table. "They killed her."

Sosimo dips his head. "That seems likely."

"How can they get away with this?" Ryder asks, eyes watering.

"We have to tell someone!" Thea says.

"I'm sorry, children. There's nothing we can do from here, and there's likely nothing we can do back in Sunta… The Erohsians have been doing this to Humans for close to a hundred years. One more death won't make a difference to them. This is why people are standing up to them. This is why Catalyst exists."

"Then I want to join them and fight," Korbin says.

"A child isn't going to win this war, Korbin. You must train and grow strong first."

"Then let's train, already. Why are we sitting around?" Korbin stands.

"I will train you as hard as you can take," Sosimo says, "but chores first." Korbin looks at Sosimo with a determined stare. "This is not negotiable."

Korbin grabs his plate and heads to the kitchen, followed by Ryder and Sosimo. Thea hugs Nero as best she can. His head stays down on his arms. She moves off to the kitchen, wiping her tears away.

"I'm sorry, Nero." Iona looks at her plate with a puddle of tears collecting on it. "We all loved her."

Nero looks at her, eyes puffy. "I know, but I'm useless. She was the only one who cared about me."

"That's not true. We care about you."

"Maybe Thea…" He flops his head back onto his arms.

"I care about you, Nero…"

Nero looks at her. "You don't have to say that." He grabs his plate and limps to the kitchen.

I've been so hard on him…

*****

"I'm sorry I've been mean to you over the years," Iona says to Nero

"What do you mean?"

"Just crabby to you sometimes."

Nero shrugs and turns back to Sosimo's training session. Ryder is wearing a circlet Artifact, while Sosimo is using another spherical Artifact to excite Ryder's essence.

"It's just, whenever we were ever doing anything away from Fae, and you were around, I'd feel really uncomfortable. Like, my hands would sweat and my mouth would go dry. It was really annoying. I don't know why it happens, but it can't be your fault."

Nero looks down, sticking his hands in his pockets.

"Can you forgive me?"

Nero glances at her briefly. "I know I've been annoying. You don't need to feel bad."

"Well, I've never had so much fun as I do exploring Kiats with you."

He smiles briefly. "It's been fun."

They turn their attention back to the training. Sosimo stops, pulling the circlet off Ryder's head.

"Did you feel anything?" Sosimo asks.

Ryder blinks and looks around as if the world were foreign to him. He shakes his head. "No. What's it supposed to feel like again?"

"I can only explain it so many times," Sosimo says. "Let's try again. You'll get it eventually." Sosimo puts the circlet on Ryder's head and continues what he was doing earlier.

"I don't understand why it's so hard for them," Nero whispers to Iona.

"So could you really use Aether?" *Maybe he was telling the truth…*

Nero dips his head. "Yeah, but something's wrong. I've tried more, but I don't feel the same. It's like I can only use it sometimes." He looks at Iona. "Maybe you should try."

"What? I can't use Aether. I've never absorbed an entity."

"I'm not so sure. I have a feeling that you might be able to."

"How?"

"It just seems like you should be able to. Let's just try. I'll be right back." Nero hobbles on his sore ankle to the Artifact rack and grabs an Artifact like the spherical one Sosimo is using with the other children. He comes back and sits next to Iona. "Your essence is like another body part. Once you can feel it, you can move it just like your arm or leg. It's just a matter of recognizing its presence. Are you ready to try?"

Wow, it really seems like he knows what he's talking about. Iona nods.

"Okay, close your eyes. Take some deep breaths and try to relax." Nero moves to his knees, picking up her hand.

She feels a slight tickle in her hand that steadily grows stronger. *What is that?* Suddenly it disappears, and she feels a strange snap of something rushing back to her hand.

"Woo, what did you do?" Iona asks, opening her eyes.

Nero smiles and shows her the little sphere. "This thing somehow pulls at your essence. It's weird, but I can use it to stretch your essence a little from your body. Then, if I jerk it away, your essence snaps back, which I was hoping you could feel."

"I could! How did you know to do this?"

Nero shrugs. "I just can see things differently. It's hard to explain. It's like a whole world of light. Let's try again."

Nero repeats the process a few more times until the sensation in Iona's hand becomes stronger.

"So that's your essence you're feeling," Nero says. "Do you feel a tension or something in it when you relax?"

Iona closes her eyes and relaxes, focusing only on the new feelings. Everything just feels right. "I don't think so," she says. "Why?"

Nero shakes his head. "Just curious. It's nothing. I want you to try to make your essence respond now. Pretend your essence is just another part of you and push it out of your hand into the world."

Iona closes her eyes, pushing against what she thinks is her essence. It responds, but not by much. "I'm not sure I'm doing it right," she says. "I barely feel anything."

"No, you're doing it right. You just need to do it more." Nero brushes his hand over his head, looking to the side with an unfocused stare. He smiles. "I have an idea." He hobbles back over to the Artifact rack. After a moment, he selects a pendant on a gold chain, then kneels next to Iona. "Now, try again."

Iona closes her eyes and tries again, this time when she feels something respond, she also feels it get pushed back into her leg. "What was that?"

"Your essence was just barely coming out of your leg. Since this pendant has Aether, I used it to push against your essence a bit, hoping you would feel it. Did it work?"

"It did! It was weird."

"Okay, go again."

They continue, and as Nero pushes her essence back, it becomes easier for her to push it out. They do it until she can easily push her essence from any part of her body.

"You're getting it, Iona. Nice job. Are you up to try to move it now?"

"Yeah! How do I do that?"

"Do the same thing, but now you need to feel the pendant with your essence. Once you get that down, you should be able to move it. Just give it a shot."

She closes her eyes, reaching out for the pendant. There is a strange snag. As she pokes it, the pendant begins to feel more tangible. She pushes it.

"You moved it!" Nero gasps. He is smiling when she opens her eyes.

"I can use Aether!"

"I knew you could."

Iona jumps up. "I'm going to show the others. Maybe I can train with them now." In her excitement, she fails to notice the smile fall from Nero's face. She grabs the pendant, hurrying over to the others. "Sosimo, I can use Aether!"

"Really? But I thought you never absorbed an entity," Sosimo says.

"I know. Or at least I don't remember. Maybe I absorbed one when I was little?"

"Perhaps, that would explain why you were so hesitant to go for one in the mountains. I've heard of a ceremony by a group of Humans called the Daynin to force young children to absorb essence; it doesn't sound gentle. It could have been a traumatizing experience."

Am I Daynin? "Where do they live?"

"They lived all over the world, but I believe most of them integrated into society a long time ago. Maybe your parents had a similar belief. Maybe you absorbed one by accident. There are an endless number of possibilities... I'm not sure you'll ever find out." Sosimo thinks to himself for a moment, putting a new toothpick in his mouth. "Are you going to show me what you can do?"

Iona hands him the pendant, which he looks at curiously. She closes her eyes and again pushes against it with her essence.

"Wow, great. It looks like you can train with us now," Sosimo says.

Ryder throws his arm around Iona. "Awesome."

"What made you pick this Icor Amulet?" Sosimo asks.

"Oh, it wasn't me. Nero grabbed it." She looks over to where they were seated. Nero is gone. Her heart drops.

16 Taunting

Nero

Nero finally slows from a gimpy jog with a heavy heart. Memories of the dream that woke him still cling to him.

Just when I thought I had a friend, I'm ditched again. He reaches the park and wanders along the empty paths, head down. A fall breeze rustles the leaves in the trees. *This might be a good place to die. Maybe they would think about me then.*

You don't mean that.

Nero looks around. *Maybe I do.*

Then you're being stupid.

Jeez... He throws up his hands. *I'm going crazy, and my imaginary friend isn't even nice to me.* "Why don't you keep your comments to yourself?"

Fine.

Nero shakes his head. *When will anything good ever happen to me?* Just out of the corner of his eye, behind a thick clump of trees, he sees a strange light. *Again? This is the third time I've seen it here.*

He runs over to the trees and sees a violet entity, similar to the one in the back of Fae's house but darker in color; orange, red, and yellow light swirls from within. He tentatively walks toward it. It slowly moves away. *Well, at least it's not attacking me like the green one in the mountains.*

Nero shifts his perspective to see Aether. Instantly, he is overwhelmed by an intense energy. *Wow, it must be strong! Maybe I can absorb this one!*

Nero lunges after the entity and it dodges him easily, zipping off behind some trees. He runs after it, chasing it through sections of thick growth. He comes close to touching it a few times, but it is always a fingernail's length away. A large root catches his foot, sending him crashing down. He lies on his back, unmoving. *I can't do anything right!* Before he knows it, tears are welling up in his eyes and he sobs. *I'll always be alone.*

After his tears run out and his head starts to hurt, he uncovers his face. The entity, which is now a lighter violet and has less swirling light coruscating from its core, is just off to the side. It is close. He reaches out for it, feeling a gentle, tingling warmth; not the same surge of power he felt when he was at the hideout with the canisters. The entity dissipates into nothing.

Did I absorb it? Nero looks at his arm. When he shifts his perspective, it looks exactly the same. *Still nothing. But what the heck happened? And why did it come to me?* He jumps up. *Maybe Sosimo will know.*

*****

Nero hides around the corner as Iona and the other children leave the training room. When Sosimo is alone, he pops out.

"Hi Sosimo. Can I ask you a question?"

"Of course." Sosimo pulls out a toothpick from his little container to chew on.

"I was wondering about entities. Do they think?"

"As I said back in the mountains, they don't really think. They only react to their environment. Similar to jellyfish in the ocean. Do you know what those are?" Nero shakes his head. "A jellyfish is a primal creature that has a very simple nervous system. To train it to do something would be impossible."

"So, it wouldn't come up to you if you were feeling sad or something?" Nero asks.

Sosimo creases his brow. "That's a strange question. They do react to emotions, but I doubt they would approach someone."

"So, if I were chasing one, would it hide behind trees?"

"No, I think that would require some sort of reasoning."

Well the violet one did. Could it be smart? Next time I find it, I should test it. "Are there different types of entities?"

"An entity is an entity. Aside from their Aether abilities, they're all the same," Sosimo says. "There are different types of essences, though, such as spirits and demons."

Nero frowns. "Spirits and demons are real?"

Sosimo nods. "Any essence that comes from a living creature is called a Vitaya. Generally, these will absorb back into the World Essence if they aren't taken or trapped. Sometimes, a person's or creature's will to live is so strong that when they die their essence resists the pull of the World Essence. They create their own protective shell. That's what you'd call a spirit. Occasionally they're powerful enough to possess living things, in which case they're called demons." Nero's face melts into horror. "You shouldn't worry about demons. They're pretty much fantasy. And spirits are few and far between. The best places to find spirits are at the Corusnigmas. Do you know what those are?"

"I've heard the name before but… not really."

"Some people think they're the original sources of the different Aether casts, but no one really knows. The Aether concentration around them is beyond any other location in the world."

Could it be a spirit? "Do spirits look like the entity we saw in the mountains?"

"No. Spirits usually take on a rough shape of their living form. They're generally confused. Part of them still thinks they're alive."

Doesn't sound like a spirit. "Are there any free entities in Kiats?"

Sosimo shakes his head. "I doubt it, someone would have captured it and used it in an artifact by now."

"What if I were to find one?"

"You're not going to find a free entity in Kiats. I'm sorry. Are you feeling left out because you can't train with the others?"

Nero looks down. "What's wrong with me? Why can't I absorb entities?"

"Keep your head up, Nero. You're always welcome to stay and practice with us even though you can't use Aether. We'll find something for you to do."

"Okay…"

"I think I have something that might be interesting to you."

Nero looks up. "What?"

"Follow me." Sosimo leads Nero to his private study and pulls a thin leather rope out of his desk drawer. The medallion hanging from it has a dark wooden center surrounded by lighter wood. It is covered in strange flowing carvings. "This was given to me many years ago. I believe it has some sort of mental Aether, but I've never been able to figure out what exactly it does. Since the other children can use Aether, maybe you should have your own Artifact. Would you hold on to it for me for a while?"

Nero shifts his perspective. He sees a pulsing green glow of Aether encompassing the entire medallion. While he watches, the dominant green glow abates and a darker green, swirling Aether is visible for an instant.

"Are you sure?" He asks. "It seems so nice."

"Yes." Sosimo pushes the medallion toward him. "Put it on."

Nero puts it around his neck, tracing the carvings with his finger. "Thanks."

"Let's get ready for dinner." He scoots Nero along.

*****

The next morning, Nero jogs to the park, reviewing his plans. He walks down the paths to the deeper parts of the park. When he is alone, he shifts his perspective. A faint trail of violet light reveals itself. After following the trail for a few minutes, he sees the entity off the path, in the thick trees and growth.

Yes! Nero jumps up and runs. *Whoa.* He catches himself. *Easy. I need to do my first test. If it's like a jellyfish, then I should be able to walk up to it calmly without scaring it away.*

He slowly walks through the growth toward the entity, trying to calm his breathing. He comes within arm's reach, and the entity has not moved. Nero moves a little bit closer, circling the entity. He slowly moves his hand toward it. The warmth tickles his skin.

Nero's shoulders drop. *Check one for stupid. It didn't even move. Maybe there's a chance I can still train it... Let's see if I can get it to change colors.*

Nero pulls out three colored cards: red, yellow, and blue. He holds the yellow card up to the entity. Nothing happens. *Great, this is going to be a waste.*

He holds up the red card and again, nothing happens. "Change colors!" *How do I demonstrate?* A thought brings a smile to his lips.

He holds the red card next to his face, holding his breath and forcing the blood to his head until his face turns red. The entity does the same.

Nero jumps up. "Yes!" The entity shrinks away and Nero calms himself.

He holds up the yellow card, and the entity turns yellow. It changes colors for the blue card as well. He holds up two cards at the same time and each side of the entity changes color to match the cards on either side: half red and half blue.

This is good! That's kind of like training it... maybe one more step.

Nero holds up one finger and the red card. Then he holds up two fingers and the yellow card. Finally, he holds up three fingers followed by the blue card. He continues this until the entity changes colors by just following his fingers.

Alright, one last test. Maybe I can get it to change to red and blue, like I did with the two cards.

He holds up a one with his left hand and a three with his right hand. The entity turns purple.

Nero throws up his hands. "Check two for stupid. Where did purple come from? You're just a jellyfish."

A bolt of energy shoots out from the Entity and hits Nero's foot.

"Ow! What the crap!" Nero jumps on one leg as numbness swallows his foot. *That hurts. Maybe it reacted to my frustration. I'll have to ask Sosimo about entities attacking.* He turns around to leave and immediately is zapped in the butt. "Ow!" Nero grabs a rock. Before he can throw it, the Entity zaps his hand. He drops the rock, thrusting his hand between his knees to relieve the pain. *Oh my gosh, that stings... Think jellyfish. If I stay calm, I can walk up to it and whack it!*

He takes a few deep breaths. The numbness fades. With a stick in hand, he takes one step forward and gets zapped. He jumps like a scared cat, running away. *Alright, this mist is going down!*

*****

In the early morning of the following day, Nero walks down the street to the park.

"Off to war, young one?" An old Borukin sweeps the front of a shop as Nero passes. Nero dips his head, avoiding eye contact. "Let Marks bring you fortune with your breakfast," the Borukin says with a chuckle. His greying, disheveled braids bounce around his head.

Moments later, Nero sees an especially large Borukin with white tattoos on his face and arms. He is walking with a young Borukin girl with braided hair. Nero changes direction, hurrying along to avoid further interaction. The colander-helmet bounces against his forehead and the cooking sheets tied around his chest rub awkwardly when he hurries. At the park, he sets down the trashcan lid and broomstick. In his thick leather gloves, he fumbles to tighten oversized hiking boots. He checks the layers of towels wrapped around his arms and legs, then heads into the park.

He strides purposeful and proud. *When I slay this evil, pink, zapping Entity, I will be a hero!*

Once again, the Aether trail leads him to the Entity. It flickers in brightness and color, settling to a dark violet as Nero continues to approach.

You're going down!

The Entity shoots a bolt of energy at Nero, who pulls up his trashcan lid to block. The lid violently vibrates, shooting pain all the way up to his shoulder. He hides behind a tree for cover.

Holy moly, that hurts! It must be zapping me harder today. It must be an evil entity, for sure.

He takes a deep breath and jumps from behind the tree. Immediately he dodges more bolts of energy, running from one tree to the next to get closer. When he has no other option, he blocks the Aether with the lid. After a second hit, his arm is throbbing in an unbearable pain that forces him to hide for a few moments.

He continues to fight, but no matter how quickly he moves, he is always forced to hide before he can get within striking distance.

He slams his back against a tree, catching his breath. The baking sheets on his chest and back have smoking holes in them. The trashcan lid is in worse shape, and the towels wrapped around his stick arm are charred. *It's going for my sword side, where I don't have my shield... smart. Maybe if I run straight at it, I'll take it by surprise and I only have to block one zap. That would let me get close enough.*

Nero dives out from the tree, charging the Entity. The first two bolts of energy zip over his head. At point blank range, he blocks an attack with the lid, temporarily knocking him off balance. It takes him two steps to center himself before he makes a wild jump, broomstick raised above his head. The Entity has long-since moved.

Nero's swing goes wide and throws him forward, leaving his broom side completely exposed. He senses the Entity's imminent attack, desperately throwing his broom up to block. The stick takes the attack, and Nero rolls over his shoulder. He lands in a three-point stance, swinging the trashcan lid around in anticipation of another attack. The stick vibrates softly in his hand while he takes deep breaths.

The Entity just flickers in brightness and color. *What the heck is it doing?* It dissolves into nothing.

Nero's heart suddenly jumps to his throat as he notices Illi has made significant amount of progress toward day. *What time is it? I'm going to be late for Sosimo's morning exercise!*

*****

Back in his normal clothes and breathing hard, Nero stumbles into the exercise area as Sosimo is just finishing leading the other children through their morning Roroonki exercises. They all look at him oddly.

Later, as the children are heading out, Iona stops by Nero. "I haven't talked to you in the last couple weeks. Are you mad at me?"

For leaving me? "No." Nero looks over to Sosimo, who is waiting. "I think Sosimo wants to talk with me."

"Okay, I'll talk to you later."

"'Kay." Nero walks away.

"I know you feel left out, and I respect the fact that you want to do your own training, but I want you to do these exercises with us. There's no reason you can't."

Nero nods. "I really meant to come back, I just lost track of time."

"I expect you to be here tomorrow morning." Sosimo turns to leave.

"Hey, Sosimo. Can I ask you another question?"

"Is this another strange one?"

"Uh, maybe"

"Well, at least it'll be interesting."

"Remember how you were telling us about the Games? Is there an event where they block Aether or something?"

"There is. It's called the Trial of Odosa. The competitors block attacks from an Aether-canon the size of Gracie. It's very impressive. What do you want to know?"

"Oh, cool. Do they use a metal shield or something?"

"No, of course not. That would be a horrible idea," Sosimo says. Nero's face grows warm with embarrassment. "Aether flows through materials differently than normal energy. A metal is the worst choice." Sosimo points to the wooden weapons hanging on the wall. "They use styks such as those, which provides a medium for Borukins to interact and store Aether."

Holy cow! That's why it didn't hurt when the Entity attacked my stick... Did it know?

"Blocking and deflecting Aether attacks is a Borukin-specific skill called Odo. It is an important part of our culture and who we are. Very few races could match the skill of even a young Borukin in this. Why are you curious? Would you be interested in going to the Games if I take you?"

"Yes, that would be fun," Nero says, smiling.

Sosimo nods. "I'll keep that in mind. Now, let's get to work. We have candy to make."

*****

"Hmmm, either you wised up or someone's baking cookies at home." The old Borukin is once again sweeping the front of his store in the early morning.

Nero dips his head, quickening his pace. He only carries the broken broomstick. *Why didn't I go another way?*

Nero hurries past an old, light skinned woman in a full-length, layered garment. The sturdy old woman looks into his eyes and smiles.

Nero yanks his gaze away, hurrying into the depths of the park. *Jeez, that was creepy... Now, where is this Entity? It's really going down today!*

It takes him just a moment to track it down. Again, the Entity flickers in brightness and then settles to a darker violet when Nero gets close.

I hope that means it's scared...

The Entity shoots a bolt of energy and Nero rolls to the side. He closes the distance, diving behind a tree as sparks shower down over his head.

Alright. I just need to block the crazy-fast lightning with this little broomstick before it melts my face off. He takes a quick breath. *Here goes nothing.*

He pops out from behind the tree. When the Entity attacks, he whips the stick up with his eyes closed. He feels an impact on the stick and jumps back to safety. The broomstick vibrates with energy. He naturally pushes against it and the vibrations settle.

Ah-ha! It worked!

He runs out from the tree, charging. A few bolts fly over his head. He rolls out of the way of a third, landing on his feet and easily blocking a final bolt with the stick. Nero slashes right through the Entity, tearing it in two. Light and mist shower to the ground.

"I got it!" He holds up the vibrating stick in triumph. "I vanquished the evil..." Nero looks around. He is alone. His shoulders sag and his arms drop to his sides. *So, right when I kinda make a friend, I kill it... wonderful.*

Suddenly, his butt is searing, and he jumps high off the ground. He lands on his feet with his hand covering the painful spot. He spins around. The violet Entity flickers with brightness. "Cheap shot," Nero yells.

The Entity shoots him again. Nero barely blocks it, dodging quickly behind a tree. He rubs his numb bottom. *I guess I'm just going to have to do better!* Nero smiles to himself and charges the Entity.

17 A Stolen Dagger

Nero

Nero blocks two quick attacks from the Entity. It is just a meter away before it suddenly falls apart. He inhales several times, charred broomstick ready. His breath is just barely visible in the cool winter morning. *Where did it go?*

He shifts his perspective to see the violet glow dissipate into the surroundings. Nero hears rustling from behind him. He spins around. The bright red, Aether glow of a person is running away.

He switches his perspective back to see a woman in brown. Soon, she is lost in the park. *What was that?* He runs forward to get a better look, stumbling on a golden glittering object in the grass. He drops his broomstick, picking up a long dagger. The engraved, dark wooden sheath is inlaid with gold and precious stones of green and red.

The handle is made from the same wood as the sheath, light grain running along its length. He pulls the dagger out, revealing a dark, double-edged blade. The triangles cut into its length are large near the base and smaller at the tip. He shifts his perspective to see a gentle pulsing red glow along the length of the sheath. There is a slight green glow between his fingers from the handle. When he slides the blade back in the sheath and removes his hands, green lines of Aether cling to his hand, as if the handle were covered in sticky slime. Eventually, the lines of Aether break. Green tentacles from the handle reach out for his hand.

Oh that's creepy. The tentacles sway like grass in the ocean as he moves his hand back and forth. *This is weird. It's like they're alive and drawn to me. What are they?*

Suddenly, there is an iron grip around his wrist. The dagger is ripped from his hand.

The old Borukin Nero had seen sweeping in the mornings, glares at him with a stare of death. "You two-handed, white-skinned,   sorry-excuse-for-something-that-uses-oxygen, thief!" He says between deep breaths.

"What?" Nero yells, partially from pain and partially from surprise. "I didn't steal anything."

The man turns, yanking Nero's arm with him. Nero resists, but the old man's strength is unyielding.

"Thought you could take advantage of an old man? Obviously, your Human brain didn't account for the speed of a well-ripened Borukin! I was right behind you the whole time."

Nero stumbles along. "I don't know what you're talking about! I just found it on the ground." Nero's tears and panic start to build.

The old man walks with a slight limp. "Save your lies for the police. You'll be in jail until you get arthritis."

"I didn't do anything wrong," Nero barely squeezes out. Tears trickle down both of his cheeks.

The Borukin drags Nero the rest of the way to his shop in silence. Inside, he throws Nero on a chair next to a phone. The medallion on Nero's neck jumps, catching the man's eye.

"Did you steal that, too?" The man grabs the medallion.

Nero fights with the old man, but is unable to stop him from pulling the necklace over his head.

Nero's head drops. "I didn't steal anything," he says between sobs.

The old man hesitates, picking up the phone. "Where'd you get this, then?"

"Sosimo gave it to me. The candy maker."

"Ha! Sosimo, the candy maker? You might as well call him Sosimo the rock trainer for the waste of talent he is." The man shakes his head. "There's no reason he would give a little rascal like you this medallion."

"But he did!"

"Well, let's see what Sosimo has to say about that." The man looks Nero directly in the eyes. "Don't think about doing anything funny. Or anything at all. Just sit there and breathe. If you must." He dials. "Hi, Sosimo. It's Saraf."

Saraf frowns. "What? No, I'm not getting needy. This is about something else. Do you know a small child, Human—I think—light hair, really skinny, cries a lot?"

"Oh, yeah?" Saraf covers the phone with his hand, looking at Nero. "What's your name, boy?"

"Nero."

Saraf's shoulders droop. He moves his hand from the phone. "Yeah, it's him. Did you give him the medallion I gave to you?"

"Well, I found him in the park with Kormick's dagger."

"That's what I think, but he says he just found it."

"You trust him? Are you sure he hasn't stolen anything from you?"

"Of course I saw the thief. I'm not getting that old."

"The one that took the dagger was dressed in brown. If I had to guess, she was a she and definitely not Borukin."

"No, the boy doesn't fit the description. I didn't say I saw him take it."

"Well, then, yeah. His story could check out. But why would she drop the dagger?"

"Errrr… or more likely she saw me coming." He lets out a sigh. "Okay fine, I'll let him go."

Relief washes over Nero. He fills his lungs with air, wiping the tears away. Saraf's shop is bursting with Artifacts. They cover the walls, shelves, and display cases. When Nero shifts his perspective, he is overwhelmed by light of every color. It shines as if the place were on fire. *Holy cow, this is incredible!* Without thinking, he hops off his chair, moving toward an especially bright glow from a display case in the back of the shop.

Saraf eyes Nero, still talking on the phone. "Are these kids with that catalyst thingy you're helping out?"

"No? Well, pardon me. Why didn't you tell me about them?"

Saraf shakes his head. "And I don't approve. Though, you do seem a bit more manageable lately…"

"You don't need to keep asking. I already said I would help even though you're going to be rustier than a sunken ship and I'm going to have to do everything."

Saraf glances again at Nero, who is examining the Artifacts. "Okay, well I need to go, Sosimo. Goodbye."

"Hey," Saraf snaps. "I said you were only allowed to breathe. What are you doing, moving around?"

"I thought that was only because I was in trouble."

"And you think you're not in trouble anymore?"

Nero looks about. "Am I?"

"Not yet."

Nero turns back to the Artifacts, sticking his nose on the display case. They are more impressive than any Artifact he has ever seen. Most of them radiate blue, while others are green or red. One has an orange glow. Nero lets his vision switch back to normal. He sees the artifacts as crystal rods, gloves, bracers, bracelets, and necklaces.

"Take your greasy nose off my case," Saraf says. He palms Nero's head, moving him away. "Do you have any idea how hard it is to keep this place clean?" Saraf rubs the glass with his shirt.

"Your Artifacts are amazing! They're way better than Sosimo's. Where did you get them?"

"Ha! Sosimo hasn't showed you the good stuff then. He was my most promising student."

"For doing what?"

"For making Artifacts. Has he not told you? Do you think people just gave these to me because I'm nice? Do I seem nice to you? No. I made them. Most of them, anyway."

"You did?" Nero asks, disbelieving.

"What? You don't think an old but surprisingly good-looking Borukin such as myself could make Artifacts?"

"I never said you were good-looking."

"I know. I'm just saying that for an old guy, I'm not too hard on the eyes."

"You *are* pretty old-looking," Nero says.

"Are you trying to get on my bad side?"

"No, sorry. What I meant is—I didn't think I'd ever meet a person that could make artifacts. They're incredible. What do all these do?" Nero sticks his nose against the case again, pointing inside.

"Will you stop it with the nose?" Saraf pulls back Nero's head and rubs the display with his shirt again.

"Sorry! What do they do?" *So many different types…*

"More than a feeble Human brain could understand." Saraf turns Nero around, pushing him away. "I'm saving you the headache."

"Please! I have a good brain. I promise."

"I'm sure you do."

I can't leave. I may never get another chance to see these. Nero sits on the ground. "I'm not moving unless you show me one. You'll have to carry me out."

Saraf looks down at him, frowning. "I took a poop bigger than you this morning. Carrying you shouldn't be a problem."

Nero rises to his knees. He clasps his hands together. "Please, sir, just show me one."

A shiver runs through Saraf's body. "Ooh, I'll do it as long as you don't use that word again."

Nero hops up and sticks his finger on the glass, pointing to a bracelet.

Saraf holds out his arms, looking at Nero's finger like he was just insulted.

Nero pulls back his finger, wiping the glass with his dirty shirt. It only smears more grease around. "Oh, sorry."

Saraf shakes his head. "Just leave it." He fumbles in his pocket for a set of keys. "Sosimo made this bracelet a long time ago. It's very impressive." He looks at Nero seriously. "Don't you dare tell him I said that."

Nero shakes his head solemnly. "I won't."

"Good. Are you ready?"

Nero nods, shifting his perspective. Saraf's body swirls with blue and red interwoven Aether. Many details of his face are still visible, completely different from the obscuring bright red glow from the Woman at Blue Horin. As Saraf reaches for the bracelet, the green tentacles fanning from it dive into his hand. Green veins of light crawl throughout his body. His natural glow dims. Nero jumps, letting his perspective shift back to normal.

Saraf is gone. Nero shifts his perspective once again. Saraf's glowing body is walking away. Suddenly the green veins in Saraf's body dim and his normal glow returns.

Saraf jumps at Nero. "Boo! Bwahaha. Did I scare you?" Saraf frowns. "You don't seem so surprised."

"What happened?"

"What do you mean, what happened? I was invisible. Well, not truly invisible. This spiffy little bracelet discombobulates your brain waves, so they can't perceive my presence. The downfall is, it drains energy faster than trying to dig up your grandma's grave to get an Amulet she promised you but didn't write in her will before the keep catches you…" Saraf says as his breath runs out. He lets out a nervous laugh.

"Is the handle of the dagger I found an invisibility talisman too?"

Saraf's eyebrows rise. "It uses the same cast of Aether, but it's a speed and strength talisman instead. Why did you ask that?"

"They both have those strange tentacle thingies coming out of them."

"Tentacle thingies? Did we change topics?"

"I don't know how to explain them, it's something I feel and see, I guess... They're kinda like—green tentacles—" Nero wiggles his fingers, looking at Saraf, uneasy. "When you touched it, the tentacles went into your hand and spread green lines of glowing light through your own blue and red glow. That scared me because when I looked for you, you were gone. When I focused, though, I saw your glow and brighter green lines."

"Red lights, green lights, tentacles... The only tentacles I can imagine are the ones mucking with your brain."

"I'm not making it up. All these Artifacts have different colors and stuff."

"Uh-huh. Whatever you say, kiddo."

"Why doesn't anyone ever believe me?"

Saraf looks at Nero for a moment. "You did recognize the handle and the bracelet. How about I give you a challenge to prove what you say?"

"What type of challenge?"

"A challenge to the death!" Saraf says with both hands open toward Nero.

"What?" Nero looks at Saraf in shock.

Saraf drops his arm. "Okay, fine, I can see you're not really into that. It doesn't have to be to the death—unless you do something completely unexpected."

Nero eyes Saraf. "What's your challenge?"

Saraf rubs his hands together. "Oh, excellent, excellent." He starts to pull artifacts from different shelves. He places them on a glass top table, prancing as he goes. "This will be a challenge of legendary dimensions." When he collects a satisfying pile, he stands next to them with a serious face, arms crossed.

"Are you ready?" Nero asks.

Saraf gives him a curt nod.

"What do you want me to do?"

"Sort," Saraf says with a quick point to the pile and crosses his arms again.

Nero frowns at Saraf, approaching the pile of Artifacts. *I could sort them by bracelets, necklaces, gloves… maybe by Aether!* He shifts his perspective. The pile glows with three different colors of light. Some of them are pulsing, some have a solid glow, and others have the weird tentacles.

Nero separates first by color, then by the type of light they emit. In the end he has rows of blue, red, and green separated into columns with solid lights, pulsing lights, and tentacle lights. All the while touching the tentacles as little as possible.

Nero stands back. "How's that?"

Saraf looks at the grid. "Holy mother of pearl. You separated them by cast and type."

"What does that mean?"

Saraf's jaw nearly hits the ground. "How can you ask that, after you've sorted them?"

"I'm trying to tell you! I just did it by color and glowiness. Sosimo hasn't taught us Artifacts yet."

Saraf raises an eyebrow, scratching his chin. "Hm, curious. It's as though you can see Aether as if it has different colors."

"That's what I've been trying to say." Nero throws up his hands. "Wasn't the point of the challenge to prove that I wasn't making stuff up?"

Saraf continues to scratch his chin. "A challenge to prove that you're not making stuff up… Good idea. I'll have to think on that."

"What? Are you okay?"

Saraf shakes his head. "Oh, yes, thanks for asking. How are you?"

"O—kay?"

Saraf pats Nero on the head. "Don't beat yourself up. It's your feeble Human brain."

Nero looks at Saraf, blinking repeatedly. "So, what are the different types of Artifacts?"

"Ah, yes, Artifacts. My favorite topic," Saraf says. "Well, there are four main branches of Artifacts. Capsents store Aether. Those are in your first column. Tursents convert Aether to a different form of energy—your second column. Sorbsents pull Aether from the user. Those are in your third column."

"You said four."

"Oh, and Carcerasents trap an essence and allow the owner of the Artifact to bring the essence into the world and control it... Borukins don't mess with those though. The mental bond they require is dangerous and it's no better than slavery."

"What do the rows mean?"

Saraf stares down at Nero. A smile creeps across his face. "How about this, Mr. Fancy-pants. Come work for me. I have a feeling I'll be able to use your little talent. Then, I'll answer all the questions that spill out of that little brain of yours. Deal?"

"What about Sosimo and the candy store? He needs me to help him there."

Saraf waves his hand. "Pfft. Making candy isn't complicated. Crush some beans, add some sugar, do a little dance... I'll talk with him." Saraf pulls Nero's medallion out of his pocket. "Here's this back. Sorry I took it from you."

"It's okay."

"Good. I'll see you tomorrow. My name is Saraf, by the way. What were your parents thinking when they named you after a maniac that nearly destroyed an entire civilization?"

"He fought to save his family! Nero was a hero."

"I'm sure that's the Human's version of it... Did it mention how his lust for power consumed him like so many Humans before? Doesn't seem like such a great idol to me."

Nero looks down.

"I'm sorry—that was a bit over the top, even for me. Just make sure you wear that name as yourself, not the one who's name you took." Saraf pats Nero on the back and Nero lifts his shoulders a little. "Now, get out of here. And don't be late tomorrow morning." Nero begins to walk out. "And make sure to wash your greasy nose!"

*****

"It seems that Saraf has taken an interest in you," Sosimo says guiding Nero into the training room. "Many Borukins would be grateful to have a chance to work with him. Count yourself lucky."

"Really? He seems a bit odd. What's wrong with him?"

"He's eccentric. He used to be the Obsentsan Overseer, which is an Artifact maker of the highest degree. Then he realized he wasn't happy, so he decided to relinquish the title and loosen up... which allowed his oddities to come out in full bloom, as you probably saw yesterday. Just don't let him fool you. He's incredibly smart."

"His Artifacts were all really amazing. I couldn't believe he made them," Nero says. "He said he taught you to make Artifacts. Is that true?"

Sosimo looks down. "It's been a long time since I've made one. Maybe too long. I'm thinking it's time to start again."

"Why did you stop?"

"It's in the past. I don't wish to talk about it." Sosimo takes a deep breath, looking at Nero. "So, Saraf tells me you have an incredible sense for Aether."

"I guess."

"Modesty's a good trait. Unfortunately, if you don't know the first thing about Artifacts, I'll never hear the end of it. We'll have private lessons every few nights. Are you ready to learn?"

"I think so," Nero says. Sosimo looks at him, waiting. "Yes?"

"Better. We'll work on that."

18 A Disappointing Purchase

Nero

Nero slips out of bed and into his clothes. Illi is just beginning to break the night's hold on the sky. He sneaks out of his room and down the hallway. Thea is on the stairs.

She turns toward him. He freezes. "What are you doing, Nero?"

"Nothing... what are you doing?"

Thea looks down. "I had another bad dream. At least, I think that's what it was. I just know it didn't feel good."

Nero sits next to her on the stairs. "How long have you had them?"

"They started when we ran away. Sometimes they're not so bad, but sometimes they wake me up."

"I'm sorry. Remember it's only a dream. It can't hurt you, no matter how horrible it is."

Thea nods. "It just felt so real. I was talking to a man that wanted me to run away so that I could help him. I wanted to, even though something about it felt wrong..." They sit in silence for a while. Thea turns to him. "You haven't been around much. I miss hanging out with you. What have you been up to?"

"I don't know. Stuff."

"Yeah, but what do you do in the mornings? I always hear you coming back before our morning exercise and you act different."

"Uh… I just kinda go to the park… and run around a bit…"

"Could I come?"

"Uh…" Nero looks down. *Would it show up if she were with me?* "It's not really that fun. It's something I like to do just by myself."

"Okay," Thea says with a tinge of hurt. She stands up, walking back to her room.

Maybe I should have said yes… It takes him a moment to collect himself before he leaves.

*****

Nero runs through the park, grabbing the broomstick that he dropped the day before. No sooner does he have it in his hand than a bolt of energy zips over his head. He blocks the second and third bolts, and rolls out of the way of a fourth. He kneels behind a tree. The broomstick vibrates gently in his hand.

This must be Aether. Could I use it? He shifts his perspective and sees that the stick is glowing green. He notices that he is subconsciously pushing against the Aether in the stick. He relaxes. The vibrations increase slightly. A tingling flows through his hand, up his arm, and under his scalp, invigorating him. He leaps out from behind the tree with an excitement that carries him well past his balance and he tumbles. The Entity is flickering.

What are you flickering about? "Think that's funny?"

Nero leaps after the Entity and they begin to spar at a higher level than ever before. The Entity easily matches Nero's new speed and strength.

*****

After Nero's exercise with Sosimo, he hurries back to Saraf's, exhausted. When he arrives, Saraf is showing out the Borukin man and girl that Nero has seen before. The girl walks away without paying Nero any mind. The man with the white tattoos on his face looks at Nero briefly before he follows.

Saraf beckons Nero in. "You're breathing awfully hard, boy. Are you sickly?"

"I just ran so I wouldn't be late. Who were those two?"

"That was Grebson and Natina. A few times a week I train her in secret before the shop opens."

"Why?"

"The King doesn't believe his daughter needs to know about Odo."

"Her dad's the King?"

"If she's the daughter of the King, that would make the King her dad. And the daughter of the King is usually a princess... so, maybe you can deduce what that means."

"She doesn't look like a princess."

Saraf smiles. "That is exactly why I like her. She has a good brain," Saraf says, ruffling Nero's hair. He stops, looking at Nero sternly. "I'm trusting you with this information. Don't tell anyone. It's not your secret to share, nor is it possible to ensure its safety with another person."

"I won't."

"I hope not." Saraf slaps his hands together. "Now, let's get this pig show started and see what you know." Saraf walks to the middle of his room, holding out his arms. "These are all different kinds of Artifacts. Do you know why Artifacts are important?"

"Because they do cool things?"

Saraf's expression shows shocked disgust. "Because they do cool things? That's the best answer your feeble brain could come up with?" He exhales sharply. "We may be in trouble." Nero deflates, looking down. "Ah, buck up. It's not completely hopeless. Once I get my hands on your brain, there's a chance I can massage some life into it, yet." Saraf's hands massage the air. "So, pay attention. Artifacts are essentially Aether programs. They allow people to use skills they may not have or are not in line with their cast. They're also so easy to use any carrot cake can do it. It's as simple as that. Now that Artifact copies are getting better, Artifacts have become a lot more affordable. Pretty much everyone and their nakok is using them. The downside to Artifacts is they're not as efficient as performing a skill without one. And the skill is limited to the strength of the Artifact."

"Is what makes Artifacts work the same thing that lets people use Aether? Wait! Do artifacts have an essence?"

Saraf throws his hands up. "Yes! Three points for your brain. Count 'em up, all for you. And because Artifacts have an essence, they strengthen with use. Just like people."

"Can any essence be used?"

"Good question. Two more points for your brain! An exciting comeback. All essences are pretty much the same, but there are advantages and disadvantages to using just any essence. There's a race called the Werrin. They are skilled in creating protective, Aether-absorbing Artifacts. It is a common practice for a grandparent to sacrifice their essence on their deathbed so their Vitaya can be used to make an amulet. They tend to be exceptionally powerful—in the hands of their own bloodline."

"Where do they live?"

Saraf slouches. "Minus ten thousand points. Non-Artifact-related question."

Nero frowns. "How do you make Artifacts?"

"With difficulty. Plus one."

"Are you going to show me?"

"Maybe."

Nero looks around. "What would you like me to do?"

"Plus ten," Saraf says with a smile and a pat on the back that nearly knocks Nero over. "Sweeping is the first order of business. Then, you can clean the bats out of my belfry."

"What?"

"Nothing. I'll find you a broom."

*****

Nero walks nervously through the streets, fiddling with the money in his pocket. *I can't believe he sent me by myself! We've always gone together.*

Nero follows the path by memory until he reaches the market. He weaves through the people, stopping at the stand of the traveling merchant Saraf had asked him to look for. The merchant is well tanned and small. He is covered by a thick, travel-worn jacket.

"Come, come! Behold the splendor of my Artifacts and relics. You will find nothing better across all of Majirin and the world. I have traveled from the Gearamonish Archipelago to the Black Ocean of Tyrona. I have been so close to the Tenebrous Miasma that a part of me was lost forever. I labored through many perils to bring you these fine items, and through my travels I've never seen their equal," the merchant yells to the crowd. He points to a board where fancy amulets of gold and precious stones hang. "These come from the land of the Werrin, in Holentor. I gathered them from a Werrin master Obsentsan directly. It pains me to part with them, but for you, my friends, I will endure the suffering!"

Nero squeezes around the shoppers until he manages to reach the display of artifacts. He shifts his perspective and looks at the items. He is first drawn to the display of hanging amulets. They all give off a weak radiance of light. Nero frowns. Of all the pieces, only a talisman attracts Nero's attention. It is still hardly comparable to Saraf's. Nero picks up the talisman, inspecting it further.

The merchant spins on Nero. "Young man! That is a fine piece you're looking at." The merchant snatches it from Nero's hands. "Unfortunately, it is too fine a piece for you to touch, unless you have one-hundred and fifty Anterren."

It doesn't seem so nice... Nero continues to look around. *I hope Saraf doesn't get mad at me if I don't bring anything back.*

At the far end of the stand, he sees a large, gnarled piece of wood covered in dried moss. It is a display for red glowing

Artifacts. He squirms through the people and looks. The red Aether flows into the wood and, just before it fades away, he sees a slight tinge of violet, similar to the fruit he found back in Ferin Forest.

Nero grabs the Merchant's attention. "How much for this wood?"

"Oh, that? That's just for displaying my goods."

"Is it for sale?" Nero asks.

"How much you got?"

Nero pulls out money from his pocket. "I have two-hundred Anterren."

The merchant plucks it from his hand and counts it. "Well, it's not much, especially for a piece that has been with me for as long as I can remember, but since you seem to be partial to it, I'll give you a discount. Deal?"

"Uh, yeah. Thanks."

The merchant clears the display. Nero bear hugs the log off the table and waddles back to Saraf's shop as quickly as he can.

*****

"Stop!" Saraf says just as Nero takes his first step into the shop. "Think carefully before you bring that dirty thing into my shop."

Nero freezes and looks at Saraf. "But this is what I bought."

"I didn't think you had much of a sense of humor, but you got me."

"No, I'm serious. This is the only thing I saw of value at the stand. Well, I think it has value…"

"I didn't know we were into collecting firewood. Did you find a particular likeness to yourself that captured your attention?" Saraf walks up to him, eyeing the wood suspiciously. "And how much did you decide to spend on this?"

"The merchant took everything."

Saraf nearly chokes. "You spent all of the money on this? I was a little worried, but I didn't imagine you'd blow it this badly." Saraf's face turns serious. "What exactly drove you to buy this?"

"I don't know. The Aether reminds me of the Aether from that katshy fruit. I figured it might be worth it." Nero looks down. "I thought that stuff was expensive. I'm sorry."

Saraf's eyebrows come together. "Katashne'n?"

"Yeah, that's it."

"What? Where did you see Katashne'n fruit?"

"By a tree in Ferin Forest."

"Sosimo didn't mention anything of the sort."

"Yeah, I didn't really tell him…"

"Why not?"

"I don't know. I didn't think he'd believe me, and my friend Korbin would have probably made fun of me."

"Doesn't sound like much of a friend." Saraf begins to pick dried moss and dirt from the piece of wood, scattering it all about the floor. Nero looks at the mess in horror. Saraf rubs his thumb against some of the exposed wood then stops. "Nero. This could be Katashne'n wood. Did you know?"

"Uh, that's—"

"Close the shop and throw the sign over the door. We're going to find out for sure."

"But…"

"No buts! I'm as excited as a little schoolgirl, and I have the patience of one as well. Follow me!"

Saraf runs off with the piece of wood over his head to the stairs in back.

The first part of the basement is a training room similar to Sosimo's, with stone walls and a small stationary bicycle in the corner. Saraf grabs the wood and puts it on a side table, below a rack of Artifacts.

"Hop on that bike. Pedal as fast as you can." Saraf runs into the back room.

What the heck's going on? Nero lowers the seat as far as it goes and starts to spin the pedals. They are attached to a chain that turns a strange mechanism: a small box with a handle, sitting at the center of several rotating disks.

Just as a burn develops in Nero's thighs, Saraf runs, grabs the hunk of wood, and disappears again. He pokes his head out a moment later. "Grab the Aether container and bring it here."

Nero shifts his perspective, noticing the small box has a green pulsing glow of Aether. He pulls on the handle, and it comes free.

The next room is a disaster. Different materials and tools are hanging from the walls, strewn about the tables, and stuffed in cabinets that will never be able to close.

"Holy cow. What happened down here?" Nero asks.

"What do you mean? This is my workshop," Saraf says with a smile.

Nero looks around, mouth open. "This place is a disaster. How is that possible? Has Sosimo seen this?"

Saraf frowns. "Just bring me the Aether container."

He puts the container down on the only clear section of table. A wooden container sits open with six crystal spheres resting in individual slots.

"What are we going to do?"

Saraf pats the Aether container. "We're going to use the Aether stored in here to charge the wood." He points to the crystal spheres. "Then, we're going to use those Adter Tursents to check its cast."

"How do we do that?"

"Each one of these crystals is fused with an essence of a different cast. When they contact Aether of the same cast, they glow. You can tell which sphere corresponds to which cast by the symbol etched on them. They are for Pahzan, Icor, Moltrik, Ru, Nesiv, and Biat Aether," Saraf says. He points to each of the crystals in order.

When Nero shifts his perspective, he sees each sphere has a different color emanating from it: red, green, blue, brown, orange, and yellow. "And what do the different Aethers do?"

"Sosimo hasn't taught you this?" Nero shakes his head and Saraf lets out a sigh. "What a slacker. Pahzan Aether allows someone to control the flow of energy, Icor Aether allows someone to interact with organic matter, Moltrik Aether allows someone to control electricity and magnetism, Ru Aether allows someone to manipulate the nuclear forces of atoms, Nesiv Aether allows someone to manipulate spacetime, and Biat Aether allows someone to tinker with essence. Got it?"

"What are nuclear forces? And what is spacetime?"

"What do they teach you kids in school these days?"

"I'm only twelve!"

"That's no excuse. I was doing quantum mechanics when I was still in diapers.

"What's that?"

"Oh, for Stone's sake." Saraf scrambles for a piece of paper and writes some words on it. "Study these things, or next week I'm going to make you and Sosimo do one-thousand pushups."

Nero looks at the list and gulps. It reads:

Thermodynamics, electricity and magnetism (emphasizing electromagnetic radiation), radioactive decay, the strong force, general relativity, and the proper Borukin form for pushups.

"Are you making this stuff up?"

Saraf waves his hand. "Bah. Let's get back on task."

Saraf opens the top of the Aether box, pulling out a flexible cable. Nero sees that it glows with green, pulsing Aether. Saraf touches the end to the wood, and the wood's Aether turns green and brightens while the container's glow lessens. Once Saraf removes the cable, the wood turns to violet.

"The wood takes the Aether from the container and puts its own cast on it. Most organic material has an Icor cast. It's the more exotic materials that have different casts." He puts the cable back and closes the container. "Now, we can test the Aether of the wood. The groovy thing about Katashne'n wood is it works with every cast and it can store an incredible amount of Aether, which makes it very valuable in making artifacts."

It also turned red when the amulets were touching it... "Does that mean each of the ball thingies should glow?"

"Yepper!" Saraf ruffles Nero's hair. "You need to stop being so negative about your feeble brain. It's proving to be decently capable."

The Entity is also violet. Is it the same? "Where do you find entities like this wood?"

"I don't think there is such an entity." He slaps his hands together. "Let's begin." Saraf takes the Pahzan sphere and touches it to the wood. The wood's Aether turns red and the sphere brightens. When Nero lets his perspective go back to normal, he sees the sphere glowing white.

"Alright, good. One down," Saraf says. He grabs the Icor sphere, touching it to the wood. The sphere again glows. When Nero shifts his perspective, the light from the sphere and the wood are both green.

Saraf tests the blue Moltrik, the brown Ru, the orange Nesiv, and the yellow Biat. All of them glow when they contact the wood. Saraf sits back in a chair. "It's Katashne'n wood alright, just covered in so much junk no one paid it any mind." He slaps Nero on the back. "You're impressive."

Nero feels his cheeks begin to glow. "How do you usually tell?"

"Without all the bark and once it's been polished up, it's a dark wood with occasional light grains running down it."

"Is that what's in the handle of that dagger?"

Saraf nods. "It is. That's why I was so angry when I thought you had tried to steal it." Saraf smiles. "Though I'm fortunate life spun its wheels the way it did. Two hundred Anterren for this is an incredible deal. I'll have to find a way to make it up to you."

"Thanks." Nero feels strangely light. "How much is it worth?"

"For a chunk this big? Depending on the quality of the wood under this mess, I would say... a golden shoed donkey... maybe even two for that matter."

19 The Hunt

Isis

Animals scurry away as the quick, heavy pounding of many feet approaches. Figures emerge from the woods, running with an unexpected agility. Their faces are hidden behind full helmets, their bodies are covered by armor, and they each carry an Aether rifle. The tallest one leads the pack.

"Is he alive?" Isis asks through the microphone buried in her helmet. Her breathing gives only the slightest hint of exertion.

"Yes, Ma'am. We took him without serious injury and got him to a medical pod at our field base. He seems quite mad though," Lieutenant Colonel Phillips replies through her earpiece.

"He's a traitor. What would you expect?"

"He's acting like a savage animal. It's hard to explain. We can barely communicate with him."

Isis gracefully leaps over a fallen tree. "How did you capture him? Could he have head trauma?"

"We were patrolling grid Alpha-Charlie thirteen when we came in contact with Uniform-Alpha. He incapacitated two of the squads, and a third is missing. The two traitors, Echo-Alpha and Echo-Bravo, were with him, but they aren't nearly as quick. The slower of the two, Echo-Alpha, sustained several shots to the legs. He was captured. A jumper picked him up shortly after."

"What happened with Echo-Bravo?"

"Before they could engage Echo-Bravo, Echo-Alpha jumped up and started to run. It took three mid-inf to drag him down and chain him. The wounds to the legs hardly bothered him."

"They must've only grazed him."

"No, Ma'am. Two shots hit him right in the meat of his left thigh, and another in his calf. He shouldn't have been walking, let alone running... Excuse me, Ma'am, one moment."

Isis's earpiece goes quiet. She quickens her pace.

A moment later, it pops back to life. "Sorry, Ma'am. You may want to hurry. We just brought Echo-Alpha back from cardiac arrest. The medic doesn't think we'll be able to do it again. Would you like me to send a jumper?"

"Negative. There aren't any landing spots. I'm only two kilometers away. I'll be there in three."

Isis kills the connection with a thought. She pushes herself faster, running through the trees at a dangerous pace toward the green arrow on her visor display. The distance indicator below her target designation rapidly falls off. In under three minutes she reaches the field base, her soldiers following in formation. A mid-infantry soldier, standing outside of a medical pod, flashes green on her display. 'Lt. Co. Phillips' hovers over his head. She acknowledges the visual, causing the glow and designation to disappear from her visor.

Phillips approaches. "It's too late. They revived him a second time, but shortly after, his heart stopped."

Isis sidesteps Phillips and enters the pod. Medics surround a bed that has a sheet draped over a body. "What happened?" she asks.

The medical captain in light infantry gear and a medical insignia on her arm approaches. "We're not sure, Ma'am. It's as if his body just gave up. The wounds on his legs were well tended. He shouldn't have died."

"Was there head trauma?" Isis asks.

"No, Ma'am, not that we could see. But his body was covered by black spots. We checked for disease and did not find a match. I can't say anything for certain."

"Could this be linked to his mental state? Could this explain why he betrayed us?"

"There's no way to tell, out here. We'll have to take him back to the lab and run some tests with the proper equipment."

"Is this an infectious disease we need to take precautions for?"

The captain shakes her head. "I don't think so. We ran blood through the analyzer and I can say with confidence that if it does spread, it's with difficultly. There would need to be perfect conditions, or something else involved."

Isis sends out a command to her squad to set up a holomap. "Alright, Captain, do what you need to do. Get me some answers as soon as possible."

Phillips follows Isis outside, where her squad has assembled a small projector on a tripod. They flip it on, and a green three-dimensional holographic map of the region appears.

"Show me Uniform-Alpha's estimated trail, and highlight our recent contact locations," Isis says. A blue trail, followed by three red blinking pyramids, lights up along the projected mountains. The trail ends at the third pyramid.

"We've been following animal carcasses for more months than I want to count and we're virtually on top of Borukin territory. Every engagement has been on its terms and it's picking us off a few at a time. That's going to change."

"Glad to hear, Ma'am."

"What's the status of the vultures?"

Phillips pulls up his wrist computer. "The two vultures are loitering at twenty-five thousand meters. Each is carrying a smart duster, two SEIBs, three umbrella clusters, and eight RPPDs."

"Primary target," she says, poking the mountains past the last red pyramid. A yellow pyramid pops up that rotates and changes in size. "Considering its path so far, we should expect our primary target to be in this area. I'm going to take my unit and another platoon of mid-infantry and set up here." She indicates an area ahead of the yellow pyramid in the valley of the mountains. "Phillips, I want you to position everyone else on the opposite side of the target from me. You need to form a line so tight mice can't slip through. Comb down the mountain. When you make contact, focus on pushing the target toward my anvil."

"Yes, Ma'am."

"You have ten minutes to deploy your men before I launch the smart duster, and then I'll set up. You may use the entire payload of the second vulture if need be. Bring both of them down to fifteen thousand meters and set them to ready."

Phillips taps several commands into his wrist computer, and the camp begins to buzz with activity. Sleek black aircraft, similar to the levitraft, begin to ferry soldiers to their locations. After ten minutes of preparations, the field base is nearly empty. Isis, Phillips, and a few squad members are huddled around the holomap.

"Assuming it has continued to move, we'll deploy here." Isis taps on the yellow pyramid, dragging it forward.

She pulls her wrist computer up, selects 'smart duster' from the second vulture and touches 'drop on target'. A two-minute countdown appears next to the package name. The last second turns over, and fingers of smoke sprout in every direction from a flash in the sky. A deep thud follows after a short delay. The tips of the fingers of smoke begin to fall, flashing intermittently with a popping that echoes over the mountains. The yellow pyramid on the holomap is covered by a spreading blanket of blue, diffusing like dye in water. Some of the blue darkens and turns red.

"That's our spot," Isis says, tapping the growing red area. "Redirect appropriately and we'll see you on the other side."

"Yes, Ma'am." Phillips types a few commands on his wrist computer and hurries off to a waiting jumper.

*****

A bird lands in a tree above Isis and her squad of perfectly camouflaged soldiers. Only with movement can their shape be distinguished.

Her earpiece buzzes to life. "We have contact, Ma'am. Grid Delta-Golf twenty-two. Converging on the target and forcing it toward you," Phillips says.

Isis steps behind a tree to pull up her wrist computer. She adjusts her squad's position with respect to Phillips's contact point, sending out the command. Her soldiers quietly move. Two grey smoke trails streak down from the sky; distant thuds make the trees quiver.

"Echo-Bravo is down," Phillips says. "But there's a new target, and it looks to be one of the other missing men. His combat suit is in shambles, but he's fast... Designating him as Echo-Charlie."

Three more spears of grey smoke strike the ground, followed by explosions. Isis looks at her wrist computer and sets up three target areas, with unique call signs, for the RPPDs.

Isis closes her computer and pulls up her weapon. She opens a channel to her squad. "Prepare for contact. Focus on the primary target, but be aware we have a new threat: Echo-Charlie. Echo-Bravo has been taken down."

Rapid gunfire explodes in the distance.

"We lost visual of Uniform-Alpha," Phillips says. "It should be heading your way. Echo-Charlie is injured. We're reining him in."

Isis adjusts her grip on the stock of her weapon. "Good work, Phillips."

Her visor picks up movement in the distance. A red indicator appears around the object, estimating its distance.

"I've got a visual. Close in!" Isis yells over the channel to her team.

Her visor displays green friendlies converging on the target. Aether fire burns the air. Suddenly a green indicator flies through the air, jerks to a stop, then falls to the ground where it begins to blink yellow. A name and a medical status pop up on Isis's display.

Isis sprints toward the target as more friendly indicators are knocked down and begin to flash yellow. Before she can assist the others, the target breaks through her defensive line, moving with unhindered speed.

"Damn it!" Isis angles her direction to intercept. With a thought, she deploys two RPPDs at the red target indicator.

When the ten-second timer reaches zero, streaks stab down and twin explosions shake the trees, wiping the target indicator from her display. On her visor, she pulls up a map, finding she is the closest to the target. Other soldiers are approaching.

"I'm making contact and need support!" she yells to her squad.

The trees give way to smoke. She slows to a walk, pulling up her Aether rifle as a man lifts himself from the ground; a new red indicator appears over him. She fires a burst, but the man instantly moves out of the way, spinning to face her. She fires again. He dodges just as easily. As his eyes settle on her weapon, he furrows his brow. A sudden violent tug rips it from her hands. The man sprints toward her with startling speed while she pulls out her side arm, firing. Even at this close range, he still dodges to the side. He grabs her wrists and they struggle, her suit straining with the effort.

I can't win this. She commands three more RPPDs to hit right on top of her. The area around her glows red and a ten second timer pops up on her visor.

9...

The actuators in her suit's arms begin to pop and give out from the struggle. Pain shoots through her arms with each one.

8...

The crushing grip on her wrists causes her to drop her sidearm.

7...

The man lets go of one wrist and punches her in the side. Her armor cracks with her ribs.

6...

She swings a desperate punch at his face, which he does not bother to block. Her fist knocks his head to the side.

5...

He straightens his head, throwing her three meters through the air.

4...

Her broken ribs slide past each other as she lands and tumbles to a stop.

3...

Isis gasps for air as the man takes a casual step toward her.

2...

With one last effort and immense pain, she fights to her feet and runs. Her suit grinds and whines with the movement.

1...

He looks up at the sky and makes a move.
BOOM, BOOM, BOOM!

The blast lifts Isis off the ground, slamming her into a tree. The impact and the incredible pain in her ribs is stunning. She remains still, despite the blistering of her skin through the holes burnt in her armor.

"Do you think I want this?"

Adrenaline kicks in. She forces herself to move. The man is limping toward her, several of his wounds bleeding freely. She struggles, on her side, to crawl away.

"I can't help what I'm doing. I just want to live," he says with a calm voice. His breathing is labored.

He pulls her up by the shoulder. Isis clutches his free arm but cannot compete with his strength. He grabs the edge of her helmet, ripping it off. For a moment, he looks at her. His right eye is a deep black. The black has spread to the surrounding flesh and down along his jaw. His face is covered with stubble. His hazel eye is filled with remorse. Isis grabs his wrist with both hands. She is powerless to do anything.

The man closes his eyes. "I'm sorry." The pressure on Isis's neck increases.

So this is my end? Pathetic... A foreign presence worms itself throughout Isis's body with such aggressive violation that she would scream if she could.

A burst of gunfire tears into the man, sending him sprawling off to the side. Isis falls to the ground.

A soldier kneels next to her and holds her head up. "Ma'am, can you hear me?" He pulls off his armored glove, checking her pulse.

"Is he dead?" Isis tries to prop herself up, but the soldier stops her.

"Yes, Ma'am. I flattened him."

"Did you check his pulse?"

The soldier glances at the unmoving man. "Ma'am, we need to get you to a medical pod immediately. You're in bad shape."

"Check it!" she yells with such vehemence that it sends pain shooting through her ribs.

Another soldier runs up to take the first soldier's position. "I'm calling in a jumper. We'll get you out of here. That was an impressive maneuver, Ma'am."

"Yeah... What's the status on Echo-Charlie?"

"Phillips and his guys took care of him."

Isis shakes her head. "We weren't prepared for this."

The first soldier comes back to Isis. "No pulse, Ma'am. He's gone."

Isis sighs with pain. "Thank the Creators."

20 Lepisents

Iona

Ryder, Korbin, Iona, and Thea tumble into the training room. They immediately sort themselves out, standing in a straight line. Sosimo watches them from his stationary bicycle. An Aether generator whirs as it charges from the motion of his legs.

"You know, you're thirty minutes early," he says. He gets off the bike.

Ryder steps forward. "We finished all the chores, so we were hoping to start with the lepisent lessons early."

"You finished cleaning the chocolate molds, wiping down the front display window, sweeping the shop floor, dusting the vintage grinders, and organizing the new candy?" Sosimo asks.

Ryder nods. "We did. We also mopped the mixing room floor, set aside the ingredients for the next mixing, took out all the trash, and washed Gracie."

Sosimo smiles. "I'm impressed."

"You smiled!" Thea squeals. She runs up and jumps on him. "I knew you could."

"Smile or not, we're still in the training room, so if you don't act like it, I won't do it again."

Thea slides off Sosimo, runs over to the others, and stands perfectly straight with her arms to her side and a straight face. The rest of the children do the same.

Sosimo lets out a huff. "You've finished all the chores and you've learned how to use Fundamental Aether well enough. There's no reason to wait any longer. Let's get started, then." A wave of semi-controlled excitement runs through the children. Sosimo eyes them as they try to contain it. "You all might be excited about shooting fire balls and bolts of lightning, but there is a lot more to lepisents than just offense. They're equally as important for defense."

"Really? But how do you defend with a lepisent?" Ryder asks.

"We'll cover defense as soon as you manage the basics. Now, hop on that bike and start pedaling, I'll need Aether to demonstrate how to use the different lepisents."

Sosimo lashes a leather harness to his forearm and brings two crystal rods from the table to the generator. The crystal rods are inlaid with wood curling around their bases.

Sosimo holds up his forearm to show the children the harness. "This is the most practical way to hold lepisents. It's cheap and it's easy to change the lepisents you're using." He shows them a slot on the top of his arm that the crystal rods can slide into. "These are the lepisents we'll be using." He flips the lepisents over to reveal carved symbols on their undersides. "Each lepisent is typically labeled by three symbols, which represent the cast, the behavior, and the type." Sosimo points to the first symbol. "Who knows what this means?"

"That's Moltrik Aether," Thea blurts out.

"Very good. And this second symbol means electricity, so both of these rods create some sort of electrical attack using Moltrik Aether."

"What's the last symbol?" Korbin asks.

Sosimo points to one of the wands with three solid circles on it. "This symbol represents its type. This one means it's a pulse lepisent." He holds up the next lepisent with three solid lines. "This one is a continuous lepisent."

"What does that mean?" Iona asks.

"It's how they're used, which is just how it sounds," Sosimo says. "Let me show you." He slides one rod into his forearm harness. "This is the continuous one." He grabs the Aether generator and a stream of electricity arcs from the lepisent to a stone, person-shaped target, blinding the children.

"Woo! Neat," Iona says, rubbing her eyes.

"Exactly what you'd expect. Once a continuous stream of Aether finds a target, it tends to stay connected. If you want to attack something else, you'll have to stop the Aether flow for an instant and change targets."

"Show us the pulse one!" Korbin says.

"Pulse lepisents require a little more finesse than continuous types." Sosimo changes the lepisent on his forearm and points it at the target. "Alright, stand back." He grabs the Aether generator. There is a heavy shock and a loud crack as a bolt of energy shoots from the lepisent and explodes against the target. The target slams against the ground, breaking off its head. "Ha. I haven't done that in ages... felt good."

Korbin jumps up. "You snapped its head right off! That was awesome. Are we going to do that?"

"Maybe, but not for a while," Sosimo says. "There was a large amount of Aether behind that pulse. If you work at it and if you're patient, who knows what you'll be able to do?" He walks over to the table and grabs smaller forearm harnesses for the children. "Everyone, put one of these on. We're going to first practice with the continuous lepisents."

The children take turns. They are all successful in making electricity hit the target with much less spectacle than Sosimo's first attempt.

Next, they practice with the pulse lepisent, which requires feeding Aether at the right rate and with the right quantity. Feeding it too fast with not enough Aether creates a backfire; feeding it too slowly just makes it crackle. After a few backfires—which the children quickly learn are a painful mistake—all of them meet with varying degrees of success.

"And when you get good, you'll be able to adjust the size of the pulse by playing with the rate and quantity of Aether you give the lepisent." Sosimo looks over the children, standing in a line once again. "Good job, everyone. Any other questions?"

"Did you burn your face playing with Aether?" Thea asks.

Iona's chest becomes so heavy she has trouble breathing.

Sosimo's body deflates. "No."

"Then how?"

Sosimo looks down. "Havityn Igor hit Kiats and destroyed my home and everything in it. I shouldn't have survived."

"I'm happy you survived," Thea says.

Sosimo looks at her and turns away. "I'm going for a walk. Please clean up." He leaves the training room.

"Smooth move, Thea," Korbin says. "He was just starting to act cool."

"I'm sorry. I was just curious," she says, playing with her hands.

*****

The children hop up from the couch as Sosimo walks in.

"Hey, Mr. Sosimo," Thea says. "Are you okay?"

Sosimo nods. "Better now, thanks. Sorry I disappeared." Before Thea can open her mouth, he claps his hands. "Let's start dinner."

In the kitchen, Sosimo slams a fifteen-centimeter-thick cookbook on the counter, flipping it open. He looks up a recipe and skims through the directions. "Thea and Nero, start chopping tomatoes, onions, peppers, and garlic." Thea grabs Nero by the arm, dragging him toward the counter. They each step up on a stool to reach it. "Ryder and Korbin, start on the stove. Iona, you can help me with the salad and rounding up the rest of the items. Let's also toast some sourdough with salt and oil. Grab the baking sheets in the cabinet."

Noises and smoke quickly envelop the kitchen. The children scurry around the stoves and counter tops, a stool always in tow. Chopped food goes to the stove and they work with little direction from Sosimo.

Iona pulls open a lower cabinet, grabbing a baking sheet. "Woo." Light pours though a few blackened holes. "What the heck?" She grabs the next sheet, which is in a similar state of holiness. Finally, the third one is in usable shape. "Hey, Sosimo, what happened to these?"

Sosimo looks at the sheets, brushing the scorch marks with his finger. "Someone melted holes in them. Looks like Aether. Do you know anything about this?"

"No. Why would anyone do that? Seems a bit silly," Iona says.

"It does." Sosimo takes the good cooking sheet, placing the others to the side to be recycled.

Iona notices her mouth is dry. She looks at the rest of the children working. Nero is frozen, peppers waiting to be cut in front of him.

Thea grabs the pepper. "Come on, Nero. What are you doing?"

Nero glances back toward Sosimo, then starts cutting some onions. *Why does he look guilty? I wish he'd talk to me...*

After an hour, they set several platters of mostly recognizable food on the table.

Sosimo sits first. "Looks good. Let's eat."

They haphazardly fill their plates, and the room is filled by the sounds of silverware and chewing.

Once the eating finally settles, Sosimo breaks the silence. "So, Nero, I want to talk to you about something."

Nero looks up, paling.

Sosimo frowns. "You're not in trouble."

The tension flows out of Nero.

"I recently purchased an essence for an Artifact project I'm working on."

"You make artifacts?" Thea asks. "I thought you were a candy maker."

"My first trade is artifact-making."

"Then why do you make candy?" Korbin asks. "Artifacts are awesome! You'd be way more cool if you made Artifacts."

"I'm not worried about being cool," Sosimo says, eyeing Korbin. "I still sell some on the side; however, my candy store has been my life ever since Havityn Igor—anyway, Nero, instead of making an artifact with it, I'll let you try to absorb it so you can train with us, if you'd like. It's a Moltrik cast."

"Ooh, yeah, Nero, you should," Thea chirps.

A little bit of hope swells in Iona. "Nero, that'd be great. You should do it."

Nero looks at the other children, and then at Sosimo. "Really?"

"Yes. Really."

"If I try and it doesn't work, will you be able to use it?"

Sosimo shrugs. "If I can catch it, yes, but if it is anything like the one in the mountains, probably not."

Nero uses his fork to play with his food. "Then, no, it's okay. You can use it for your artifact."

"Are you sure? You may not have another chance for a long time."

Nero nods. "I don't want to waste it for you. I don't think it'll work."

Poor Nero.

"Come on, Nero! You're just being scared," Korbin says.

"Korbin, cut it out," Sosimo says. "It's his choice, not yours."

"Yeah, but he's always scared. It's the truth. Ask everyone."

"Drop it. Nero's being very considerate for letting me use it. You should take a lesson." Sosimo turns to Nero. "Thank you, Nero."

Silence blankets the table for several minutes. They pick at the last bits of their dinner.

"Is everyone still wanting to participate in 'capture the orb'?" Sosimo asks. "We're about a month out."

"You're going to let us?" Korbin asks.

"Yes. You've practiced enough. I think you can handle it just fine."

"Yay!" Thea throws her arms in the air.

Sosimo looks at Nero. "You don't have to participate. They'll be using Aether. It could be really hard on you."

"I don't want to be left out. I'll be careful."

"Okay. It might sting, but it won't kill you. I'll register you all and get us tickets for the second to last day of competitions. We'll get to see the finales of the strong man competition, and Aether weaving. It should keep you all entertained."

"What happens on the last day?" Ryder asks.

"There's a closing ceremony and the finales to Stone's trials. They include the Trial of Odosa that we'll get to see the prelims for, the Trial of Borutaress that is a no-holds-barred combat between two Borukins, and The Trial of Orinda... It's a tough day to get tickets for."

"What's the trial of Orinda?" Iona asks.

Sosimo lets out a sigh. "It used to be a fabulous battle of honor and friendship between the best Borukin and a Drake. Do you know who Drake are?" The children shake their heads. "They're a powerful race of shifters. They exist as two different forms, both of which are lizard like. One is bipedal about the size of you children; the other form is large with a long body. Unfortunately, the Trial of Orinda has turned into a vicious battle against creatures that don't deserve to be killed."

"Why'd they stop fighting Drake?"

"The relationship between the Borukins and Drake became strained, and the Drake pulled away. When the Drake were leaving for their island, there was a skirmish and one was captured. She was tormented and forced to fight in the trial. When she started killing Borukins in only a handful of minutes, they replaced the Drake with creatures more manageable. No one has challenged her in a long time."

"Her?"

"Yes. Her name is Testrel."

"And she's still alive?"

Sosimo nods again. "I suspect she will be for another hundred years. She's held captive in the Orinda Museum."

"Can we see her?" Iona asks.

"I'd rather not. It's a despicable place."

"Please, Mr. Sosimo?" Thea clasps her hands together. "What if we never get to see a Drake ever again?"

"You probably won't... I'll think on it."

*****

In the training room, the children form a line in front of Sosimo. They are just about to start their morning exercise when Nero runs in, jumping into position next to Iona.

Iona sniffs the air. *Is that smoke I smell?* Nero's clothes look to be more battered than usual. Little bits of wood are hanging from his hair. *What's he been doing?*

"You just barely made it on time," Sosimo says, frowning. "Did you light yourself on fire?"

Nero's lets out a breath. "No—it was an experiment—" He glances away from Sosimo.

"Oh, yeah? You're not burning down anyone's house, are you?"

Nero shakes his head vigorously.

"We'll talk after. Let's begin our exercise."

They go through the traditional Borukin Roroonki morning exercise, moving fluidly from one move to the next. When they finally finish, Nero tries to leave, but Sosimo stops him. The other children run off, but Iona sticks around, pretending to finish some stretching.

"Where are you off to so fast, Nero?" Sosimo asks.

"I'm just trying to get to Saraf's on time. He doesn't like when I'm late. And I need to shower."

"Why do you smell like smoke?"

"Umm..." Nero looks at the ground.

"Just promise me you aren't doing anything dangerous that could harm you or others. Fire is not something to play with. It can quickly get out of control."

"I wasn't playing with fire. I promise."

Sosimo stares at Nero for a moment. "Alright. Have a good day."

Nero nods, disappearing out the door in a breath.

Iona walks over to Sosimo. "What do you think he was doing?"

Sosimo shakes his head. "I haven't the faintest idea, though there seems to be a faint wisp of residual Aether around him."

"But I thought he couldn't use Aether."

"I know. It's strange."

"Can I ask you a question?"

"Sure," Sosimo says. "What is it?"

"You said there was a group called the Daynin or something, that forces their young to absorb entities. If it's so traumatic, why do they do it?"

"It just gives your body more time to adapt to Aether so you're more effective when you start training. The reason it's traumatic is because babies usually don't have the desire to take the essence. The conditions the ceremony uses to ensure success are not very pleasant."

"How would we know if I'm a Daynin?"

Sosimo shrugs. "There might not be any way to tell. I didn't think they were still around. There are any number of ways you could've absorbed an essence, so it's hard to say where to even start." Sosimo eyes Iona's blue-gemmed necklace. "Can I see that? You said you've had it as long as you remember, right?"

Iona takes it off, handing it to him. "I have."

"It's beautiful." Sosimo looks closely at an engraving on the silver under the gem. "This writing, do you know what it says? I've never seen anything like it."

"What?" Iona takes her necklace and looks at the engravings. "I thought they were just designs. You think it's writing?"

"I can't say for sure but it looks that way to me. At least it's not random."

"What could it say?"

"Your guess is as good as mine, Iona. I'll think on it and let you know. Let's get ready for breakfast. I'm starving."

*****

"Can you believe Nero this morning?" Korbin asks while the children wait for Sosimo to prepare their next lesson. "All his clothes were trashed. He must've been doing something really stupid."

"I don't know. It could've been cool," Iona says.

"No way, not our little Sammy." Korbin shakes his head. "Cool isn't in his dictionary. I wouldn't be surprised if he did it just to get attention because he's jealous."

Sosimo turns and walks toward Korbin, staring him down. "Do you know who your family is?"

Korbin shakes his head, shrinking down. "No. They died."

"Your family is alive, Korbin."

Korbin looks at Sosimo with surprise.

"Your family is Ryder, Thea, Iona, and Nero. This is your family. You need to look out for each other, because in the end, they're all you have. Do you understand? Even if you don't always like Nero, he's your family. Treat him as such."

Korbin dips his head. "Yeah. Okay."

"Don't forget it." Sosimo steps back, takes a deep breath, and looks at the others. "Alright, let's get on with training. Put on your harnesses. Today, I want to touch on defense. A Borukin's high Aethersotto allows us to interact with Aether using a styk to defend ourselves. You all, on the other hand, will have to use Aether from your lepisents for defense. Today, I will teach you how to block, destabilize, or deflect an attack. Let's begin. Korbin, hop on the bike for me."

Sosimo puts a lepisent into his forearm harness and walks over to the Aether generator. It is connected to two devices with lepisents in them pointing at a target wall. He adjusts the knobs on the two devices resting on the table. "These will take in Aether and power the lepisents. They're both exothermic Pahzan lepisents; one is a continuous type, and the other is a pulse type. Ryder, hit the button on the left when I tell you." Sosimo grabs his dark, polished styk and touches it to an exposed wire of the Aether storage container. He walks in front of the target wall. "Okay, Ryder."

Ryder hits the button. A small red fireball emerges from the lepisent. It wobbles as it moves just faster than a walking pace. Sosimo shoots another fireball. It collides with the first, releasing a wave of heat as they both disappear.

"Woo," Iona says, touching her face.

"When I use the same cast, they interact quickly. Depending on how much Aether I use, I can stop the attack, slow it, or plow over it." Sosimo walks over to the table and switches his lepisent. "Again, Ryder."

This time, Sosimo shoots a black shimmering ball that is barely visible. When it hits the fireball, they both disappear.

"That wasn't very exciting," Thea says.

"That was endothermic Pahzan Aether reacting with exothermic Pahzan Aether. Basically, hot and cold, which makes warm. Right? There are all sorts of interesting interactions between types of Aether, so keep that in mind. Now, Aether can only exist in our space for a time proportional to the user's Aethersotto. When this time is up, the Aether will destabilize and release its energy. If we mix different types of Aether, they won't cancel like before, but the rate of their destabilization will increase."

Sosimo switches his lepisent, touches the Aether storage container again, and readies himself in front of Ryder.

A ball of crackling electrical energy shoots from Sosimo's lepisent and collides with the fireball from Ryder. They form a churning ball of fire and electricity hovering in the middle of the room. After a heartbeat, the ball pops, sending out a wave of crackling heat. The air smells of ozone.

"That attack would've lasted another second or so if I didn't use my Aether to destabilize it. Again, Ryder."

This time, Sosimo shoots a much smaller ball of electricity to collide with the fireball. The fireball angles oddly away from Sosimo, hitting the wall to the side of him.

"It takes much less energy to change the direction of something than to stop it completely. This technique requires more skill. It was only possible because I'm using a lepisent of a different cast. When my Aether interacts with the lepisent's Aether, there is a bond I can use to nudge the incoming attack away from me."

Sosimo demonstrates how pulse lepisents and continuous lepisents interact. When he finishes, he looks over the children. "What methods you use will come down to the situation and your own style, but regardless, your resourcefulness and conservation of energy is the key to survival. Always keep an open mind. Any questions?"

*****

Sosimo pulls out a nice wooden case with a latched lid, placing it on the table. "It's time to check the type of Aether you all are capable of using."

Iona, Thea, Ryder, and Korbin crowd around for a better look. They are covered in sweat and scorch marks from another day of training.

Sosimo pops the latches and opens the case. Inside are six crystal balls. Each is etched with a unique symbol. "These are called Adter Tursents. They're used to test Aether cast." Sosimo quickly reviews the Aether casts that correspond to each ball. He calls Ryder forward. "We'll start with you, Ryder."

Sosimo pulls out the Pahzan Adter Tursent and places it in Ryder's hand. "Now, just like a lepisent, try to transfer Aether into it."

Ryder closes his eyes for a moment. Then, he looks at Sosimo. "I couldn't feel anything. Am I doing it wrong?"

Sosimo shakes his head. "Not at all. It'll feel natural when you match with the sphere." Sosimo gives Ryder the Icor Adter Tursent. Again, nothing happens. The Moltrik Adter Tursent also does nothing. "Hm, well, I'm glad I borrowed a full set."

"Why's that?" Ryder asks.

"Ru, Nesiv, and Biat Adter Tursents are difficult to come by and they're just as unlikely. Let's try Ru." Sosimo holds his breath as Ryder tries the Ru Adter Tursent. He exhales when nothing happens. "Okay, good. Now the others."

It is only when Ryder tries the Biat Adter Tursent that it glows. Ryder opens his eyes and smiles. "I felt that one."

Sosimo takes the sphere from him. "Hm, interesting. You could go your entire life without encountering Biat Aether."

"What can he do with it?" Thea asks.

"Adter Tursents are unable to differentiate between different branches of a specific cast, so we'll just have to wait and see what his abilities lean toward," Sosimo says. "There are three main branches of this type of Aether. The Biat Aether, Take, lets someone absorb essence. All Humans have a sliver of this. The only difference is that Humans can only interact with a weak essence such as an entity or one from a broken shell. On the other hand, someone with this branch of Aether can interact with an essence directly, so they don't necessarily have to kill the Aether-being in order to absorb their essence. People with Take Biat Aether also have the ability to make puppets."

"What's a puppet?" Ryder asks.

"A person can use Aether to pull the essence out of an individual. Instead of absorbing it completely, they leave it partially connected. Through this link, the person has the ability to manipulate the individual like a puppet. If they are skilled, they can control the other individual perfectly. You'd never be the wiser. You think they're your friends, but next thing you know, they're stabbing you in the back. If you have this branch, I don't ever want to see you do this."

Thea shakes her head. "Ryder would never do that."

"I'd expect not," Sosimo says.

"What are the other branches?" Iona asks.

"Destroy Biat Aether is equally as horrible as making a Puppet. It lets you unravel someone's essence from the inside out, killing them in that moment or sometime later. It can be used to harness a large amount of Aether."

"Oh, gosh. That sounds awful," Ryder says, disgusted.

"Yes. It is. Now, the last branch is something special. Creation Biat Aether allows someone to shave off some of their essence and imbue an inanimate object with life. It is incredibly difficult to do. I've heard a person has the ability to make the new essence have whatever cast they desire. Someone could create a rock creature with Pahzan Aether to act like a guardian."

"That sounds awesome!" Korbin jumps up. "You should totally learn how to do that, Ryder."

Sosimo chuckles. "If he has this branch he could, but it'll take a lot of work." Sosimo looks at Ryder. "I hope you realize how lucky you are that absorbing this entity didn't kill you."

"What? I could have died?" Ryder glares at Korbin. "I thought absorbing weak essence like ours was okay."

"Yes, but if the Biat essence has the Take branch and it's strong enough, it will absorb your essence. Then, it either kills you or takes over your body. You need to be careful. Don't play with things you don't understand."

Ryder nods. "Okay."

"Good. Now, let's move on. Korbin, come up here."

Sosimo hands Korbin one Adter Tursent after another until the Ru Adter Tursent glows. Sosimo lets out a breath. "Oh no."

Korbin's smile falls away. "Why's that bad?"

"Ru Aether has a higher potential for destruction than any other Aether cast. It can level buildings and poison the land.

We need to keep this an absolute secret, or you may get expelled from the city. I'll think on this more, but you must promise not to use Aether outside of anything I've taught you."

Korbin looks down at his feet.

"It's alright, Korbin. It's not your fault. It's just a big responsibility. Promise me you won't try anything unless you talk to me, or someone else with experience." Sosimo waits a moment. "Korbin. Promise me."

Korbin looks up and nods. "I promise."

"Good. Now, let's check the final two casts, just in case."

The remaining two Adter Tursents do nothing when Korbin tries to make them glow.

"Wait a second," Iona says. "I thought you said all Humans have some Biat Aether. Why didn't it glow?"

"Good observation. No Human would activate the Biat Adter Tursent normally. A Human's ability with Biat Aether is greatly limited. It's really only a fraction of one of the branches so the Biat Adter Tursent doesn't even register the partial talent." Sosimo signals Iona to step forward. "You can go next."

Iona tries to activate all the Adter Tursent spheres. Only the Icor Adter Tursent glows.

Sosimo takes the last sphere from Iona. "Icor Aether is the most practical of all. It's my cast as well. Depending on the branches you're capable of, you may be able to heal people, augment your strength and or speed further than typical Fundamental Aether, increase your physical resistance, and read or manipulate minds."

Read minds? That would be interesting. I could figure out when Korbin is causing trouble… "How do you learn this stuff?"

"With time. When you're older I'll show you what I know." Sosimo turns to Thea. "Now you, Thea."

Thea holds the Pahzan Adter Tursent. It glows.

Sosimo nods. "Okay, good. That's a pretty common cast to have. You've got the potential to freeze things and make fireballs. It should be useful. Let's check the others, just in case."

Thea holds the Icor Adter Tursent and it glows as well.

"Okay, you're at least a bicast. That's impressive."

Sosimo hands Thea the Moltrik Adter Tursent. She focuses on the sphere and it glows as well.

"Wow, a tricast. That's even more impressive. Moltrik Aether allows someone to manipulate electric and magnetic fields and also chemical bonds if they're really good."

Thea then tries the Ru and Nesiv Adter Tursents with no success. The Biat Aether, however, glows when she uses it.

Sosimo stares at the glowing sphere for a long moment. He reaches out his hand, hesitates for a moment, then takes it. "Huh." His eyes wander as he rolls the sphere in his hand.

"What? Isn't that good?" Thea asks.

After a moment, Sosimo makes eye contact with Thea. "It's curious. I'm not sure what it means, but this happens to be the exact same casts the Seekers of the Drebin have."

Thea's face loses color. "Does that mean I'm a Drebin?"

Sosimo shakes his head. "No, no. It's not possible. You know how I told Ryder he was lucky the entity didn't kill him? An essence from a Seeker would do that to anyone that tried to absorb it. Instead of killing the person, it overwhelms them. They're just a shadow of their former self, completely driven by the essence and by Drebin beliefs... So, if this was a Seeker essence, you'd most likely have lost your mind and run off to try to join them. Fortunately, you haven't, which is a good sign. I'm just curious what the Erohsians were doing with these essences..." Sosimo shakes his head, shrugging his shoulders. "Or perhaps they're not from the Erohsians... I'll have to ask some Humans I know in Sunta next time I'm around."

Sosimo puts the last Adter Tursent in the case, latching it shut. "Well, you all certainly have some interesting casts.

Now, go start on your chores. I'd like to talk with Korbin in private."

The other children gather their stuff and leave the training room. Iona glances back to see Sosimo lead Korbin over to a chair, a hand on his shoulder.

I hope he's okay. She turns, following Ryder and Thea.

21 The Smoking Boy
Nero

The dark violet Entity forces Nero to back up to a large tree. His broomstick is packed with so much Aether, it vibrates harshly in his hands. *Can this thing blow up?* He draws as much Aether as he can to augment his strength, but it hardly seems to make a dent. *Please don't blow up. Please don't blow up!* He glances around in the early morning darkness for easy cover, seeing nothing. *I don't think I can block anymore.*

The Entity shoots a bolt of energy at him. He reacts with the broomstick. *Oh no!* His body tenses, pushing against the Aether. The impact creates a small pop to the side. A ring of smoke rises from the ground.

Did I just deflect that?

The Entity flickers briefly and attacks again. Nero focuses on putting pressure against the Aether in his broomstick. He sends another bolt of energy ricocheting off his stick.

This is awesome! Now I don't have to worry about this thing blowing up in my face! A smile creeps across his lips. He advances, pushing the Entity back to earn himself some breathing room. "Not so tough now, Mister I-can-use-Aether-but-I'm-still-just-a-blob-of-mist. Or is it Little Piggly Pinky?"

The Entity grows darker, only a hint of violet visible. It fiercely attacks, driving Nero back on his heels. He swings the stick wildly to keep up.

"Alright! I take it back. I like pigs. I like pink!" Nero dives out of the way, blocking a shot. *I need to go on the offensive, or I'm going to get smoked!* He deflects another few attacks. Each time the stick is knocked around like he is blocking a ball. *Wait a second! If I can deflect the attacks, I wonder—*

He grips the stick in both hands, settling on the balls of his feet. Everything seems to slow. A small spot on the Entity brightens, and it releases a huge bolt of energy. Nero steps into it, swinging with all his might. He connects with what feels like concrete. There is a moment of calm, then the stick's vibration increases painfully.

A bright flash, and a surge of energy propels Nero through the air. He trails smoke like a streamer, hitting the ground and tumbling backward into a bush. Pain stabs him in the stomach each time he tries to take a breath, reducing him to short gasps. Slowly, his breathing comes back. The ache throughout his entire body takes over. A strange, smoky smell tickles his nostrils. He closes his eyes.

Ouch.

Hurried footsteps crunch through the surrounding area. *Great… Maybe if I don't move they won't see me.*

"Are you okay?" Comes the voice of a young girl.

Dang. Nero claws his way from the bush, struggling to his feet. The same Borukin girl and man he had seen in the morning at Saraf's are looking at him: Natina and Grebson. *Princess! What do I do?* The girl's eyebrows are furrowed in worry, but the man's face is completely neutral. He has the Aether cast symbols of Pahzan, Icor, and Moltrik tattooed onto his face. Nero quickly glances around. To his relief, the Entity is gone.

"What are you doing in that bush?" Natina asks.

"Uh—I was—um… sleeping. If that's okay?"

The girl tilts her head, frowning. "Why are you smoking?"

"I don't smoke!"

"No, look at yourself. You're smoking!"

What is she talking about? Nero looks at himself. He is definitely smoking. He tries to clear the air with his hands to little effect. "Oh, that? Uh... that's normal," he says, coughing.

She raises her eyebrows. "It's normal for you to look like you're roasting over a smoldering fire?"

Yeah, that was pretty stupid. Nero looks around in the plants for inspiration. *Maybe I can change the subject.* "What are you doing back here? No one's ever back here."

"Grebson," she says, indicating the impressively large Borukin, "wanted us to walk through the park before training. We heard a big explosion, so we came to look. And we found a roasted Human boy."

Nero's shoulders drop. *Was it that loud?* "You're not going to cut me any slack, are you?"

"No. It's pretty ridiculous. Did you blow yourself up? What were you doing?"

"Nothing," he spurts out. *Did she see anything?* "You know. The usual."

"I'd sure like to know what the 'usual' is."

"Uh..." Nero steps from one foot to the other, avoiding eye contact. A few moments of silence pass.

"Alright, Natina. We should go." The deep voice of Grebson startles Nero.

Natina shrugs. "Fine. He was getting boring, anyway." She turns and stomps off.

Nero swallows as Grebson walks up to him. "You work for Saraf, don't you?" Nero barely manages a nod. "Good. I'll see you later." Grebson turns to follow Natina.

Nero slaps the sides of his thighs. *What did I do this time?*

*****

Nero hurries into Saraf's shop after Sosimo's morning exercise, his hair still damp from a quick rinse.

"Smoke-flavored today, Nero?" Saraf asks, chuckling.

Nero sniffs his shirt. *Still?* He hurries to do his morning chores before Saraf can say any more. *Where am I going to find another broomstick?*

Later that morning, the bell on the door jingles for the fourth time.

"Did you leave something, Grebson?" Saraf asks.

"I'm here to talk about the boy."

Nero glances up to see the massive Borukin staring down at him. *Here it comes…*

"I know he doesn't look like much, but his brain isn't as feeble as you'd expect," Saraf says.

"That's not what I want to talk about."

"Well, it's hard to find good work these days, especially when the people that I train leave," Saraf says, looking straight into Grebson's eyes. "I don't have the luxury to be picky, even if he's not Borukin."

"Can he use Aether?"

Saraf beckons Nero closer. "Can you?"

"I don't know." Nero cannot look either of them in the eye.

Saraf holds up a hand. "Don't let that answer fool you. I don't think his brain is properly connected to his mouth."

"Aether or not, he seems to have enough time in the morning to light himself on fire. I think we should put him to work," Grebson says.

"I've already put him to work."

"I can see that, but I was considering using him to motivate Natina during her training."

Saraf walks over to Nero. He lifts Nero's arm. "He's a bit skinny. I'm not sure how much motivation he'd provide."

Nero pulls away, glaring at Saraf.

"True. But just having another person doing some of the exercises might help encourage her," Grebson says. "She'll have someone to relate to and work with."

"Hmm, I just had a thought." Saraf scratches his chin. "It's a bit out there… but even though Nero's particularly skinny, and his mouth isn't connected to his not-so-feeble brain, Natina and he might be able to relate. Then we could push her harder."

The tattoos on Grebson's arms ripple over his flexing muscles. "That's a good thought, Saraf."

Saraf smiles. "The old man's still got it."

"You agree?" Grebson asks.

Saraf nods. "Might as well. I'll just have to check with Sosimo."

"He's with Sosimo?"

"He and a few other rascals, as I hear."

"Children? Is he getting better?"

"Why don't you call him and find out?"

Grebson holds up his hand and walks out.

Saraf waves Grebson off. "Thanks, Grebson. You have a good day, too," he says melodramatically. Saraf turns to Nero, thumping him on the back. "Well, I sure hope she doesn't hurt you."

"I can take it. She's just a girl."

Saraf smiles. "That's exactly the kind of thinking that'll get you hurt."

*****

The drone of the Aether generating bike hums in the background.

"Is this all I'm going to do?" Nero asks as he pedals.

"Have you seen the size of your legs?" Saraf asks. "They're toothpicks! This'll do you some good." He turns to Natina. A device with a lepisent rests on a table, pointing at Natina. Saraf puts his finger on the button. "Alright, Natina. Are you ready to start your Odo training? We'll pick up where we left off with Odosa."

Natina nods. She's holding a light brown piece of polished wood in front of her. "I'm ready."

Saraf taps the device. A small fireball shoots out of it. Natina whips up her styk to block it, creating a puff of smoke that curls away from a scorch mark midway up the styk.

Saraf frowns. "Come on, Natina. Focus."

Natina tightens her grip on the styk, scowling at the lepisent fixture.

"Relax. It won't work if you're tense," Saraf says.

Another fireball shoots at her. Again, there is a puff of smoke.

Natina looks from the scorch mark to Saraf. "What's wrong? I did this yesterday!" She quickly glances at Nero, avoiding his eyes.

"It'll take time," Saraf says. "Everyone has to work on it. You're making good progress. Now, try again."

This time, the fireball winks out of existence as soon as it touches the styk. Natina pumps her arm in the air and Saraf smiles.

I can do that! "Could I try?"

"Odosa is a Borukin skill," Saraf says. "To absorb Aether into a styk is not something everyone can do."

"I think I can do it."

"I'm sure, and you'll think that right up until a fireball takes your face off. Then what am I supposed to tell Sosimo?" He turns back to Natina. "Again."

No one ever believes me! Nero looks down at the handlebars and tries to push his frustration into the pedals.

Little fireballs shoot from the device, faster and faster. Natina absorbs most of them, but a few explode in smoke. Saraf continues to release fireballs at her until sweat covers her forehead. When he finally stops, Natina smiles.

Saraf nods at Grebson, sitting to the side. "You were right."

"Right about what?" Natina frowns.

Saraf waves his hand. "Never mind. We're here to train, not chitchat. As you know, blocking Aether attacks relies on absorbing energy. The blocker must become one with her styk. If you don't block correctly, damage will be done to the styk. If you block too much, it'll fill up and explode. There are several techniques you can use to avoid overload. We will start with the easiest, called Odomi. It's simply Aether deflection, and it's a great skill to use when you have no other choice. It's actually a bit easier when your styk has Aether in it. The only problem is that unless you're deflecting it at an enemy, you waste the Aether.

"In order to deflect, you need to focus on keeping the Aether and your styk from merging." Saraf points to a target drawn in chalk on the wall. "Try to aim there."

Ooh. Could I deflect attacks back at the Entity? Maybe if I don't try to hit the Aether the broomstick won't explode?

Saraf sends out a fireball and Natina blocks it. "Focus, Natina, keep the energy between your styk and the fireball separate. It's a matter of stopping the Aether." This time, the fireball hits her styk and wavers for an instant before shattering in a shower of sparks. "Good, that's better."

She soon is deflecting the fireballs in every direction except the target area. A ring of smoke rises from another scorch mark on the wall, right over Saraf's head.

Saraf straightens. "Okay, seriously. Aim for the target."

Natina continues. The walls are soon covered by marks.

Saraf looks around, shaking his head. "You did well, but I'm more impressed with the mess you've made. We'll definitely have to work on aim."

"Maybe if you'd show me how, I'd do better," Natina says, taunting. "Can you even do it anymore?"

Saraf raises an eyebrow. He looks at Grebson, who shrugs. "Alright, fine," Saraf says. "I'll show you after you and Nero are done sparring."

Natina jumps up. "Great!"

Nero slows his pedaling. "We're going to spar?"

Saraf beckons Grebson over. "Will you charge the Aether container for the demonstration while I train the little ones?"

Grebson nods and relieves Nero. After adjusting the seat height, he flips it up to a higher gear and the hum that filled the room before turns into a loud drone.

"You two are going to do something, Nero," Saraf says over the noise. "I hope it's going to be something we can call sparring, but that depends on how quickly you catch on."

Saraf takes half an hour to go over general grappling moves with Nero while Grebson oversees Natina's styk sequences.

"Oh, boy. We're going to have to practice this on our lunch breaks, Nero. You need some work... but the show must go on." Saraf leads Nero over to Natina. "Alright, Nero. I want you to try to take the styk from Natina." Saraf eyes Natina. "Just don't hit him with it. This is a grappling exercise."

"Uh... How am I supposed to do that?" Nero asks.

"Just go after it." Saraf pushes him forward, but Nero resists. "Try something we just practiced."

Natina waves the styk in front of him. "Are you scared because I'm a girl?"

"A giant girl," Nero says under his breath.

"What did you say?" Natina takes a step forward.

"Nothing." Nero squeaks just before he lunges for the styk.

There is a blur of movement and the wind leaves Nero's lungs.

Natina looks down with a smirk. "Did I hurt you?"

Saraf pulls Nero up. "I'm glad Natina is showing a bit of fierceness, but jeez Nero. Did you pay attention to anything I just went over?"

Nero fails several more attempts, the last of which leaves him on the ground once more, struggling to catch his breath.

"Okay, I think we should call that enough before we break Nero. We'll have to come up with a way to even it out." Saraf turns to Grebson. "How's the charging of the Aether container?"

"It's good enough for the demonstration. Nero, take over for me." Grebson hops off the bike and goes to the fireball generator.

Saraf picks out a short styk. He holds it lightly in one hand, readying himself. "Just one right now, Grebson."

Grebson turns up the knob on the device. The air around the fireball generator crackles with energy. A large, fast-moving fireball shoots out. In a flash, Saraf flicks his wrist and deflects it directly into the center of the target. "See? Piece of pie."

Natina claps her hands. "That was great. Do more!"

"Alright, Grebson, shoot a couple at me."

"Are you sure you don't want your normal styk, old man?" Grebson asks.

"Who are you calling old?"

"Suit yourself." Grebson leans over to Nero. "Just keep on pedaling, boy," he whispers out of the corner of his mouth.

Saraf easily deflects the first fireball at the target. Before it lands, another one is blazing toward his chest. He flicks his wrist and again deflects the fireball perfectly. Grebson shoots fireballs at him as fast as he can. Saraf dodges and ducks around some while sending the rest at the target. He even deflects some in mid-spin, behind his back. Eventually the lepisent Grebson is using backfires and sputters.

Saraf looks at him, breathing deeply. "Did you forget how to count?"

"You expect me to pass up an opportunity to try to get even for all of the stuff you put my brother and I through?" Grebson asks, smirking.

"How'd that work out for you?"

"Well, you're pretty fast for an old man."

"That I am!" Saraf turns to Natina. She is beaming. "How was that?"

Grebson glances at Nero, who is still pedaling. He adjusts the knobs on the lepisent fixture and shoots a much smaller fireball, scorching Saraf's pants.

"That was low, Grebson," Saraf says, looking at his burnt pants. "These were my favorite."

"A wise man once told me to never let my guard down."

"I can't imagine you keeping any wise men for company, you baboon."

"You're probably right," Grebson says. "I'd like to talk to you upstairs before we leave, if you're done with lessons for the day."

Saraf puts the styk back. "Very well, let's get it over with. Please clean up before you leave, Natina." Saraf and Grebson walk upstairs.

Natina grabs a rag, fills a bucket with water, and begins to scrub a blackened section of wall.

Nero walks over with another rag. "Would you like help?"

"Even after I kicked your butt?"

Nero shrugs.

"Sure, then. Thanks." She throws the single braid of her hair over her shoulder.

Nero starts to scrub. "It seems like everyone here has long hair and tattoos. Why's that?"

"It's a tradition. The tattoos represent Borukin accomplishments and their status. Family crests are on our backs, accomplishments go on the chest and stomach, military rank goes on the arms, Corusmin achievements go on our faces. Only the King is allowed to tattoo his scalp."

"And the long hair?"

"The length of your hair shows how long you have been out of service. Only warriors that are in service shave their heads."

"Even the girls shave their heads?" Nero asks, mouth open.

"The women in the military do. Why wouldn't they?"

"I've never seen a woman with a shaved head."

"Well then maybe you should open your eyes. I'll do it one day. It is a great honor."

"What does Corusmin mean?" Nero asks.

"A Corusmin award goes to a person that has made it to the monolith of a Corusnigma. Do you know what those are?"

"Really strong areas of a particular Aether cast?"

Natina nods. "Yeah, basically. At the center of each one is a monolith. Getting there is very dangerous. Only very skilled Borukins attempt it, which makes it one of our greatest achievements."

"What do they look like?"

"I've never seen one in real life, but I've seen pictures. They're all different, depending on their cast of Aether. The Nesiv Corusnigma has giant rocks floating in the air. It's really cool looking. To get to the monolith you have to go over bridges that span the rocks and traverse areas where the gravity is random and unstable."

"That sounds pretty awesome. I'd like to see that someday."

"Yeah, me too." They work in silence for a few moments. "So, what were you doing in the park when Grebson and I found you?"

Should I tell her? After a moment of scrubbing, he speaks. "I was playing with this entity thing I found in the park."

"An entity? In the park?"

"Yeah. It's violet and red and yellow, and it shoots electricity at me. We kind of have a little sparring challenge. It's really fun."

There is a moment of silence until Natina laughs. "An entity! Ha! You almost got me, Nero. Come on, be serious. Were you playing with fireworks? You really should be careful with that stuff."

Her disbelief punches him in the gut. "I know..." *She doesn't believe me, either...* Nero turns back to scrubbing in silence on a dark burn mark. "Aren't you a princess?" he asks when it finally disappears.

"Yeah." Natina avoids eye contact, focusing intently on a small scorch mark.

"Shouldn't you have servants to clean up for you?"

"What's that supposed to mean? Am I not allowed to work like a normal person?"

"No, I didn't mean that. I just figured servants would clean up after you. Since you're a princess."

Natina lets out a puff of air, relaxing her shoulders. "There usually are, but for Saraf to train me, he demanded I take responsibility for my own actions and clean up after myself. Usually Saraf and Grebson help and it's fun. It makes me feel like I belong, instead of being detached from everyone. That's the lame thing about being a princess. Everyone is afraid to talk to me."

"But it's pretty cool that you have a body guard. Grebson looks like he could really kick some butt. He's the biggest Borukin I've ever seen."

"It's cool if you like having no privacy and always asking permission to do things. It makes it hard to have friends... But Grebson is my favorite of all my bodyguards so far. He's not as scared of my father as the others, so he lets me have some fun once in a while."

"What did he do to get all his tattoos?" Nero asks.

"He won't talk about it, but a lot of people respect him. He was a great competitor in the Games and he completed three Corusnigmas. He probably would have gotten four if he tried. There's not a Borukin alive with four Corusmin achievements."

"Why didn't he?"

"He was going to the Nesive Corusnigma, but a really bad Havityn hit Kiats. It killed his whole family. Only his brother survived. He hasn't competed since and he gave up going for achievements. My dad says he became a hunter for the crown. He was the one that ended the Murderess. Do you know who that is?"

"Korbin has an action figure called the spider murderess. Is that the same?"

"Oh, yeah. There's only one like her."

"I didn't think she was real."

"She used to be the most feared woman on the planet. She'd leave tokens for her victims. If you ever got one, your days were coming to an end, no matter what you did."

"Scary."

"Yeah." They work for a few minutes in silence. "Are you excited for the Games? They're less than a month away and there are going to be three planets in Axiom on the last day so it could be extra exciting! Are you going to watch? What's your favorite event?"

"Uh…"

"My favorite is the Trial of Odosa. It's on the last day. My brother, Kamin, is competing this year. He might even give Overseer Carason a run for her money, but I don't think he really has a chance. She's in charge of all the schools in Kiats. She's also my idol. No one can match her. I hope one day I can be that good. Then I could compete in the Games and my dad would be proud of me."

Dad… Nero works another scorch mark. *Must be nice to have parents.*

After another half hour of cleaning and sparse conversation, they finish and Natina and Grebson leave.

In the afternoon Saraf closes his shop and Sosimo appears, dragging behind him a large container on wheels.

Nero greets him at the door. "What's that for?"

"It's a large Aether container. It's tradition to make an Artifact from your own blood and sweat, so I've been charging this thing for the last couple of weeks." Sosimo pats the container. "Unfortunately, this beast is heavy. It's the only way to easily store Aether for a long period of time." Sosimo reaches into his backpack. "This is the essence I'm going to use." He pulls out a cylindrical container with small silver windows, handing it to Nero. There is a gentle white glow coming from inside.

"This is just like the containers we found back home!"

Sosimo nods. "I'm not surprised. It's a pretty common design. The metal keeps the essence from escaping, and the windows allow you to see if there's anything inside. Give us a hand with the doors while Saraf and I lug this elephant downstairs."

In the workshop, Saraf opens the door of a sizable metal container that sits a meter off the ground. In the middle of the container, there is a sphere that stands on a metal rod like a lollipop. Protruding from the side of the container is a small plank. It reaches to within five centimeters of the sphere. A coil of wire lies at the bottom.

"Sosimo, may I see your net and vessel?" Saraf asks.

Sosimo opens a small box on the cart and hands Saraf a crystal rod with inlaid red wood. He then takes out a metal webbing of the same shape with a fixture as its base, and places it next to the case.

Saraf inspects the rod. "Not bad. It looks like it's going to be a pulse lepisent, though I would've concentrated the wood more toward the end. This is redwood?"

"It is."

"Interesting. Not my favorite, but this is your artifact." Saraf sets the rod down and picks up the metal webbing. He pushes down a little clip, and the webbing detaches from the fixture. The webbing separates into two pieces, that he then closes around the rod. "See this, Nero?" He holds up the crystal rod. "This is the vessel we'll turn into an artifact. The metal mesh around it is the net." He points to the fixture. "This is the base. Got it?"

Nero nods. "Easy peasy."

"Now, there are two parts to an essence: the core and the shell. The core is what channels the Aether and defines the essence's characteristics. The shell provides an anchor to our world and physical protection. It can take on many forms. For an Aether being, it's their body. For an Artifact, it's the vessel. For a free essence, such as we have, it's an Aether barrier."

He puts the fixture on the plank and plugs the coiled cable into it. "This cable will energize the base, which will attract the core of the essence while the sphere will attract its Aether shell." Saraf closes the door to the container. "Sosimo, are you ready?"

Sosimo screws the essence vessel into the side of the container and rotates a door release mechanism. "Alright, it's free."

Saraf pulls Nero over to two switches. "This one powers the base and this one powers the sphere." He flips the switch for the base, and a little green indicator light goes on above it.

"Shouldn't we flip the other one, too?" Nero asks.

"We need to let the core settle on the base. If we don't give it time, both the shell and the core will get pulled toward the sphere, which doesn't help us." Saraf waits for several moments, then he flips the next switch. "They should be separated now." He opens the door to the large container. Floating over the fixture is a tiny white star.

"Is that the core?" Nero asks.

"It is. The only thing keeping it from dissipating right now, since it no longer has a shell, is the energy from the base."

"What happens to the shell?"

"It's mostly Aether. We'll use it in the next step, along with the Aether Sosimo brought." Saraf grabs the rod in the metal webbing and slowly connects it to the base. The core brightens as it is forced inside the vessel. "The vessel will provide the protection from the outside world, but it won't fully bond until we turn the power off on the base. Before we let it bond, I'm going to force Aether in a specific manner through it. The core will mimic and take on this same Aether behavior temporarily. Before I stop putting Aether through it, we'll turn off the power, which will permanently bond the core to the object and set its properties to the Aether I was using. The actual design of the vessel determines if it is a continuous or a pulse-type lepisent." Saraf turns to Sosimo. "So, what behavior did you want?"

"I would like electromagnetic radiation with a spread of frequencies topping out at three hundred gigahertz."

"Wow, do you want a cherry on top, too?"

"If you can manage, sure, but I think you have your work cut out for you already."

"That I do. This would certainly be useful to fight an advanced race that relies heavily on machines."

"That's the point."

"So that's why Sosimo needs your help!" Nero says. "Your cast is Moltrik and Pahzan and Sosimo's is Icor."

Saraf looks at Sosimo, smiling. "Not bad for a Human, eh?"

"Not bad at all," Sosimo says.

"There are ways to make Artifacts that aren't your cast," Saraf says. "However, it's tricky, never works as well, and requires special tools. Let's set the properties and finish the process."

Saraf removes the base from the large container, putting it on a stand in the middle of the room. Sosimo brings over a crystal sphere that is attached to a cable from the long-term Aether storage.

Saraf palms the sphere and touches the Artifact in making. He closes his eyes. "Here we go."

Sosimo pulls Nero back. "It's going to be rough at first." He places his hand on a switch. "I'll cut the power to the base as soon as Saraf stabilizes the Artifact."

Large sparks begin to arc between the Artifact and the rest of the room. Sosimo steps in front of Nero, shielding him. Saraf grimaces and his breathing grows more and more labored. Waves of energy pour from the end of the lepisent and the stray bolts of energy striking the surroundings lessen.

"Is it there yet?" Nero asks, peeking around Sosimo.

"Not much longer. It's almost settled."

The sparks disappear, and a continuous wave of energy radiates from the tip of the lepisent.

Sosimo flips the switch. "Alright, Saraf. That should do it."

The energy cuts out. Saraf opens his eyes, blinking. He grabs the edge of the table for support. Sosimo hurries over to help him to a seat.

Sosimo smiles. "Not bad for an old man."

"Old man!" Saraf grunts. "I could still run circles around you if I had to…" He puts his hand on his head. "Oy. Maybe I am getting old."

22 Odoki

Nero

"No, no, no. You need to focus. Strike it like it's a giant hawk trying to nip your ears off," Saraf says, sitting next to the fireball generator. "It should come off your styk faster than it started."

"But shouldn't I be adding to its Aether as well? How am I supposed to do that when my styk is empty?" Natina asks, waving the piece of wood in front of her. She's wearing a pair of clear safety glasses.

"Yes, but you can't jump over a pair of donkeys if you don't clear the first one... first. Odoki is a very delicate skill. Any Aether in your styk can overload it if you aren't practiced. It takes time to control how much and how fast you transfer Aether through Odoki. Just like deflecting Aether, it'll take time and practice. Trust me, this is the best way. I've had many of my styks blow up on me because I tried to rush it. We need to start small, adding energy through the physical contact."

Is that what happened to my broomstick when it exploded? Nero continues to pedal the bike. "Why does the stick explode?"

"Odoki puts a lot of strain on your styk. If you have a lot of Aether built up and you have poor control, all the energy will empty instantly. This can exceed the Aethersotto of your styk, which will cause it to overload and explode. Same goes if you do this with an attack that's too powerful. Your styk won't be able to handle the stress. A true master can modulate exactly how much energy releases from their styk."

"Why would you risk it?" Nero asks.

"It's the fastest way to drain energy from your styk. So, you would use Odoki if your styk is almost maxed out, or if you simply want to go on the offensive to change up the tempo of the battle. It could potentially give you an edge. It's also much faster than trying to deflect or block, so if you're desperate, Odoki will help speed up your defense."

"If you're adding Aether to the attack, what happens to the cast?"

Saraf raises his eyebrows and smiles. "That's a very good question. And to think I used to make fun of your feeble brain. When you deflect an attack, nothing happens to the cast. When you perform Odoki, though, the cast of the attack will change to the same one of your styk. Though your styk doesn't actually absorb the attacking Aether, the two become one for just a moment." Saraf turns back to Natina, placing his hand on the fireball generator. "Remember, there are two important aspects to this Odo form. First, you need to swing and make contact, which can be challenging in and of itself. Second, you need to focus on driving your stick through the Aether. For especially powerful attacks, it may feel like you're hitting something as hard as Grebson's head. You must keep your styk moving forward. This is a good mental trick for keeping your styk strong. Ready?"

Natina nods weakly. Saraf hits the button. A fireball grows at the tip of the generator. When it reaches the size of an apple, it detaches, wobbling like a droplet of water from the faucet. Its colors swirl, orange and red, twisting in on each other. Natina curls her lip, swinging with her whole body. The blob of fire brightens as she makes contact. It flares yellow before it zips toward Nero. He dives from the bike as it explodes against the wall. The momentum from Natina's swing spins her in a circle before she catches herself. Grebson chuckles.

Saraf looks at the giant scorch mark on his wall, shaking his head. "Nice hit, slugger. You didn't need to murder it. You nearly took off Nero's head!"

Nero dusts himself off. "That was awesome!"

Natina smiles at him. "Thanks."

"Could I try, Saraf?" Nero asks.

Saraf frowns. "You're going to keep asking until I let you, aren't you?" Nero nods. "Well, I suppose we can give it a shot one day. You must earn the right, first. You need to have your basic physical skills down. When you become proficient in Roroon, then we can give it a try. But it's your fault if you get hurt."

Nero smiles. "Deal!"

"Good." Saraf turns to Natina. "We'll have to figure out a better arrangement, so you don't destroy my training room. At this rate, it won't be long before there's nothing left. In the meantime, let's move on to Odora. You can't do much damage by drawing Aether from your styk." Saraf walks over to a rack to grab a leather strap. He ties it around Natina's waist. Then, he ties her right arm, styk in hand, behind her back. Saraf hops on the bike and starts to pedal. "You two know the drill. We'll warm up before we give Natina any Aether."

Nero walks over to Natina. They circle one another before Nero attacks. It takes him a few tries before he gets hold of her. They wrestle. Even with one arm tied behind her back, Natina is a close match for Nero. They grapple and strain to get the upper hand, and finally, Nero slips a foot behind Natina, pushing her to the ground.

Nero throws up his hands in triumph. "Got you!"

Saraf claps. "Holy smokes, I didn't think I'd live to see the day. Looks like those little muscles of yours actually work. Now, Natina, come over here and charge your styk. This time when you fight, I want you to draw the Aether from the stick for extra strength."

"That hardly seems fair," Nero says.

"And I'm getting old and my back always hurts. Is that fair? Hardly, but I'm not complaining," Saraf says.

Natina walks over to the Aether storage container, touching it with her styk. She walks back to Nero, smiling. "Why'd you stop dancing?"

Nero and Natina wrestle again. Again, it is a close match. Nero just barely manages to throw her down. He does a celebratory dance as she gets up, glaring at him.

"Just let the Aether flow into you, Natina, and the rest should happen naturally. Don't try to fight or resist it," Saraf says.

Natina closes her eyes for a moment, concentrating. A smile spreads across her face. "I think I got it."

Nero stops dancing. *Great...*

Natina lunges at Nero with surprising agility. He dodges her hand once, but the second time, she comes around and grabs his arm. She spins him around once then throws him to the ground. Natina starts to dance. "What'cha going to do now, skinny boy?"

Nero jumps up and tries to wrestle with her, but her speed and strength are too much. He lands on his back again.

"Alright, good job, you two. Practice a few more times. I'll be right back." Saraf hops off the bike, walking into his workshop.

"You know this is so unfair, right?" Nero asks.

"Yeah. It's too bad you can't draw Aether."

But I can! I just need to grab onto the styk. I think...

When they start again, Nero manages to just slide by one of Natina's lunges. She swipes again. He goes low, throwing her off balance. He grabs the styk in her hand as she tries to regain her balance. It vibrates with Aether and he opens himself up, letting it flow into him. He feels a surge of strength and he tosses Natina. She lands with a thump on her tied arm, yelping.

Oh no!

Nero and Grebson hurry over. Saraf is close behind.

"What happened?" Saraf asks.

"It looked like Nero got a lucky throw. Natina landed on her arm," Grebson replies.

Saraf gently unties her arm and she immediately cradles it, face stoic but ashen. "Who thought of tying her arm behind her back anyway?" Saraf asks.

"That was you, Saraf," Grebson says.

Saraf shakes his head. "What a nakok-wit." He pulls Natina to her feet. "Let's get you upstairs and take a look."

Saraf and Natina walk upstairs. Grebson stares Nero down. "I saw what you did." He reaches down to pick up the styk.

Nero looks down. "I'm sorry. I didn't mean to hurt her, I promise. Please don't tell the King."

"Don't be ridiculous. You drew Aether from the styk, didn't you?"

Nero nods. "I think so."

"How?"

"I'm not sure. I just did. I can also block and deflect Aether attacks."

"I didn't believe her, but there's something unique about you."

"Her who?"

"Only a few races other than Borukins can perform those skills. Humans definitely cannot, but you're different. Meet me before Illi rises tomorrow morning where Natina and I found you in the park. Come prepared. I want you to show me what you can do. I hope for your sake, you don't disappoint me."

Nero swallows. "Okay." *What does that mean?*

*****

Nero enters Sosimo's shop, which has a steady flow of customers scanning the candy. Two children excitedly run past him as he walks through to the back, and then to the second floor. He finds the other children training with Sosimo.

Iona and Ryder are working together. A small pit forms in Nero's stomach.

Thea runs over to him immediately, grinning. She holds up her arm, a lepisent strapped to it, and points it at Nero. "I just womped Korbin with this!"

Nero ducks.

Sosimo walks over to meet him. "Come on, Thea. Don't point that at people's faces." She lowers the lepisent, a little embarrassed. "Why are you home early?"

"Saraf made me take the rest of the day off because I was feeling bad. He said: If I'm not going to be here in spirit, then go waste space somewhere else."

"That sounds like him. Why were you feeling bad?"

"I accidentally hurt this girl he's been training."

Sosimo pats him on the back. "Don't feel too bad. I'm sure it's nothing serious. He seems pretty happy with your help, so you must be doing a good job in general."

"Yeah. At least he doesn't make fun of my brain anymore."

"We need to get back to training. Stick around afterward, Nero. I have something you might be interested in seeing." He directs Thea back to training.

Korbin stands up, groaning when he sees her coming.

Nero sits and watches the other children blast each other. Seeing Thea hit Korbin in the middle of his chest with a shot of Aether brings a smile to Nero's face.

He shifts his perspective and looks at the children's swirling Aether. Ryder has a yellow glow, Korbin has a brown glow, and Iona has a green glow. Thea, on the other hand, has a bright combination of red, blue, green, and yellow Aether. Each color though, is less vibrant than that of the other children. Nero looks closer, noticing that only her head glows with green Aether. The Aether from the rest of her body mixes around her neck, pushing toward her head, but the green Aether always surges back.

That's cool! What does it mean?

At the end of the training, the children are blackened. Sosimo sends them to clean up.

He walks over to Nero, shaking his head. "Not the prettiest sight, huh?"

Nero smiles. "It's fun to watch, though."

"It is. Wait here. I have a curio to show you." Sosimo hurries upstairs.

Iona sits down next to Nero. "Hey, so how's it going?"

"Alright. You?"

"I'm good. Playing with lepisents is pretty fun."

"It looks like it."

"Thea's doing the best. The rest of us are pretty equal. It's tough, but I enjoy it. What have you been doing? Are you still exploring the city at all? Any adventures?"

Nero shrugs. His eyes focus on nothing. A smile plays at the corners of his mouth. *A few.*

"What about working for Sosimo's friend? Is that fun?"

"Yeah, it's pretty sweet. Saraf has all sorts of cool artifacts and junk. Last month, they let me watch them make a lepisent. It was totally awesome."

"How did they do it?"

Nero's eyes light up. "So they got this essence and put it into a box and then flipped some switches that pulled the essence apart to separate its core from its shell. Do you know what that is?" Iona's eyes glaze over. "Well the core is the part that—"

Sosimo stomps back down the stairs holding a case. "Here it is, Nero," he says. He removes a single-sided black metal sword. It has two slots above the guard, carvings and other materials are inlaid in the blade. "Has Saraf ever shown you one of these?"

Nero shakes his head.

"Probably because he doesn't have one."

"Why's it special?" Iona asks.

"Here, Nero. What do you think?"

Nero shifts his perspective. Most of the blade is blurred by a gentle pulsing glow churning with red, blue, and green Aether. Violet lines fan out from the slots above the guard. The edge glows violet, too. Occasionally, a touch of Aether arcs from the main body and the violet lines flare with the same color. The edge stays incredibly crisp. "Wow, this is interesting. I see that it is mostly Pahzan, Moltrik, and Icor Aether. It has some strange lines from these slots to the edges, like the Katashne'n wood. What does it mean?"

"Saraf wasn't kidding about you. It's called a Porlimin sword. They're very difficult to make. They accept spherical tursent Artifacts that augment the Aether the blade cuts with. The two slots give you an instant choice of which Aether to use. The Aether you sensed in the body of the blade provides extra strength and protection. If you look carefully, you'll notice that the edge of this blade isn't even metal. Although, it'll still slice right through your finger."

Nero looks at the blade, running his finger on the edge. Sure enough, he sees a wood grain in the edge. His finger starts to bleed. He sticks it in his mouth, handing Sosimo the sword.

"I told you so. It is Katashne'n wood, just like you thought. Anyway, I thought you'd appreciate it."

Nero pulls his finger briefly out of his mouth. "It's really cool. How much was it?"

Sosimo shakes his head. "You don't want to know." Sosimo puts the sword back in the case. "So, did you remind Saraf we're going to the second to last day of the Games tomorrow?"

Nero nods. "What time are we leaving?"

"A little after eight in the morning. We'll skip the morning Roroonki so you can all sleep in. It's going to be a long day."

Yeah… Hopefully that's enough time for Grebson to kick my butt.

*****

Nero hurries through the park with his latest broomstick from Saraf's shop. Illi is just peeking over the horizon. He slows as he gets closer.

I wonder where he is.

Be careful. He's hiding.

Nero stops, readying his stick. There is a flash out of the corner of his eye. He spins to block a ball of Aether. It feels like nothing compared to the Entity's attacks.

Grebson steps out from behind a grouping of trees. He has a silver gauntlet on each arm. When Nero shifts his perspective, the gauntlets glow red and blue. Grebson himself has a detailed green glow, revealing all of his features. The styk in one hand has a fainter green glow, while the container he holds in his other hand has an extremely bright, pulsing glow. Nero lets his perspective shift back to normal.

A sliver of a smile touches Grebson's mouth. "Good. You at least have enough skill to perform Odosa." Grebson exposes the top of the container, transferring the Aether into his styk.

Nero lowers his broomstick, smiling. Grebson's expression grows serious, he thrusts his hand outward and a stream of lightning arcs from one of his gauntlets. Nero throws up his stick. The electricity grabs onto it viciously.

I've never dealt with this before. The attack pushes him back, but he continues to block. His stick begins to vibrate. *What am I supposed to do?* He starts to draw some of the Aether for strength, but the incoming Aether is coming in faster.

Grebson cuts the attack, following with two fast-moving balls of fire. With his increased speed and strength, Nero easily blocks them. He dives out of the way of a third, deflecting a fourth straight back at Grebson. Grebson blocks the fireball with a flick of his styk.

Grebson looks at Nero, surprised. "I guess she was right. Let's see what you can handle."

"Who is 'she?' Natina?"

Grebson hurtles another fireball at Nero. Nero blocks it. The attack knocks him off balance. Grebson starts to raise his left arm.

Great. Not again.

The electricity races toward Nero. This time, Nero tries to push the energy away from his stick. He feels the attack slam into the wood, knocking him one way and ricocheting off to the side, scorching a tree. Another fireball flies at him, a stream of lightning following behind. He deflects the fireball back into the lightning. The Aether mixes together until it explodes, allowing Nero to move to the side easily.

That was cool.

Nero dives, as another fireball zips over his head.

"Damn, boy. Saraf won't believe this. How much can you take?"

Nero starts to smile. Three more fireballs fly at his face. He deflects the first fireball into the second. They disappear in a flash of heat. He blocks the third.

That works awesome. I'm going to have to use that against the Entity.

He barely pulls his stick up in time as a huge fireball crushes into him. He rolls backward, popping back to his feet quickly. A stream of lightning grabs onto his stick. His hands sting and his teeth begin to chatter as the broomstick is loaded with Aether.

He rolls to the side, swinging hard. The electricity arcs into the trees. This time, as he reaches his feet, he jumps one more time. He feels the heat from another fireball wash over him. The broomstick vibrates uncomfortably in his hands.

I'm not sure how much more it can take. What did Saraf say about removing the stored energy? Grebson readies another attack and Nero widens his stance, digging his toes into the ground. *BAD IDEA!*

Grebson releases the fireball. Nero swings. The broomstick in his hand feels as though it has hit a moving truck. He clenches his teeth, driving through it. The energy travels painfully up his arms. Suddenly, it calms. Nero opens his eyes. There is a haze of Aether all around him.

I'm alive! He sees a gigantic ball of Aether flying toward Grebson at incredible speed. "Uh-oh."

Grebson's eyes grow large. He pulls up his styk. The ball of energy slams into the stick, knocking Grebson off balance. The energy zips high into the air. Nero watches in amazement.

Wow...

BOOM!

The morning sky lights up as the ball of Aether releases its energy, jostling the treetops. Nero readies himself, looking at Grebson. Fire flares in Grebson's eyes. He shoots out a dangerous stream of lightning at Nero, which latches instantly onto the broomstick. Before Nero can shake it off, two massive fireballs slam into his stick as well. The vibration in Nero's broomstick reaches a critical point and explodes in his hands, sending him spinning into a bush. He hits his thigh on a rock, landing face down. Every part of Nero's body aches from millions of pinpricks, his hands feel like they are on fire, his thigh is throbbing, and his ears are ringing. Grebson pulls him out of the bush, a rag doll, and sets him gently on the ground.

"You alive, boy?"

Nero grunts, squinting to see. Grebson is standing over him, a touch of concern in his scowl.

"Sorry. I lost my temper. I'm not as disciplined as I used to be. If it was an even fight, it would have cost me."

"You think I could have beat you?"

"No. I'm saying that if we were evenly matched and I behaved like that, you would've won. You still have a lot to learn, and you're small. If this was a real fight, I would've just cracked your skull and been done with it."

Nero holds his head. "You might've done it anyway."

Grebson looks at his eyes. "You don't look concussed. I think you're fine. I'm not usually impressed, but you are more skilled than I could have imagined. Your instincts are good, even though you're timid in normal life. It threw me. I'll have to urge Saraf to let you train fully now, though I'm not sure it would be good for Natina."

"Why not?"

"Your skill is beyond anyone your age, or even years older. You might not be a good challenge for her. Who trained you in Odo?"

Nero looks around. "Uh, no one." Grebson gives him a look. "I just played in the forest—by myself." Grebson is still unconvinced. "I listened very closely to Saraf."

"That I can see." Grebson reaches down, picking up a sliver of Nero's shredded broomstick. "Another thing that made me doubtful was your styk. I thought you were holding a broken broomstick."

"I was."

Grebson's eyes narrow. He looks closer at the wood. "It does seem to be standard wood. Why were you using it?"

Nero shrugs. "I'm not sure; it was the only thing I had, and it worked better than a metal shield."

"Are you serious?" he asks. His deep voice rattles Nero's skull.

"Oh, yes. Metal doesn't work at all when blocking—"

Grebson throws up his hand. "I know. Every Borukin infant knows. So, the only reason you were using the broomstick was out of convenience?"

Nero nods.

"Well, then, I shall be interested to see what you can do with a decent styk. You do realize your Odoki I deflected could have killed someone? You nearly caught me off guard."

Nero looks down. "I'm sorry."

"It's not your fault. You should just be more careful, so you don't hurt someone by accident. If that had hit me, I would have deserved it for not paying attention. That's probably why I lost my temper. You scared me."

"I scared you?"

"Your attack certainly did."

"But aren't great warriors fearless?"

"Who's to say I'm a great warrior?"

"I just thought—"

"No one is fearless, Nero. If they are, then they're either lying or stupid." Grebson looks around. "We should get out of here. We're bound to have drawn some attention." Grebson turns to leave, but stops. "I need to give you something." He reaches into his pocket, pulling out a shiny brown stone. There are six blue gems evenly spaced around it. "A friend wanted me to give you this."

"Who?"

"It doesn't matter. Just don't lose it. And don't show it to anyone."

Nero takes the token, looking at it. He can sense a very faint hint of red Aether when he shifts his perspective. "What is it?"

"It's a symbol of protection." Voices float faintly toward them. Grebson turns. "Let's get out of here. People are coming."

Nero hobbles back to Sosimo's, his leg aching. He hops in bed with an hour to spare and sleeps peacefully.

23 The Games

Iona

Iona snaps awake. *The Games!* She throws off her covers. "Come on, Thea. It's time to get up!" Thea stirs in the other bed, but moves no further.

Sosimo, wearing his standard long sleeves, looks up from making breakfast as Iona enters. "Mornin', Iona. Food's pretty much ready, so help yourself." Iona grabs a plate, filling it with eggs, bacon, and toast. "I'm going to wake everyone else," he says.

She takes a seat at the table by herself. *Nero isn't up yet? That's got to be a first.*

A few moments later, Sosimo comes back. The other excited children trickle in behind him. Nero is last. He looks like he just came out of a dryer filled with rocks and dirt. He is fighting to keep his eyes open, limping on one leg.

Sosimo frowns. "Jeez, Nero, rough dream?"

"I was fighting..." Nero bites his tongue, looking down. "I just bumped my thigh. It really hurts."

"A Charlie horse. Those are the worst," Sosimo says.

"What's that?" Korbin asks.

Ryder turns to Korbin and punches him in the thigh. Korbin falls from his chair in agony. "That's a Charlie horse."

Sosimo lets out a short laugh. "My brother and I used to do that all the time. How'd everyone sleep?"

"What was that giant explosion?" Thea asks. "It woke me up."

"Me too," Ryder says. "The sky was glowing afterward."

"I'm not sure," Sosimo says. "I saw the news before breakfast. They said it was some sort of Aether explosion. Probably some dimwit showing off for the Games. Things like this happen before big events."

Iona watches Nero pick at his food without looking up. *Maybe it scared him.*

After they finish breakfast and brush their teeth, Sosimo pulls out bikes for all of the children.

"Why do we have to ride on bikes?" Korbin asks. "Can't we just take Gracie?"

"It'll be much easier to get around on bikes," Sosimo says. He gives an old purple bike to Korbin. "It's not far."

"Stop whining, Korb," Ryder says. "It'll be fun, watch." He rides a red bike in wobbly circles around the alley.

Korbin jumps on his bike, mimicking Ryder with an equally unsteady demonstration. They all take a moment to acquaint themselves with their two-wheeled transportation before Sosimo leads them away on his bike, which looks more like a motorcycle. The crowds of people they pass soon overflow onto the streets. No cars are present.

They reach the cliffs where they see Illi just above the ocean. Its light burns along the water, illuminating the large stone structures.

Sosimo stops at a bike rack. He pulls out a giant chain, strings their bicycles together, and locks them. Sosimo points to a giant museum of black marble crisscrossed with white lines. Two carved Borukins stand on either side of the large double doors. Each has one hand holding up the roof. "That is the Orinda Museum, where the history of the Games is kept. I'll show you around before we visit Testrel, the imprisoned Drake. Then we'll head to our seats in Stone's Coliseum. Sound good?"

All but Nero hop in excitement. "Yeah!"

"Let's go," Sosimo and Thea say at the same time.

"Jinx!" Thea says quickly. "I got you!" She points at Sosimo, running in place.

"How do I play?"

"You can't talk." Thea runs over and punches Sosimo in the leg. Her hand crumples and she holds it up. "Ahh," and falls to the ground.

"Are you okay, Thea?"

Korbin shakes his head, looking down at her. "She's dead. I've seen this before. Once when an enemy punched Captain Konquer in the stomach, he flexed, and it sent a shockwave through the guy's body and killed him. Killed him just like that." He snaps his fingers.

"Is that so?" Sosimo reaches down and picks her up by the armpits. He tries to set her on her feet, but her legs are limp. Eventually, her head rolls to the side, her tongue flopping out.

"I'm telling you, she's deader than a slug in an oven. There's no hope."

"I can see that, but we can't leave her here." He throws her over his shoulder. "Maybe we can feed her to Testrel."

Thea squirms. "No, Mr. Sosimo, I'm alive. I was just joking."

Sosimo sets her down. "That's good, because I don't think you would be very tasty."

"You wouldn't really feed me to it, would you?"

He pats her head. "No, Thea, I was just joking. Let's go."

Sosimo pushes into the flow of people and the children fight to stay in his collapsing wake. They reach the large steps of the museum, then the double doors that make even the Borukins look small. There is a short entryway lined with statues of vicious creatures. Sharp claws, horrible teeth, and spikes reach toward the children from every direction. The creatures look like they will spring to life at any moment.

Sosimo points as they walk through the entrance. "These are the main creatures the Borukin warrior fights in the current form of the Trial of Orinda."

"Are these real monsters?" Korbin asks.

"No, Korbin. Unfortunately, they are just creatures that have been turned into something violent. In their natural environment, they'd probably leave you alone. Except that one," Sosimo says. He points to a large bat-creature the size of the children. Its wings are spread; its mouth is an open snarl with sharp serrated teeth. "They're called Shirako bats. They can be found at the edges of the Tenebrous Miasma. They're pack hunters and will attack virtually anything. They circle and nip at you until you bleed enough to lose consciousness."

Sosimo hurries them through one of many revolving doors to the main chamber that expands in every direction. The magnificence of the stonework and the high dome are quickly diminished by the gruesome decor. The paintings below the curve of the dome are all Borukins covered in gore and battling monsters. Their expressions are wild and lusting for battle as they wade through the death they had caused. Along the perimeter of the floor are statues of life-sized Borukins locked in eternal combat.

Iona blinks her eyes as her vision turns red. She nearly runs into Sosimo when he stops abruptly. The corners of his mouth turn down and the toothpick in his mouth snaps. The children look at him for several moments until he finally speaks.

He lets out a breath. "Let's get through this room quickly. It's a disappointing display of what Borukins are turning into. In the past, this room was peaceful. It used to be a room for honor, not savagery."

He leads them past a series of statues of heavily armored Borukins thrusting bladed and spiked weapons of lurid design. They are all statues of the competitors in the Trial of Orinda.

Sosimo quickens his pace as he approaches the end.

"Who's this one? He looks familiar." Nero stops, pointing to a statue of a Borukin fighting off two flying creatures with razor sharp teeth.

"No one," Sosimo says.

"Hey! It says Grebson," Nero says. "Is this the same one that I see with Saraf?"

"It is."

"He must be famous," Korbin says. "Nero, can you get me his autograph?"

Iona's chest grows heavy.

"What good is fame, Korbin, when you're not there to protect your family?" He looks at Korbin for a moment before turning away. "Let's go see Testrel and get out of here."

The children look at each other, dumbfounded, before following along. They walk to the back of the museum into another large opening. A sign in red reads: 'The Borukin Killer.' A large cage fills the center of a solarium. It is surrounded by Borukins. Red, green, and yellow light coruscates about the room as the serpent-like creature breathes. It is long and coiled more times than Iona can count. Occasionally, an arm or a leg is visible where thick chains hold it in place. It has barbs running along its snout, and two large horns jutting straight back from its forehead.

"Woo." Iona moves closer to Ryder. "That's her? She's huge."

"A truly magnificent race…" Sosimo says.

"What are those chains doing to her?" Nero asks.

"They're keeping her from moving. Duh," Korbin says.

"Korbin, you should learn to respect Nero's questions. He sees things none of us can."

Iona glances at Nero, who looks hurt. *What does that mean?*

They continue to walk toward the Drake. Iona feels suddenly tired as they get closer to the cage.

"Ultimately, Korbin, you are right," Sosimo says, "but there is more to it than just steel. Normally this cage would be no more than tissue paper to her if she wanted to escape, but the chains about her legs are specially made so they continually drain her of Aether. Testrel generates so much Aether they use her to power the surrounding buildings."

"Holy moly, that's a lot of Aether," Thea says, bouncing on her toes.

When they reach the Drake's head, the children lean over the railings, trying to be as close as possible.

Iona watches her body rise with breaths taken as though they are inconvenient and not worth taking. *I'm sorry, Testrel. I wish I could help you.*

Testrel's eyes open. The Borukins gasp. Iona looks directly into the black iris of an eye almost as big as her head. She cannot move. After a long moment, Testrel lets out a breath, closing her eye.

Sosimo puts his hand on Iona's shoulder. "That's the most I've ever seen her move."

The Borukins around the cage chat excitedly amongst themselves.

"But it just opened its eyes," Thea says.

Sosimo nods. "I know. It's sad, but she's still got life left in her. Hopefully, they'll let her go before she gives up completely."

"Why don't any of her friends come and rescue her?" Nero asks.

"I don't think they know she's alive," Sosimo says.

*****

After the museum, they take their bikes to the Coliseum, locking them up near the largest of the three connected stadiums. In the boisterous crowd, Sosimo leads them under the high edged stadium to stairs that fan out and rise a third of the way up its height. Their tickets are checked, and they enter a corridor filled by a number of food, drink, and souvenir vendors set up between the entrances to the different sections of seating. Finally, they reach an entrance to their section.

Light envelops them. It takes Iona a moment to adjust, and a moment longer to comprehend the sheer size of the stadium.

The arena is an expanse of polished red granite. Borukins are scattered all around, dressed in immaculate white robes, performing stretching and movement routines. In the center, there is a raised platform of onyx in front of a giant cannon.

At the near end of the arena stands a large rotating apparatus with five long spars sticking out from the center. A Borukin with a shaved head, body covered in white tattoos, pushes each spar to rotate the assembly. On the far side, a giant screen shows the announcer interviewing the various competitors. Their names and notable achievements are listed below.

"Neat." Iona pauses, absorbing the whole scene.

"Come on, children," Sosimo says. "The sooner we get to our seats, the better."

They climb halfway up, and Sosimo directs them to a row with open seats.

"What's that big thing they're pushing?" Iona asks once they are all relaxing in the warm morning light.

"It's an Aether generator, similar to the bike we use for practice. The competitors in these games require an impressive amount of Aether, which is stored under the arena."

"What's the cannon thing for?" Iona asks.

"That's for the Trial of Odosa. It's just a larger version of the device that shoots out Aether in the training room."

"Woo! They're going to try to block Aether from that?"

Sosimo nods. "It's humbling, isn't it?"

"How can anyone even do that?" Korbin asks.

"You'll see soon enough."

"What else will we get to see?" Thea asks.

"After the Trial of Odosa, there are the finals to Stone's Lift, and then Aether-weaving," Sosimo says.

"Aw, but I wanted to see the fighting," Korbin says.

"The preliminaries for the Trial of Borutaress are in the next stadium," Sosimo says. "We wouldn't be able to see both, and trust me, the competitions here are something you don't want to miss."

The competitors disperse as the announcer steps up to the little platform.

"Ladies and Gentlemen, welcome to the Games. Please settle in and prepare yourself for some amazing performances today. Our great King and liberator, Layton Stone created the Games as a means to keep our skills sharp and ready at a moment's notice. As we approach the last days of the Games, we will begin Stone's Trials: the backbone of what truly defines us as Borukins." The crowd cheers, and the announcer waits until they settle down. "One of these is the Trial of Odosa. It was chosen by King Stone to demonstrate our abilities to defend against even the most powerful Aether attacks. It also demonstrates that our fortitude never falters!" The crowd cheers again. "Now, it is with immense honor that I introduce the competitors for this great trial."

The announcer begins to read names. The crowd cheers for each one with varying degrees of enthusiasm as the Borukins in their white robes and styks of assorted shapes approach. They all bow toward the King's private box then sit in a row of seats. "Prince Kamin Ramas Jr.!" A large, stern Borukin follows the same procedure and sits with his styk across his lap.

"Jesler Coffman!" Another Borukin approaches and sits. "And finally, the truly unbelievable Overseer, Melanie Carason!" When Melanie enters the arena, the crowd erupts in a deafening roar. It lasts up until she bows and takes her seat. "Now, before we begin, please join me in showing our respect to Etta Mayes for the singing of our National Anthem."

The Borukins in the crowd stand and put their fists over their hearts. Etta takes the platform.

After the anthem, the announcer takes center stage one last time. "Good luck to the competitors today, and may Stone give you strength!"

The head official steps up to the center platform, minor officials on either side. "The Riner Ratio will be set to zero for the preliminaries. We'll open the competition at one-point-five on the Boltz scale." One of the minor officials holds up a flat board with a cup on it. The head official picks up the cup, shakes it, then slams it onto the board, upside down. She takes the cup away, looking at a single die left on the board. "We'll start with Icor. First up is Emery, followed by Kessler, with Latham in the hole."

The officials step down. A few of the competitors start warming up again while others remain seated. The head official walks over to the cannon and confirms the settings for the machine. A young Borukin settles herself on the center platform, facing the cannon. She signals with her head; the official waves a green flag. A bolt of white energy launches out of the cannon in a flash, crashing into the Borukin's styk.

"Oh wow!" the children say in harmony.

"It's only getting started, children."

Three judges in yellow run up to the competitor and inspect her white robes, the head official approaching. One by one, the yellow judges hold up white flags. The head official does a quick scan, then holds up her white flag. "Pass!"

A light applause rolls through the crowd.

"So, what's going on?" Ryder asks.

"The preliminaries are just used to weed out the contestants," Sosimo says. "They will continue to up the total energy of the attacks for each level while rotating through Moltrik, Pahzan, and Icor Aether until only four competitors are left."

"Why not the other casts?" Nero asks.

"They're not as common and the ones selected are the typical ones you'd have to fight against."

"How do you get eliminated?" Iona asks.

"In order to pass, the contestant's robes must be unscorched. They wear white so it's easier to tell."

They turn their attention back to the competition. With each new level, the intensity of the cannon dazzles the children. The number of competitors begins to dwindle. With just a handful of competitors left, only Kamin hasn't entered.

He continues to sit in his chair with a rigid back, his styk on his lap, and his hands on his knees. The activities move around him, but he remains perfectly still, only blinking on occasion.

Ryder points at the King's son. "Why hasn't he done anything yet?"

"He must be confident enough that he doesn't feel he needs a warm up. He placed third during the last Games, so it should be interesting to see how his skills have developed."

"Do you think he'll win?" Nero asks.

"I doubt it," Sosimo says. "Jesler beat him pretty significantly last time around... And there isn't a Borukin alive that can match Madam Carason's Odo. She's the Overseer to the Borukin schools of education and martial arts. It puts her in control of one of the only political bodies that carries any weight, compared to the King. She's an exceptional lady: open minded, thoughtful, and the reason why it was so easy to get you all in school."

Eventually, there are only five competitors left. One readies himself, and the cannon fires. A bright blast engulfs the competitor. Streams of fire shoot everywhere; the roar of energy rattles Iona's teeth. After a moment, silence blankets the arena. The Borukin is left in the center, breathing heavily. The judges run up and start to verify his success when one raises a red flag and points to the competitor's elbow. The competitor throws up his hands, arguing with the judge. The other judges look at his elbow. After a moment of study, they throw up their red flags as well. The competitor shakes his head and sits off to the side. The prince, for the first time, gets up and talks with the official.

"See that?" Sosimo asks. "Since that competitor just failed, this will be the last level, so the King's son has finally decided to enter. If any of the other competitors fail as well, then their burn marks are compared in a tiebreaker."

Madam Carason, Jesler, and another competitor pass and take a seat to the side. Finally, Kamin casually walks up and takes a relaxed, ready position. The cannon fires; he blocks.

Once the energy clears, the judges run to inspect him. None of them raise their red flag. Kamin walks out of the arena, unconcerned.

"So, is that the end, then?" Ryder asks.

"Yep, those are the four competitors for tomorrow," Sosimo says.

"I wish we could see it. Does it get a lot more powerful?" Ryder asks.

Sosimo nods. "It'll be impressive."

Workers flood the arena, removing the Aether cannon and the onyx platform. Another group of Borukins bring in a tall, framed structure on wheels. They anchor it to the ground. At the base of the tower, others expose a channel in the arena floor. The channel is a little narrower than a Borukin's shoulders. It has metal bars spanning its width, so it looks like a ladder laying on the ground. The same group of workers enter the arena again, pulling a large chunk of sandstone on rollers. They manage to maneuver the stone to the middle of the tall structure where they attach a thick steel cable to a harness wrapped around it. The cable runs up the center of the structure and back to the ground, ending in a hook. Four large, thick Borukins walk into the arena, followed by their coaches and assistants. They begin to warm up.

"Holy cow. Those guys are huge," Korbin says. "They must be twice the size of you, Sosimo."

"And they aren't all men, Korbin."

"Oh."

"How does this one work?" Thea asks.

"These are the finals of Stone's Lift competition. Each competitor is latched onto the cable connected to the giant stone and to an Aether supply. They use the Aether to modify their strength to pull the stone up the tower while they traverse the ladder. If there is a tie for distance, then the quickest one to get there wins."

The first competitor walks up to the channel. His helpers secure the metal cable to his harness and another lighter cable to his belt. He positions himself with his hands and feet on the metal rods in the channel and nods to an official. A three-tone starting signal goes off, and the Borukin starts to traverse the ladder with astonishing speed. When he reaches halfway, his pace begins to slow, and he struggles to reach the next rung. He pulls up, but before he can grasp the rung, his other hand slips. He is ripped from the ladder, flying through the air. A loud clang rings throughout the stadium as the stone is caught. The competitor tumbles to a stop. He picks himself up and bows to the audience, which meets him with a roar of approval.

"I don't understand, Sosimo," Ryder says. "If they're using Aether, why do they get tired?"

"Well, even though they have all the energy they need, their muscles still fatigue and lose their effectiveness. They still need to train their bodies to handle the load."

The next competitor starts and falls off at a shorter distance than the first. The third just barely finishes, and the fourth makes it all the way without showing even a hint of exhaustion. The crowd applauds as the competitors bow and leave the arena.

During the following intermission, Sosimo takes them back into the corridor with the concession stands, game stalls, and stores. The walkway is packed with Borukins of all ages trying to buy food and jostling each other. Smaller groups brag about their success at the stalls that test skill in mini-versions of the competitions. The Borukins playfully shove each other as they wait for the results.

Sosimo pulls them over to one of the stands. "Alright, this is a Borukin favorite. It's great for energy. Who wants to try it?"

"What is it?" Thea asks. The vendor wraps rice, a dark gooey sauce, and white meat in seaweed.

"It's seaweed, rice, a plum sauce, and crab. Very tasty."

Thea wrinkles her nose. "Ew. I don't like crab."

Nero steps up. "I'll try it. I'm hungry."

Iona looks at him and raises her eyebrows. *Wow, Nero going first?*

Sosimo thumps him on the back. "That's the spirit." Sosimo turns to the servers and orders one for Nero.

Nero takes a tentative first bite and then scarfs the rest. He shrugs. "It's pretty good. Can I please have another?"

Sosimo continues to feed them snacks, daring the children to try new foods. Finally, when they are stuffed, he brings them back to their seats.

Soon, more workers bring a wood platform to the center of the arena. The stadium roof begins to close, blocking Illi's hot afternoon light.

"What's going on?" Iona asks.

"They're making it darker, so you can see the light from the Aether weaving," Sosimo says. "In all your life, you won't find a better demonstration of Aether manipulation especially since we have Delue and Ratami in Axiom today. Prepare yourself."

"How do they win?" Korbin asks.

"Aether weaving is a subjective competition, so whoever gets the best score from the judges wins."

A Borukin is introduced and enters the arena. He walks toward the platform in slippers and a long baton in each hand.

"The platform is charged with Aether," Sosimo says. "They don't wear shoes so they can absorb Aether through their feet while keeping both hands free."

The performer places his slippers to the side, steps on the platform, and bows toward the King's private box. The main lights dim, casting the stadium into darkness. Only a few small lights illuminate the weaver and the arena perimeter. Music starts, and the weaver begins to move his hands. He summons up creatures of Aether that race around the arena.

They cascade together, forming a torrent of changing colors, which morphs into new shapes, seamlessly synchronized with the music. When the music ends, the lights come back on and the spectators cheer. The Borukin bows to the King once more, stepping away. After a few minutes, his scores show up. The crowd cheers again. Another performer follows with a similar performance.

When the next performer takes her place on the platform, Sosimo nudges Thea. "Okay, watch this one. Rae Mezlerra is going to be amazing. Hopefully she doesn't get herself into too much trouble."

"What do you mean?" Iona asks.

"She likes to make honest statements. Usually, people with power aren't pleased with her."

The woman bows to the King and the lights dim.

Birds above and a forest below take shape from the darkness. People tend to the finely-detailed forest. A newcomer arrives. One by one, the newcomer convinces the people to harvest the forest. The weather grows dark. The ones who are not convinced protest, but are ignored. Large trees fall; their wood carried away, leaving the forest devastated in no time. One enormous tree is left.

The cutters approach. A few protesters stand in their way. They fight while the weather storms around them. After many fall, the cutters eventually triumph. One cutter looks to the bodies scattered around, then to the large tree, then to the destroyed forest. They plant themself in front of the other cutters moving toward the last tree. The weather again matches the tension as the one cutter argues with the others. One at a time, the other cutters look around. The tension in their bodies lessen. They turn to the fallen and weep. The weather turns light, the people move out to plant seeds, convincing the cutters they encounter to become keepers. The music and lights from the Aether slowly fade away.

The crowd erupts in applause.

"Hm. This should be interesting," Sosimo says.

"Why?" Iona asks. "That was amazing."

"It was also a stab at the royal family. The King won't tolerate that well."

"It was? What did it mean?" Nero asks.

"I believe it's expressing her frustration with the corruption and deviation from our roots. She'll probably go to prison for it." Sosimo points at the results screen. "Here, look. The scores are coming in."

The audience falls silent at first, but as soon as the score from the second judge pops up, an uproar of boos and complaints ensues. Each of the scores is much lower than the previous competitors.

"What's going on, Sosimo? Someone's messing up," Korbin says.

Sosimo nods. "They're not messing up; they're just too scared to vote in favor. They don't want to bring the King down on them." The last score pops up, and it is a perfect ten out of ten, which spurs the crowd into cheers. "Unlike that judge…"

"What's going to happen to them?" Thea asks.

"It depends how mad the King is. Hopefully, if the judge keeps her head low, she'll avoid most of the mess."

After the crowd settles, the final competitor performs and comes out with the highest score. The canopy in the stadium opens and Illi's late afternoon light creeps in. Several podiums are set up for the finales of the day, medals awarded to each of the competitors. Rae Mezlerra does not even make the podium.

"And that concludes another fantastic display of Aether weaving," the announcer says. "Now, I hope the children are excited, because it's finally time to see what our young are capable of in Capture the Orb!" The crowd cheers. "If you were accepted to the game, please make your way to the arena to check in. We'll be starting soon."

"That's your cue, children. Remember: if you get hit with Aether or knocked over, you're out. Also, keep in mind that the arena is set up to give Borukins going for the orb Aether, so they'll be able to use lepisents, just like you. Good luck. I'll be watching."

The children clamor down the stairs toward the arena where they check in with a Borukin.

Iona watches Ryder and Nero walk to the red team, while Thea and Korbin wait for her on the blue team. She smiles. *I hope we beat them.*

They walk toward an older Borukin girl who is separating the other children into two groups. "Humans?" She says with a bit of disappointment. "Can you at least use Aether?"

"Heck yes," Thea says. "We'll smoke anyone who gets in our way."

The Borukin girl smiles. "I like it. Well, obviously you'll be taking lepisents. We'll start you off on defense, so go over there." She points to one of the groups.

"What?" Korbin says. "I want to be offense. I'm going to get the Orb!"

"Yeah, and Stone's mother was an Erohsian... I tell you what, if you prove yourself, I'll let you make an attack run with me."

Korbin grudgingly accepts and the Human children join the defense group with a few Borukins that Iona recognizes from school.

Once the rest of the children finish filing into the arena, the competitors select their Aether objects. The offensive team mostly gets lepisents, while the defensive team only gets styks.

The game starts with a blue explosion of Aether in the center of the arena. The children yell in excitement. Iona and the others watch from a distance as the children at the boundary take turns advancing on the other side only to be pushed back.

"This sucks," Korbin says. "We should go up there and get some action."

"Protecting the orb is important, too," Iona says. "I'm sure there'll be someone any moment."

Eventually, one of the larger children from the other side runs past the defenders and zaps two others with Moltrik Aether that leaves them convulsing on the ground.

"Woo!" Iona says and points. "Here comes one now."

The boy just barely dodges a volley of Aether from the Humans. He glares at them for an instant then runs to the side of the Arena.

"Get him!" Korbin says, running after the Borukin.

"Yeah!" Thea starts running.

Great... Iona looks at the orb and the other defenders then chases after her friends.

Thea catches him. He blocks a couple of Thea's attacks with his lepisent, but she quickly overwhelms him. He falls to the ground.

"I got him!" Thea says, dancing.

Korbin kicks the dirt. "He was totally mine."

The boy slowly starts to get up. "Stupid Humans. Why don't you go back to your babysitter?"

Korbin steps toward him. "Who are you calling stupid? You're the one that just got toasted by a girl a quarter your size."

"I toasted your buns on high!" Thea says as she dances. "Totally well done and crispy."

"You better show some respect or you'll regret it."

Thea stops dancing. "I'm sorr—"

"What are you going to do?" Korbin asks. "You're out. It's game over for you. Do you want a tissue because it looks like you're going to cry? You poor baby—I mean Borukin."

Yells erupt from the other side of the field. A large skirmish breaks out. Kids rush to the fray, followed closely by the officials.

Korbin looks at the fight then back to the Borukin boy. "Uh oh. That doesn't look good for you."

The boy scowls. He turns his lepisent on Korbin, zapping him twice. Korbin falls to the ground, thrashing.

"Hey, that's cheating! You can't do that," Thea says, stomping her foot. She looks around to get an official's attention, but they are all turned away.

He turns and shoots at Thea. She jumps out of the way, just in time. Another group of Borukins join him. They all start shooting at the girls. Thea and Iona block a few attacks but are overcome. Moltrik Aether courses through Iona's body, making her muscles clench painfully and sporadically. She falls to the ground, curled into the fetal position.

"Jerrik, we saw you got zapped by a little girl and came over to see if you needed help braiding her hair," a Borukin girl says. The others laugh.

"Shut your dumb face, Sadie."

"Jeez, take a joke."

"Whatever." Jerrik glances in the direction of the distracted officials then turns to the Humans. "These Humans think they're better than us." He zaps Korbin again. "What are we going to do about it?"

They zap the girls as well, laughing. Thea starts to whimper.

"So pathetic," Jerrik says.

Ryder runs over. "Hey, stop. They're out." He looks at Iona. "Are you okay?"

Iona nods, trying to stand up.

"Go get the orb and mind your own business," Jerrik says.

"These are my friends."

"Then you should join them." Jerrik shoots Ryder.

Ryder defends but is hit and falls to the ground. The Borukins laugh and zap them all once more.

Nero steps in front of Iona and Thea.

The Borukins stop, frowning at him. "Oh you, the wannabe. What are you doing out of the corner I put you in? What do you expect to happen now? A little thing like you... and you found a styk. That's so cute. Get out of here before we hurt you like the rest."

"Go get help," Iona barely whispers.

"Leave them alone."

Jerrik grins. "You asked for it." He shoots a ball of Aether at Nero.

Nero hits the ball of Aether into another boy who falls to the ground in spasms.

Iona pain's is suddenly an afterthought. *What?*

"Get him!"

Nero blocks, dodges, and sends their attacks back at them, putting several down.

"How are you doing this?" Jerrik asks.

"It's called Odo. Have you tried it?"

Was that a comeback?

Jerrik growls and points to Sadie, who has a styk. "Give him a free lesson in Roroon. If you break any bones, I wouldn't hold it against you."

Sadie steps forward, attacking Nero in perfect form. Nero clumsily blocks a few of her strikes, but she hits him in the elbow and the leg, causing him to curl over. She follows through with a strike to his ribs, which he takes with a grunt. He wraps his arms around her styk as he falls to one knee.

Sadie smiles. "Are you teaching me the 'grab the styk and call for mommy' technique?"

She tries to pull her styk free and her smile falls away. Sadie puts her foot on Nero's shoulder, pulling with all her might. The styk won't budge. Nero whacks her in the knee then the hand, causing her to let go and stumble backward.

"Did you seriously just let him take your styk from you?" Jerrik asks.

"I couldn't draw. He's cheating somehow."

"Yeah, good excuse." Jerrik grabs a styk from another Borukin. "Let me show you how it's done."

Nero straightens himself as best he can, holding his two styks up.

The Borukin charges. Before he can get to Nero, Sosimo knocks him over. "Enough!" He looks at the shocked Borukin children. "You are all a pitiful example of Borukins and should be ashamed. Get out of here before I do something stupid."

They run off. Iona pushes herself up, noticing the game is over. Everyone is filing out of the Arena.

"They were such cheaters," Korbin says once standing.

Sosimo nods as he helps Thea up. "They were, but I was more pleased to see you all standing up for each other. That's family." Sosimo turns to Nero. "That was the sloppiest and most oddly impressive demonstration of Odo I've seen in a long time. You didn't tell me you were actually performing Odo with Saraf. Maybe you should train with us sometimes, too. It looks like the others could use more practice with defense."

"Yeah, that was awesome!" Thea says. She hugs Nero. "Thanks for making them stop. It really hurt. How did you do it?"

Nero shrugs. "I saw them hurting you all and I didn't know what else to do."

"Thanks, Nero," Korbin says quietly.

"How are the ribs? I saw you take a good shot to the side." Sosimo gently pokes Nero's side and moves his arm around. Nero grimaces. "It's going to be sore, but I don't think there's any serious damage. I think you all deserve some ice cream. What do you say?"

"Yeah!" Thea leaps up. She grabs Nero's hand and pulls him toward the exit.

24 Recuperation for Body and Mind
Isis

Do you think I want this?

Isis opens her eyes. Her heart is racing. It takes her a moment to remember where she is. When she does, she sees an Erohsian doctor reviewing the holographic screen on her wrist computer.

The doctor smiles, closing her computer. "Good morning, Isis. I'm glad you finally got some sleep. How are you feeling?"

"Meh." Isis closes her eyes, waiting for a wave of nausea to pass.

"That's from the accelerators. You'll be feeling like that for a few days, as much as we had to pump into you."

"When can I leave?"

"Well, let's see. You had multiple third degree burns from shrapnel melting through your armor. You have a sprained shoulder and a broken wrist. Your spine is bruised, and a number of your ribs are broken. There's some minor internal bleeding. The base of your skull is fractured from when your helmet was ripped off. Your throat is bruised. Overall, you should be here for a little over a week total."

"That's unacceptable."

"Were you listening? If it weren't for the accelerators and other treatments, you'd be in the hospital for months."

"You need to do better."

The doctor's eyebrows rise. "I heard I was treating a female Erohsian officer and had a glimmer of hope you'd have some sense."

"Don't talk to me about sense. The only reason Erohsia is anything is because the men have the drive to get things done. If I'm to keep up, I can't be in here a week. They'll show me no mercy."

"Like the way they showed the Humans no mercy when they took their land?"

"Oh, don't tell me you're one of those touchy-feely Human sympathizers. They're a dangerous race, and they need to be monitored."

"Any race is dangerous with too much power," the doctor says. "How do you think they feel about us?"

"Please." Isis throws up her free hand. "I'm not sure if I'm nauseous from your sympathizing or from the drugs. Will you just get me something for it?"

The doctor lets out a sigh, nodding. "There was a General Belshiv to visit. I told him you needed rest. Will you permit visitors now?"

"No. I'm not in the mood."

"Okay, then. I'll be back soon with something for your nausea." The doctor walks out.

Isis repositions herself, looking at her bed stand. She sees her wrist computer and carefully reaches for it. The holographic screen pops up perfectly in front of her.

Isis has a long list of messages, several from General Belshiv. *I'll deal with that later.* She calls the field doctor from the medical pod.

After a moment she appears on Isis's screen. "Ma'am, how are you feeling?"

"Wonderful…"

"I'm not surprised. I'm still impressed we cut you out of your armor in one piece."

"Did you find anything about what the heck we were chasing?"

"As you know, all of the targets were killed. The primary target was shot multiple times and he was confirmed dead on site by a soldier on your order."

"Were you able to confirm as well?" Isis asks.

"After stabilizing your condition and sending you to Sunta, I ordered the bodies of the targets to be brought back and isolated. It seems, though, RIGID found my preliminary report interesting and snatched up the bodies before I could examine them."

"Damn. Anything that could drastically enhance a soldier to the level we saw would definitely catch their attention. Did the spooks take everything?"

"They missed a few blood samples I had stashed. I was able to look at them more closely."

"What did you find?"

"Well, I'm not so sure our soldiers were actually traitors."

"Why?"

"They all have an infection. It seems to have a tremendous effect on the body, so it could have easily affected their minds. Whatever it was, we only saw the tip of its full potential."

"The infection? What do you mean?"

"It was developing, turning into something else, becoming more efficient. That's why the later targets were faster and stronger than the first ones we took out. In their blood, I found three distinct components. The first one was normal Erohsian cells. The second, was cells that were infected and mutated. I'm guessing those are the source of their increased strength, speed, healing, and Aether abilities."

"And the third component?"

"It's hard to tell. All I found were remains of something foreign."

"What do you mean by remains?"

"Whatever it was, it was coming apart. I think this explains why the victim we had in the medical pod died so quickly. The infected cells showed an increased rate of degeneration, which leads me to believe they have some sort of dependency on this foreign body."

"Wouldn't you expect some sort of degeneration after death?"

"Yes, of course, but not this quickly or to this extent. If this foreign organism disintegrated and the infection spread to the heart, the heart would fail. I'm just grateful we didn't see further progression of the infection. I'm not sure we'd recognize them as Erohsians. And to think how hard they'd be to kill…"

"We'd find a way."

"I imagine you would. Is there anything else?" the medical officer asks.

"No. Keep me informed if you learn anything new."

"Yes, Ma'am."

Isis hangs up, then calls her secretary.

"Hello, Ma'am. I'm glad to see you up. How are you feeling?" he asks.

"Wonderful. Anything come up since I last checked in?"

"The scientist, Alec Frey, called. He says he'd like to talk to you about an item of mutual interest when you're available."

Isis sits up straight. "Really?" She feels a sharp pain in her side and settles back down. "Did he say anything else?"

"Nope. I asked if he wanted to leave a better message, but he insisted on talking to you directly."

"Okay. Is that all?"

"There's one interesting turn of events with the Human uprising, but it can wait until you're out."

"What happened?" Isis asks.

"It appears they're gaining a bit more momentum. Do you remember the Human Art Lively?"

"Yes, he's an Erohsian loyalist, correct?"

"That was correct. He just flipped sides. He had a large public speech where he criticized every Human policy we have. He said that Catalyst is the only hope the Humans have if they ever want to escape our tyranny. We had to send in the riot squads to calm the Human crowd, which, of course, further upset them."

What flipped him? "Did the terrorists get to him?"

"Potentially. We have reports that say he was acting a little odd. He could have been drugged. We're trying to talk with him, but we can't locate him. I'll let you know if there are further developments."

"Good. I should be out within the week. Send me the reports as soon as you can."

"Yes, Ma'am."

"Any word on the orphans?"

"We still haven't been able to learn the identity of the Borukin who helped the children."

"Did you request entry information from the Borukin Gate?"

"Yes, but they still can't recover the records. Much was destroyed by the Drebin."

"Keep looking."

Isis ends the call and takes a deep breath, trying to get through the nausea and frustration. *I hope there's a bucket nearby...* She closes her eyes. After a moment, her stomach settles.

I can't help what I'm doing.

She awakes with a kick, relaxing the moment she sees her hospital room. *That's getting to be annoying.* Her heart settles after a minute, and she calls Alec.

"Isis, I heard the news. Are you okay?" Alec asks, concern playing across his face.

"I'm fine. What did you find out?"

"Right to business, as usual. Even a hospital bed can't curb your spunk."

Isis rolls her eyes. "Cute. So, what'd you find?"

"Seriously, Isis, how are you?" Alec looks at her, his vibrant blue eyes intent.

She hesitates for a moment, then lets out a breath, her face relaxing. "I'm okay. Having a little trouble shaking the bastard, but I'll manage. Thanks for asking."

Alec smiles. "Of course. Now, since you're not dying, let's get to business. I've been doing research... I've found three pieces of active ancient technology similar to the one you found. They're dated to the same time, within the uncertainty of the measurement. Your piece, though, is in much better condition than the others. It's amazing."

"Any idea of what they do?"

"The other three pieces are called Braunstadt pieces. They're named for the person who first made the correlation between them. No one's had any luck cracking the tech, so there are only theories."

"And what might some of these theories be?" Isis asks.

"The one I like suggests that each one is connected to one of the six Corusnigmas located around the world."

Isis lets out a breath. "If you're going to suggest they're some kind of key to opening the monoliths, I might fire you."

"You wouldn't, and we both know it. I'm the smartest scientist in Sunta, and I know you have a thing for me."

"Oh please, get over yourself," Isis looks away, hiding a small smile.

"Why are you so against the idea?" Alec asks.

"Of you and me?"

Alec assumes a stern expression, which is belied by a twinkle in his eye. "Can we please keep this professional, Isis? I'm talking about the Corusnigmas. What makes it so hard to believe that they can be opened?"

Isis lets out a huff. "I can't imagine it's possible for that amount of power to be contained, let alone harnessed. I know the ancients were capable of some impressive feats, but this is too unfathomable."

"Is it? The other theory says they're natural concentrations of Aether. What gets me, though, is why there are exactly six. Why is there exactly one Corusnigma for each cast? It's too perfect for a natural occurrence. There's something in them, something of the purest form, with unimaginable possibilities."

"Wow, Alec, you continue to surprise me. I didn't think you had this sort of hunger for power. Perhaps you're more like your peers than you think."

Alec lets out a short laugh. "Not quite, Isis. I don't see this as a tool to take over the world. I see this as something to bring the world together. If we were to unlock the secrets of the shrines, the races of the world would have to share them. It would be the common ground pulling us together."

"I'm glad you have so much faith in people, but my experience tells me they would rather fight to the death for this sort of power than share it."

Alec looks down for a second, then into Isis's pale blue eyes. "That's where we differ."

Isis shakes her head. "If the Corusnigmas were meant to be open, then why is it so difficult? How many people have died trying to unlock the monoliths?"

"Many, but if they knew what they were doing, if they had a key… I just need to get my hands on one, and take it to—"

"Is this all that you have for me? Speculation?" Isis asks. "It's giving me a headache. And here I expected you to have something of interest."

Alec takes a moment, then offers her a half-smile. "And I'd hate to ever disappoint you. If you don't distract me further, I'll give you something that'll pique your interest."

"The anticipation is unbearable," Isis says sarcastically. "Please, before I lose it."

Alec glares at her, shaking his head. "It looks like the spooks in RIGID got your item, but seeing that they're as helpless as they are, about a week ago, they called me in to help with a preliminary analysis. Oh, and by the way, their equipment is much nicer than mine."

Isis rolls her eyes. "I told you—I'm working on it. It's not easy to approve half the things you request."

Alec smiles. "As long as you're trying. Anyway, after using their fancy equipment, I was able to run some tests of my own design."

"What did you find?"

"Besides a mind-bending conundrum?"

Isis scowls at him, trying to hide a smirk.

"Alright, I'm getting to it. This is a very strange piece. It didn't behave as I'd expect a Braunstadt piece to, at least from what I've heard and studied. I tweaked the experiment a touch, which delivered some interesting results."

"That's good, isn't it?" Isis asks.

"I guess that depends on your definition. I don't think this piece is pure ancient."

"What? But I thought you said it was?"

"Don't get me wrong—there are still ancient elements to it, but there's something else there, too. It's like it's a hybrid of different technologies from different races."

"Does that mean it isn't as old as we thought?"

"No. I ran that test as well, and it definitely originates from the same time as the other Braunstadt pieces."

"Did you find any hints on the non-ancient part?" Isis asks.

"The parts are meshed perfectly together, which makes it very hard to actually detect the differences. It had to be someone with extensive knowledge of ancient technology, or someone with the help of the Lost Race to make this piece. It makes me wonder if the other pieces are also hybrids... But there's no way to tell unless I get my hands on them. I probed the newer technology with much more success."

"And what did you find?"

"Well, you're not going to like it."

"I will decide that for myself, Alec. What'd you find?"

"It's very similar to ancient Human technology."

"Don't be ridiculous. The Humans are morons. Plus, weren't they enemies with the Lost Race then?"

"Yes, I know. I triple-checked my results, and I found the same thing every time. Maybe this piece was made under a peace treaty, or something like that? We know their conflict was settled right around the end of the Second Age."

"Are you sure you aren't losing your mind?"

"I'm just following the facts, Isis. Maybe you're the one slipping from reality. Did you bump your head a little too hard this time?"

Isis rolls her eyes. Her face grows serious. "Did you tell all of this to the RIGID personnel?"

"I may… have left out a few details."

"Good. Hopefully when they mess this up, we can get it back."

"I made the suggestion that I should take the lead, but they weren't very amused. I wouldn't hold your breath."

"I'll see what I can do to stir things up."

"I'd expect nothing less from you. Well, Isis, I hope you feel better. I'll talk to you soon." He hangs up before she can answer.

Isis smiles to herself, her finger hovering over the end call button. She lies back in her bed, thoughts drifting. She finds herself staring into the mirror of a dark bathroom. She flips on the light, and to her horror, one of her eyes and the surrounding skin are completely black. She jumps back but the mirror image of herself does not move. It just stares.

I just want to live.

Isis jerks herself awake to find her fists clenched and her heart racing. *Damnit! Why am I letting this get to me? You're stronger than this!* She closes her eyes, visualizing rows and rows of Erohsian military vehicles and troops. She imagines every detail of the vehicles, their conditions, the uniforms of the troops, the perfect lines on their armor. Her breathing slows. A beep from her wrist computer disturbs her. It is General Lark.

"Congratulations on a successful mission, Isis. I knew you'd get it done. There aren't many others with the perseverance to drive their battle group for as long as you did.

From the sounds of it, you were tracking no more than a ghost."

"Thank you, General, but certainly you called for another reason? Not just to congratulate me."

The General smiles. "Let's just say the last day of the Borukin Games has produced some interesting results."

"Oh, yeah? So, your trip to Kiats and your visit with the King, went well?"

"Of course, but it's not that. I found someone you'll be interested in talking to."

"Are you going to tell me? Or are you just trying to torture me?"

"Torture, of course. I'll tell you when you get out of the hospital." The General ends the call.

Damnit, Richard! Isis shakes her head, flopping onto her pillow. *Did he find the Borukin?* She takes a deep breath, her fatigue washing over her. There is a moment's struggle, but her eyes soon close.

A soldier kneels next to her, holding her head up. "Ma'am, can you hear me?" *He pulls off his armored glove to check her pulse.*

"Is he dead?" *Isis tries to prop herself up. The soldier stops her.*

"Yes, Ma'am. I flattened him."

"Did you check his pulse?"

The soldier glances away. "Ma'am, we need to get you to a medical pod immediately. You're in bad shape."

"Check it!" *she yells.*

The soldier leaves her to stare up at the trees and the grey sky she cannot fully focus on. What's taking him so long?

"I said to check his pulse! What are you doing?" Isis hears nothing and rolls over to look around. There is no one to be seen. She stands up and finds the remains of a mid-infantry soldier. The armor is hollow. A skeletal hand covered in slimy goo protrudes from one of the sleeves.

Someone grabs her around the neck from behind. Panic stabs through her chest as she claws at her assailant's hands.

Warm breath tickles her ear. "You didn't think it'd be that easy, did you?"

"It wasn't easy at all. But I still got you," she says, almost whimpering.

He lets loose a vicious laugh. "Oh, Isis, we're just starting to have fun.

25 The King
Nero

"Next time I tell you no, and you think otherwise, you have permission to kick me in the butt," Saraf says when Nero limps into his store. "I heard they're calling you the wee Borukin, for Stone's sake. For how well you sense Aether, I should have figured you'd be able to perform Odo. Did you pick it up from watching Natina?"

"A little."

"Did you learn from Sosimo?"

Nero shakes his head.

"Then where?"

Nero looks off to the side, inspecting some of the Amulets.

"Out with it, already. You're giving me an ulcer."

"There's this smart Entity or something I play with in the park," Nero says, just above a whisper. "I've been using broom sticks to defend myself from its Aether."

"That explains everything..."

Nero looks up. "It does? Do you know what it is?"

"I've been wondering where my broomsticks have been going! Come on, Nero. I'm not that old and gullible. Where did you come up with the idea of a smart entity?"

Nero's head drops. "I knew you wouldn't believe me."

"You're serious?"

Nero nods.

"A smart entity?"

Nero nods again.

"For all the times you've proved me wrong and surprised me, I'd be stupid not to take you seriously. You'll have to show me, but for now it'll have to wait."

Nero barely catches a package as it bounces off his chest. "What's this?"

"A package, you broom wit," Saraf says. "Open it."

Nero rips off the wrapping. His excitement plummets. *Clothes?* He pulls out a nice tunic, holding it up. "Uh... Thanks. This is very... nice."

"Yeah, I'm sure you really like them. Hurry up and put them on."

"What? Really? Do I have to?"

"Yes, you do. If you're going to accompany Natina today, that is. Your ratty clothes won't cut it."

"What?"

"Natina wants you to join her for the final day of competition."

"Really?"

"Yep."

"You don't mind?" Nero asks.

"No. This may be the only opportunity you'll ever have to go to this event and besides, Delue, Ritami, and Lagia are in Axiom today. This does not happen often."

"And if I want to go, I have to wear these clothes?"

"It's a horrible price to pay, I know. Can you manage?"

Nero looks at the clothes one more time, nodding. "I'll try."

*****

Saraf leads Nero through the crowd at the base of the stadium until they reach a small guard stand. Saraf talks with the guard for a moment, who sends for a royal assistant.

After a few moments of waiting, the royal assistant approaches Saraf and Nero. "Are you the Human child, Nero?"

"This is him," Saraf says.

The royal assistant signals with his hand, turning toward the door. "Follow me."

"Have fun, Nero," Saraf pats him on the back. "Try not to hit your head on anything hard. Remember to take the steps one at a time."

"You're not coming?" Nero asks.

"Who'd run the shop? You'll have fun with Natina. Go."

Nero reluctantly leaves Saraf and follows the assistant through a side entrance. The assistant leads him up flights of stairs. They pass a few ticket checkpoints and people of all sizes and colors, all finely dressed. They are adorned with Artifacts and jewelry. Using the trained eye Saraf gave him and his sense of Aether, Nero quickly sums up each Artifact he sees. Some are nothing more than precious stones. Others shine with Aether as bright as Saraf's finest items. The assistant finally brings Nero to a door where a large Borukin royal guard stands, tattooed arms crossed. Her head is shaved. Her torso and shoulders are covered in red armor trimmed with gold and her styk is strapped across her back.

"This is the boy Natina requested," the assistant says.

The guard raises an eyebrow. "He's a bit small, isn't he?"

"He's a Human, what do you expect? He's also now your responsibility." The assistant leaves.

The guard looks Nero over one more time then knocks on the door. "Natina, the Human is here."

The door opens and Natina's head pokes out. "Nero!"

Natina grabs Nero's arm and pulls him into her private box, which looks out at the same arena Nero saw yesterday. A small table to the side has an assortment of snacks and drinks.

"Where's Grebson?" Nero asks.

"He doesn't go to the Games for some reason, so the woman is watching me for the day."

"I think I saw a statue of him yesterday at the Orinda Museum. Did he really compete in the Trial of Orinda?"

"Yeah, I think so, but no matter how hard I try, he never tells me anything about himself. It's incredibly annoying."

Natina points to the table. "You can have some food if you want. And sit down. The opening ceremony's about to start."

A large Borukin with a shaved head walks to the center of the stadium and the crowd begins to cheer. Nero watches the big screen. His skin crawls at the hardness of the King's face. *Yikes...* Ivory tattoos run up his neck, wrapping around his head like a crown. They cover his muscular arms, exposed from his short-sleeved gold tunic.

Natina points. "That's my dad!"

The King holds up his hands, settling the crowd. "Out of the ashes we arose in the Second Age, with King Stone leading us. The world was scarred, and our King was tired, but he would not rest until he saw us fit to survive. Knowing we must always be ready to meet any challenge that threatens our country, he came up with the Games. These games provide us with incentive to hone and test our might! He created three trials, which in the simplest way describes our unmatched abilities. Three trials to test the strongest Borukins. Only the fiercest take part in Stone's Trials, and today they will compete in this arena. First is the Trial of Odosa. A trial that defines the core of the Borukin's defense." The crowd cheers. "Second is the Trial of Borutaress. A trial to demonstrate our effectiveness in combat and why we are feared as warriors!" The crowd cheers even louder. "And finally! We have the Trial of Orinda! A trial that represents our honor and a taste of the nightmare we'll summon if we are backed into a corner." The crowd roars. The King looks out at the stadium, raising both fists in the air. After turning to face all the spectators, he walks out of the arena.

"I can't believe your dad's the King," Nero says.

"Yeah... He's scary."

Nero nods his head. A silence passes between them.

"So, what do you think of these seats?" Natina asks.

Nero walks to the window. "We're so high. It's awesome."

"It is a great view... I wish we were closer, though. You can't hear or feel the excitement from way up here."

"Why don't you go closer then?"

"This is my box. I don't have tickets for the lower area."

"Aren't you a princess, though? Can't you watch from wherever you want?"

"I guess… That's a good idea."

"What?" Nero asks, suddenly nervous.

"We should go down and get a closer view."

"But I thought you said we need tickets?"

"Yeah, but you just said I'm a princess. I don't think they'd mind."

"Are you sure? I don't want to get in trouble."

"Yes, I'm sure."

Natina grabs Nero's arm, pulling him out of the room.

The guard turns to her in surprise. "Are we going somewhere, Princess?"

"Yes, we are. We're going to get a better view of the competition."

"But you're supposed to watch from your private room."

"It's too high up. Besides, you can't see. Wouldn't you like to get closer to the action?"

A flash of desire passes over her face, but it quickly turns somber. "It's not my job to tell you what I want."

"I saw that!" Natina says, smiling and pointing. "Are you coming, then?"

"I'm assigned to you, my lady. I will follow you to the Tenebrous Miasma if that's where you're going."

"Really?"

"Of course, but I wouldn't recommend it."

"Maybe down the road then. Let's go." Natina turns and hurries off.

The guard looks at Nero then gestures onward. Natina hurries through the crowd, always descending when possible. At the bottom level, she walks up to an usher in a red uniform checking tickets, right at the arena level. The usher's face is curious as Natina approaches. He looks annoyed when Nero stands next to her, and worried when he sees the guard hovering behind them.

"Excuse me, sir," Natina starts. "Do you mind if my friends and I sneak into this section to watch up close?"

The usher looks at the guard then back to Natina. "Do you have tickets?"

"No, that's the thing. My dad, the King," she says with emphasis, "got me a private booth up high, but I want to be close and with the people."

The usher swallows. "The King?"

"Yes, my dad. I'm not sure what he was thinking. I asked if I could have a closer seat, but he must have been too busy."

"Uh. There are no open seats here. Would you like me to kick someone out?" He asks, stammering.

"Oh no. I don't mind standing. We'll even try to stay out of the way, if you think that's okay."

The usher lets out a pent-up breath, relaxing. "Yes, I think that would be fine, Princess. Enjoy the Games. Let me know if you need anything." He steps to the side.

"Thank you." They all hurry past.

Natina walks down the longs steps to the railings. She stops, mostly out of the way of the spectators behind her. The conversations around them turn to whispers.

In the arena, the four contestants Nero saw yesterday are just wrapping up their warm-up routine. Each one is wearing a different-colored headband. This close, Nero can fully appreciate the size of the Aether cannon. It is several times taller than him. *Holy moly, that's a big cannon.*

The guard rests her hands on the railing. "I've been to the Games many times on duty, but this is the first time I'll actually get to see the finale of the Trial of Odosa. I must admit I'm as excited as a little girl."

"I know exactly how you feel," Nero says, mostly to himself, still in a state of awe.

Natina looks at Nero and her guard, smiling. "I'm glad we came down here."

"Young Human, you don't realize how lucky you are. Many Borukins would sacrifice quite a lot to be this close and with your company."

Nero turns to Natina. "Thanks for inviting me, Natina."

"It was the only way I could think to make it up to you for all the times I slammed you in training."

"How's your arm doing?" Nero asks.

"It's fine now. I just tweaked it," she says, moving it around. "Did you draw from my styk when you threw me?"

Nero nods.

"This little Human got the best of you, Princess?" The guard asks.

"This 'little Human' is the wee Borukin. I watched him yesterday. He defended his friends from the attacks of several Borukins using Odo... I wish I had friends like that..."

I'm your friend.

The guard looks at Nero, nodding. "Impressive. I've never heard of a Human using Odo before."

Nero's cheeks flush. He inspects the railing.

"Alright, ladies and gentlemen," a voice booms over the stadium speakers. The same announcer from yesterday is standing on the center platform for the trial. "The Trial of Odosa is about to begin! In green we have Kandis Khan, making her first ever appearance in the finals. In red, we have Prince Kamin Ramas Jr., the returning champion of the Trial of Borutaress and the Trial of Orinda. He's hoping to best his third-place finish in this trial. In yellow, we have Jesler Coffman, the Trial of Odosa's runner-up last time around, sights set on the gold. Finally, in blue, we have Madam Carason, the Overseer of the Schools, an Odo Grandmaster, holder of the current record for Odosa, and reigning champion for the last three Trials of Odosa." The competitors bow, and the stadium erupts in applause.

"How do you think your brother will do, Princess?" The guard asks.

"I'm not sure. I don't talk to him much, but I heard he's planning on winning this one."

"Really? He thinks he can beat Madam Carason? If he wins the Trial of Odosa, Borutaress, and Orinda he may be the youngest to ever do so."

An official meets the four participants on the platform. He holds out a leather pouch and each of the competitors removes a small clay chip. The official looks at each of the chips and orders the competitors in a row.

"And we have the order!" the announcer says. "Kandis in green is first, Jesler in yellow is second, Prince Kamin in red is third, and finally Madam Carason in blue. Minimum starting level is set for three on the Boltz scale."

"Do they do the same thing as they did yesterday?" Nero asks.

"Not at all," the guard says.

"Today, each competitor takes a turn declaring the cast and intensity of the attack," Natina says. "If the competitor passes their challenge, then the others must try it, as well. You'll see." She points toward the arena. "Just watch."

Kandis steps up to the official to talk with him. The official punches a few buttons into what looks like a giant calculator, then nods to her. The official speaks into his small microphone.

"Kandis has made her choice," the announcer says. "She'll start the competition with Icor Aether at five hundred and fifty thousand joules and five hundred thousand watts, which puts us at three-point-one-three on the Boltz scale."

The woman in green steps up to the platform. The canon fires at her in a bright stream of energy. The judges check her; she passes. The other three competitors follow in order. They all pass. The official talks with the competitor in yellow. He again punches some numbers into the calculator, nodding.

"Alright, we're moving along nicely!" The announcer's voice echoes through the stadium. "Jesler has picked Moltrik Aether at five hundred and fifty thousand joules and six hundred thousand watts, which puts us at three-point-two-zero on the Boltz scale."

The crowd cheers. Jesler steps up to the platform. Again, each one of the competitors passes. The official walks up to Kamin next. Kamin says something, but the official hesitates, looking at him in surprise. Kamin waves his hand, noticeably irritated, and the official jumps to punch the numbers into his calculator. The official speaks into the microphone on his collar.

"This is quite the surprise." The speakers crackle to life. "Prince Kamin isn't wasting any time moving things up. He has picked Pahzan Aether at two million joules and eight hundred thousand watts, which is three-point-three-seven on the Boltz scale. If you don't remember, this already surpasses the winning level from the last competition. A brave move, indeed."

"Wow, he's confident," the guard says. "He must really be going for it."

Kamin walks up to the platform, readying himself. The red flash swallows the entire center of the arena. Nero feels a deep thud in his chest. Streamers of fire and smoke arch from the center of the explosion, slowly trailing to the ground.

"Oh, wow, that was awesome!" Nero says. His eyes adjust to the evaporating haze to reveal Kamin standing in the center, steam rising from his clothes. "How did he survive that?" *I'll never be able to block something that big.* He shifts his perspective. The arena is filled with bright red Aether, with concentrated bubbles swirling around. After a moment, they pop, spewing their contents.

"He's a Borukin. That's what we do," the guard says.

The judges circle around and hold up their success flags. The crowd cheers. Madam Carason glares at Kamin as she approaches the platform. She passes, too. The other two fail. Kandis is escorted from the arena with an injured arm.

"It looks like we just have Madam Carason and Prince Kamin left. Let's see how the Madam plans to counter," the announcer says.

Again, the official seems to be surprised by her demand. After she urges him on, he punches the numbers into his calculator and then speaks to his microphone.

"Madam Carason is going for the record!" the announcer yells into the speakers. "She's picked Moltrik Aether at eighteen million joules and six million watts for a four-point-two-six on the Boltz scale!" The crowd cheers.

"Princess. Thank you so much for taking me down here," the guard says. "This is the most excitement this competition has had since Madam Carason broke the record, and that was over twenty years ago."

After a decent length of waiting for the Borukins to turn the giant cog and generate the Aether, Madam Carason approaches the platform. She settles into her ready position and nods toward the canon operator. The crowd falls silent.

"You two might want to plug your ears," the guard says out of the corner of her mouth. She moves to take her own advice.

Natina and Nero mimic the guard just as the canon fires in a blinding flash of electricity. The shockwave of Aether knocks Nero off his feet.

"Wowee!" The guard picks up Nero. "Can you believe that? You got leveled and we're not even in the center! Are you okay, Human?"

Nero steadies himself, nodding. "I think so." His hair is standing on edge. When he grabs the railing, he feels an electric shock.

The guard laughs. "And, Princess, I assume you're okay."

"Yes, thank you," Natina says.

The judges swarm around Madam Carason to inspect her white cotton robes. The head judge holds up the pass flag. The crowd goes wild. After waiting again for the canon to be charged, Kamin approaches the platform. Nero loops his leg and arm around the pole and plugs his ears again. He shifts his perspective and sees Kamin's sharp red glow assume a ready position. There is another faint red shimmer of Aether just in front of him.

What's that?

Kamin nods and the blue Moltrik Aether in the canon surges, releasing a flash of energy. Just as the Moltrik Aether strikes Kamin, the red shield about him flares. A fraction of a second later, the platform is lost in a burst of blue light. The Aether rattles Nero again, but his firm grip saves him from getting knocked down. When the haze clears, the judges run up to Kamin. They throw up the pass flag. The crowd cheers wildly.

"Wow, Natina," the guard says. "I didn't think he was that good. I thought most of his skill was in combat."

"I think he's been practicing a lot," Natina says.

"He must be."

"Are you allowed to use Aether when you block?" Nero asks.

"You can use whatever natural Aether you have. A Borukin's Aetheratin is so low, though, it wouldn't be useful in countering an attack. Not compared to the effectiveness of our styks."

"Are you allowed to use Artifacts?"

"No. Only the styk is permitted. It is the purest form of Odo."

"Do you think he could have used something he wasn't supposed to, like an Aether shield or something?" Nero asks. "Is that even possible?"

Natina looks at Nero fiercely. "My brother wouldn't cheat."

"Careful, boy," the guard says. "If Natina doesn't beat you up for saying those kinds of things, then someone else will. Aether shields exist in the form of Amulets, or from someone with Pahzan Aether and enough Aetheratin to make it effective, but cheating has some very severe consequences. It hardly ever happens. Accusing the Royal family of it would not be good for your health."

The official approaches Kamin. When the prince responds to his question, the official freezes. Kamin smacks the official out of his daze, making him stumble to the side. The official punches the number into his calculator with shaking hands. He pulls the microphone on his collar up to his mouth and speaks.

There is a long pause before the announcer says anything. "Pardon us for the delay, we need to check the rules and regulations for the next round."

Murmurs float through the crowd. Some nearby spectators ask questions of Natina directly. She shrugs and shakes her head. "I don't know what he's doing."

After another long pause, the announcer finally begins. "Prince Kamin has chosen to attempt Pahzan Aether at one hundred million joules and sixteen million watts which puts us at a four-point-seven-five on the Boltz scale." The crowd gasps.

"Natina, what is your brother doing?" the guard asks.

"What do you mean? I don't understand," Natina says. "I don't know anything."

"The whole point of the white cotton robes is to regulate the maximum level they attempt, since the slightest singe will fail you. This is mostly for safety reasons, so the risk of serious injury is minimized."

Worry unfolds on Natina's face. "I still don't get it."

"Your brother has just requested a level that is so far beyond anything that has ever been attempted, it may kill him."

"I have to stop him!" Natina moves to jump over the railing but the guard grabs her.

"He is a grown man and he's making his own decisions. It's just surprising… but if he's made the challenge, he must have some hope of succeeding."

"Are you sure?"

"Yes. Would your brother throw away his life so easily?"

Natina relaxes a little. "No."

"Well, then, there you have it. Let's hope your brother's faith in his skill is well placed."

After a long wait, Kamin finally approaches the platform, readying himself. The guard plugs her ears with some tissue, kneels down, and has Nero and Natina stand in front of her with their ears plugged. She grabs the railing around them. Nero shifts his perspective and can now see a stronger shimmering shield in front of Kamin. A faint trail of red Aether leads off to the nearby spectators. There are three bright, swirling sources of Aether where the trail originates; two are red and one is a combination of red, blue, green, and yellow.

The canon fires with a flash that instantly drowns the world in red Aether. The heat wave slams into Nero, taking his breath away and prickling his skin. He opens his eyes and the arena is filled with streaking Aether that crackles with energy. Kamin's form slowly resolves through the haze, several meters back from where he started.

"He made it!" Natina says.

The guard raises her hand. "Ah ha, he did. That's unbelievable. Is it possible he'll actually pass?"

The judges quickly scurry up to Kamin to inspect his clothes. Each judge responsible for a section of his clothes waves the approval flag, except for one who is hesitating at Kamin's shoulder. Nero feels a strange surge of Aether. He shifts his perspective to see a green wisp emerge from the strong sources of Aether in the crowd. The wisp weaves its way toward the judges and splits into many. Each wisp dives at an individual judge. In response, green walls of Aether flare up against the attack. The walls, however, provide minimal resistance to the incoming wisps, which break through and latch on to the judges' heads. A slight moment of confusion passes before they begin to move about normally. They all review the area in question and after some deliberation, the head official raises a green flag and the crowd cheers.

That was Icor Aether, he's cheating! "Uhh, what would happen if he got caught cheating?"

"Why are you asking this? What do you think you saw?" Natina asks.

The guard turns to them. "This is not something to talk about, even for you, Natina. For your own good, quit this line of thought." Nero nods and looks down. "We need to worry about Madam Carason now, anyway. I hope Stone is with her."

"Can she just quit?" Natina asks.

"She could, but it would destroy her reputation," the guard says. "It would be better for her to lose than to step down."

"Even if it could kill her?" Nero asks.

"Yes, but let's not think about that."

When the Borukins finish charging the Aether storage, Madam Carason steps up to the platform. Her entourage fights to remove her, but they have no luck persuading her. She shoots Kamin a look of disdain before she readies her styk. The guard, Natina, and Nero take their same positions and the canon fires. In the blast, Nero feels the same flow of Aether, but then a strange pop. When the haze finally clears, there is a blackened heap off the end of the platform, on the arena floor. A medical team rushes to her with a stretcher. The crowd is dead silent.

"This is a heart wrenching turn of events," the announcer says. "But be assured, this is the best medical team in the city. Our prayers are with you, Madam Carason."

The medical team carefully moves her onto a stretcher and carries her out of the stadium.

"Your brother is just as ruthless as your dad!" Someone yells from the crowd.

Natina looks in their direction, but the Borukin says no more. "Is she going to be okay?" Natina asks, tears in her eyes.

"I hope so," the guard says. "Let's take a walk during the break."

They walk around the stadium, mingling with the glum spectators. The lines for the mini-games and the vendors are virtually nonexistent. Circles of Borukins have their heads dipped in prayer. The music from the performances in the arena is the only thing combating the dreary energy of the crowd.

By the time they return to their spot, life is flowing back into the stadium. When the last performance ends, the announcer takes the center.

"It is now time for the Trial of Borutaress! The competitors will be Talik Indair, a veteran warrior who has more medals than can be counted, against the returning champion, who needs no introduction, Prince Kamin Ramas Jr.! We all know the rules: first one to surrender or be incapacitated loses."

The two competitors approach each other from different sides.

"After the last competition, I'm not sure what to expect," the guard says. "I don't think Talik will have much of a chance against Kamin."

"Begin," the announcer yells.

Two spheres of Aether appear above the ground, each one close to a competitor. The competitors jam their styks into the blobs and they wink out of existence. With incredible speed, Talik and Kamin close the distance and attack. Their styks sound like a drum roll as they pound against each other. With each contact, the styks release pops of energy and light. They buzz and crackle as they slice through the air. Kamin retreats from Talik's flurry of attacks.

"Wow, it looks like Talik might have a chance after all," the guard says.

The fight continues for several more minutes. Talik's swings are slowly speeding up, Kamin's becoming more frantic. Talik attacks harder. A single blob of Aether appears across the arena four meters off the ground. Both competitors see it instantly and take off running. Kamin easily leaves his competition behind.

"Look at that!" The guard points excitedly. "Kamin must have been saving his energy. Watch carefully, now, this is a big moment in the battle. Talik will try to make a move to strike Kamin while he is exposed and going for the Aether."

As they approach the Aether, Kamin glances back and slows, allowing the gap between them to close. At the last moment, Kamin jumps high toward the energy. By the time he passes just over the ball of Aether, he swings his styk down like he is chopping wood, propelling the ball of Aether directly at Talik. Talik is too close to properly defend.

The ball explodes against his chest, engulfing him in flames and sending him spinning backward. He hits the ground and tumbles to a stop. Kamin finishes his aerial maneuver with a graceful flip, landing on his feet.

The smoking and charred Talik attempts to rise, but falls back to the ground. Kamin slides his styk into the holder across his back and walks out of the Arena. There is a stunned silence and sparse applause. Another medical team runs out to Talik to help him out of the arena.

"That was faster than I expected," Nero says.

The guard nods. "That might be some sort of record. I've heard that Talik is no pushover, either, which makes it all the more impressive." The guard looks around. "Alright, Princess, we need to get you up to the King's box; the Queen requested you be present after the Trial of Borutaress."

"Am I going?" Nero asks nervously.

"I suppose so," the guard says. "The final trial will happen when the moon Stybris is in Axiom later tonight so we have some time to kill anyway."

After a short wait to let the crowd thin, the three climb up through the hordes of people until they finally reach the King's box. They are let inside by several guards after a security check. Natina quickly sees her dad and moves toward him. He is among the largest Borukins in the box. His shaved head and its crown-like tattoos give him an unrivaled presence. He is talking with several older Borukins with long hair, a smaller light-skinned person in a military uniform, and Prince Kamin.

"Aether rifles, generators, and accelerators. They have their use, but they are just toys," the King says to his companion in a deep, booming voice. "What else can you offer?"

Natina stops behind him. "Excuse me, Your Highness, where's the Queen?"

The King turns to Natina, his lip curled. "Natina. How dare you interrupt me. Have you not been taught better?" Natina cowers. The King shakes his head, turning his back on her.

Natina stands there for a moment until the guard finally puts a hand on her shoulder to move her away. "Don't take it personally, Natina. He's a very busy man."

Nero glances back at the King and notices the face of the smallest person in his company for the first time. He is an Erohsian. Bolts of panic race through his body. "Why is there an Erohsian here?" Nero asks.

"He's an Erohsian General, if I heard correctly," the guard says. "Politics probably."

Oh no. Nero turns his back to the King. "Hey, Natina, do you think we can leave?"

"No, not yet. I want you to meet my dad."

"How about your mom?"

Natina nods. "Yeah, okay. She'll be happy to see me. We can find my dad later."

"Natina!" Both Nero and Natina jump, startled by the blasting voice of the King. "Come."

Nero's body goes rigid and Natina drags him toward the King and the Erohsian General. Natina performs a small curtsy. Panicked, Nero does the same.

The King raises one eyebrow. "This is your friend, Natina? A Human?"

"Yes, your highness. His name is Nero."

"Nero? An ironic name for someone so small." The King signals to the General. "This is General Lark of the Erohsians. He is my guest at the Games."

The General moves his eyes from Nero and dips his head. "Pleasure to meet you, my lady."

"The pleasure is mine," Natina says with another curtsy.

"Are you proud of your brother?" the General asks. "I hear he's going to compete in the Trial of Orinda, as well. Perhaps he'll be the youngest to win all three."

"There is no doubt about that, Richard," King Kamin says roughly.

"Of course, Your Highness. After his success so far today, I would expect nothing less." The General looks at Nero one more time. "Excuse me, Your Highness, I need a moment." He dips his head and moves away, pulling up his wrist computer as he does.

"Nero," the King says. "Have you bonded with an essence? Can you use Aether?"

"Um... Well, kinda, sometimes." Nero shifts uneasily, unable to take his eyes from the Erohsian consulting his computer.

The King turns to Natina. "Your choice in friends is disappointing. This one is nothing but a spineless child."

"He's not just a child!"

The King's face turns cold. "Do not dare raise your voice at me."

The Erohsian General pops back beside the King and holds up his wrist computer. He points to something on the holographic screen and whispers into the King's ear. His eyes fall on Nero, who is holding his breath.

The King points to Natina's guard. "You, grab him."

The guard hesitates for a fraction of a second, then firmly grasps Nero's arm.

The King walks up to Nero. "So, boy, it seems you have been getting into some trouble with my friend here."

"Your highness, if we move quickly, we may be able to question this one and capture the others as well," the General says.

The King shakes his head. "You can have this one, but I am not about to let you snatch up every Human child in Kiats. That would cause me more trouble than it is worth."

"Dad, you can't take him," Natina yells.

The King flashes her a fiery look. "Enough."

"These children may have some very important information," the Erohsian says. "We would be in your debt."

"You're already going to owe me if I give you this one. Besides, if they were so important, you should not have let them escape in the first place. Borukins have a certain respect for Humans. Allowing children to disappear would just fuel the unrest I am dealing with. Would you rather I let this one go?"

The General shakes his head. "No, Your Highness. I understand your concerns. We appreciate your sacrifice."

"Good." The King looks at Natina's guard. "I will watch Natina for now. Lock the boy up."

The guard dips her head. "Yes, Your Honor." She turns, pulling Nero through the crowd.

Nero stumbles after her, trying to sift through the shock of the rapidly collapsing situation. Tears begin to well up in his eyes.

The guard looks down at him apologetically.

26 On the Other Side

Iona

Sosimo's face turns hard while he holds the phone to his ear. "Go on… Taken? How did this happen, Saraf?"

What's happening? Iona sets down a stocking list.

"What's going on?" Ryder whispers to Iona as the other children gather in the storage room of the candy shop.

Iona shakes her head. "I don't know."

"You let him go to the final day of the Games with the Princess?" Sosimo asks. "She's the one you've been training? Did you not think to mention that to me?" Sosimo shakes his head. "Well then, what happened to Nero?"

The children turn to each other, wide-eyed, mouthing. "Princess?"

"Alright, thanks for the information. I'll call you if I need anything."

"No. I don't want his help." Sosimo's shoulders sag. The toothpick in his mouth snaps. "Fine, but this doesn't fix anything."

"Okay. I'll let you know how it goes tonight. Bye."

"What's going on?" Thea asks.

"Nero got himself into some trouble." Sosimo looks away, clenching his cylindrical toothpick holder in his fist.

"Did you say he was with a princess?" Thea asks.

"Yeah, and he seemed to have met the King as well. And the King seemed to want him locked up."

"But he's such a wuss," Korbin says. "How could he get into so much trouble?"

"What could Nero have done to deserve that?" Iona asks.

Sosimo shakes his head.

"Well, shouldn't we do something to help him? We need to rescue him if he's in trouble. He's family," Korbin says.

Sosimo gives Korbin an approving nod. "Yes, he is. There's nothing we can do at this moment. Tonight, someone will come over to explain the situation. Then we can start planning. Finish up here, then get ready for dinner." Sosimo walks off.

"How was he hanging out with a princess?" Thea asks.

"I wonder who's coming over tonight," Ryder says. "Sosimo doesn't look happy about it."

Iona nods. "No, he doesn't."

*****

As the children and Sosimo are cleaning after dinner, the doorbell rings. They hurry to the main entrance. Sosimo opens the door to a Borukin half a head taller than him. His face has three ivory tattoos of the Aether casts and his arms, at least what can be seen of them, are covered in tattoos. Iona suddenly becomes antsy. Her hands start to sweat. The two Borukins lock eyes for a moment in a tense silence. Sosimo's jaw clenches about the toothpick in his mouth. The other Borukin's arms flex.

"Grebson," Sosimo says, almost growling.

"Sosimo," Grebson says in the same tone.

"Let's just get this over with." Sosimo steps to the side, allowing the large man to enter.

Grebson glances over the children. They drop their eyes immediately. "Natina demanded that she come along."

"The Princess?" Sosimo asks.

Grebson nods.

Natina steps from behind Grebson, holding out her hand to Sosimo. She forces the worry from her face. "It's a pleasure to meet you, Sosimo."

Sosimo shakes her hand. "You as well." He turns to the children. "This is Nero's family. Ryder, Korbin, Iona, and Thea."

Ryder shakes her hand first, coming up a few centimeters shorter than her.

"So, you're the one that got Nero in trouble?" Korbin asks.

Sosimo flicks Korbin on his arm with the back of his hand. "Korbin, stop. She's here to help."

Korbin rubs his arm. "Okay, jeez, I just don't see how she could help."

"She's probably thinking the same thing about you." Sosimo turns to Natina. "We appreciate your help. We can talk at the table."

*****

"What happened to Nero?" Thea asks as soon as they are seated around the dining room table.

Grebson eyes her. "From what I've heard, it sounds like King Kamin asked the guards to grab Nero."

"Why was he there in the first place?" Sosimo asks.

"I'm sorry, I didn't know this would happen," Natina says. "I don't have many friends, so I invited him."

Sosimo looks back to Grebson. "Where were you? Why didn't you help him?"

"You know I don't go to the Games anymore. Even so, there wouldn't have been anything I could do. Nero did nothing wrong. The King made a demand, and no one was going to stop him."

Sosimo looks at Grebson for a long moment. "Why, then?"

"Did you hear that Madam Carason died after the Trial of Odosa?"

"Yes." Sosimo dips his head. "More bad news."

"It is," Grebson says. "Kamin Ramas Jr. is now the head of the schools, which greatly extends the King's power."

"I can only imagine what that'll mean," Sosimo says. "But, what does this have to do with Nero?"

"The King is making a push for power on all fronts. One of which is through technology. He's pursuing an agreement with the Erohsians."

"Erohsians?" the children cry out.

"Ah," Sosimo says. The tension releases from his face. "And there was an Erohsian with him?"

Grebson nods. "Some general. Apparently the Erohsians want to make a deal with the King to help handle the rebelling Humans." Grebson turns to the children. "Now, why would this general be interested in you all? The general showed Natina a picture of all of you."

The children sink back, looking at Sosimo nervously.

"From what I can work out," Sosimo says, "they stumbled upon some Erohsian essence specimens that were stolen by Catalyst. They opened the canisters and absorbed the essence. Now, the Erohsians are chasing them."

"And Nero absorbed one of these?" Grebson asks.

"It was just me, Korbin, and Thea," Ryder says. "Something funky happened when Nero tried. It just evaporated."

Grebson nods in thought. "It's interesting that a general would care about these children and a few essences. I wonder if there's something else going on."

"Especially with the amount of effort they're putting into the search. They nearly shut down Blue Horin when I was smuggling them out. I wouldn't be surprised if we're missing something."

"Did the Erohsians get Nero?" Thea asks. "What are we going to do? This is horrible."

Grebson shakes his head. "Not yet."

"What do you mean?" she asks.

"If you'd let him finish, Thea," Sosimo says. "I'm sure he'll get to it."

"The King has taken Nero into custody. He plans on hand-delivering Nero to the Erohsians when he visits them in Sunta. That's in a little over a month. He's using it as a show of good faith," Grebson says.

"Do you know if they'll come after the others?" Sosimo asks. "Should they go into hiding?"

"I doubt it," Grebson says. "If word gets out, the King will be lucky to avoid protests because of Nero. It wouldn't hurt to be more careful, though. Maybe you should pull them from school since Prince Kamin will be taking over."

"He can't just take Nero like that," Iona says.

Sosimo shrugs. "He's the King, he can get away with a lot. I don't have legal guardianship over you, so there's no real proof Nero was in Kiats at all. They might try to hide the whole thing. It would be my word against the King's, which wouldn't go very well."

"What about my word?" Natina asks.

"You're too young. Yours would probably just get you into more trouble than it's worth." Sosimo turns to Grebson. "Do you know when they're leaving?"

"I believe their plan is to leave Kiats in one week, and drive to Sunta so the King can make some stops in the mountain towns along the way. I believe he also wants to stop at the Moltrik Corusnigma so Kamin Jr. can attempt the trial in order to quell any disputes of his new position as the Overseer of the schools."

"So that gives us plenty of time to rescue him before they leave," Ryder says. "We're going to go get him, right?"

Korbin throws his fist into the air. "Definitely. We owe him one."

"Yes, we're going to rescue him," Sosimo says. "There's no telling what the Erohsians would do to him, or if they'd ever release him. Unfortunately, we may need to exercise more patience than you'd like. I think we'd do better pulling off a rescue mission in Sunta."

"But that means we'd leave him locked up until they got there," Thea says. "Why would we wait so long?"

"I don't like leaving the boy trapped for that long, either, but Sosimo's correct," Grebson says. "We couldn't go toe to toe with a bunch of Borukins. Sosimo's and my skills combined with your Aether abilities just aren't enough. The Erohsians, on the other hand, are particularly vulnerable to Aether. The appropriate skills would give you kids a significant advantage over them. Especially if we hit them when they aren't geared up... like at the Borukin welcoming banquet."

"What do you mean by 'you kids'?" Ryder asks.

"He means this is your task," Sosimo says.

Korbin's mouth drops. "You're not going to help?"

"A few Human children have a better chance sneaking in and out during the welcoming party than a couple of ugly Borukins," Sosimo says. "You'll have to do the actual rescuing. We'll be helping every step of the way, so you won't be completely on your own."

"Who are you calling ugly?" Grebson asks.

Sosimo shakes his head. "You're just as much of a pretty boy as Saraf."

"Not even close."

"Uh-huh." Sosimo looks at Grebson, eyebrows raised. "Anyway. These children are making good progress with Aether, but another month of specialized training for real situations will do nicely. Do you have any ideas for sneaking them in?"

"I can help," Natina says. "I'm not sure how, but I'll do whatever I can."

Grebson nods. "Good. We'll need it." Grebson turns back to Sosimo. "I also heard you may have some contacts in Sunta that could be useful?"

"Does Saraf tell you everything?" Sosimo asks.

"What would you expect?"

Sosimo lets out a grunt, lowering his voice. "Perhaps we can talk privately?"

Grebson lays a hand on Natina's shoulder. "Would you care to test these Humans' abilities? We need to make sure they'll make the cut."

"Sure, what would you like?"

"See if any of them can take you down. Keep it simple. Use standard Roroon."

"She's a princess," Korbin says. "What if I hurt her?"

"She's also bigger than you, Korbin," Sosimo says. "You should worry more about yourself."

"If any of you can take her, I'll be impressed," Grebson says.

Korbin jumps up. "That's a challenge."

"Okay, take it to the training room," Sosimo says. "We'll join you soon."

The children run off. Iona is last, following slowly. Just before the training room, she stops.

Natina is bigger, stronger, and better trained. We don't have a chance... unless we can use Icor talismans. She stands at the doorway for a moment before turning back the way she came. *Maybe Sosimo will let us.*

Iona hurries back to the Borukins but stops just around the corner when she hears the tension in Sosimo's voice.

"Why are you helping?" Sosimo asks. "I'm sure you could care less."

"I'm not the man you think I am. Things change."

"Situations change. People rarely do. What's in it for you?"

"It's not about us," Grebson says. "It's about the boy. Can we put our baggage aside for the time being?"

There is a long pause before Sosimo speaks again. The tension gone from his voice. "I agree," he says, low and barely audible from outside the dining room.

"Tell me about Nero."

Sosimo lets out a long breath. "His ability to sense Aether is astonishing. He describes it as though he can see Aether. I've never heard of anything like it."

"And his Odo is equally as impressive."

"It is," Sosimo says. "I thought he was only practicing Roroon with Saraf. How long has he been doing Odo? And why didn't anyone tell me?"

"Roroon is all he's been doing. He said he learned it by listening to Saraf and playing in the park… but he moves too well to not have been practicing with Aether. Natina told me he said something about an entity once, and Saraf said something about a smart entity. Have you heard of this?"

"He did ask me some odd questions a while back. But a wild entity in the middle of Kiats. And a smart one?"

"Or something else. I scanned and searched those woods to no avail. I must have missed it. His skills are far too advanced for him to not have had some help."

"Based just on his little demonstration during the Games?"

"I didn't see what he did at the Games, so I can't say, but I tested him myself. I was not easy on him. Did you hear the explosion over the park in the morning a few days back?"

"You're not serious," Sosimo says.

"He performed Odoki and I barely blocked it in time."

How could Nero have almost beat Grebson?

"He almost hit you? Are you getting rusty?"

"That… or soft," Grebson says. "He's a good kid; he listens well and he tries hard. We need to save him."

"Maybe you have changed."

There is a small pause.

"It's just strange that he can manipulate Aether at all," Sosimo says. "I scanned him with an Aether detector and it didn't even register."

"There's plenty I don't understand, but machines make mistakes. I'm surprised you'd put so much faith in one."

"They have their uses occasionally."

"How about the other children? They're capable?"

"Yes, they're doing well with Fundamental Aether and Artifacts. They absorbed some unique essences. Thea's a quadcast and will be quite the handful if she keeps training. Ryder's Biat Aether, and Korbin is... Ru."

"Damn, that's going to make his life hard. As long as they're proficient with Fundamental, it's a good start. What about the other girl?"

"Iona has Icor Aether, but she doesn't remember absorbing an essence. Someone must have forced her when she was very little."

"I thought that culture died off many decades ago."

Iona's heart jumps. *Did my parents die, too?*

"So did I," Sosimo says.

"Back to the problem," Grebson says. "You do have some contact with Catalyst, correct?"

"Yes, but it's more business related."

"Do you think they'd give us a hand? I'm sure it wouldn't take much to convince them to join in a mission against the Erohsians."

"I agree. We're definitely going to need them if we're going to get the children back to Sunta. I've been advising them on some new talismans that can fool the Erohsian identification sensors."

"That could come in handy. Are we going to come up with disguises for them?"

"We'll have to see how the talismans work," Sosimo says. "At the very minimum, we'll make the boys grow their hair out and trim back the girl's."

"Very original, Sosimo."

"The oldest tricks are usually the best, but it's risky. Do you think it's the right decision to send the children on a rescue mission?"

"It's our best option. We'd have no chance to pull this off against Borukins, but they do against Erohsians. Besides, I have a friend that will most likely be interested in helping."

"*A* friend?"

"Something like that," Grebson says.

"Well, we'll need any help we can get. Are we done here? I want to see how Natina is doing with the Humans."

"Yes, but you'll only be disappointed."

Iona hears chairs move away from the table. She hurries back to the training room before they see her. She is greeted by a loud smack as Korbin lands on his back.

Ryder laughs. "Oh man, Korbin, you just got beat by the princess again! That's three in a row."

Korbin jumps to his feet. "Oh, whatever, Ryder. I bet you can't do any better."

Natina puts her hands on her hips. "Yeah, Ryder. Or are you scared?"

"How are they holding up?" Grebson asks when he and Sosimo come in.

Natina shakes her head. "Not so good. Ryder's too scared to grapple with me."

Ryder exhales. "Fine, let's go." He steps up to Natina.

Korbin hurries off to the side, grinning and rubbing his hands together eagerly. "You're going to get your butt kicked so hard."

A moment later, Ryder hits the ground. Korbin jumps on him. "I told you so!"

They wrestle. Thea circles, pretending to be an announcer. Grebson watches with a faint shadow of amusement, Sosimo is shaking his head.

Natina walks over to Iona. "You're Iona, right?"

Iona nods. "I am."

"Nero mentioned you."

"What did he say?"

Natina shrugs. "Not a whole lot. It's hard to get him to talk. I wasn't sure if he was just nervous because I'm a princess, or if that's how he always is. What's he usually like?"

"He's quiet, but sometimes he'll do stuff that surprises you… Like when we were running from the Erohsians a few months back. All of us but Nero got captured by some traffickers."

"Oh no. What happened?" Natina asks.

"Some stupid kid posing as an orphan tricked us. He got us locked in a prison cell on this giant ship. We thought we were all doomed, but next thing we know, Nero comes in and rescues us. It was amazing."

"Wow. How'd he do that?"

"We're not sure. Apparently, someone helped him, but I still wouldn't have expected it in my entire life."

Natina nods. "He seems to be full of surprises."

"It wasn't always like this," Iona says. "He used to be scared of everything."

"What changed?"

Iona shrugs. "I'm not sure. So much has changed for all of us."

They look at each other for a moment then turn to watch Ryder and Korbin wrestle.

"So, you're all from Erohsia?" Natina asks. "What do you think of the Erohsians?"

"Bah. They're horrible. We call them Minis because they're so small. They're always pushing Humans around, trying to control us. Only Catalyst stands up to them."

"That's the Human resistance group, right?"

"Yep, they're great. I hope one day me and the others can help."

"I'm sure they'll let you, especially if we rescue Nero."

Iona smiles. "I hope so."

Grebson walks up to Natina and Iona. "We should leave. Are you ready?"

Natina nods. "It was good to meet you, Iona."

Natina says goodbye to everyone else. Sosimo walks the two other Borukins out.

"Can you believe Nero's been hanging out with a real princess?" Thea asks the rest of the children.

"Yeah, how the heck did he pull that one off?" Korbin asks.

"She seems okay, though," Iona says. "But I want to know what's up with Sosimo and Grebson. They don't like each other."

"Maybe it's just because Grebson's bigger," Korbin says. "He's huge. Those tattoos on his face are so cool."

"Come on, Korb, don't be ridiculous," Ryder says. "I doubt Sosimo cares about that."

"Well then, why do you think they're like that?"

Iona drums her fingers on her thigh. "Could they be related?"

"Like brothers?" Thea asks.

"Yeah, maybe," Iona says.

Ryder shrugs. "I haven't got a clue. I just know we're going to need them both to get to Sunta and rescue Nero..."

"I'm scared to go to Sunta," Thea says softly.

"Me too, but Sosimo and Grebson are smart. They'll come up with an awesome plan," Ryder says.

Thea looks down. "I know. I'm still scared."

Ryder looks at her, then the others. "If Nero were an animal, he'd be a gentle orange butterfly."

"Is it because he's cute?" Thea asks.

"What? No! Really?"

Thea looks down blushing. "Whatever."

"Okay... is it because he always gets pushed around, like, by the wind, but it doesn't really bother him?" Korbin asks.

Ryder shakes his head.

"How about because he looks harmless but if something tries to attack him, he's actually poisonous and they totally regret it?" Iona asks.

Ryder nods. "Yeah. He is way tougher than he looks."

The children nod their heads, smiling at each other.

"We don't have a choice," Korbin says. "We need to rescue him even if that means going back to Sunta."

27 A Cell of a Room
Nero

Nero shudders from the remains of his nightmare. He buries his face into the thin pillow, wrapping the ends around his head. *What am I going to do?*

"Hey, Nero."

He barely hears the voice. *Just leave me alone!*

"Nero, it's me. Come on. Talk to me for a second."

Nero rolls off his stomach and sits up, pulling the black hood from his head. He stares with bloodshot eyes at Natina.

Natina offers a small comforting smile. "How are you doing?"

Nero looks around his cell. "I'm a prisoner here and I'm being dragged back to Sunta. It's the end of the world!" Tears well up in his eyes.

"It's not the end of the world."

"It's the end of my world. The Erohsians will never let me go."

"Did you forget about your friends?"

"My friends? What are they going to do? Do you think they care? Korbin's probably excited I'm gone."

"Stop it, Nero! You're being stupid."

Nero hangs his head, throwing his hood back up. *It's the truth...*

"I'm your friend, and the others do care about you. Korbin was the most eager to rescue you."

Nero wipes his eyes. "Really?" His voice is just over a whisper.

Natina smiles, nodding. "Really. Just know we're all thinking about you."

A small smile teases the corners of his mouth.

Natina peers around the cell. "So, are they treating you okay?"

He shrugs. "I guess. It's really boring."

She reaches down, picking up a pile of books at her feet. "Luckily, I thought of that. I brought you some books." She hands them to him. "Here are a couple on artifacts that Saraf let me borrow, and here are a couple on different Borukin Aether skills that Grebson said you'd be interested in. And this one, is one of my favorites."

Nero grabs the last book. "What is it?"

"It is a true story about the last expedition to Bellicove Island."

"I thought no one ever goes there."

"It's mostly because of this story."

"Really? What happens?"

Natina smiles. "I guess you'll have to read it to find out."

"Thanks." Nero sets the books on his bed. He pulls the hood off his head and holds out his dark sleeve. "So, what's up with all these black clothes? They're kinda cool."

"Remember what I told you about the tattoos? They define the person. The black robe is a symbol of removing who you are. It doesn't really work in your case, but in general, the dishonor is a powerful deterrent to crime." She looks at him for a long moment. "Do you really think my brother was cheating?"

Nero shrugs. "It looked like someone was helping him."

"How could he kill Madam Carason?" There is a knock on the door outside the cellblock and Natina turns away. "That's my signal from Greb I'm out of time. The King and everyone are heading out tomorrow, you included. Since I'll be traveling along, I'll try to say hi more often. I'll talk to you soon."

"Thanks for coming."

"Of course." Natina lingers for just another moment before she leaves.

Nero sits back on his bed, grabbing the book that Natina said was her favorite: The Last Expedition. He props his pillow against the wall, crosses his legs, and cracks it open.

*****

Everyone in the chamber gasped in surprise; everyone cramped around the edges and everyone packed into the staggered sections of seats. Even the three individuals atop the intricately carved, dark, wooden structure at the head of the chamber couldn't hide their apprehension.

These were the members of the Anterren Council and the leaders of the three dominant races. On the left sat the large, dark-skinned Queen Jarmin of the Borukins. Her white tattoos crawled up her neck and over her shaved head as though they were a crown. On the right sat the small, light-skinned Dictator Ulis, of the Erohsians. He looked like a child compared to the Queen. In the middle sat the olive-skinned Madam President Dema of the Humans. All of them were covered by the dark blue robes of the Anterren Council. Golden linings were visible on the hoods hanging down their backs and on the edges of their cuffs.

Under the high vaulted ceilings, on a small podium, a confident Borukin stood facing the council. He bore the weight of all the stares in the room. Four white tattoos, of different Aether casts, graced his face. His modest, pale green outfit moved gently with his breath. He was the only one in the chamber, including myself, who was breathing.

I watched as Dictator Ulis's face twisted from shock into anger. He slapped the arms of his throne. "This is absurd!" the Erohsian yelled. "How dare you make a mockery of this council and waste our time with such requests. I shall have you arrested."

"Enough." Queen Jarmin stood, holding a hand up to the Erohsian Dictator. "I will handle my own." She turned to the Borukin on the platform. "We've known each other for a long time, Rolk. I would go as far as to consider you a friend."

I looked at my husband on the platform, hardly able to contain the pride I felt. He dipped his head toward the Queen. "As would I," he said.

"If you were any other person, I would laugh at this request," the Queen said.

"You're actually going to consider this?" Dictator Ulis asked.

"Before us stands Corusmin Master Rolk Arman, the only Borukin in the last five-hundred years to have come as close to understanding the Corusnigma as the Great Queen Temas. He has made it to the monoliths of the Moltrik, Icor, Pahzan, and Nesive Corusnigmas. I have no doubt he could complete the Ru Corusnigma if the Ruians hadn't poisoned their land. His proficiency in Odo is second to none and he is capable of what most have only dreamt of, so if there is anyone who has the right to propose something that no one else has done, then it is he. All I ask is that we hear him out."

The Human President Dema stared down at Rolk. "I have heard from many of my own that you are a sensible man, with honor above most, and bravery matched by only a few," she said. "Because of this, I wish to hear you out."

The Erohsian dictator threw up his hands. "As if we don't have anything better to do! Shall we invite a circus for the next meeting?"

President Dema turned to the Dictator. "Ulis, the council has decided. It will happen." She held his gaze for a moment before turning back to my husband. "Now, Rolk, before I make any decision, I would like to know three things. What can you hope to gain with an expedition to Bellicove Island? How can you justify the risk when all previous expeditions have ended in disaster? And, finally, why now?"

Rolk dipped his head. "Thank you, Madam President, for giving my wife and I this opportunity to present our case. We'll be sure to remark on each of your questions. If you don't mind me answering out of order, I'll begin with the last. Why now? I believe this is a perfect time to make such an expedition. We are in a time of peace. Our three races have never had a stronger bond." He held up his hands to the council then to the chamber filled with a diversity of races. "Which is shown by the presence of this great council and all of the people gathered here. In these times of peace and prosperity, it is our duty as a civilization to advance our culture and ourselves. How is it that we've been content for so many years with such large gaps in knowledge of our history and of the world? We know very little of anything prior to twelve hundred years ago, besides that which is in the Book of Creation."

"And what if that time period was censored for a reason?" Dictator Ulis asked.

"Perhaps it was… or maybe it was truly lost in conflict. Either way, we'll never be able to avoid the same mistakes unless we can look at the lessons from history," Rolk said. "The Creators and the Lost Race have vanished from Anterra. What could be responsible for such a demise? Is it something we should prepare for or is the threat contained, as the Book of Creation states? No one can say, which is what leads us to the motivation for such an expedition.

"The only sure remnants of the past are the six Corusnigmas scattered about the world. And due to the extreme danger they pose, we can barely scratch their surface. A large part of this is because we don't understand what we're dealing with. We're fumbling in the dark when there's a banded Celequore ready to pounce; it's far from safe and hardly ideal." He paused and looked at each of the council members. "Now, there are two other areas that haven't been explored because of the danger they pose, yet we know there are certainly ancient ruins to be studied: The Tenebrous Miasma and Bellicove Island. If we were to unlock the secrets of one of these, then perhaps we will be better suited to unlock the secrets of the others."

"But if they're all so dangerous, how can you justify proceeding with one over another?" Dictator Ulis asked. "The Tenebrous Miasma has been known to swallow entire ships."

"The Tenebrous Miasma is another matter entirely. I'm not saying this won't be dangerous. What I'm saying is if we can minimize the risks, the payoffs could be substantial."

"And, how do you plan on minimizing the risks?" Dictator Ulis asked. "This expedition will need to be made up of all our races for it to be approved, and no one will be as strong or as capable as you. Can you guarantee their safety?"

"I don't want you to believe my talents and achievements have made me reckless. Life is too precious to waste on the pursuit of glory, and nothing is worth the lives of an entire expedition," Rolk said. "Being such, I only dare make such a request upon the foundations of a discovery my wife has made, so I'll leave it to my wife, Nix Armen, to address this last point."

I took a deep breath and stepped forward. "It is a great honor to present our case. I thank you for giving us the opportunity."

"You and your husband have done the Borukins many great services," Queen Jarmin said. "It is the least I can do. Now, tell us about your discovery."

I dipped my head toward each of the council members and took another breath to let my heart settle. "Anterra is composed of many different races, each with a unique set of abilities. The number of races that share the same base genetic makeup is beyond what anyone expects to have happened naturally. So, even though the Erohsians have different beliefs than the Humans and Borukins, we all can agree the Creators made each race for a specific purpose." I paused and noted the general agreement of the council members and the audience, which I used to fuel my confidence. "In order for the Creators to take advantage of our skills, they would have to communicate with us, which is why we all speak a variation of the same language. The Ethnohaps are the exception, however. Why would our Creators make such a xenophobic class of races that are difficult to communicate with?"

"There are plenty of theories on that topic," Dictator Ulis said.

"I agree, but the reality of the situation is, our Creators wouldn't make something if there wasn't a purpose. Without communication, the Ethnohaps would be next to useless to them."

"That will be a difficult thing to prove in so little time, Nix," President Dema said.

"I shouldn't need long." I nodded toward one of my attendants, who brought forth a container with both hands. I opened the lid and removed a glowing green sphere the size of a cantaloupe. In the center, yellow wisps of light curled around themselves. The audience gasped. "Have you seen its equal?" I asked the council members, then the audience. No one commented. "This was a gift from the Vasugian Ethnohap after we were able to communicate with them, using this." I took a staff with a crystal orb at the top from another assistant close by. I tapped it on the ground. The orb, held in place by thin pieces of metal wrapped about its body, gave off a gentle blue light. I felt the Aether wash over my face.

"This light has been shown to calm the Aquarian Ethnohap race, and I theorized they were not unique in this matter," I said. "When we brought the light to the Vasugians, they were equally calm, and we were able to learn a little about their culture. It was still difficult to communicate, but the outright hostility was gone."

"Where, exactly, are you going with this?" Queen Jarmin asked, her voice patient.

"Well, we know from the few reports on Bellicove Island there is an Ethnohap race living there. Likely, they are responsible for the immense danger. Why would they be any different from the other Ethnohaps? I think there's a good chance they'll react similarly to the crystal orbs, allowing us to safely explore the island."

"It sounds like a dream," Dictator Ulis said. "You have no proof for the theory."

"That's true," I said. "But there is only one way to find out. My husband and I would like to take an expedition to the island. Once we arrive, we will go out with a small group to test the theory. If it fails, then it fails. There will be little, if any risk to the expedition's safety. If it succeeds, then we continue. The entire expedition will be conducted with careful reviews of safety for everyone, following each new discovery."

President Dema reviewed some notes, then looked at me. "The potential rewards for an expedition of this nature are unimaginable."

"So, you've made up the decision for all of us?" Dictator Ulis asked.

President Dema shook her head. "Absolutely not, I'm simply stating my mind. It's the decision of the council as a whole, as this will be a joint endeavor of our three great races. Rolk and Nix Armen, we have heard your proposal and we shall consider it. You are dismissed."

*****

The bars on the cell door rattle, waking Nero from his comfortable daze.

Two royal Borukin guards stand at the door. "It's time to go. The caravan is moving."

Nero grabs the one book he brought with him to the temporary holding cell and slides between the hulking masses of the guards. They lead him outside, where Natina is waiting with an unknown bodyguard.

Nero eyes the bodyguard with Natina. *Where's Grebson?*

The prisoner guards dip their heads. "Princess. What can we do for you?"

Natina steps forward, chin up. "We've been on the road for several days now. Has the prisoner given you any trouble?"

"He is a non-bonded Human boy. He won't give us any trouble for the entire trip. I guarantee it," the female Borukin Guard says.

"Just as I'd expect from you two, Bresta. Now, remember, we need him in decent shape when we arrive, so he can be presented to the Erohsians. Perhaps you can make sure to take him out of the prison truck and walk him every time we stop?"

The male guard shakes his head. "Sorry, Princess, but that's against regulations."

Natina shrugs. "Suit yourself, Jaice, but I hope you'll be able to find new jobs when we get to Sunta and you make a fool of my dad."

Jaice frowns. "How so? There's no chance he'll escape while we're watching him."

"And I have no doubt in your abilities, but if the prisoner is unable to walk during the presentation, then how's that going to look for the King? He'll be furious. Who do you think he's going to blame?"

The guards' eyes widen. They look at each other.

"You said it yourself. He's an easy charge. Which would you rather risk? On the other hand, I could fetch the King so he could tell you the same thing." Natina begins to walk off.

Bresta holds up her hands. "No, Princess. Please don't bother. It would be… wise to walk the prisoner under the circumstances, especially due to the extended duration of the trip."

Natina dips her head. "That is an excellent point." She turns and walks away with her own bodyguard.

Nero is led to the four-doored prison transport vehicle and put in the back seat with his other books. Once the rest of the Royal caravan starts to move, they follow suit. Nero pulls out a book and starts to read.

*****

The six of us held on, our dinghy battling through the waves. We hopped over some and smashed through others, propelled by the constantly whining engine. A steady wind flowed over the island, channeled by rocky cliffs on either side of a small cove. The tropical forest loomed over a diminutive beach: our target. The breeze kicked up white caps on the waves, spitting a fine mist that collected on my face along with the spray of our small boat. Salt water tickled my tongue and burned my eyes. Shaded by thick cloud cover, Bellicove Island was exactly what I expected for a place with such ominous history.

The small Erohsian leader, Seader, in a dark, skin-tight body suit and a vest of pockets, tended the steering at the stern of the dingy. His eyes were hidden behind the visor of his combat helmet.

"I've been thinking. In order for this to work," he yelled over the ocean and motor, "we need to be fully engaged with the Bellicoven Ethnohap before we try to activate the staff. It's the only way for us to be certain it will repel them."

"Seems like that's a bit overboard," said Onk, the Human leader. Both he and his second, Fording, wore the standard Human military fatigues with lepisents fastened to their forearms. "Can't we just turn the thing on and see if they leave us alone?"

"Leave us alone?" Seader asked in a caustic tone. "I would never have imagined a Human turning down an opportunity to fight someone."

"What are you trying to say, Mini?" Onk snapped.

I slammed my bo staff styk against the floor of the boat. "Quit it," I said, eyeing them until they both looked away. "Now, Seader, what were you saying? I agree with Onk.

Turning the staff on from the get-go would be the safest option."

"It'd be the safest, but our goal is to test the staff's effectiveness and ensure the safety of the entire expedition. If we turn the staff on when we arrive, then there's no way to tell if the staff's working, or if the Bellcoven are just waiting for a good time to attack. However, if we can repel them with the staff while we are fully engaged, then we guarantee the staff will do the job we expect."

Rolk nodded, a dark, sword-like styk strapped across his back. "That's a good point."

"Oh, come on," Onk said, looking at the large metal container sitting at Seader's feet. "If he's so smart, then why'd he bring a rifle when we're going up against an Ethnohap race that specializes in projectiles? It's going to be useless out there."

"It's not a rifle," Seader said. "It's an Aether-cannon, and it's going to change the way people look at Erohsians. We'll no longer be helpless against all your Aether, so you better start showing us some respect."

"Ha! Can you even pick it up?" Onk asked. "I'm sorry. I don't find you Mini's very intimidating when you look like a little child with a big squirt gun. Just leave the fighting to the ones who can do it."

Rolk grabbed Onk by the shirt and pulled him close. "Enough," he said slowly in his deep voice. "The Erohsians are an important part of this mission. They have a role, just like you. Don't forget that."

Onk fell back to his seat and readjusted his shirt. "Alright, I'm just giving him a hard time." He turned, looking out to the island. "Can you hurry this thing up? I need to get on some solid ground before I lose my breakfast."

Seader shook his head, turning his attention back to the approaching beach, moments out.

Rolk stood at the bow of the dingy, using his legs to absorb the undulations of the boat. "Onk and Fording, as soon as you can, form up a defensive barrier against projectiles. We'll fall in behind. That will be more effective and safer than relying on our individual amulets."

"You got it," the two Humans responded in unison.

"May Stone's courage flow through us," Rolk said, his voice rising over the waves and the engine. "Marks's sword guide us, and the lost blood nourish us!"

Seader slammed the boat onto the beach. Everyone lurched forward. The Humans used the momentum to launch themselves ahead, and it was just a moment before everyone else joined them. Seader's second-in-command, Maizy, disembarked with medical gear. In both hands, she carried a detector that had analog meters and colored light bulbs.

"We're set. Ready to move on your command, Rolk," Onk said, his eyes scanning the trees. "We can hold this extended barrier against projectiles for some time. I'll let you know when we're pushing our luck."

"Thank you, Onk and Fording. Now, if everyone is ready, let's move forward. Maizy, keep me posted on the Aether levels in the area."

The small Erohsian with her large medical pack moved the Aether detector around. "A bit higher than normal, about two-hundred and twenty-five milliSorvin. I'll let you know if it rises."

We moved forward slowly. I carried my bo staff out in front of me, ready to activate the blue light-emitting orb attached to its top at a moment's notice. Seader took heavy steps, straining under the weight of his fancy new weapon. We reached the edge of the forest and continued inward for fifty meters until Rolk brought us to a stop near a clearing.

"Alright, that's far enough," he said. "I don't want to put us in too deep a hole if we need to retreat. We'll exchange blows with them but try not to kill anything. Nothing needs to die for this test."

"The Aether levels here are noticeably higher now. About five-hundred and fifty milliSorvin," Maizy said. "It looks like it might level off, though."

"Thanks, Maizy." Rolk turned to Onk. "Could you attract some company?"

Onk smiled. "Fording makes more noise than me, she'd be better for this task." He looked at Fording.

Fording nodded. "Of course."

Fording put her hands together as if she was holding an invisible ball. Suddenly, they were filled with a coruscating sphere of energy, light escaping through the gaps in her fingers. The ball doubled in size, and Fording gently pushed it away from her. It oscillated like a water balloon as it moved away at walking pace. With a flick of her wrist, it sped off into the forest. Just as it was about a stone's throw away, Fording clenched her fist and brought her elbow to her side. The ball of energy shimmered for a second then exploded in a bright violent flash that shook the trees, causing the birds to fly away.

"Hopefully that'll do it," Fording said, taking her position next to Onk.

We waited for almost a half hour until Onk broke the silence. "This is why I hate defense. I have no patience for doing nothing." His head snapped to the side. "Oh, hey, I think I saw something." Suddenly, his hand made the tiniest of movements and a shower of dirt splashed up from the side. "Whoa, those things got some zip. Stay tight, I wouldn't want anyone getting nipped."

There was another splash of dirt to the side. I turned my head just in time to see a Human-like shape hanging from the branch, swinging out of sight. Soon, projectiles were zipping through the air, leaving glowing streaks of light that looked like a crisscrossing of spider webs. Some would smash into the dirt while others sunk deep into trees with puffs of smoke.

"Alright, I think they're attacking us," Onk yelled over the noise. "So, any time you're ready to use your little crystal thingy!"

"No, not yet," Seader yelled. "They need to come at us directly. I want to see them react to the light."

The projectiles eventually stopped. Rolk raised his styk. "Be ready."

My heart accelerated, and I prepared myself.

A creature swung from a tree and landed on the ground only meters from us. In that moment, I could see the intelligence in its eyes. Although it was Humanoid in shape, it crouched on all fours with a glowing, dagger-like object in one hand. Its skin was covered in grime. Moss hung from its minimal clothing. Its eyes left me and snapped to Seader. It was on him before he could pull up his weapon. They tumbled to the ground. Rolk swung his styk with incredible speed and strength into the Bellicoven's side, knocking it off Seader and sending it back through the trees. More of the Bellicoven swarmed us from all sides.

The smell of ozone filled my nose. The Humans used their lepisents to release balls of energy through the air, leaving trails of popping Aether in their wake. Onk used Moltrik Aether to create blue-hued balls of energy crackling with electricity. Fording used Pahzan Aether that smoked and swirled as though a fire was trapped inside. The balls of energy would strike one of the Bellicoven, knocking it to the side or off a tree, but they were quick to bounce back.

I fended off a couple of Bellicoven, struggling to keep track of the others preparing to pounce.

Seader scrambled to his feet, holding his side. "Alright, now!"

There wasn't a moment's hesitation. I slammed my staff into the ground, activating the orb. A soft blue light illuminated the clearing, and the Bellicoven immediately stopped their charge. They scurried off into the forest. Some of them in mid-leap twisted in the air, desperate to escape. They hit the ground near me and immediately scurried back to the forest. Others climbed the trees, occasionally looking back. Eventually, they all disappeared.

"Hot damn, that pickled my back hair," Onk said. "Well, if that doesn't prove Nix's theory on the orbs, then I don't know what will."

Seader nodded, still holding his side. "If it repels them in a heated attack like that, then it works for me. Thank the Creators it worked," he said while looking at a smear of blood in his hand.

Maizy rushed over to him.

"So, you approve of proceeding?" Rolk asked, sliding his styk across his back.

"I do," Seader said. "But we really need to consider how to deal with this race. Just in case."

Maizy stood up. "It's nothing but a scratch. It looks like the new matrix armor took the brunt of the damage. They must have got you with some nasty Aether-infused weapon. Nothing else would have sliced through it like that."

"All the more reason to make a plan to deal with this race," Seader said, his voice raspy.

"Well, let's get back to the ship and do so," Rolk said. "We'll have to be extra careful when exploring the island, so we don't overextend ourselves." Something caught his eye and he pointed. "Nix, are those ruins?"

I looked in his direction. There, barely visible, was a crumbling moss-covered wall of old grey stone. "I believe they are," I said.

Seader shrugged his small pack from his back and knelt over it. He pulled out a device, threw the strap around his neck, and stood. "I brought the dater; shall we see if all this hassle is worth it?" He asked.

"Quickly, if you are up for it," Rolk said.

Seader led the way and scanned the ruins with the dater. After a few minutes, the device beeped. "Wow, these ruins go back way before the Corusnigmas. They're thousands of years old."

Onk slapped my husband on the back. "Rolk, looks like you and Nix did it again."

Rolk grabbed my hand, squeezing. "Let's just hope, by Stone's fortune, these aren't the only ruins we find."

"I have a feeling this is only the beginning," I said, squeezing his hand back.

28 Practice Makes Perfect
Iona

Korbin is mid push-up when Sosimo enters the training room.

Sosimo pulls the toothpick from his mouth, raising an eyebrow. "Doing a bit of extra exercise, Korbin?"

"Just trying to get stronger," Korbin says, red faced.

"This wouldn't have anything to do with getting your butt kicked by Natina, would it?"

"No…" He looks up at Sosimo and his face is even redder. "Maybe a little. I can't be beaten by a princess!"

Sosimo pats him on the back. "Natina is a well-trained Borukin. There's nothing to be ashamed of." He turns to the rest of the children, clapping his hands. "Alright, let's get started. Over the next few weeks, we'll become familiar with some skills and tools Grebson and I think you'll need." Sosimo moves to the artifact rack, selecting a Moltrik lepisent. "The most important skill we'll be working on is using Moltrik lepisents to stun someone. We'll also practice team work to focus attacks on a single target. It will drastically increase your stunning capabilities." Sosimo places the lepisent down and takes a bracelet from the wall. "These are invisibility talismans. You'll be using these and Moltrik talismans to trick the security system. It will help you sneak through Demeeurj Tower, which is the massive Erohsian building at the center of Sunta."

"Oh, cool, we're going to become invisible?" Thea jumps with excitement.

"It's more of a trick of the mind, but it has the same effect," Sosimo says. "It will even affect each of you, so the tricky part is working together when you can't see each other, which we'll practice. We'll also be training with doormen." He picks a rod with a red pointed end and a blue pointed end. "The Erohsians may have some heavy-duty doors, and these gals will take care of most anything in your way. They're loud, messy, and take a week or more to recharge, so this is a tool of last resort."

"How do they work?" Iona asks.

"Each one has three components to it." Sosimo shows the red point and the blue point. "This is the hot end and this is the cold end, which are conveniently labeled. The hot end will melt the locking mechanism. The cold end will cool the metal after you've opened the door."

"Why would we need to cool it down?" Ryder asks.

"Because melted metal is extremely hot, and you may not have time to let it cool down naturally before you squeeze through. The cold end is also a protective shield. It will cool any metal that gets flung at you when you're trying to pry the door open." Sosimo points to the center. "The center is what you use to pull the door open. It uses Fundamental Aether to latch on to the door, so you can open it when the lock is melted and the door is hot."

"Couldn't we use our own skill to pull it open?" Iona asks.

Sosimo nods. "You could, but the skill required to multitask is at the edge of your current training. Plus, this is a Borukin device. We don't have the Aether reserves to use on tasks like that, so we make self-sufficient tools. It'll also be a great way to save Aether. Grebson and I will set up some training exercises for the bracelets and the doorman later. For now, we'll start to practice with the Moltrik lepisents."

"Is Grebson your brother?" Thea blurts out.

Sosimo looks at her then down. "Yes."

"I thought your family was killed?"

"They were, and so was his. I tried to save all of them... but I failed." Sosimo crushes the toothpick in his mouth. "If he wasn't off pursuing his trophies, maybe we *could* have saved everyone."

"Fae always said a relationship with a grudge goes bad like a container of milk," Thea says. "But I'd never forgive him either."

Sosimo looks at her, frowning. "You'd never forgive him?"

"No. Not ever."

"But Grebson is his family," Korbin says. "And Fae always said if you keep carrying around your baggage, you'll be too tired to live your life."

"It sounds like Fae was a smart lady."

"She was." Thea's eyes well up.

Sosimo kneels down and hugs Thea. "We can work on this together."

29 The Moltrik Corusnigma
Nero

Nero sets one of his books on the back seat of the prison truck as the royal caravan comes to a halt. They have arrived at the Borukin Gate on the west side of the Siroté Mountains. Construction equipment is scattered around in every direction as Borukins work on upgrading the walls and defense turrets.

"I'd like to see the Drebin try that again," Jaice says when they pass through the wall.

Outside the Gate, tanks and burly vehicles arrayed in a defensive position provide cover during construction. Nero looks over the number of Borukins stationed there during the construction. He cannot count them all. His eyes drift past them to the north-west, where he had felt something when they were fleeing to Kiats so many months ago. *Was that the Drebin?*

The caravan splits off the main road following the Carn River to a road along the foothills. Nero sits up. "Where are we going? Isn't Sunta along the Carn?"

Jaice turns around, nodding. "We're going to the Moltrik Corusnigma first. The King wants the prince to pass the trial."

"Are we going to be able to see it?"

"We'll walk around the area, but I doubt we'll see the attempt."

"That'd be great if we could. I've heard of the Corusnigmas. They sound awesome. Have you ever seen one?"

Both of the guards shake their heads.

"I know there's a lot of Aether and stuff, but what makes it so hard to get to the center?"

"It's the randomness and the concentration of the Aether that's the tricky part. If you're caught in just one flare up, you'll be lucky to survive," Bresta says, eyes forward, driving. "The Moltrik Corusnigma doesn't have any major physical obstacles. The real dangers are the electric forest, the magnetic morass, the molecular igniter, and the spotlight."

"What are all those?" Nero asks.

"They are the smites of the Corusnigma. They're manifestations of the different branches of the Moltrik cast: one for electricity, one for magnetism, one for chemical, and one for light. The electric forest and the spotlight will be pretty obvious if you see them. The molecular igniter is the most dangerous; it'll break chemical bonds in your body, and there's no physical signs. The magnetic morass is the least dangerous because it's just an extremely high magnetic field. As long as you don't have any conductive material on you, the effects only slow you down."

Nero looks down the road through the front window. *I really hope we get to see it.*

*****

"How much farther do we need to go?" Seader asked, irritated. His combat helmet hung off his backpack and a steady flow of sweat dripped from his face. The thick humid air of the tropical forest was oppressive.

A Human excavator stepped over clumps of vegetation, hacking through the growth with a machete. "Not much farther, sir," she said with derision.

The six of us, we who made the first steps on to the island together, had been surveying the different discoveries on the island. It had been three weeks now. Each new set of ruins was an exciting discovery; some big and some small. All seemed to have the markings of our Creators. We just needed to catch one break before it all fell into place and we could start to truly understand.

"Patience, my friend," Rolk said. "We'll get there in time."

"How can you ask me to have patience?" Seader demanded. "If this Human is accurate, the new area matches the description of the Last Sacrifice. Finally, we'll be able to put to rest the differences in our teachings."

"As long as you're prepared to be disappointed," the Human leader, Onk, said, slapping at the bugs around his face. "It's so amusing that, even to such a logical race, it's not obvious that the Creators brought about the Final Days. Their sacrifice was nothing more than an effort to fix their own mistake."

Seader shook his head, wiping the sweat off his sunburnt forehead. "You Humans and Borukins are fools. It was your rebellion that brought about the Final Days. If it weren't for the love of our Creators and their sacrifice, none of us would be here."

"Oh, please," Onk said. "You've placed them on such a high pedestal that you'd lick their shoes clean if they–"

"For Stone's sake, enough already," I said fiercely. "We don't know what we'll find, but until then, let's not start this debate. It never goes anywhere."

Onk and Seader grudgingly agreed. We all continued in silence.

No more than fifteen minutes later, a Borukin military officer ran up to us, sucking in deep breaths of air. "Corusmin Master Rolk, I've just got news we've had multiple sightings of cressen."

"What!?" Seader gasped.

Rolk held up his hand. His hard, professional façade only showed the slightest hint of fear. "Calm yourself, Seader." He turned back to the Borukin officer. "Can you be certain?"

The officer nodded. "Yes, certain. We have four independent sources who have seen the tell-tale yellow eyes. They are watching us."

"How many?" Rolk asked.

"At least two, possibly three. They were seen on the ground and in the trees. We're not sure if any are aerial."

"That's it, then," Seader cut in. "We need to pull out. We're unprepared for this kind of threat."

Onk let out a puff. "Leave it to the Erohsians to be the first to run."

"Don't, Onk," Rolk said sharply. "This is serious. Seader is right to be concerned."

Seader glared at Onk. "Of course I am. How did you not know cressen were here, Rolk?" Seader asked, the strain obvious in his voice.

"No one's made it this far before," Rolk replied. "Take a second to think. We need to look at this in the right light. Running away at this point does us no good, but I do think we should make plans to pull out and reassess the situation."

"Reassess the situation?" Seader cried. "There's no other option but to pull out. You and the moronic Humans can stay and fight, but I'm not sticking around to get massacred."

Onk stepped forward. "What are you trying to say?"

Rolk put his hand on Onk's chest to stop him. "Onk, enough. Seader, get a hold of yourself, for Stone's sake. I've encountered cressen before. Just because they're dangerous doesn't mean they're always hostile. We've made it this far. We've been here for over three weeks. Who's to say we're even in danger? Cressen are simple creatures. They're easy to read. We just need to avoid their trigger and we'll be fine. If we were going to trigger them, we would have already done it. Now that we know they're here, we can take the necessary precautions."

Seader shook his head. "As if it's that easy."

Rolk nodded. "It is." He turned to the Borukin officer. "Inform everyone that we're in non-hostile cressen territory. That means no hostility to anything. Do not move any more ruins. No more exploring. Have everyone regroup at the camps and wait for further details."

The Borukin nodded. "Right away, Corusmin Master."

Rolk turned to Seader. "We'll be alright. We'll continue with our plan to see the newly discovered ruins and help the people get back to the ship. Then we can come up with a new plan."

Seader pulled his large weapon tight to his body. "Cressen might be simple, but the Anterraktor isn't. Where there are cressen, there's always a guardian. What if we encounter it?"

Rolk held up his hands to our surroundings. "Everything we've encountered is incredibly old. I bet the Anterraktor has been around for a long time, so it's most likely hibernating. As long as we don't do anything stupid, we won't trigger the cressen, and we'll be fine. Trust me on this."

"This is a big risk," Seader said.

"I know. I'll take responsibility for whatever happens." Rolk turned back to the excavator. "Now, if you would, lead the way."

Her face pale, the excavator began again.

We walked for over an hour through the dense forest, following cairns and markings on the trees. The path was difficult, always uphill. Unexpectedly, the vegetation fell away as we reached a cliff. The cliff wrapped around a large area of sunken ground. It looked like someone had taken a giant scoop out of the landscape. In the center of the hole were ruins consumed by vegetation. Even at this distance, I could tell they were immense. Six circular structures surrounded a hexagon-shaped clearing made of stone.

"'In the crater, we took our last breaths, with the trap set, there was nothing left to do but wait for their arrival,'" Maizy said, looking off at the massive bowl in front of them.

"Orinda 3:14, the Battle of Orinda," Rolk said. "I can see why they're thinking this is the location of the Last Sacrifice. We wouldn't be the first to make such a claim, though." He turned to the Human excavator. "What have you learned so far?"

"We found what looks to be a sealed ruin. It runs underground at the edge of the large, flat surface. We haven't a clue how to open it," she said. "We also discovered that, just like the Corusnigmas, we were able to match each of the structures with a unique Aether signature, suggesting each structure seems to have been tied to one of the Aether casts."

Rolk pointed to one of the six main structures, the one that was massively damaged. "Do you remember which cast was associated with that structure?"

"I believe that one had a Biat signature."

"Hmmm," Rolk tapped his knuckles on his hip. "I wonder if there's significance in that. Why would the Biat structure be destroyed? And why is the Biat Corusnigma at the center? Are the Aether levels elevated?"

"Slightly," the excavator responded, "but nothing close to the Corusnigmas. Whatever the purpose of this structure, I believe it failed."

"Do you have any guesses as to what happened?" I asked.

The excavator shrugged, shaking her head. "Nothing solid. It looks like something tore itself out of the Biat structure. The others seem to have failed at head stones located on the large hexagon surface."

"Enough talk," Seader said. "I'd like to see them up close, so we can make our own educated opinions."

The excavator flashed a look of frustration, dipping her head. "Of course. We have to follow the edge of the cliff for a while, then we can follow the old road to the center," she said, pointing the way with her finger.

The path was better traveled than our earlier path, so we made good time. We covered the distance in thirty minutes and arrived alongside the severely damaged structure we had seen from above. Stones and debris were scattered among the vegetation. The structure was riddled with cylindrical voids of varying depth. There were plants growing in each of the openings.

"This is just a large storage container," Seader said. "I bet these holes used to create a matrix of wood, or another high Aetheratin material before it decomposed."

Rolk nodded. "I agree." His attention wandered away from the structure before he turned back to the excavator. "Has there been a thorough survey of this crater?"

"Not yet, sir. We were mostly focused on the center," she replied.

Rolk marched off in the direction he had been looking. We began to follow, but he held us back with a raised hand. "Just wait a moment. I feel something." He continued through the forest and disappeared as he pushed through a thicket. I held my breath. "Alright, everyone," he yelled back. "I think it's safe."

We moved forward, struggling through the same vegetation that he had. It opened to a small clearing. Rolk was standing in the center, hands out, as if he were warming them in front of a mesmerizing fire. I could feel a hint of radiating Aether, now that I was closer. I could only imagine what he was feeling.

"What's the Aether coming from?" I asked.

Rolk shook his head. "I'm not sure, but it seems to be centered here. I feel like the Aether is contained by something. There's a lot more to it than what I'm sensing." He closed his eyes for a moment. "Onk, come here, but not too close. I need to borrow some Aether."

"Are you sure this is wise?" Seader asked.

"It hasn't reacted to me yet. A touch of Aether won't do anything." Rolk pulled out his styk, holding it toward Onk. Onk touched it with a small spark of Aether. "Thank you." Rolk turned back to the empty air and held up one hand, his fingertips scintillating with Aether.

The Aether latched onto something, and a flare of light bloomed from the center. We covered our eyes. I pulled my bo staff forward, preparing for whatever was to come, but fortunately nothing attacked us. I blinked away the spots in my vision. Once I could see, a watermelon-sized sphere was bobbing in the air in front of Rolk, glowing.

"Wow, that's curious. It's like the Aether made it take shape." Rolk reached out and touched it. "There's a lot of Aether in this thing. It's impressive. I've never seen anything like it... it feels alive." He stepped away from the sphere and approached Seader. "Could I borrow your Aether

Equipment? I'd like to take some measurements."

"NO, STOP!" Seader yelled.

We turned just in time to see Onk touching the sphere. There was a large crack, and a bright wave of energy sent Onk flying and tumbling along the ground. I covered my face and felt the warmth of the Aether pass through me. It set my skin tingling.

Rolk rushed over to kneel beside Onk. "Are you okay?"

Onk shook his head. "Yeah. What happened?"

"I'm not sure," Rolk said. "The sphere reacted to you in a way I wouldn't have expected. You shouldn't have done that."

Leaves slapped our faces. The swirling wind picked up, quickly turning into a roar. The trees and plants rustled. I had to cover my face from the pelting of leaves and twigs. I peeked through my hands at the sphere, to see it melting into a glowing ooze that fell to the forest floor. It bubbled into a mist, then evaporated into nothing. The colors around me began to dim and the edges of the world blurred.

"It's causing an Aether shift," I yelled over the noise. I could only imagine the amount of Aether necessary to cause such a shift.

The sphere melted away and the wind calmed down. The leaves gently glided back to the forest floor. The color and sharpness of the natural world came back—almost completely.

"Is that it?" Seader asked.

Rolk stood up. "No. There's something here with us." He stepped toward the center of the clearing and slowly rotated, his styk poised.

Suddenly, light caught my eye. I turned to look. Ten orange claws burned into existence, floating in midair, swaying ever so slightly. Before we could react, they lunged at Onk. Onk instinctively released a blast of Moltrik Aether from his lepisent. The bolt of electricity exploded against the being and sent an electrically charged mass flying into the vegetation.

A Human-sized creature rose from the storm of electricity; its claws glowed even brighter. Streamers of electricity traced out its invisible body. Its wolf-like head snapped directly toward Onk, and it launched itself at him on stocky legs, its massive gorilla-like arms tearing up the ground. Rolk leapt toward the creature, swinging. Just then, the last bit of electricity faded from the creature's body and it faded from view. Once more, only its claws were visible. Rolk toppled to the ground as his styk passed through the creature.

This time, Onk and Fording were ready. They both blasted the creature with Aether, knocking it back into the forest. The fiery energy of Fording's Pahzan Aether interwove with Onk's blue Moltrik Aether, blending across the creature's body and occasionally jumping to the surroundings.

"It's a virker," Rolk yelled. "It's made of Aether. Physical attacks are worthless alone."

"They don't exist," Onk yelled. "It's impossible."

I stepped beside Rolk, bo styk ready. "We can have that discussion after we've dealt with it."

Rolk held out his styk to me. "Take some of the Aether I pulled from it. When we attack it with Aether, it will temporarily be drawn closer to our realm. We can attack it directly then."

I grabbed his styk and pulled some Aether from it. "Thanks."

The virker leapt at Onk again, and the two Humans countered with their Aether attacks. This time, the virker was barely slowed down. With the Aether still coursing over its body, I swung my styk at the creature as if I were going to deflect an Aether attack. My styk struck the creature, driving it to its knees. I followed through with the other end of my bo, but it jumped out of the way, slashing its claws at my leg. I pulled back just in time, though the searing heat of the claws still singed my skin.

The Humans attacked again, knocking the virker off balance, and Rolk leapt closer. His styk connected once in the creature's side making it stumble, but it blocked Rolk's next few attacks. Rolk dodged swipes from the claws and swung at the virker again. With no apparent effort, the creature grabbed his styk and raked Rolk's chest with its other hand. My heart seized while I watched my husband clutch his chest and fall to the ground.

The creature turned back to the Humans and flicked away their Aether attacks with ease. It launched itself at Onk, sinking its claws into his shoulder, and driving him to the ground. Fording grabbed at its arm, but she was easily tossed into the vegetation. The virker raised its other set of claws to strike Onk's neck. I forced the thoughts of Rolk away and rushed to help. Just as the virker began to swipe, a pale green blur slammed into it.

The virker's arm flared with Aether as a large, hairless, dog-like creature bit into it. There were spikes along the length of the new creature's body, larger at the joints. Its cat-like paws dug into the virker, and the wounds flared with light. The virker struggled with the new creature only to get pounced on by two more. Yellow eyes flashed. These were the cressen. A hairless, monkey-like cressen dropped from the trees onto the group.

Even with the cressen hanging off of its arms, the virker struggled to its feet. Aether spewed from its wounds, a thick mist that slowly settled and eventually burned away in an orange glow. Again, the colors of the forest began to fade.

The virker slowly brought one arm around to grab the cressen. Its claws sunk into the cressen's back. Red blood painted the cressen's pale skin.

A sudden bright flash blinded me, and the world disappeared.

The ringing in my ears was the first sign I was still alive. Each following pain, whether it was sharp and stabbing or large and throbbing, was another confirmation. It took me a moment to sort out that I was upside down against a tree, most of my weight on my head and twisted arm. I could feel blood rushing to my face, and sticks poking me. As my sensations began to work themselves out, I could tell I wasn't suffering any life-threatening injuries. I hoped the others fared as well.

What happened? I pulled myself out of a clump of vegetation at the base of a tree and looked around as dirt and clumps of plants sprinkled the ground from above. There was a large crater where the virker and cressen had been. A great chaotic buzz of Aether filled the air. The color and normality of the world quickly returned, and the buzz of Aether settled.

The others in the group were stirring from similar tangled positions. I let out a great sigh of relief when I saw Rolk walking toward me, his hand on his chest. I struggled to my feet and rushed over to him. The gouges across his chest were cauterized from the Aether burns and the bleeding was minimal. He would live.

"What was that?" Rolk asked.

Seader brushed dirt off himself and patted his weapon. "Yeah, sorry about that. It's still a bit crude but at least it got the job done."

"I've never seen anything like it," Onk said. "It didn't even leave behind essence."

"That's because it's brand new," Seader replied with a smile. "It's an Aether weapon, the first of its kind. It seems to have passed its first field test with flying colors. I told you you'd soon be respecting the Erohsians as an offensive force."

"You just evaporated the cressen along with the virker," Rolk said. He paused and let silence fill the air. Not a single creature could be heard. "We've just started a war with the Anterraktor."

"But you promised it wouldn't be an issue," Seader said.

"That was before you started killing cressen," Rolk turned to me. "We need to pull everyone back before it's too late. We won't have much time before they form up and attack. May Stone be with us. We're going to need him."

*****

After a half hour of waiting in the truck, the guards finally bring Nero out to stretch his legs. The cool, salty air of the ocean tickles his nose, vivifying his senses as he fills his lungs with a long, deep breath. The caravan is parked on a large shelf with mountains protruding into the grey clouds on either side. The shelf reaches toward the ocean and suddenly drops away. Goosebumps cover Nero's body and the tingling of Aether runs over his skin. He shifts his perspective. Immediately, his senses are drowned by an intense blue Aether from beyond the edge of the shelf. After a moment, his senses adjust, and the light around him is muted. Waves of blue Aether radiate outward, varying in brightness, as though a blue star is hidden just below the edge. Every few minutes, deep thuds of thunder echo between the mountains.

"Are you okay?" Bresta asks.

Nero lets his perspective shift back and looks at the guard. "I've never been around so much Aether..." He points toward the edge of the shelf. "Are we going that way?"

She nods. "We'll head off to the right ridge. Let's hope to stay out of the way of the King and prince. I think the prince is done, so it shouldn't be a problem. Remove any metal from your pockets and body. Stay between us in case there are any hot spots." Bresta hands Nero a little tube that looks like a pen with a clip on it. "Put this on the collar of your shirt."

Nero looks at the tube and notices it is hollow down the center with glass on one end and a white film on the other. "What is it?"

"It's a radiation dosimeter. In case we get hit by stray radiation, it's good to know what we've been exposed to." She then holds out a set of earplugs. "And put these in."

"What for?"

"To protect your ears. Don't ask stupid questions."

The two guards remove their styks from the truck and check the lepisents strapped to their forearms. Nero takes his spot between them, and they start toward the edge of the shelf. The ground falls away and reveals another shelf fifty meters below. They can hear the faint sound of waves crashing against the rocks below. Fog flows down the mountains like little streams. It passes around boulders, slides off cliffs, and collects in troughs, until it reaches the lower shelf. The fog spills across a flat, grey-metallic surface that extends for hundreds of meters. A few silver streaks run through the surface at random. In the center is a pyramid no taller than a small house. It is made of the same grey metallic material. A beam of light shines from the top of the pyramid, arbitrarily scanning in every direction.

Suddenly, a vortex of light and energy swirls about the peak of the pyramid. It coalesces until there is a bright flash. A blue bolt of lightning arcs out, burning a line in Nero's vision. It reaches across the shelf and strikes the ground. There is a sharp crack, followed by a concussion that hits Nero in the chest. He instinctively throws his hands over his ears, even though he is wearing earplugs.

A forest of electrical tendrils sprouts from the ground where the bolt struck. They reach up toward the sky, whipping in the air for a moment before gradually fading to nothing. Two more bolts of lightning strike other parts of the shelf in quick succession.

"That's the electric forest, as I bet you could tell. Not even the strongest Borukin could survive one of those," Jaice says as echoes of thunder bounce between the mountains. "The beam of light coming from the top of the pyramid is the spot light. It might look harmless, but there is a large range of electromagnetic radiation in the beam. Radio waves, microwaves, x-rays, and gamma rays—which is why we wear the dosimeters. You want to stay out of the beam at all costs, or down the road you will regret it."

He points to the shelf and sweeps his hand around. "The only sign of the molecular igniter is the grey, shiny metal you see making up the whole shelf. That's silicon. It's what's left of the natural granite when it's broken down into its constituent components. The few streaks you see are aluminum and other elements. The last smite is the magnetic morass. It's pretty harmless as long as you are clear of metal. The worst it'll do is slow you down... which is bad enough if you get caught by one of the other smites."

"And it's really possible to get by all of that?" Nero asks.

"That's what makes it such an achievement. In order to make it to the monolith at the center, you need to sense the Aether and avoid it accordingly." Jaice points to a group of Borukins hiking up a trail from the lower to the higher shelf. Their faint chant carries over the distance. "It looks like the Prince made it. He's becoming a great Borukin."

Nero shifts his perspective and watches the currents of Aether. It concentrates in knots right before a smite occurs. *So that's how you'd avoid it.* For the first time, he sees several Humans wearing khaki colored clothes, standing along the ridge of the upper shelf. A few are standing at the outer edges of the lower shelf. Nero points to them. "Who are those people?"

Jaice dismisses them with a wave of his hand. "Spirit hunters. They pillage the Corusnigmas in order to capture and sell spirits."

"Why would anyone want a spirit?" Nero asks. "It wouldn't be wise to make artifacts out of them. The thoughts of the person the essence belonged to could mess with how the Artifact behaves."

"That's correct... but they're not making Artifacts with these spirits. The behavior of spirits is partially due to the memories caught in the essence. There are ways to extract the memories and study them. A lot of people, especially nimus extractorians, buy the spirits for these memories. Because the Corusnigmas are dangerous, they fetch a nice price."

"But why would you care about old memories?" Nero asks.

"The Corusnigmas date back to at least the War of Salvation. We lost a lot during the War of Salvation... a lot of history... a lot of technology..." Bresta says. "Somehow, the spirits here are tied to the Corusnigmas and are equally as old. Historians like to use these memories and attempt to piece together the past."

"That seems like it might be important," Nero says. "Why don't you like them?"

"The past is the past. We should focus on the present and the future. The conflict back then killed a lot of people, so I say let it rest. Besides, it doesn't seem right to sell people's spirits to be dissected and put under a microscope. I wouldn't want it done to my essence."

Jaice points once more to the group of Borukins climbing to the upper shelf. "Let's head back so we can catch the King and Prince before the marking ceremony."

On the way, the hairs on the back of Nero's neck stand on end and the air buzzes with Aether. Nero comes to a stop.

"Something doesn't feel right." He shifts his perspective but doesn't see the telltale signs of any of the Corusnigma smites.

The guards slow down, raising their styks. "I may feel something as well," Bresta says after a moment.

His perspective still shifted, Nero watches as wisps of blue Aether seep from the ground, twisting as they grow, slowly collecting in a humanoid shape the height of the Borukins. Streaks of electricity race through its limbs and arc outward from all over its body. When the Aether finally stops collecting, the edges of the spirit form the fuzzy facial features of an old man. He looks directly at Nero and smiles, a strange crooked smile. The old man raises his hand and begins to approach. *What the heck?* Nero takes a step back, letting his perspective shift back to normal. Only the outline of the spirit is visible now. Its color has turned to the blue of an electrical spark accompanied by a constant crackling. The guards step in front of Nero, which causes the spirit to stop and cock its head to the side.

Out of nowhere, a stream of fire slams into the side of the spirit, knocking it off balance. The spirit spins around, and the hard outline of its shape explodes with wild hairs of electricity. Two streams of electricity from the spirit's hands scorch the ground, shattering the boulder where the spirit hunter hides.

Jaice jumps forward and strikes with his styk, disrupting the spirit's attack. The spirit quickly turns on the Borukin to blast him with Aether. He barely blocks it and is knocked off his feet. Bresta catches the streams of Aether with her styk, using it to power her pulse lepisent. Two fast moving fireballs slam into the spirit's leg, bringing it to its knees. Bresta springs forward and strikes the spirit's head with her styk. It tumbles to its side.

The spirit dissolves and coalesces on its feet, but before it can attack again, pulses of Aether from converging spirit hunters catch it. Wild streams of electricity whip around the spirit as it stumbles backward. It tries to focus on one of the spirit hunters, but the barrage is too consistent, its attacks are poorly aimed. Finally, the spirit crumples to its knees and its outer shape melts away as though it lost what was holding it together. A melon-sized shining star hovers in its place.

One of the spirit hunters rushes over to draw it into a small device. She closes the device, tucking it into the front pocket of her jacket. "Yee haa! That was a powerful spirit." Her hair is grey, tied back by a bandana covering her forehead. The sides of her face are hidden behind the high collar of her jacket. She turns to the Borukins. "It would have electrified you gargantuan masses if it weren't for us."

Jaice walks up to her. "It may have done us no harm if you wouldn't have attacked it."

The woman rolls her eyes. "It was a tormented spirit. There's no rhyme or reason with them."

Jaice shakes his head. "You're a fool."

King Kamin and the Prince run up with an entourage of other Borukins. Nero notices three Humans with them. One is older, with the loose clothes of an academic. Another man is wearing modest clothes and has an emotionless face. The last, younger, has spiked hair, tight pants, and a vest.

"What's going on here?" King Kamin roars.

Bresta dips her head. "There was a powerful spirit that these Humans," she says waving her hand toward them, "enraged."

The woman spirit hunter steps forward. "What she's really trying to say is, we saved their lives. I believe a reward is in order."

The King turns to her. "Be gone, hunter. Your kind isn't respected by Borukins."

The woman shrugs. "You heard the King. He doesn't appreciate our protection. Let's move out."

The King turns to Nero and the guards. "What do you think you're doing?"

The weight of his ire nearly causes Nero's legs to buckle.

"Taking the boy out to stretch his legs," Bresta says, strain in her voice.

"He's a prisoner. He doesn't need to stretch his legs."

"I'm sorry, Your Honor. Natina recommended we take care of him, so he is presentable for the ceremony with the Erohsians."

"Did she also tell you to make a fool out of yourself in front of the spirit hunters? Just get him out of my sight, you worthless Borukins," the King growls. "I don't want to see him until the ceremony."

The guards both dip their heads. "As you command." They grab Nero and shuffle him back toward their vehicle.

"Do you think we're in trouble?" Nero asks from the backseat.

"Just be quiet," Jaice barks.

Nero's shoulders slump and his nerves begin to overcome him. *I hope I get rescued soon...*

A communication device beeps. Jaice picks it up. "Hello... Okay, we'll do so." He puts the device down, turning to Nero. "Looks like you're going to have a visitor."

"Who?"

"A Human. The King gave him permission."

What, now? Nero leans back and starts to pick at his pant leg.

Shortly, Bresta steps out of the truck and meets the three Humans Nero saw with the King earlier. While they talk, Nero shifts his perspective. The Humans glow much brighter than the Borukins. Their swirling Aether obscures their shapes, whereas the guard has very sharp features. The old man and the younger man with spiked hair have Pahzan Aether. The modestly dressed man with no facial expressions has a mixture of Pahzan, Moltrik, Icor, and Biat Aether. *Wow, they're as bright as the woman from Blue Horin. Are these the same essences I saw at the Games?*

Jaice soon gets out of the truck as well and the old man takes a seat in back with Nero.

The Human holds out his hand. "Hello, Nero. My name is Vilhelm." Nero looks down and sits on his hands. Vilhelm closes his hand, smiling. "It is good to meet you. The King says the Erohsians are looking for you and your friends. Do you know why? Did you and your friends find essence containers?"

Nero remains silent.

"This is really important. I need to know your story."

Still silence.

Vilhelm lets out a breath. "Nero, you can trust me. I'm on your side." He pauses. "Can I tell you a secret?" Nero looks up at him. Vilhelm smiles and leans in close. "I'm part of Catalyst."

"Really?"

"Yes, but don't tell anyone. I hate the Erohsians just as much as you. You can trust me. Tell me about the essence you found."

"I thought Catalyst was good, though."

"What? Of course, we're good. We're trying to liberate humankind." Vilhelm pauses and looks at Nero. "Why would you say that?"

Nero looks down. "Because you helped the Prince kill Madam Carason," he says quietly.

"What?" There is a moment of silence before Vilhelm lets his body relax. He puts his hand on Nero's shoulder. "I am just as sad as you are that Madam Carason died. If I could go back and save her, I would in an instant. I promise.

"Then why did you help shield the prince from the Aether canon? You helped him cheat."

Vilhelm looks at Nero for another long moment. "Because Catalyst needs allies, and the King asked for a favor. He promised me no one would get hurt. To my great sorrow, it was not the case. You must not tell anyone. Your life depends on it. The King would not be happy if he found out you knew. Do you understand?" Nero nods, and Vilhelm smiles. "Now,

I've told you a secret. It's your turn. How did you know that we helped Prince Kamin?"

Nero slips his hands out from under his legs and fidgets with the bottom of his shirt. "Because I can see Aether."

"That is truly incredible."

Nero looks up in surprise. "You believe me?"

"Of course. Why wouldn't I? How does it work?"

Nero shrugs. "I'm not sure, but when I relax, I can see all the different types of Aether people have."

"So you can see my Aether?"

Nero nods. "You're Pahzan, just like the guy with spiked hair."

"And the other?"

"He has several different types, just like my friend Thea." Nero bites his tongue.

"So you opened the canisters?"

Nero looks back down and continues to fidget.

"This is important, Nero. I promise I mean you no harm. Being Human, we've only got each other. We're as good as family. You can trust me." Vilhelm waits a moment. "Did you open the essence containers you found?" Still, Nero is silent. "Why were you so surprised when I believed you?"

"Because no one ever believes me."

"Have you been able to do this all your life?"

Nero shakes his head.

"Perhaps it started when you absorbed an essence?"

"I can't absorb essence. I think something's wrong with me."

"Maybe I can help you. What happened?"

"I tried to absorb an essence, but when I touched it, I passed out. My friends said it evaporated or something."

"Did you happen to see any markings on this container?"

"Yeah but I can't remember what they were... The one I opened was really dim... I guess it was too dim though."

Vilhelm's eyes grow wide for a moment. "Are you sure you opened it?"

Nero nods. "I wanted to absorb it, but then I felt bad... and stopped... then I fell over. I saw my whole life flash before my eyes."

"Hmm." Vilhelm swallows then nods slowly. "That is very interesting. I think I have a hunch about what's going on."

"You do?"

"Yes, but I'd like to scan you. Do you mind?"

"Sure, but nothing'll happen."

"Yes, of course. I just want to see for myself." Vilhelm opens his coat and pulls out a complicated hand-held Aether detector. He scans Nero, but the detector picks up nothing. He looks at the detector in surprise and pushes a few buttons. Still, nothing. "Yep, just as expected..."

"What does it mean?"

"I want to confirm my guess first. I'd hate to tell you anything but the truth. If we're friends, though, I'm sure I'll be talking to you again soon."

I can't believe he knows! This could explain everything. Nero nods. "Yes, I'd like that."

"Now, tell me about the other containers. You and Thea opened one each, what about the other three?"

"Ryder and Korbin each opened one."

"And the fifth?" Vilhelm asks.

Nero shrugs. "It was broken when we found it."

Vilhelm nods. "That makes sense. And you said Thea is like my friend? How is she doing since she absorbed the essence? Is she acting the same?"

"Yeah. Our friend said the essence she absorbed wasn't too strong, so she should be okay."

"Hmm, well I'm glad to hear it. I'd very much like to meet your friends, do you know where they are?"

"No." *But they're going to rescue me.* Nero smiles to himself.

"Ah, but you know where they will be. They're going to come for you, aren't they?"

Nero looks at Vilhelm. His face turns hot.

Vilhelm smiles warmly. "Don't worry. I told you, we're on the same side. Maybe I'll be able to help. It sounds like a perfect job for Catalyst."

"Really?"

"Yes, of course. I'll see what I can do. It'd help if I knew who you were staying with in Kiats, though. That way, I can make sure their plan will work. It'd be horrible if they were captured, too."

"Sosimo's really smart though. They won't be caught."

"Sosimo, the candy maker?"

Nero winces and looks down. "Yes."

"Ah, Sosimo, a great man. We're already friends, so I'll be sure to talk with him. Well, Nero, it's been good to meet you." Vilhelm knocks on the window and Bresta opens the door. "Good luck."

Nero watches Vilhelm and the other Humans walk off. He grabs his book and smiles at the thought of being rescued.

*****

"Cover me," Onk yelled. He stopped to turn toward our pursuers.

I pulled up my styk, looking for incoming projectiles. I had abandoned the blue crystal emitter long ago. For now, the Bellicoven were set on killing us. Onk shot several balls of Aether at the cressen running after us. His attacks were sluggish, and the cressen easily dodged them. I knocked two projectiles out of the air and used the last remaining bit of Aether in my styk to force two more into the ground.

"Dammit," Onk yelled. "The Bellicoven are slowing down my attacks."

"Let's link, then," I said, eyeing down the incoming cressen. "We can take care of both."

"Okay, let's do it!" Onk held out his hand. I took it.

I followed Onk's Aether tickling my fingers to its source, tracing it through every part of his body and collecting the whole of his essence together. I summoned up mine as well and let their energies blend. The sudden flow of Aether that immersed me was intoxicating, yet it was shared with a sense of fear and a wild fervor. The image of the glowing claws of the virker ready to strike, a burning pain in my shoulder: they were echoes of Onk's thoughts. The Aether reserves we shared flowed deep, yet my normal connection to Aether was slightly numbed.

Onk used our high Aethersotto to overwhelm the two Bellicoven in the trees. He pulled them from their perch, slamming them into the oncoming cressen, tangling them up in a jumble of limbs.

I reached through the Aether to a spot high up behind the cressen and Bellicoven, forcing open a link to myself. The Bellicoven and cressen were quick to untangle themselves and prepare for a direct attack from us. A slight smile reached the corner of my mouth as I forced a continuous Moltrik attack through the link. Electrical tendrils of Aether reached out from the single point behind our enemies. It latched onto them, causing their bodies to go rigid. I fueled the attack with Onk's reserves until all of them fell to the ground, unconscious. It cost us almost all the Aether we shared.

Onk let go of my hand. "Nice job."

Instantly, the anxiety fell away, and my natural calm returned. "Thanks," I said, "but it's not going to give us much time."

Rolk stood over a recently fallen cressen. A trace of blood stood out, bright against the white of his heavily bandaged chest. "We need to keep moving. I don't want to get caught by the Anterraktor."

Onk ran over to the dead cressen. A mist was rising off its body. It swirled around itself, a bright little star of light forming.

Rolk stopped and looked at it, then to Onk. "Are you sure?"

"We don't really have a choice at this point, Rolk," Onk said. He walked over to the glowing star and touched it. It jumped into his finger. Onk stopped breathing, clamping his eyes shut for just a moment. "Okay, good," he opened his eyes. "That should help. Let's go."

Onk took off. We followed him through a thick section of growth that opened to a large clearing. He began to run, but stopped suddenly and started to back up. "Uh-oh. I think I triggered another one."

There was a bright flash. A shock rippled through us as another sphere began to vent Aether.

"Take cover!" Seader yelled, whipping his Aether canon up toward the sphere.

With the previous blast still fresh in our memory, there wasn't a moment's hesitation. We all fell to the ground. I covered my ears and shielded my face, gritting my teeth. The blast resonated through my bones. Bits of plants and dirt pelted me all over.

Rolk stood up, brushing dirt and debris from his clothes. "That's one way to take care of them," he said, assessing the results. "How many more of those shots do you have?"

"That was it," Seader replied. "So let's not disturb any more of them."

Burning pieces of vegetation gently fell to the ground. Sparks of Aether jumped through the air, illuminating an array of dormant virker spheres. The ones within a fifteen-meter radius of the destroyed sphere began to release their Aether and awaken.

"Holy crap," Seader whispered, his Aether canon hung loosely by his side.

"Yeah... We're screwed," Onk said.

Rolk scanned over the spheres then slung his styk behind his back. "No, you're not." Rolk put both hands on my shoulders and looked me in the eyes. "Nix, I have a plan that will keep everyone safe, but you need to lead them back to the beach... alone. I won't be able to come with."

"What are you talking about? We can all make it back," I said, grabbing his arm. "We just need to hurry."

"Maybe us, but not many others will survive if we just run." He moved my hand into his. "I can perform a Seteress Kimkariki. It will stun enough of the Bellicoven and cressen to give everyone enough time to escape."

"A Seteress will kill you," I said, knowing he was fully aware of the consequences. "Where would you even get enough Aether?"

He nodded to the awakening virker.

I shook my head, feeling a panic that I hadn't felt for a long time. "No. This is ridiculous."

"This expedition is my responsibility. It has to be done."

I squeezed his hand with both of mine. "At least let me help."

He pulled my hands up to his lips. "I need to know you'll survive. Please, at least give me that."

"It's too much… You're a part of me. How can I go on if I'm no longer complete?"

"You will. I have no doubt. You are strong. I wish there was another way, but these people had faith in me and I have to protect them… and you. Please. Do this for me?"

I dipped my head, letting the tears fall freely.

He pulled me in tight and squeezed. "I love you," he whispered before pushing me away. "Now go!"

It was the hardest decision of my life, but I knew there was no point in fighting him anymore. His mind was set, and there was a job to do. I hardened my resolve and turned back to the world, which had lost a lot of its color. The edges of the trees and our surroundings blurred as Aether flooded the forest. The virkers were well on their way to awakening. There would be hardly enough time to put a safe amount of distance between Rolk and us. I turned to the others in the group, running toward them. "We need to get moving!" I yelled.

"What about Rolk?" Onk asked.

"He's going to give us a window to escape. Let's not waste it. Now move!" I grabbed Maizy, the small Erohsian, and began to run as fast as I could; the others followed.

It wasn't long before I felt the surge of Aether rip through me. I could feel it ignoring me, but the overwhelming flood that passed through us still made my head go fuzzy. I tumbled to the ground. It was unbelievable what Rolk could do when he put his mind to it. I could only expect such a ferocious farewell from my Rolk.

It took me several minutes to find my bearings and let the dizziness pass. The Humans and the Erohsians were all unconscious. A few minutes passed before the Humans were conscious and semi-functional. We didn't know how long the Erohsians would be out, so we carried them back to the cove.

The beach was in chaos when we got there. Boats were making trips back and forth between our ship and the beach. The wounded and unconscious were ferried first, while the remaining people were scrambling to pack up. A defensive perimeter was set up, but it had little use. Anything hostile in the forest was unconscious after the Kimkariki. The rest of our expedition escaped with minimal casualties and injuries, thanks to my husband's final act.

Part of me wanted to go back for him, but I knew in my heart that even he couldn't survive a Seteress and risking myself to check would be a waste of his sacrifice, a sacrifice that will weigh heavy in my heart 'til the day I die.

30 Now to Execute

Iona

"This afternoon, Natina will throw a fuss over her ceremony arrangements," Grebson says to Sosimo and the children. They are all seated around a kitchen table in the loft above Sosimo's Sunta candy store. "She should get authorization tomorrow morning to send out a Borukin servant to pick up more help. This is the first big challenge, but he should pick you all up if you play the part. She'll also have him pick up one of those Erohsian solar system projections everyone is crazy about these days." Grebson turns to Sosimo. "I'm assuming you've made the modifications and sold it to the shop we discussed."

"I have," Sosimo says. "It'll drain the children's Aether and project different biometric signs for the Erohsian sensors. They'll register as four random children. Have Natina ask for a pink Illi, it's the only one in the shop of that color."

"Good. I sneaked in the rest of the equipment, including the new Erohsian Moltrik ID talismans. Are you going to tell me what special favor you promised your friends in order to get those talismans *and* their assistance?"

"Nothing at all," Sosimo says. "They were, surprisingly, willing to help. Perhaps they saw this as a good time to field-test the talismans. They could have any number of their own motivations."

"Who are your friends again?" Iona asks.

"Just friends," Sosimo says. "You'll meet them after the mission."

I wish he'd just tell us.

Grebson stands up. "I'll see you children tomorrow. May Stone's courage flow through you, Marks's blade guide you, and the Lost Blood nourish you." Grebson turns from the table and leaves.

Sosimo sits back down and sighs. "This should be an interesting rescue mission, but I think we can pull it off."

"What did Grebson mean by all that?" Ryder asks.

"It's an old saying we use. It means: may you have the courage, the skill, and the strength to finish the task ahead. It dates back to the Age of Creation when King Stone and the Human leader Jezebel Marks fought to free us from the Creators."

"What about the Lost Race?" Iona asks.

"The Lost Race was the first to rebel against the Creators. It was also said they were the closest race to the Creators' image, a perfect race. There was a great bond between the Humans, Borukins, and this race; nothing was impossible when they were together. However, they created the Drebin which was nearly the end to all of us. At the end of the War of Salvation, the Lost Race was... removed from the world."

"How is that possible?" Iona asks. "Were they killed off?"

Sosimo shakes his head. "It was a really rough time in history. No one is really sure what happened. They simply ceased to exist." Sosimo stands up. "I'll make us some lunch, then we can go over the plan one more time.

Thea clutches at her chest once Sosimo leaves. "I'm so nervous."

Iona nods and drums her fingers on her thigh.

"So am I," Ryder says.

"Me too," Korbin says.

All the children look at him in surprise.

"What?" Korbin asks.

"You never admit to being nervous," Iona says.

Thea jumps up. "Yeah. Like never, never."

"This is serious now. It's the real thing." Korbin looks around. "We could get in real trouble…"

Ryder pats Korbin on the back. "We'll be alright, Korb. We've never practiced so hard in our lives."

"Do you think we can pull this off?" Thea asks.

"We better," Ryder says. "Nero is depending on us."

*****

The children walk in the shadows cast by the buildings from the mid-morning light. The Human district in Sunta is a maze of repetitive streets and apartment towers. The only source of color and personality is the clothing which hangs to dry from the windows and small balconies. Other Humans walk or bike to their jobs, or gather at inlets to the large public transit that travels between the buildings above. Higher than the skytrain, vehicles zip along the barely visible skyways and even higher than that, levitraft and other aircraft fly unrestricted.

Iona takes a breath with every other step. Her nerves are in a constant battle with her fatigue, played out on her fluttering eyelids. All of the children, in their ratty clothes, are in a similar state after completely draining their Aether before setting out.

"So, what's the ball for again?" Thea asks.

Ryder rolls the worn-out rubber kickball in his hands. "It does something so the Erohsians can't see us with all of their stuff. We have to keep it close until we get the other package, which will then take over."

"I wish we didn't have to get drained. I'm so tired," Thea says, dramatically dragging her feet.

"I know. It stinks, but this is the best way to sneak past the Erohsians."

"What do you think the Borukin we're going to meet looks like?" Thea asks.

"Like a Borukin," Ryder says. "I'm sure we won't miss him."

"But what if he doesn't show?"

"Sosimo and Grebson have thought of everything for this mission. I'm sure he will." Ryder turns to Thea. "Do you have any other questions?"

Thea shakes her head. "No."

They continue to walk down the streets, guided by the directions that Ryder has memorized.

"Are you sure we're going the right direction?" Thea bursts out as though the question was pent up inside.

Ryder lets out a breath. "Yes, Thea. We're almost there."

"What if something goes wrong?"

"Sosimo will be watching. Don't worry. Now, enough questions, Thea... Jeez."

Thea looks down at the street. "I just want to rescue Nero and be done with this."

Iona nods her head. "We all do."

Finally, the claustrophobia of the pressing apartment buildings eases. They see a large cement court with hoops and goals. Other children are scattered about, yelling, playing with balls, and chasing each other around.

"This is it." Ryder drops the ball and kicks it to Korbin. "Let's kick the ball until he comes. Just not too hard."

The children play with diminishing enthusiasm, continually looking around. Ryder constantly forces them to participate. Suddenly, silence falls upon the playground and the children turn around. A light grey, seven-person truck stops at the edge of the gaming area.

"Minis!" A child yells.

Instantly, the Humans scatter, leaving only Ryder, Korbin, Thea, and Iona. They all watch the vehicle as a large Borukin steps out, glances at his watch, and surveys the area.

Ryder picks up the ball. "Okay, here we go. Let me and Iona do the talking."

The Borukin with his large, hasty strides crosses the concrete quickly, eyeing the children as he comes. "Why'd everyone run?" he asks the children.

Ryder steps forward with his chest out. "Because they thought you were a Mini."

"And why didn't you run?"

Iona now steps forward. "Because we aren't scared of you or them."

The Borukin smiles with a chuckle. "Good. Can any of you use Aether?"

Ryder shakes his head. "No, why?"

"I'm looking for a few non-bonded Human children. Are you interested in making some money?"

"We're not supposed to talk to anyone who works with the Erohsians," Ryder says.

Iona grabs Ryder's arm. "But we could buy a new ball." She looks down at her ratty shoes. "And some new shoes."

"It's just for the day, and it won't be hard," the Borukin says. "It looks like you kids could use a little extra something."

Ryder turns to the Borukin with scrutiny. "Okay, we're listening. What's the job?"

"The Borukin Princess needs your help," the Borukin says.

"A princess?" Iona asks with feigned excitement.

The Borukin nods. "The one and only Princess Natina."

"What does she need?" Ryder asks, also with exaggerated excitement.

"She needs help with a royal ceremony for the Erohsians." The Borukin bites his last words.

"A ceremony for the Minis?" Ryder says. "I don't like it."

"You will be paid nicely, I promise," the Borukin continues quickly.

"How much?" Iona asks.

"Enough to buy you all new shoes and a new ball."

Ryder holds up a finger. "Give us a second." He pulls the other children into a huddle. "Okay, let's just give him a second to sweat." Ryder whispers to the other children. "I think it's going just how Sosimo wanted." They break the huddle and Ryder approaches the Borukin who is looking at his watch. "How much are you offering?"

"Twenty Anterren each," he says.

Ryder thinks for a moment. "Well seeing as this is for the Minis, we're going to need forty."

"Twenty-five."

"Forty-five."

The Borukin frowns. "That's not how you bargain."

Ryder shrugs. "We said we weren't scared of you, so don't try to cheat us. This isn't something we want to do, and from the looks of it, you're in a rush, so it's either forty or you can go find some other kids." Ryder looks around. "Might be tricky, though."

The Borukin lets out a sigh. "Fine, but we need to hurry. The Princess is waiting." He sets off across the concrete, and the children jog to keep up.

He reaches the Erohsian truck and opens the back door. Ryder drops the ball and climbs in first. When Iona hops in and sits down, the bracelet on her arm suddenly turns cold and her fatigue doubles. *That must be the solar system.* She looks up front and sees a package on the dash wedged against the window.

An Erohsian escort in the driver's seat looks back at the children, and then at the Borukin who is scrunched in the front seat. "Are we ready to head back, then?"

The Borukin grabs the package, placing it on his lap. "We're all set."

The threat of being in the same car as an Erohsian is quickly surpassed by their fatigue. Within ten minutes, they are sleeping.

"Hey, kids, wake up," the Borukin says, twisting awkwardly to see them. "We're almost there."

Iona blinks her eyes and looks out the window. The car is just pulling down a ramp under a very large building. Darkness overtakes them as they enter a garage.

"You're a sleepy bunch. I hope you have more energy when the Princess is around, or we'll both be in trouble." The car comes to a stop at a security gate.

Iona's tiredness evaporates as armed Erohsian guards approach the truck from both sides. One of them signals for the Erohsian escort to roll down his window. "Please state your business."

"Business pertaining to the Royal Princess of the Borukins."

The guard uses a device to scan the escort's eye and looks through the information on a holographic display. "It says you're responsible for one Borukin and are authorized to bring back an Erohsian solar system and four non-bonded Human children. More servants for the banquet tonight?"

"They're for the Princess's honorary ceremony," the Borukin says. "She's making some last-minute adjustments."

The guard looks at the back of the truck. "We'll need everyone to get out and be scanned before you pass."

"Of course." The escort undoes his seat belt and exits the car followed by the Borukin and the children.

Iona holds her breath as the guard walks down the line, scanning the identification and Aether of each of the children.

The guard reaches the Borukin with the package. "And this is the solar system? Please remove it from the package."

The Borukin carefully removes a dark hemisphere and holds it out to the Erohsian.

The guard scans it. "Aether's a bit high... but still under the regulation limits." He hangs the scanner from a strap around his neck and takes the projector. A small button on the side generates a holographic display of the solar system with a pink star in the middle. A small grey planet rotates quickly around Illi, followed by three blue and green planets. A larger, pale green planet trails the first four. The rest of the planets are much bigger. A white planet with faint pink clouds is followed by the largest planet, which has dark orange-brown clouds at its equator and yellow poles. The next planet is pale green. A brilliant blue planet with streaks of white clouds is next and last, a red planet, only slightly smaller.

He clicks it off. "A pink Illi?"

The Borukin shrugs. "Children..."

"Okay, then, everything checks out. You may proceed," the guard says, handing the Borukin the package.

Back in the car, the children relax. Without the adrenaline from the security checkpoint, their fatigue hits them full force. After winding deeper into the parking structure, the escort finds a place for the truck and shuffles everyone out. The children drag their feet as he escorts them to an elevator, where he uses an eyeball scanner to reach the sixtieth floor.

They funnel through the elevator at the sixtieth floor and walk down a hallway through a set of propped-open double doors. There is a large terrace sheltered by a half-domed ceiling of glass. From every angle, the room looks out at the buildings of Sunta to its boundaries. Looking straight up, Iona can see the building continue toward the sky, too many floors above to count. The terrace is populated with tables covered in white cloth. At the close end, facing toward the city, is a stage where Natina and other Borukins are rehearsing. Grebson is standing off to the side, watching. His focus shifts to the group of children as they enter.

"No, no, no, no, NO!" Natina stomps her foot. "This is NOT good enough."

The Erohsian escort walks up to the stage. "Excuse me, Princess. We have finished your errands. Please let me know if you need anything else."

Natina quickly glances at the escort. "I will." She hops down from the stage to approach the children and the Borukin. "You were sure taking your time."

The Borukin dips his head. "I'm sorry, Princess. I went as fast as I could."

"Let me see the solar system."

The Borukin pulls it from the box and turns it on. "It was the only one with a pink Illi. I was lucky to find it."

"That will do." Natina turns her attention on the children. "And these are the Humans you found?" She walks around them. "They're not much to look at." She grabs Korbin's arm and lifts it up. "This one is nothing but skin and bones."

Korbin's face turns red. He pulls his arm back.

Iona suppresses a smile.

"I'm sorry," the Borukin says. "I didn't know there were aesthetic requirements."

She waves her hand, walking back to the stage. "They'll do."

Grebson moves forward. "I'll take them to get changed."

"Be quick about it. We're short on time." She hops back on stage and continues her instructions.

Grebson dips his head, moving to the Borukin. "You must forgive the Princess's short temper. She is anxious about the new additions to her ceremony."

The Borukin hands Grebson the package. "I understand. I can't imagine what she'd be like if you didn't give me those tips on where to find the pink solar system and the children. It saved me a lot of time."

"I'm glad, for both of our sakes, it worked out." Grebson turns to the children. "Follow me." He leads them out and to a small side room beside the elevator. "So far, so good," he says to the children. "This is where you'll be when you're waiting and resting."

He opens the package and pops off the bottom of the solar system projector. One by one, he pulls out small crystal slivers and hands one to each child. Instantly, the bracelet on Iona's wrist warms. Her incredible fatigue lightens.

Korbin shakes his limbs. "That was horrible."

Grebson hands them each a candy bar. "This should help bring back some of your energy."

"How do those things work?" Iona asks, holding the crystal up to the light.

"They're talismans that have their drawing part and their conversion part separated. The bracelet draws your Aether and sends it to the conversion part. An Aether sink—what was in the projector—continued to absorb the Aether from the conversion part, so your Aether levels stayed exceptionally low. It's a clever little Artifact Sosimo made." Grebson points to some clothes lying off to the side. "Those are yours. Change and wash up a bit. You'll have to practice with Natina first, but then you'll have some time to rest and eat. After your ceremony, Nero will be up. Hurry back here and grab your gear from the cabinet under the water jug. There is a Moltrik pulse grenade, and an extra doorman and invisibility bracelet for Nero as well."

"But Nero doesn't have Aether to use it with." Thea's confusion is knit into her brows.

"Just tell him he can draw from the doorman if he needs." Grebson opens the cabinet and places the solar system projector in it. "Make sure to bring this out with you. We don't want to leave any trail."

"Okay, we will," Ryder says.

"And remember, half the plan is escaping. It will be easiest if it stays quiet. Only make your move when you're confident you'll have some privacy, and minimal surprises. You'll also want a good place to hide the unconscious Erohsians, so your best bet will probably be the holding area." Grebson walks to the door. "Don't be long. I'll be waiting outside."

The boys and girls wash up with some paper towels and a little bit of water and change into yellow gowns with hoods.

"Can you believe she said I was skinny?" Korbin asks.

Thea laughs. "Yeah, that was funny. I almost giggled."

"She's a really good actor," Ryder says. "If I didn't know any better, I'd be scared of her." He pats down his outfit. "Everyone ready?"

Grebson leads the children back to the banquet to be pulled into Natina's relentless drive for perfection. She berates the children at every opportunity. She coaches them to carry a large chest on their shoulders, keeping their heads down, and moving around the stage with Borukin dancers. At the end of their performance, they kneel at the center of the stage while Natina rehearses the presentation of her gift and her speech.

After several hours of repetitive practice, she finally releases them. The children stumble back to their little room, and before Korbin can begin to complain about Natina's drive, they see a meal waiting for them.

With stuffed bellies, their nerves begin to nag them. Thea spastically moves about with anxious conversation, Iona sits in the corner with her head against the wall, Korbin fidgets with whatever he can get his hands on, and Ryder paces around the room, pushing on his front teeth with his thumb. After what seems like a whole day of waiting, they are served one more small meal and informed the banquet will commence.

We can do this.

*****

Iona waits in the hallway, hood pulled over her head, supporting the ceremonial chest with the other children. The double doors leading to the banquet room are closed, but the applause coming from the other side is still audible. When the applause dies, an assistant does one last check of the performers and opens the doors.

The dancers lined up in front of the children quickly move, exposing Iona to the full view of the guests. Borukins and Erohsians alike in formal attire are situated about tables. The centerpieces of glass flowers glow ever so slightly in an array of colors.

Iona quickly dips her head. *There's so many people.* Her heart begins to race. *There's so many Erohsians...*

"We can do this," Ryder whispers. "Just like we practiced."

He steps forward with the chest, and the rest of the children are forced to enter the room. The second step comes easier, and soon they are moving toward the stage where the dancers have already begun. They pass by tables, easily within arm's reach, and every time Iona sees a face out of the corner of her eye, she dips her head lower, hoping the hood will shield her from the Erohsians hunting them.

After executing their practiced maneuvers, they end kneeling beside the chest, facing the audience. The bright lights of the stage cast the dining tables in darkness while the city lights twinkle like a field of wildflowers through the glass dome of the terrace.

Natina approaches the chest and pulls out a green carving of a Drake twisted about itself. "General Lark, I would like to present you with this statue of a Drake as a symbol of the time you spent with us when we shared our beloved games with you."

The audience claps politely. A moment later, the hard rubber soles of an Erohsian thud across the stage. Iona sees the grey boots walk right by her from beneath her hood.

"Thank you, Princess Natina," the general says. "I will never forget my time in Kiats. It was a great honor. I hope our races can continue to share what we both hold dear, as there is a lot we can learn from one another."

The audience applauds again, and the general and Natina leave the stage, followed by the dancers, then the children with the empty chest.

Almost done! Iona forces herself to walk at the same pace as the others, but her body only wants to run.

They leave the banquet room, drop off the chest, and fight to maintain composure until they close the door behind themselves in their own private room.

Thea jumps up. "We did it! That was so scary. I thought for sure someone would recognize us."

"Shh," Ryder says. "We still have the hard part to go, so don't relax just yet." Ryder removes the gear from the cabinet under the water jug, handing it out. "Get dressed. We don't have much time until Nero's up."

They change their clothes to match the servant uniforms of the other Humans at the banquet, strapping the lepisents under their sleeves. Finally, Ryder exchanges their old ID talismans with fake Erohsian ones and packs up their previous clothes and the solar system projector into his gear bag. Iona puts the large pulse grenade in a sling.

Ryder hands the bag to Korbin. "I'm going to go take a look. When the ceremony with Nero is almost over, I'll come back and get you." Ryder slips out the door.

Thea paces about the room. "This is nerve-racking."

Korbin nods. "Tell me about it. Nero better be happy to see us."

"I'm sure he will be," Iona says.

Ryder dips back into the room five minutes later. "The ceremony is wrapping up. We'll hang out in the hall until Nero passes, then follow him." Ryder hands out a clear string with knots to Korbin, Thea, and Iona. "Alright, let's go invisible. It's just like we practiced with Sosimo and Grebson."

Each child blinks out of view as they put on the bracelets. When they have all disappeared, the door cracks open. A moment later Iona feels a tug on the string and follows the pull into the hall. Two Erohsian guards in formal attire emerge from the banquet room, leading a small figure dressed in dark robes. *That must be Nero.* Iona holds her breath as the guards pass. She only starts to breathe when the tug on the line in her hand brings her back to reality. *We're okay. They can't see us.* The guards lead Nero down the hall and to one of the elevators that goes to the higher portions of the building. *Hopefully, this goes better than practice...*

The elevator opens and Nero is forced toward the back. Iona imagines Ryder taking his position in the corner of the elevator and Korbin moving in next. One of the guards selects a restricted level higher up and scans his eye for clearance. He pushes the close door button right as Iona feels a tug on the line; she squeezes through sideways as it shuts. She squishes up against another invisible body and the door, keeping as far away from the Erohsians as possible.

Iona looks at Nero under his black hood and sees him smiling, staring right back at her. *Can he see us?*

One guard smacks Nero on the side of the arm. "What are you smiling about? The only prisoners who go to this floor are the ones that never leave with their minds intact. They're going to put your brain through a blender, Human. What did you do to deserve such a ceremony?"

Nero dips his head.

"Okay, then. Hold your tongue while you can, because it's a luxury you won't have when they start working on you. There's really no reason they'll hold back—" The guard holds his hand up to his ear piece. "Yes, we have him, and we're on our way now… Yes, sir, we'll change the plan. We should be there shortly." The guard looks down at Nero. "Well, it looks like they're not wasting any time. You're going straight to Capping and Extracting. Aren't you a lucky one?" he asks, selecting a floor several stories higher.

The elevator continues upward. Iona tenses for the coming task, visualizing the seamless movements they practiced with the Borukins.

Please, don't trip.

The elevator stops, and the door begins to open.

"I'm not going," Nero says to the guards. He looks at the other children out of the corner of his eye.

The guards look at each other, smiling. "So, there's a little fight left in you after all?"

"I always find it funny that you can make just about anyone lead the way to their end with the proper encouragement," the other guard pulls out a thin retractable baton. "Isn't that right?" he asks Nero. Nero shakes his head.

The guard whacks his leg with the stick. Nero lets out a yelp, sinking just a little before righting himself.

The guard hits his legs again. "Lead the way and I'll stop." The stick lashes out two more times.

"Okay!" Nero cries, tears in his eyes. "I'll go."

"Who says you can't teach a Human?" the guard holding the elevator open says.

The other guard chuckles. "Isn't that the truth?"

By the time Nero exits the elevator, the rest of the children are already out and waiting by the side of the hall. Nero looks at Iona, showing a quick smile.

Thanks, Nero.

The guards prod Nero down the hall and direct him to a secured metal door.

"This is the end of the road. If you're going to beg, now is the time to do it," one of the guards says.

Nero remains silent while the guard has his eye scanned. The door clicks and he pulls it open.

"Suit yourself," he says, pushing Nero through the door.

Iona crosses her fingers as the last guard enters the doorway and the door closes. She visualizes Ryder sliding a thin piece of metal in the doorjamb to block the latch from catching. "Did you get it?" She whispers.

"I think so," Ryder says. "Everyone good with the plan?"

"Are you sure it's a good idea to throw the grenade so close to Nero?" Thea asks.

"I'll only do it if I have to," Iona says.

"And Grebson said he can take it," Ryder says. "We have to keep with the plan. When you're ready, Iona."

Iona drops the line, pulls out the large cylinder grenade, and feels her way around Thea and Korbin, up to Ryder. "Okay, I'm ready."

"Let's do this." Ryder opens the door.

Iona rushes through, quickly trying to make sense of her surroundings. She picks out Nero, but freezes as five light-infantry Erohsian soldiers, the two guards, and a few scientists turn toward the door. *Soldiers?*

Suddenly, she is slammed from behind and topples over with a yelp.

"Hostiles. Take cover!" a soldier yells.

Iona struggles to untangle herself from the mess of limbs. The soldiers move away from Nero and take cover behind tables and other electrical equipment.

"Throw it," Ryder yells.

Iona pulls herself free and throws the grenade at Nero.

31 Getting Out is the Hard Part
Nero

"This is the end of the road. If you're going to beg, now's the time to do it."

Nero keeps his head down. *We'll see what you say when my friends rescue me.*

The guard opens the security door. "Suit yourself," he says, pushing Nero through.

The room is large and surprisingly open. There are several well-kept consoles in the middle with holographic displays and several larger projectors to the left. On the right, there is a closed doorway. In the far back is a single chair on a small platform. It has light brown leather padding and arm rests with straps. Above it are metallic arms, curled up like a spider hanging from a web. Three scientists turn, and five light-infantry soldiers snap, weapons at the ready.

"Declare yourself," a soldier yells.

"Private Bramble and Private Marcus, escorting the Human prisoner for probing by orders of Dr. Grantov," one of the guards stammers, looking at the weapons trained on them.

Dr. Grantov walks forward. He is wearing a white uniform and is cradling a small clear container with a metal object in the center. "Yes, finally. Bring him here. We have work to do."

The guards push Nero forward. "Is the prisoner really so dangerous? Why all the muscle?" Bramble asks.

Dr. Grantov strokes the clear container. "The light infantry are escorting an important item. I hope he'll have some information on it. Strap him into the chair. We'll begin immediately."

Nero gawks at the soldiers. He shifts his perspective and sees a slight blue glow around their bodies, crisscrossed by gentle pulsing red lines. *How are they going to get past these guys?* His heart starts to accelerate. Bramble and Marcus shove him forward.

Two assistants appear and lead Nero toward the padded chair. The arms above the chair make small movements as they approach. Nero resists their pull, imagining the capping device scrambling his brains. *Where are they?*

The door to the room opens; everyone stops to look. Nero shifts his perspective to see Iona's green glow with the darker lines of the invisibility talisman woven over her body. Korbin and Thea slam into her. They tumble through the doorway with a yelp.

"Hostiles. Take cover!"

The soldiers fan out, ducking behind the tables and equipment.

"Throw it!" Ryder yells.

Iona throws a blue glowing object at him, the size of a soda can. It bounces on the ground and rolls to his feet. Its brightness intensifies.

Uh-oh. With hardly a thought, he kicks the object at the closest group of soldiers preparing to fire at his friends.

The glowing object slides under the feet of one of the soldiers. "'Nade!"

The object erupts into a pincushion of electrical bolts of energy. The electricity pierces the surrounding lab equipment, moving in straight lines unless metal is in its path. The metal guides the electricity, until it reaches an edge, where it fragments outward like the roots of a plant. Sometimes, the electricity swirls in midair like little eddies in a stream.

Nero is caught by the expanding front. His whole body goes rigid. His vision darkens and his head begins to feel light. His body is released after a few moments and he sinks to one knee.

Nero's guards and the scientists fall unconscious, along with the soldier standing directly over the explosion. The two soldiers on either side of the explosion fall to their knees, and one who was farther away staggers backward, tumbling into Nero.

The children run forward, using their lepisents to zap the soldiers who are struggling back to their feet. The soldier who tripped over Nero untangles himself and pulls up his weapon. Korbin shoots him with Aether, making the soldier's suit glow. It does nothing to slow him down. Korbin dives out of the way as the weapon cracks sharply, scattering pieces of the lab equipment everywhere.

"Together!" Ryder yells.

Ryder, Iona, and Thea zap the soldier and Korbin joins in as soon as he rolls back to his feet. The soldier shakes violently from the Aether. His suit brightens. With his perspective shifted, Nero sees the red lines surrounding his body glow more intensely as though they were little streams of lava. Then, as if a light bulb had just burnt out, the lines flash and disappear. The soldier crumples to the ground.

"That was messy," Ryder says. "At least there aren't any alarms yet."

Korbin walks over to help Nero up. "So far, that's an improvement over your rescue mission." Korbin pulls up a guard's hand and uses his fingerprint to unlock Nero's cuffs.

Ryder points to the last soldier they knocked out. "Yeah, but did you see Nero take out this one? Nice job."

"I meant to do that," Nero says and rubs his side. "Thanks for coming."

"You're family." Korbin smacks Nero on the back. "Of course we'd come."

"That was a lot tougher than I thought," Iona says. "Do you know why there were actual soldiers?"

Nero looks around and sees the doctor lying on the ground. The clear box is just a finger width from his hand. Nero picks it up and looks at the metal piece secured inside. His heart jumps. "Hey, Thea!"

Nero hurries over to her with a smile from ear to ear.

"My necklace!" Thea gives Nero a hug. "I can't believe you found it."

"Nice find, Nero," Ryder says. "You'll be Thea's hero forever now."

Thea, Korbin, and Iona wrestle with the clear box, trying to crack her necklace free, while Ryder hands Nero some clothes and gear from his satchel.

He gives Nero one of the invisibility bracelets. "And here's an invisibility bracelet for the way out, if we need it."

Nero takes the bracelet. "But I can't use Aether to make this work."

Ryder pulls out a spare doorman from his pocket. "Grebson said you could use this, somehow?"

Nero shifts his perspective and sees the bright pulsing glow of the doorman. *Can I really use this like the stick in the park?* He reaches out to it with his essence. With a little coaxing, he feels Aether flow into him. "Yeah, cool," he says, smiling. "I can definitely use this."

"Moltrik Aether works really well against the Erohsians, but since we don't have a lepisent for you, you can use this if you need." Ryder hands him a dart gun. It is the same design he used in Blue Horin Bay. "Grebson made it."

Oh, great. "Thanks," he says with less enthusiasm.

"Of course." Ryder turns away while Nero changes, touching his small earpiece. "Hey, Sosimo, we have Nero and are getting ready to leave. What should we do with the guards? There were a lot more than we expected." Ryder looks around and notices a series of cells in the side room. "We could lock them in the prison cells... Okay, we'll do that and remove their helmets… Yes, we'll be careful." Ryder takes his finger off his earpiece and walks to the other children just as they are breaking open the box. "Help me put the Erohsians in one of the cells over there."

"What for?" Korbin asks. "Can't we just leave?"

"Our exit is way below us, so we'll want to sneak as far as we can before the alarms go off," Iona says. "They won't be sleeping for much longer."

Ryder nods. "Exactly."

The children walk into the cell room made of steel. There are electronic panels on each door.

"Hey, look." Iona runs up to a cell. "Somebody's in here."

Lying on the bed with an I.V. drip and health monitor equipment is a man, covered by a blanket. Other than the heart monitor continually beeping, he appears to be dead.

"He looks Human," Korbin says. "What are they doing to him?"

"I wonder if they're drugging him," Iona says.

Thea grabs two bars of the cell and sticks her face as close as possible. "He looks sick." She then turns to Ryder. "We should free him."

Ryder looks at the eye scanner security mechanism on the door, similar to the device the guards used.

"Korbin, help me pull the smart-looking Erohsian over here. Let's try scanning his eyeball," Ryder says.

Ryder and Korbin drag the Erohsian over to the door and hold his eye open to the scanner. A prompt for a security code comes up.

"Dang. That's not going to work." Ryder looks around and shakes his head. "I'm not sure what to do. Let's finish moving the Erohsians into the other cell, then I'll ask Sosimo. Iona, will you remove their helmets… or any other communication devices they might have?"

Iona nods, and the children get to work moving the Erohsians. When Ryder goes for the fifth soldier, on the far side of the room, he stops and turns toward the others. "Hey. Who knocked this one out?" Everyone shrugs.

"Could the grenade have got him?" Korbin asks.

Nero looks at the Aether and notices the pulsing lines of red are still present around the soldier's slightly glowing body. "He doesn't look like he got zapped like the others."

Iona shrugs. "I don't think we should waste time arguing about results."

"Good point." Ryder grabs the soldier's arm and pulls him into the cell with the others.

They lock the cell and Ryder touches his earpiece again. "We're all done, but we ran into a little situation. It looks like there's a Human in one of the cells. Should we try to free him?"

"No, he's not awake. It looks like he's being drugged or something. We tried to open the cell, but it asked for a code as well... No, we haven't used any of the doormen yet... Okay, we'll give it a shot and leave soon."

"What did he say?" Thea asks.

"Sosimo says that it's our call. His friends who are helping us would probably appreciate it, but we need to hurry. Our ticket out of here won't be around all night. They're setting up at the fortieth floor now."

Thea jumps up. "I say we save him. No one should be left here." Her shoulders drop and she looks to the others. "It's sad."

"We can spare one doorman," Iona says. "Can't we?"

Ryder nods. "It should be okay."

"Then let's do this. Put on your glasses." Korbin pulls out his doorman, locks onto the cell door, and blasts it with a jet of Aether.

The heat causes the security panel to curl up, hiss, and pop almost instantly. Liquid metal drips down the bars until he can pull the door open. Korbin flips the doorman over to use the cold end. Instantly, the heat on the children's faces vanishes.

"That was awesome," Nero says. "Did Sosimo teach you that?"

Korbin spins the doorman around in his hand. "He sure did." He slides it into his pocket.

The children step into the cell to inspect the man. His face is speckled with black, and on the far side, his eye is consumed completely by black. His chest moves ever so slightly.

"What did they do to him?" Thea asks.

"I saw this guy in the industrial district!" Nero says.

Korbin turns to him with his eyebrows raised. "Oh, yeah? Was he at your birthday party, too?"

"Not now, Korb. We need to get him up," Ryder says. "Pull that thing out of his arm."

Iona pulls off a piece of tape holding the I.V. down and removes it from his arm. A drop of blood almost too dark to be real beads at the spot.

Thea shakes the man's chest and smacks his face. "Wake up. We need to go." After a moment of prodding, he remains unconscious. "What are we going to do?"

"Great. This is just what we need," Ryder says. "I guess we can try to carry him out."

Iona shakes her head. "That's a big risk. We could all end up in here if we try. We won't be able to sneak or move as quickly as we need to."

A piercing alarm suddenly hammers on the children's eardrums.

Korbin throws up his hands. "Dang it, why does this always happen?"

"What are we going to do?" Thea asks, her voice shrill.

"We need to go," Ryder says. "We don't have a choice."

"So we just leave him?" Thea asks.

"It's horrible, but we have to. We can't carry him thirty some floors while we're being chased." Ryder touches his earpiece. "An alarm just went off. We have to leave the other person. He's not waking up... We'll hurry." Ryder turns to the others. "It sounds like the alarm isn't because of us, so it'll actually provide a little cover. But we still need to get the heck out of here, and fast." Ryder dashes out of the cell. He freezes. "Oh, no."

A thick metal security door has slid over the exit. The children run up to it.

"This is a big door," Korbin says.

"Thank you, captain obvious," Iona says, eliciting a glare from Korbin.

Ryder inspects the multiple locking mechanisms. "This is going to be really hard."

"We'll have to work together," Iona says.

Ryder points to the four corners of the door. "I think there is a bolt in each one of these locations. A lot thicker than what we practiced on."

"We only have four doormen left. That means Nero won't be able to use Aether," Iona says. "He won't be able to use the invisibility talismans."

Great. This far to get left behind again. Nero looks down.

"If we don't get out, it doesn't matter." Ryder turns to Nero. "We won't leave you, okay?"

Suddenly Ryder's eyes grow wide and he looks past the other children. He raises his arm with the lepisent but before he can use it, a flash of Aether pulses through them. Nero feels fogginess creep into his mind. He shakes his head clear. The other children's eyes have glazed over, and they are perfectly still. Nero turns around to see a slim figure of a woman covered in a tight dark suit, a mask, and goggles with golden lenses.

Nero lifts up his doorman but the woman snatches it out of his hand with amazing celerity.

Nero glances around in desperation as the woman stares at him. *What am I going to do?*

The woman shakes her head, disapproving, and Nero shrinks down. She casually hands the doorman back to him, indicating for him to move to the far side, where she leads the mindless children one by one. Once there, she takes Ryder's earpiece out and puts it in his pocket. Then she puts each of the children's fingers in their ears, where they remain. She motions for Nero to do the same, which he does immediately. He shifts his perspective and sees a green haze clinging to all of the dazed children's heads.

The woman, who has walked back to the door, is cloaked in the same dim white Aether as the surroundings. Nero can barely distinguish her. She holds up her hand, and red Aether spills from her suit. A massive fireball slams into the barrier, making the metal flex for just a moment before it wraps around the fireball and smashes into the wall on the other side of the exit. The explosion leaves the air crackling with Aether. The red of the woman's body quickly fades back to white. The sprinkler system kicks in and the cold water makes short work of the small fires, spitting steam where it splashes on red hot metal. Nero's clothes are soaked through, and he feels a chill run down his spine.

The woman turns back to Nero and waves goodbye with her fingers.

Nero half-heartedly waves back. "Uh."

She then shimmers out of view. Nero tries to sense her Aether, but he sees nothing.

Ryder and the rest of the children blink the glaze out of their eyes. "What the heck just happened?"

"This crazy person in black stunned you all, or something, and then just blew the door apart," Nero says waving his arms.

"And then just disappeared?" Korbin asks.

Nero nods. *But not with any invisibility bracelet* I've *seen before...*

"What did she do to us?" Thea asks. "That felt familiar."

"It was some sort of Icor Aether. I'm not sure," Nero says.

"How about we continue with the getting out of here?" Ryder moves forward. "We can worry about it later. I say we skip the invisibility and just run like crazy."

Korbin nods. "Good plan."

Ryder leads the way through the puddles of water and back toward the exit. He dips his head into the hallway and jumps back into the room. "Dang it, we have more company."

Iona pushes through the children. "I have an idea! Get your lepisents ready!" She pokes her head out and turns the cold end of the doorman on the water as three Erohsian security guards run down the hall.

The water coating the walls and floor turns to ice. The guards let out a yelp as they lose their feet. They slide down the hallway, desperately clawing at the ice to slow themselves down.

Iona jumps back in and pulls up her lepisent. "Now!"

The children zap the guards as they slide past the door, turning them into lumps that continue to slide, inert, for another ten meters.

Korbin smiles. "That was fun."

Ryder laughs. "Yeah, it was. Good thinking, Iona. Let's go."

They all cautiously walk across the ice, running as soon as they are clear of it. Nero draws from the Aether of his doorman to keep up. They plow through the door to the stairwell and run straight into a group of Erohsians with weapons. They are all rapidly descending. Ryder tries to pull up his lepisent, but before he can use it, the group of Erohsians continues past. The children bump into him and come to a stop at the door.

"Whoa," Korbin says.

Ryder throws his finger to his lips. "Shh."

Nero shifts his perspective and sees a green chaotic flow of Aether around the Erohsians running down the stairs. *That's strange.* "Something isn't right. They don't seem like normal Erohsians."

"I'm not going to complain if they ignore us," Ryder says. "I'm not sure what's going on anymore."

"Did they see you?" Iona asks.

Ryder nods. "Definitely, but they didn't even flinch. Let's just follow them, I guess. We can give them a little space."

After a moment, the children begin their descent.

"Do we really have to run down thirty floors?" Nero asks from the back of the group. The repetitive motion of the stairwell makes his head spin.

Iona glances back, still plummeting down the steps. "We got you on the seventy-fifth and we need to get to the fortieth, so yeah."

Nero stumbles down several stairs. *Oh great.*

After ten more flights, echoes of fighting from below bounce up the stairwell. They freeze.

"It sounds really close," Thea whispers. "How are we going to get by?"

"Err." Ryder taps the railing. "The stairwell is our only option, and we need to keep moving. I don't know what to do."

Iona peeks down the center of the stairwell. "We might be able to sneak by."

Ryder nods. "Okay, I'll go down a little and see where the fighting is coming from. I'll wave you all by if it's clear." Ryder tiptoes down another floor and sees an exit propped open by a body of an Erohsian soldier. The sound of multiple weapons firing echoes into the stairwell. "Okay, let's just make a run for it. The fighting is in the hallway."

"What's going on?" Thea asks.

Ryder shakes his head. "The Minis are fighting each other... but who cares? Let's just keep moving. Go first, and I'll follow behind."

Thea runs by first, followed by Iona, Korbin, and Nero. Ryder takes up the rear.

"Hey, stop!" an Erohsian soldier yells from below.

Nero instantly freezes. Thea screams. Ryder pushes past Nero, scampering down to Thea.

"What happened?" Ryder asks.

Nero forces his legs to move. He finds everyone standing in front of four Erohsian soldiers posed like statues. Nero shifts his perspective and notices a green shimmer over their heads; they have the faintest blue Aether visible throughout the rest of their body. He looks at Thea, and the normal green Aether around her head is almost completely gone. After a moment, though, the green pushes the red, blue, and yellow Aether back down past her neck.

Thea looks at Ryder, then back at the dazed Erohsians. "They were coming from below. They scared me."

"But what happened to them?"

"I just closed my eyes and screamed. When I opened my eyes, they were frozen."

"She used some sort of Aether," Iona says. "I saw it happen."

"I think that's the same thing the stealth woman did," Nero says. "It looks like what happened to you all."

"But how?" Korbin asks. "She doesn't have a lepisent. And we didn't learn how to do that."

A trampling of feet from above floods the stairwell. "Run!" Ryder pushes Thea and Iona forward. Nero follows after Korbin. They jump down groups of steps at a time, barely keeping their feet. The floors fly by, but no matter how fast they go, the Erohsians always seem to be behind them. A stairwell exit opens just as Nero passes. He slams it into more Erohsians attempting to join the pursuit, buying a little more time.

Floors pass by, and the children's Aether reserves wear thin. They begin to slow.

"This is it!" Ryder yells.

Thea slams through the door at the fortieth floor, followed closely by the others. Nero catches a glimpse of Erohsians coming from below. He sprints through the door. Just as he crosses the threshold, he feels a sharp stinging in his shoulder. The whole right side of his body goes numb and he stumbles forward, hitting the ground. He struggles to his feet and tries to keep running, but his body will not respond. Korbin turns and begins to come back, but blasts from the Erohsian weapons zip over his head, forcing him to go on with the others. Rough hands seize Nero, while the other Erohsians run after his friends.

Nero's mind begins to clear, and panic takes over as he sees Korbin disappear around the corner.

"We got one, Ma'am," one of the Erohsians holding him says. "We're still chasing the others, but they have nowhere to go on this floor. We'll cover all exits."

No. I can't get captured again. A tingling sensation runs up his spine and over his scalp. *I don't want my brain to be put through a blender!*

Erohsians continue to flow past him. They pull him to the side.

"Nice try, kid, but you're ours now."

The tingling covers his entire body, turning to sharp pinpricks. His face burns; darkness narrows his vision. All sounds grow far away, like his ears are stuffed with cotton; a deep anger infests his mind. Nero begins to tremble. *I don't want to go back. I won't!* He grabs the Erohsian's arm and twists it around so they face each other. "No, I'm not!"

The terror in the soldier's eyes is clear behind his visor. He desperately shoves a stunner into Nero's side. There is a sharp bite, and the stunner explodes in the Erohsian's hand. Nero continues to twist, forcing the man to his knees.

Violet speckles Nero's vision and then, everything goes black.

32 It Couldn't Be Worse
Isis

Isis watches from her seat. The young boy she had seen almost a year ago in New Lur walks off the stage with an escort of Erohsian guards. They are all dressed for the ceremony.

So much show... She shakes her head. *Should at least be a real escort.*

Isis bites her lip as the ceremony continues. She forces herself to talk politely with the other people at her table during the short breaks between presentations. She even stands up after the Erohsian and Borukin speeches about the new age of friendship to come. Finally, the ceremonies conclude, and the food is served. She grabs her knife and fork, slides them into a tender herb-roasted chicken breast, and slices a piece. Steam rises from the fresh cut, bringing with it an assortment of flavors that tickle her nose.

CRACK. CRACK. CRACK.

Everyone in the half-domed banquet hall drops their utensils and turns to the entrance; several have already ducked under their tables. Flashes of Aether weapons zip through the doors, shattering sections of the glass dome behind them. An Erohsian guard stumbles back from the entrance and slumps to the ground. Other guards slam the double doors closed and rush to wedge them shut with furniture.

"We're under attack!" Someone yells.

Thanks, moron. Isis calmly pulls up the holographic screen on her wrist computer to access the building security system as the banquet hall erupts into chaos. She clicks on the emergency button, which triggers the alarm.

Almost immediately, a video feed of the security officer pops up. "What's the situation, Ma'am? We detected weapons fire on the sixtieth floor."

"The banquet hall is under attack by unknown hostiles. Send in help and set up a combat channel for notifications and orders through me."

"Yes, Ma'am." The video feed cuts out.

Isis selects a security camera of the hall outside the banquet room. A group of Erohsians take up defensive positions and prepare a charge to blow through the doors of the banquet room. *Erohsians? What is going on?* She takes one last sip of her drink before getting up.

The guards inside the banquet room have gathered at the door. They continue to stack anything they can find on the barricade.

Isis grabs a pistol from one of the injured guards. "Pull that junk out of the way. I need to open this door."

One of the guards stops and looks at her. "Ma'am?"

"Do it. I'm not asking." She looks back at her holographic screen. The security camera shows two Erohsians finalizing the charge on the banquet door. They stand up and run back for cover. Just as the door is cleared, Isis pulls it open, fires her pistol randomly down the hall, and snatches the explosive. She dives out of the way as Aether rounds tear chunks out of the door. In an instant, she looks over the explosive and pulls out the electronic detonators. She turns her eyes away just as they pop, singeing the tips of her fingers. She lets out a breath. *That was too close.*

She waves the other guards back to the door. "What are you waiting for? Barricade the doors."

The thuds on the doors from the enemy slow. Isis pulls up her wrist computer. The hostiles have moved forward again, kicking at the doors with little effect.

Good, only one explosive with them.

She pulls up the combat channel and sends a note that the hostiles appear to be Erohsians in military uniform. Isis walks over to General Lark and the massive Borukin King, who are surrounded by guards. The Borukins stand a meter taller the Erohsians in the dining hall.

"I thought this place was secured, General," King Kamin says, his eyes ablaze with indignation.

"It is, Your Majesty," the general says. "Don't worry. You and your family are completely safe."

"Safe? I am not worried about safety. It is your complete lack of competence that insults me." The King turns to Isis. "Who is attacking us?"

Isis looks at the general and back to the King. "We're currently looking into it. They appear to be disguised as our own military."

"How can you propose a partnership when you cannot even protect the most important building in your city?" the King roars. "You Erohsians are just as weak as I thought." He turns and begins yelling commands to the Borukin guards.

"What in Anterra is going on, Isis?" General Lark asks.

"I don't know, sir. I stopped their first assault and barricaded the door. I don't think they have any more explosives to break through, so it should hold fine. Reinforcements are on their way. I'll have this wrapped up shortly."

"Keep me updated, and for the Creators' sake, don't let anything happen to the Borukins."

"Yes, sir." Isis moves back to the secured doors. There are faint thuds coming from the other side. Erohsian guards are scattered behind make-shift cover. On her holographic screen, she finds the reinforcements are only a few floors down.

"Reinforcements are almost here," Isis says to the guards. "When they arrive, I want to hit the hostiles from both sides. They look like Erohsians, so watch your friendly fire."

Isis pulls the security camera of the hallway back up on her holographic screen and taps on one of the hostile Erohsians. A profile of an Erohsian soldier pops up. He has an elevated Aether level.

What does that mean?

She taps on the other hostiles, noticing that they all have higher Aether levels than typical Erohsians. She sends a note over the combat channel to link hostile Erohsians to elevated levels of Aether.

Friendly indicators of Erohsians appear on the far side of the hallway. Flashes of light zip down the hall, exploding off the barricades of the hostiles. The ones working on the banquet doors give up and move to face the new threat.

Isis signals the guards and they clear the doors. The hostiles are cut down from both sides in a matter of minutes. None of them try to surrender.

Isis crosses the hallway to meet up with the light infantry soldier leading the reinforcements. "Good work, soldier," Isis says. "I want this floor completely secured. Mix up your soldiers and the guards to maximize effectiveness. The Borukin royalty is our number one concern. Do you understand?"

"Yes, Ma'am." The soldier moves off.

Isis puts on an injured soldier's helmet, synchronizes it with her wrist computer, and programs it to mark all Erohsians with elevated Aether levels as hostiles. She accesses the building's security system and scans for other alarms and notifications. Two pop up. One alarm shows a breach in the door to the roof and another shows a fire alarm in Capping and Extraction. She pulls up the video feed of the room and sees a frozen picture of light-infantry soldiers being consumed by a bright flash. An error message runs across the bottom. She switches the view to the hallway outside Capping and

Extraction and sees a mangled door, covered in ice. Sprinklers add to pools of water. A few soaked Erohsian guards are just starting to pick themselves up. *What's going on here?*

She rewinds the video feed until there is a bright flash. She hits play, and the video shows an immaculate hallway. After a series of events that leaves the hall a complete disaster, she sees a group of Human children leave the room, scurrying across the ice. Isis's heart jumps and she freezes the picture, zooming in on their faces. *Them! Why weren't they detected?* She taps on each child and an Erohsian officer identification pops up. *Because the system doesn't register them as Humans...* She clenches her fists. *How?*

She removes the security clearance on the fake IDs and puts a target flag on them. The security system tracks them to the sixty-fifth floor, moving down the stairwell.

She opens a public channel to the security officer. "There are unauthorized Humans in the building, somehow using Erohsian identifications. They are heading down the stairwell. I've marked their IDs. We need them brought in alive and with minimal injury. Notify everyone to set their weapons to stun. I'm going to take a group and personally cut them off in the stairwell. Check the system to see if there are more fake IDs out there."

"There's a group of five soldiers on their way up," the security officer says. "They're at the fifty-fifth level and will stop anything from getting by."

"Perfect." She closes the channel and grabs two banquet guards and two soldiers, instructing them to follow.

The door to the stairwell swings open, and red hostile indicators pop up on Isis's helmet. She starts firing her pistol immediately as hostile Erohsians burst through the door. One falls to the ground, but the rest flood into the hallway. She jumps behind cover as a barrage of weapon fire fills the air.

Other friendly Erohsians quickly converge on the hallway and their strict training brings the firefight to an end after another few minutes.

Isis gathers the Erohsians with her once again, running back to the stairwell with more caution. Once in, all she hears is the patter of footsteps from below.

She checks the location of the Human children on her wrist computer and sees they are a few stories down. "They've passed us," she says to the Erohsians following her. "Catch them!"

She begins to descend, stiff from her freshly healed injuries. The light infantry soldiers quickly pass her. Just a floor down, she runs into a group of Erohsians in the middle of the stairwell, rubbing their heads and blinking at each other.

"What are you doing?" Isis asks. "You were supposed to stop the children."

One of the soldiers looks at her. "We ran into them, but they stunned us. We weren't expecting it."

"How could you let a bunch of Human children stun you?" she asks incredulously.

"I'm sorry, Ma'am."

"Just get moving! We can still catch them."

Isis pushes through.

She opens a channel to the security officer, bounding down the steps as best she can. "The Humans got past us. They're heading down. Send up as many as you can, and we'll trap them between us. Have anyone else available converge on the stairwell."

The officer acknowledges her, and Isis closes the channel to focus on running. The swarm of Erohsians in the stairwell slowly builds. More appear at every floor.

"We're coming up on them now, should make contact in a matter of seconds," an Erohsian soldier says over the channel. "We see them. They're exiting the stairwell at the fortieth floor." Isis continues to jump down, several stairs at a time, and hears an Aether weapon fire. "We got one, Ma'am." More weapons fire.

"I'll be there soon," Isis says. "What about the others?"

"We're still chasing the others, but they have nowhere to go on this floor. We'll cover all—" Static cuts him off.

"What was that?" The static continues. "Repeat. You're breaking up." *What is going on?*

Isis looks at her wrist computer. The holographic screen is flickering. She jumps down another few stairs, past the forty-third floor, just as a wall of Moltrik Aether expands upward from below. She clenches her teeth an instant before the Aether hits her.

$$*****$$

"Ma'am. Are you all right? Can you hear me?"

Isis's vision clears, and she finds herself looking at the light-infantry soldier bent over her. The lights in the stairwell are flickering.

Isis props herself up against the wall, holding her head; the helmet she was wearing is lying off to the side. "What happened?"

"We're not sure. Some sort of Moltrik Aether surge." The soldier offers her his hand.

Isis takes it and lets him pull her up. "What's the damage?"

He shakes his head. "No idea, Ma'am. I've just been working my way down and checking the injured."

"Carry on, then." Isis wobbles for a second as she reaches for the hand railing. "How long ago did it happen?"

"About thirty minutes ago."

Wow... She descends, one step at a time. The soldier watches her for a moment before moving to others.

Erohsians are scattered around the stairwell in varying degrees of consciousness. Several fresh soldiers run from one fallen body to the next, assessing for critical injuries. Isis arrives at the fortieth floor.

The Erohsian security officer is issuing orders to anyone capable. He sees Isis and approaches her. "Ma'am. I'm glad you're on your feet. I wasn't sure where you ended up."

"What are you doing up here?"

"After the event, all of the electronics were fried from floor thirty-six to forty-four. My position at the security center was useless, so I had someone cover my station and hurried here to assist however I could."

"How bad is it looking?" Isis asks hiding her concern.

"Actually, there don't appear to be any life-threatening injuries."

Isis lets out a breath. "That's good news. What happened?"

"I'm not entirely sure. We caught the boy from the ceremony on this floor, like you heard over the channel. Suddenly, the video cameras died, and the sensors on the floor started to fluctuate. The event occurred shortly after."

"The boy from the ceremony? He was measured with no Aether. Are you sure it was him?"

"The computers modeled the event. They pinpointed his location as ground zero, rating the event as a minimum of a four on the Boltz scale."

"A four in a single event?" Isis says, incredulous. "That can't be correct."

The officer shakes his head. "I have someone picking through the data, but it's a mess piecing it all together. We have to use the data from several floors away. It's too hard to say at the moment. We'll confirm with the soldiers closest to the event when they regain consciousness."

"What happened to the boy?"

"We're not sure. When I arrived, he wasn't here."

"How about the others? Are you still tracking them?" Isis asks.

"I'm sorry, Ma'am. They got away."

"What!? How's that possible?"

"There were other Humans who set up a zip line from this floor to one of the adjacent buildings. They were using fake IDs as well. As soon as we discovered it, we sent people to secure the building, but they had already escaped through the basement using some of the old Human tunnels."

"Damn those tunnels. They should've been cleared out a hundred years ago. Did you figure out how the other children got in?"

"Reviewing the security tape, we established they sneaked in as extra servants for the Borukin ceremony."

"And have you found out how they fooled our sensors?"

"No, Ma'am. It's something that masked their biometric and Aethiometric signal. The terrorists are getting smart."

"I wouldn't go that far. They're Humans, after all. Did you try to track them before the banquet? That should give us a hint about their current destination."

"We tracked them all the way back to where the Borukin and the Erohsian escort picked them up. But, again, the sensors failed for some reason."

"Did you talk with the Borukin and escort?"

"No chance. The Borukin royalty is extremely angry. They won't communicate with us. They think a group of anti-Borukin Erohsians was responsible. We did talk with the escort. He said that nothing seemed out of the ordinary. The escort did comment that the Borukin was overall harmless, and very nervous about being late for the Princess."

Could the Princess be involved? But why would she be part of an attack on her own people? She is friends with the boy... but I can't imagine she'd go that far to save him. "Any information on the Erohsians attacking us?"

"Nothing much. I checked their backgrounds, and they're all Erohsian military. I don't know how they hid this from the mind sweeps."

Isis shakes her head. "Their tactics were sloppy. Just because they're traitors doesn't mean they'd lose all their training."

"A puppeteer, then?"

"It seems unlikely, just because of the number of puppets." *It also doesn't explain why their Aether levels were elevated.* "How'd they get in?"

"It looks like some of them worked themselves in through normal security access. The first group disrupted the roof security equipment, and the rest parachuted in with supplies. The Humans who set up the zipline came in first. They sneaked down using the same fake ID technology the children had. I believe the attack on the banquet was supposed to be a distraction for the boy's escape."

"All of this for one boy?" *They were all working together... but why such a big distraction when they could sneak around so effectively? Something's not quite right.* "Continue with what you're doing and let me know if you find out anything more."

"Yes, Ma'am." The officer starts to walk away.

Isis clicks on her wrist computer, but it does not respond. *That's great.* "Hey, do you have a com I can use? Mine is fried."

The officer pulls a small grey rectangular object out of his pocket. "I brought a few just for the occasion." He tosses her the communication device and continues his duties.

Isis places her thumb in the center of the screen. A welcome message with her name appears. "Call General Lark," she says, holding it up to her ear.

"Isis, I've been searching for you. Come up to my office. We need to talk."

"Yes, sir. I'll be right there."

Isis walks up a few floors to an elevator with a working panel and takes a ride almost to the very top of the building. She enters the general's office and surveys the glowing horizon. It ends sharply at the plains, as though Sunta is an island of light in the dead of space.

He closes the holographic screen on his computer, signaling for her to sit. "I'm glad you made it unscathed."

"What did you want me up here for?" she asks.

"I'm not sure if you're aware, but your target escaped."

"I'm aware of that. Along with all the children rescuing him."

"No, designation Uniform-Alpha."

Isis's heart skips a beat. "What? What do you mean he escaped? I thought he was dead."

"He was, but as soon as the spooks got hold of him, they saw an opportunity for a new weapon and started his heart so they could study him. His body is impressively resilient."

"But how did he escape? After the trouble we went through to take him down, they can't possibly be that stupid."

"They said he was almost completely brain dead. They didn't think he would ever recover. They wanted to probe his mind to see if they could learn something... The cells in the probing room were up to the necessary security level, and they kept him under watch and heavily sedated just in case."

"What kind of watch?"

"Three light-infantry soldiers and an additional two were watching the ancient artifact you recovered a year ago."

"What was that doing in the extraction room?"

"They were going to use it to speed up the probing process on the Human child."

"Tell me that's at least safe."

Lark shakes his head. "I have no good news for you today."

Isis let's her head fall back. "So these children somehow managed to take out the soldiers, free the boy, take the artifact, and set free one of our worst nightmares?"

"Unfortunately, that's not the end of it."

"How could it get any worse?"

"The surge of Aether that destroyed the security door of the probing room was recognized by the sensors." He eyes her, taking a breath.

Isis throws up her hands and lets them fall. "Oh, just tell me."

"The Murderess."

"Impossible."

Lark shrugs.

Isis runs through her memory. "The last person who had any info on her was a Borukin hunter. He claimed she was dealt with permanently. That was over ten years ago."

"I thought the same."

"Was she behind the Moltrik event?"

"No. I had someone look into it. The signatures were different."

"Well, then, who was the target?" Isis asks. "I'm guessing one of the Borukin royalty. Revenge perhaps?"

"Actually, the Borukins were unharmed, and there was no word of one of her tokens. You know how much of a fuss they make. Perhaps she didn't have a target."

"She always has a target. How can you be certain it was her? Could it be an imitator?"

"Maybe, but other than the door getting blown off its hinges, there was no sign of her on any of the sensors. The only thing capable of that is her suit."

"So it was either her, or someone with her suit... Fantastic." Isis runs her thumb over the edge of her ear and looks at Lark. "Have you talked with the Borukin royalty?"

"With difficultly. They're enraged and will be heading home immediately. Luckily, no one was killed or injured too badly in this fiasco. It'll take some time to get things back to where they were. Unfortunately, we aren't going to have a treaty anytime soon."

"That's it!" The general looks at Isis and she continues. "The attack on the banquet wasn't a distraction. Catalyst just wanted to frame us and hurt our treaty with the Borukins; a treaty would make their efforts more difficult. They must have had other motivations for rescuing the boy, and then somehow gotten the support of the Borukin Princess... They also must have a new way for controlling individuals. I'll have to review the data to see if there are any hints, so we can avoid this in the future." Isis lets out a breath. "This is their biggest offensive yet. Catalyst is getting bolder."

"As the new Brigadier General of Security for the city center, I hope you have a good plan to counter them."

Isis lifts herself up. Suddenly, her pains are nothing. "Thank you, Richard. I'll get on it right away."

The general smiles. "No, you won't. We have everyone available hunting for the Humans and Uniform-Alpha. Not even you could provide additional help right now. I order you to get yourself looked at and catch some rest. It sure looks like you could use it."

Isis glares at him. "Yes, sir."

Isis's small communicator beeps as she enters the elevator. Seeing an incoming call from General Belshiv, she puts the communicator back in her pocket and leans against the elevator wall. *I'll deal with that later. I have Humans to hunt.*

Epilogue
Days later…

"Are you sure this is the right decision?" Saraf asks.

Sosimo pulls a toothpick from his container. "We don't have much choice. Kiats isn't safe for them."

"But with the rebels?"

"I know. It's not ideal. But they will be safe there… for now."

"And what of Nero?"

Sosimo sighs, putting the toothpick in his mouth. "He'll stay with me for a few more days, then he has to go as well."

"Will that be enough time?"

"He's coming back to his old self. I think it'll be enough… It will have to be."

Nero pokes his bleary-eyed head around the corner. "Sosimo?"

Sosimo briefly covers the phone. "One second Nero. Alright, Saraf, I have to go. I'll call you tomorrow."

"He should come back to Kiats so we can figure out what's happening to him."

"And keep him locked up all by himself?" Sosimo says, hushed. "He needs his family. We'll talk more tomorrow."

"Yeah, fine. Give him my best."

Sosimo hangs the phone up, walking over to Nero and kneeling. "What can I do for you, Nero?"

"Am I a bad person?"

Sosimo frowns. "What? No. Of course, not. Why would you say that?"

"I had a dream I hurt people."

"It was just a dream."

"But it felt so real."

"Would you like to talk about it?"

Nero shakes his head.

"Okay then. Would you like to help me with some Artifacts?"

"Yes, please."

"Great. I could use your eye on something." Sosimo leads Nero up a floor to his Artifact workshop. "It's a new shield project. I think you'll find it interesting."

The Story Continues in:
Catalyst

Thank You!

I really appreciate your interest in my work. I have a great story arc for these characters planned. Your support makes it all worthwhile.

Upcoming works:

Catalyst
Nero and his family have found a sanctuary where they can thrive, but a corruption that reaches into their core will jeopardize all that they have built.
Coming 2020

The Tenebrous Miasma
When Iona is forced to travel to the edge of the known world, hints to her legacy suggest her growing powers are still in their infancy. In order to bring her family home, she'll have to muster everything she can manage... and more.

Malatras
In the aftermath of betrayal, an old relationship takes on a new facet as they piece together their shattered world.

Newsletter and Website:
My website grows along with Anterra; blakevanier.com. If you'd like the latest updates, please join my newsletter.
blakevanier.com/newsletter-signup/

If you like the story, please leave me a Goodreads review and an Amazon review. Also, please share with your friends!

goodreads.com/author/show/15724437.Blake_Vanier

amazon.com/Blake-Vanier/e/B07XCCLQ27/ref=dp_byline_cont_ebooks_1

Acknowledgements

I would like to thank my wife, Heather Passe, for pushing me to rewrite the whole thing and to allow me to bounce things off her. When I'm straying, she is instrumental to keeping my characters on their path.

Kate Klein was the first person to read it from beginning to end, which was huge. She helped me add more layers to my characters.

When I received the professional edits from Clara Cuthbert, it looked like she had used a dagger for how much red was on the page. It was tough to look at, but in the end, resulted in another rewrite which improved it greatly.

Terri Hofer, Laura Passe, and Allison Youngblood had great comments and edits.

Abdulaziz AlObaid has been a great support and incredibly encouraging.

So many others have helped me in one way or another. James Mason, Stéphane Béland, Barry Solway, Sam Mesker, Nick Derimow, Tim Plummer, Cove Sturtevant, Seth Wilberger, Rachel Ross, Lauren Brenkle, John Graham, Barrett Sleeper, and Francisco Gonzales.

Thank you everyone. Writing can be brutal. You all helped me make this better than I could have on my own.

Glossary

Please visit blakevanier.com/anterra for more information on Anterra

Accelerator

Erohsian technology that drastically increases the healing rate.

Adter Tursent

Artifact designed to absorb a specific type of Aether and emit light. They are commonly used to determine the specific cast of Aether in question.

Aether

A complex form of energy that exists in the higher dimensions, which overlap the four everyday dimensions in normal experience. Through essence, Aether can be brought into the normal dimensions and converted into useable energy.

Aetheratin

A measure of how much Aether someone or something is capable of storing.

Aethersotto

The measure of how quickly something can use Aether (power output).

Aether Branch

Refers to the subset of skills of a particular Aether cast. It is common to have a certain cast of Aether, but not be able to perform all the skills associated with that Aether. The person would then only be able to use some of the branches of that Aether cast.

Aether Cast

Type of Aether. Casts correspond to the six higher dimensions. When pulled into the normal dimensions, different casts of Aether create unique effects on the world.

Aether Shift

A condition in which normal dimensions begin to merge with higher dimensions due to a very high local density of Aether. Various side effects can occur depending on the cast of Aether causing the shift.

Amulet

A specific type of Artifact designed to protect the user from incoming attacks. An Amulet draws Aether from its own Aether reserve and operates independently of the wearer.

Ancient Technology

Any technology that may have been derived from the Creators. Most of this technology was lost during the War of Salvation.

Anterra

The Name of the planet.

Anterraktor

A creature that is said to be the guardian of the planet. They employ the use of cressen to do their bidding, but are formidable in combat and Aether themselves.

Anterren

The currency of Anterra.

Artifacts

Objects infused with at least a part of an essence. The essence is 'programmed' in a sense to manipulate Aether in a desired manner.

Bellicove Island

An island that has been forsaken long ago. There are ruins that date back to the Creators, but no record exists to explain their purpose.

Biat

A cast of Aether that allows for the manipulation of essence. Manipulations include the abilities to absorb essence, destroy essence, and create essence.

Blue Horin

A city on the Blue Horin Bay. It is a thriving seaport where many races come to trade.

Boltz Scale

A system of measurement used to quantify essence strength. It factors in both Aetheratin and Aethersotto into a single number for comparison with other essences.

Borukin

A dark skinned, large race with arguably the highest Aethersotto on the planet. They are skilled artisans and combat experts.

Capsent

A basic Artifact used to store Aether for use.

Carerasent

An Artifact that has bound part of an essence, imprisoning it. An individual can use a mental link to release the essence, which allows the essence to manifest a physical form. The individual's control over the summoned essence will vary greatly.

Catalyst

A Human organization rebelling against the Erohsians in a bid for equality.

Continuous Lepisent

A type of lepisent which creates a continuous stream of Aether from the user's input.

Corusnigma

A geographical area of incredibly high Aether concentration. Six such locations exist throughout Anterra, each with a specific Aether cast. At the center of each is a monolith of unknown purpose.

Coteress

A temporary bonding of two or more essences. The bond results in Aether abilities that are the addition of the individuals with a fractional loss.

The Creators

A race worshiped by the Erohsians and believed to have lived on Anterra millennia ago. The Erohsians believe the Creators created all the races that exist on present day Anterra.

Cressen

Aether creatures that are guided by an Anterraktor. Cressen are created from the babies of normal animals in Aether-saturated areas. The Anterraktor chooses an animal before it is born. Once picked, the animal will develop similar attributes as their mother but will be significantly augmented in all respects.

Daynin

A group of Humans who would force their children to bond with an essence at a young age. This bond would allow the child to grow up and develop with their Aether abilities, arguably making them more proficient when they are grown.

Drake

An ancient race of reptilian shifters. They retreated to their own island after a conflict with the Borukins. They are recorded throughout history, especially during times of conflict.

Drebin

The people who believe a Savior is the protector of all the races and will eventually deliver Anterra from suffering. They are one of the few examples where races of every kind have united for a common cause.

Entity

A very basic essence that exists in the world. They have basic instincts, similar to that of a jelly fish.

Essence

A connection from the normal dimensions to the higher dimensions. During use, the connections may grow and develop complex formations. These formed connections to the higher dimensions will create something analogous to a neuro-network, allowing the essence to process thoughts and memories.

Erohsian

A small Humanoid race with high intelligence. They have very basic Moltrik Aether capabilities.

Fundamental Aether

A set of Aether skills that focus around one's essence. These Aether skills allow for the transfer of forces from one's body to the rest of the world. A side effect of Fundamental Aether is an increase in stamina and strength.

The War of Salvation

An event that was responsible for the removal of the Lost Race from Anterra and the creation of the Drebin. It culminated in a world war against the Drebin.

Human

A race of people who are born without a substantial Aether ability. The only natural Aether ability they have is to absorb essence. The first essence they absorb determines their Riner Ratio and their Aether skill sets. Subsequent absorbed essences will increase the individual's Boltz value.

Icor Aether

A cast of Aether that manipulates the body. The manipulations include reading and manipulating minds, drastic increase of strength and speed, healing, and increased physical resistance.

Invisibility Talisman

A type of Artifact which draws Aether from the user and converts it into mental Icor Aether, then uses the Icor Aether to influence organic minds such that the user appears invisible.

Jasmeer

A small Borukin town in the Siroté mountains.

Jazebel Marks

The leader of the Humans during the War of Salvation.

Katashne'n Tree

A tree that is highly dependent on Aether, thus is only found in Aether-saturated areas. For whatever reason, a Katashne'n tree is very difficult to find, even after it has been found once. The wood has incredible Aether properties, one of which is its affinity to all casts of Aether. Katashne'n fruit is also a prized commodity for its high levels of Aether and its stimulant-like characteristics.

Kiats

The Borukin capital.

Kimkari

A Borukin combat art that focuses on handling attacks from multiple sources.

Layton Stone

The leader of the Borukins during the War of Salvation.

Lepisent

An offensive Artifact that takes in Aether of any kind and outputs a specific cast of Aether that the user may not have. Even if the user has the specific Aether cast, a lepisent eliminates the need for the user to develop the challenging skills to use Aether in such a way. The user can then focus time learning to use lepisents in general and expand their versatility.

Levitraft

A vehicle that utilizes a Yerantol cage for the sake of transportation.

The Lost Race

A race of beings that were removed from Anterra at the end of the War of Salvation. It is believed that they worked hand in hand with the Humans and Borukins to stop the Drebin from taking full control. Exactly how they disappeared from the planet is unknown.

Majirin

The largest continent of Anterra. Majirin is the homeland for Erohsia and Boruk.

Moltrik Aether

The cast of Aether associated with electricity and magnetism. This Aether can manipulate electric fields, magnetic fields, molecular bonds, and light.

Nesiv Aether

The cast of Aether associated with the manipulation of spacetime. Most commonly, Nesiv Aether is used to create gravitational sinks, or to shield mass from an external gravitational field.

New Lur

One hundred years earlier, the Erohsians assaulted the Human capital city, Bahsil. Nearby, the Humans destroyed all the weaponry and equipment in the city of Lur before fleeing. In more recent years, the Erohsians attempt to revive the once heavily industrialized city, calling it New Lur. New Lur is the Erohsians' attempt to give pride back to the Humans to encourage them to work.

Nimus Extractorians

People who extract memories from essences. Typically, this is for historical reasons. They are also called Essence Historians.

Normal Dimensions

These correspond to the everyday four dimensions in which the world is often perceived: one temporal and three spatial.

Obsentsa

The Borukin art of making Artifacts.

Obsentsan

A Borukin term for an Artifact maker.

Odo

A Borukin skill in which the subject uses a styk to manipulate Aether from an external source.

Pahzan Aether

The cast of Aether associated with energy transfer. These transfers of energy include adding energy, extracting energy, and using Pahzan Aether as a shield which absorbs other forms of Aether.

Porlimin Weapons

Aether-based weapons of exceptional make. They are designed to accept different Artifact spheres which can augment the type of Aether the blade cuts with. Often one weapon will have multiple slots. This allows the user to change the Aether the blade is using instantly.

Pulse Lepisent

A type of lepisent which creates a short burst, or multiple short bursts, of Aether from the user's input.

RIGID

A top-secret agency of the Erohsians that deals with national security and advanced weaponry.

Riner Ratio

The ratio of an essence's Aetheratin to Aethersotto. It is used to judge how someone uses and interacts with Aether.

Roroon

The Borukin art of hand to hand combat. The typical training includes callisthenic movements that Borukins use for exercise and meditation.

RPPD

Rocket Propelled Pinpoint Detonator. The pinpoint detonator has a guidance system that is capable of hitting stationary geo-referenced targets with high precision. The rocket will propel the explosives to high speeds allowing for quick delivery, especially when used in tandem with a Vulture.

Ru Aether

The cast of Aether associated with nuclear forces. It is the most feared Aether cast due to its potential for destruction and misuse.

Seteress

The act of severing one's own essence from one's physical being. This allows the person to circumvent the physical restrictions of the body when using massive amounts of Aether. The result, however, is unstable and death of the individual is inevitable.

Spatsentzin

A region where a large number of essences have bonded to the surroundings. This elevated occurrence of bonding drastically increases the Aether concentration in the area and often leads to a substantial Aether shift. The bound essences may still have connections to their once living selves and may interact with the world in a positive or negative manner.

Spirit Hunters

People who hunt for strong essences in the hopes of selling them to Essence Historians. They typically hunt essences around Corusnigmas.

Sorbsent

A specific Artifact that draws Aether from a user. A Sorbsent is typically integral in the design of talismans.

Styk

A Borukin tool that allows the user to interact with and store Aether. Many Borukin art forms have developed around this tool. Typically, Styks are made of materials that have a high Aetheratin, such as wood and other organic materials.

Sunta

The capital of Erohsia.

Talisman

An Artifact that draws Aether from a user and uses it to augment a specific set of their attributes, such as speed and strength.

The Tenebrous Miasma

Is a large region in the ocean of notorious hostility toward adventurers. Erohsian satellite imagery and flybys have revealed a series of large islands. Any effort to get close to these islands has resulted in disaster.

Trial of Kimsa

One of Stone's Trials that takes place during the end of the Borukin games. The trial of Kimsa is a test of a Borukin's effectiveness in combat.

Trial of Odosa

One of Stone's Trials that takes place during the end of the Borukin games. The trial of Odosa tests a Borukin's ability to defend against large Aether attacks.

Trial of Orinda

One of Stone's Trials that takes place during the end of the Borukin games. The trial of Orinda is a test of a Borukin's ability to continue in the face of monumental odds. This trial is the culmination of the games and of all Borukin skills.

Tursent

A type of Artifact that converts Aether from one source into a specific type for a specific function. These are the base for lepisents.

Virker

Believed to be creations of the Creators that no longer exist. A large part of a virker is said to reside in the higher dimensions.

Vitaya

An essence that is part of a living organism. A Vitaya is exposed to the world when the organism dies.

Vultures

Erohsian high flying unpiloted aircraft. They are capable of sustaining flight almost indefinitely. Some are used to hold a variety of deployable weaponry, and some are used for surveillance.

World Essence

The name for Anterra's essence. It is believed that a life of an essence begins and ends with the World Essence. There has been no direct, scientific proof for its existence, however, several experiments are currently in development.

Yerantol Cage

Is an invention that minimizes the effect of gravity on the mass inside the cage. The cage is essentially a potential energy buffer, which allows mass to be moved to different potential energies with near perfect energy recovery. Most importantly, the constant acceleration needed to maintain position in a gravitational field is greatly reduced. To start, the Yerantol cage is energized to the potential energy of the equivalent maximum elevation. As the cage rises, energy is drawn from the cage to account for the increased potential energy of the cage's contents. When the cage descends, the potential energy of the contents refills the cage.

Zarta

An Aether creature of high intelligence. The similarities between Zartas and insects have left most evolutionists dumbfounded. The similarities constitute one of the strongest arguments that the Creators were actually responsible for the different races of Anterra. When the Zarta grows, it uses its strong Aether ability to project limbs, causing its natural limbs to atrophy and fall off. Zartas have hard exoskeletons under a soft hair, very effective eyes, and a bird-like beak.

About the Author

In high school I got the bug to create a story from a friend named Frankie. In 2008, taking the train home from an internship at Lockheed-Martin, I got the idea that was the seed for my Anterra series. I finished school with the series outlined and the first few chapters complete. When I finally thought it was done, I reworked a lot of it. Then, with some constructive criticism, I rewrote almost the entire thing... then I did that at least one or two more times... It was painful. Thankfully, we are finally there and I can begin to share this story with you all.

When I'm not working on the story, I'm either working on software that processes satellite data for solar and atmospheric science on satellites, working in the shop making things with a cnc milling center, or practicing Brazilian Jiu Jitsu.

Made in the USA
Coppell, TX
03 December 2019